You

Are

My

Reason

A Novel

by Kitty Berry

ISBN: 9781073419609

Cover Design by Golden Czermak

Compatible Companions Trilogy:

You Are My Reason (Book 1)

My Forever Maybe (Book 2)

After You (Book 3)

Warning: This book is for mature readers only. It contains adult themes that are sexual in nature.

Character Glossary:

The Stone Series:

<u>Sliding (Book 1):</u> Introduces Tate Taylor and Brooklyn Adams. Brooklyn has a sister named Katrina. Tate's cousin is Damian Stone. Mac is introduced as is Sven, both military men.

<u>Stoned (Book 2):</u> Features Damian Stone and Sydney Cooper. Damian's sister is Drea Stone.

<u>Siblings (Book 3):</u> Introduces Sebastian Morison.

<u>Second Chances (Book 4):</u> Tells the story of Pete Roman and Raina Montgomery. Their friends are Todd & Amanda, Willie & Sofia, Chris & Tracey. Raina has a brother; Elliot and her father is Sven from Sliding.

<u>Screen Play (Book 5):</u> Phoenix Doyle and his sister Arizona meet up with Bailey Connors and Hunter King. Bailey's best friend is Randi and her brothers are Bryan and Derek. Hunter's brother is Graham. The King Brothers were Sydney's bodyguards in Stoned.

<u>Stealing Home (Book 6):</u> Pete Roman's parents are Rick and Lori; their story is told in this book. You'll also meet Jonesie. His island was the island used in Sliding.

<u>Surrender (Book 7):</u> The story of Bailey Connors's best friend, Randi and her brothers, Derek and Bryan.

<u>Starting Over (Book 8):</u> Graham and Hunter King get their story in this one. Graham meet Emory Dawson.

<u>Silence (Book 9):</u> This is a continuation of Starting Over

<u>Survivor (Book 10):</u> Dr. Wilson Anderson is introduced and will get his story in The Anatomy of Love Trilogy.

<u>A Stone Family Christmas (The Holiday Edition):</u> No new characters are introduced.

The Anatomy of Love Trilogy:

<u>Anatomy of Love (Book 1: Dr. Wilson Anderson):</u> Dr. Wilson Anderson meets Sloan Hale. His daughter is Scarlet and will appear again in Vines of Ivy.

<u>Anatomy of Love (Book 2: Dr. Caine Cabrera):</u> Caine meets Katherine Mills

<u>Anatomy of Love (Book: 3 Dr. Jessie Holt):</u> Dr. Jessie Holt is reunited with Cindy Baxter. Cindy was Brook and Sydney's doctors and she knows Damian Stone.

Stand-Alone Novels:

<u>Vines of Ivy:</u> Introduces Jason and Rae Cohen and their friend Boden. Their son is Troy. Troy's high school friend is Lance. When he moves to college, he meets Scarlett Anderson from The Anatomy of Love Trilogy.

(An AOL Trilogy carry-over)

Compatible Companions Trilogy:

<u>You Are My Reason:</u> Elliot Montgomery from Second Chances (The Stone Series Book 4) is grown up and finds a love interest in Courtney Knight. She's the daughter of Katrina Adams (Brooklyn Adams Taylor's sister from Sliding) and has a sister named Bridget. Amanda from Second Chances is also reintroduced.

<u>My Forever Maybe:</u> This is a continuation of the story You Are My Reason

<u>After You:</u> This is a continuation of the story You Are My Reason

1

The crackle of the ice under my feet as I walk through the city streets of New York remind me of my youth in Vermont. The slush on the pavement, seeping through my shoes, not conducive to the inclement weather, sends a chill up my spine. The sensation has me tightening the muscles in my neck which causes me to roll the kinks from my shoulders.

It doesn't matter that it's obvious I'm now an adult living outside of the Green Mountain State, my mind plays tricks on me and I'm stopped short as a memory of another time surfaces. I physically feel the alteration in my system, my waning confidence has me scanning the streets for a distraction. It's only moments before one comes into view.

Fighting off my natural desire to approach the man who has caught my eye, I remind myself that this feeling will be fleeting. Another notch on my already scarred bedpost, not so much.

"Hey Court, wait up."

Lost in my internal conflict, I hadn't heard Ace Lyons at first.

"Where you rushing off to?" he yells.

Ace Lyons is the last person I need to be near right now. Well, maybe not *the* last, but wherever Ace was, *the* very last person I need to see, is never far behind.

Ace was recently released from basic training after being caught with his pants around his ankles and his dick inside his commanding officer's wife. His father called in a favor with Mac, the head of security at my stepfather's company, and that's how our path's crossed.

Turning toward the guy that struggles with keeping his dick out of places it doesn't belong, I also spot his partner in crime, Callan Black. Like I said, never far behind. And Callan is *the* man I don't need to be near right now.

Callan Black is a strong, high strung whiz on a computer. The Brainiac could hack into anywhere. Like Ace, his dick's ability to hack into women's panties is what my issue is at the moment. Lord knows he's had the all-access ticket into mine since the day I first laid eyes on him. He keeps it secured in his pocket and pulls it out when he needs it. Yup, he's an asshole.

Ace and Callan are always where the other one is. Always. So, I guess it's appropriate that they like to take their women together.

Running into them right now is a recipe for a fucking disaster.

I heave in a gulp of air. Moving in their direction, I plaster on a fake smile. "Ace," I greet with a gentle kiss to the corner of the mouth that has explored every inch of my body as much as it has my sister's. "Callan" I say without moving to offer him the same level of affection. He's my poison and dangerous. I suspect Ace has it bad for my sister, so a kiss to the corner of his mouth isn't going to hurt anyone. Callan Black and I, on the other hand, have history. It might be short, but our secret hook-ups are starting to fuck with my head. Callan claims he's never had feelings for a woman, so why he's picking now and me to fuck with is anyone's guess. So, like I said, dangerous.

Callan cracks a smile, my kiss for Ace and lack of one for him has not gone unnoticed.

"I'm on my way out" I shiver as a gust of cold wind blows my hair into my face and I finally answer Ace's question about my activities.

The familiar sensation of coldness hitting my skin reminds me of another time and place. One I don't want to remember. One that I run from in my sleep and avoid with the distraction of men when I'm awake. And in there lies the problem.

Before I can avoid his touch, Callan's finger pushes back the clump of hair now sticking to my glossed lips. "New color?" he asks trying to suppress any further comments about where he'd like to see that new color slathered, I'm sure.

Callan and my secret hook-ups are not public knowledge, but our ménage with Ace and Bridget wasn't a secret. My sister and I had been sleeping with men together since high school. My stepfather knew that Bridget and I had slept with the two men standing before me and leading me into temptation like Eve to the forbidden fruit. My mother and aunt lectured Bridget and I on keeping up appearances and pushed us in the direction of our new friend, Scarlett Anderson in hopes that her innocent nature would brush off on us. It's where my latest idea came from. One I'm trying to hold on to long enough to get out of this ice castle of a city and sink my toes into the pink sands of paradise.

Where these two men won't be. Where no men will hopefully be. I need this to be a male-free experience to be able to pull off my plan.

"I think Bridge is still inside. Bobby's gone for the day," I shrug. "I'm sure she'd like to hang out, Ace" I say as I back away like prey in the wild.

Callan chuckles. "Just Ace, huh?"

He's trying to goad me into admitting that I don't want him to fuck my sister or any other girl for that matter, but I refuse to give him that satisfaction. Instead, I shrug again as I watch Ace's eyes flame with fury over the thought of his friend fucking my sister.

My sister had confessed to having her panties wet and in a bunch over Ace Lyons before I'd even washed my skirt with the stain from him on it. After that, I've tried my best to avoid the guy that my sister insists can be her reason for living. Yes, she's a drama queen, my sister. But she was my drama queen and after Scarlett's Friendsgiving, we'd agreed to work on changing our promiscuous ways. What I can't tell Bridget is that this leopard can't change her spots. Well, not yet. Not until my one-year contract with Compatible Companions expires, that is.

"And what about you, beautiful?" Callan asks with charm to spare.

"Been there, done that, Cal. Anyway, I'm in a hurry. I gotta go."

"Where you going?" Ace questions.

"I need to do a few things before Bridget and I leave for a few days."

"Leave?" Ace asks, and I know by the tone of his voice that he returns my sister's feelings and then some. "Where are you taking Bridget?"

"Calm down, big guy. It's only ten days. Bobby has a friend of a friend that owns a property in paradise and he's sending us to give my mother a break."

"That's bullshit. Why didn't Bridge tell me?"

"Dude," Callan says. "Can you whine a little more or…"

"Fuck you, man, okay? I'm just asking. Drop the shit about feelings, it's getting old."

I knew I was right. He has feelings for my sister, and I'd bet he's as ornery as he is because the idea of spending ten days without seeing her is already pissing him off.

Looks like Bridget's plan to gain his attention by making his heart grow founder through distance was working before she'd even left this concrete jungle. I'd have to think about letting her know that she already has Ace eating out of her hands. It might be more fun, though, to watch her freaking out just for a little while. It's going to be a long plane ride and I'm sure to get bored. It could be a fun distraction.

Did I mention that my sister could be a drama queen?

I answer Ace's question. "Maybe she didn't tell you because she didn't think you'd care. Maybe she figures that you'll just find another girl to fuck while she's gone. You know, out of sight, out of mind" I state without ever taking my eyes from Callan's.

"I care," Ace says then turns toward his friend and raises a hand. "Fine, I fucking care. Shut the fuck up now, okay? I said it, I care."

"Good luck with that," Callan scoffs, pissy because I suspect that he possibly cares a little too. Maybe about me. "I'm outta here. See you later," he says then turns toward me. "Make sure you don't get a tan line, Court. Your tits will look even better bronze. Go topless for me."

So maybe he doesn't care all that much, then.

"You're such an asshole" I say as I turn and leave Callan Black and Ace Lyons on the busy New York City street.

As our private seaplane skims across the crystal blue waters of the South Pacific, I ponder the idea of leaving behind my deep-rooted coping mechanism and the year-long contract that is breathing down my neck.

Was it even possible to change my ways? Did I need to? Maybe my match would be receptive to an open relationship. I try to scan over the contract in my mind, but I had barely scanned it over as I signed it, so it's no use. When I return, I'll have no choice but to meet up with my match on New Year's Eve.

What the fuck was I thinking?

As I'm questioning the logic of this hiatus from my inevitable miserable year, I hear my sister ask, "Dealing with Uncle Tate's shit pays off sometimes, right?"

I glance in her direction and shrug a bare shoulder because it makes me wonder if my latest poor decision will pay off. It might not in the sense Bridget refers to in this instance, but it will pay up. Yes, a year from now, I will be substantially wealthier. Three hundred thousand dollars wealthier. Not that it's really about the money. Bobby more than keeps Bridget and I comfortable in the lifestyle he'd grown accustomed to before marrying our mom, but you never know when that's going to end. If history repeats itself, Bobby's time with us is soon going to come to an end.

And that's what I had been thinking when I signed my name on the dotted line and became one of Compatible Companions' employees. Well, that and the sex.

I needed to get out on my own two feet and take Bridget with me. My mother and Bobby deserved to enjoy one another without the pressures we were creating in their marriage.

I shrug to myself and I consider the sex angle to my plan. If I was signing on to a year-long contract with a male who had matched up with my profile, I'm guessing his main request had to have been sex and lots of it. The distraction I'll surely need. Now, I can only hope that he's not ninety-three and in need of a little blue pill to make him semi-erect.

Thinking that's really all I can hope for, I sigh. I mean, actually finding someone that can be my lifelong compatible companion was a joke, right? Prince Charming was only in children's fairytales and my life was the furthest from a happily ever after.

I learned that lesson the hard way. Men were liars and cheaters who turned their backs on their responsibilities. See, my brain is clearly based in reality, but my psyche, now that's a different story.

"Did you hear what I said," Bridget asks. ""Dealing with Uncle Tate's shit pays off sometimes, right?" she repeats.

"I guess, but you know that Bobby only did this to get us out of his hair, give mom a break before Christmas, and because his security team was spending more time securing us to his desk than they were securing anything else."

Bobby Knight, our stepdad should be running for the hills any second. He and my mother have been together longer than either Bridget or I had expected already.

Bridget smirks. "Yeah, the Ace and Callan thing really pushed his buttons."

And yet Bobby Knight remained. The man must be a masochist.

"I guess this is pretty cool," I say as we're deposited onto the pink sand. "If we're going to try to turn over a new leaf, we couldn't ask for a better place."

I leave out the fact that my fingers are crossed that this place will be one without men lurking about and making it challenging. Yes, the D is my kryptonite.

"You're sticking with Adams, huh?"

I shrug again, this time my shoulder raises at our middle name. I told my sister that if we were going to try to reinvent ourselves, we'd need new names, at least for this trip to paradise. Courtney and Bridget were sex-crazy, promiscuous sluts with daddy issues longer than the dicks they liked to suck. Adams and Maddie had clean slates free of skeletons in their closets.

I took our middle name then reversed the letters for my sister's alias. Viola, we were reborn!

And now here we were with the chance of a lifetime to reinvent ourselves into women who were respected for more than their ability to suck and ride cock.

Now, don't get me wrong, those are skills that come in handy, but sometimes a girl wants a man to look her in the eyes and actually care about their conversation. You know, before he takes her from behind in a bathroom stall of a nightclub.

Pushing thoughts of my night not long ago with Callan away, I sigh.

And so it begins. I'll transform into the perfect young lady with class. I'll tuck my ghosts away and see what it's like to live life from the advantage point of innocence. For the next ten days, I will live as someone new. Every decision I make, everything I do will be based on the opposite of my natural instincts. My very own Bizarro World, if you will. I'll live life as others around me do every day, free from the pressure to hide a past that has shaped their present. Able to tuck away their worries over a future that looks bleak without dropping to their knees.

It'll be easy without the temptation of my usual vise.

For ten days, I will be Adams.

It doesn't take Bridget or I long to strip out of what little clothing we had worn to get to our private island getaway. After our plane from New York had landed in the hot tropics, we'd pretty much donned nothing more than a tube top and a sarong for the ride over to the compound in the seaplane. And now that we've plopped our bags down in our respective rooms and changed into our bikinis, we were ready for some serious sunbathing.

The pink sand and crystal blue waters were an oasis in front of me. When I was a little girl growing up in the freezing temperatures of Vermont, I was convinced that I had been a mermaid in another life. I waited for countless days for my very own Prince Eric to show. When he didn't, I found solace in every sea urchin with a dick. But now that I'm where I feel at one with the environment, maybe I can finally channel my inner spirit animal and reach that illusive state of Zen.

"Maybe I should be Ariel instead of Adams" I state as I pull the string on my bikini top and lay on the lounge chair. Burned nipples be damned.

Bridget covers her eyes with her celebrity magazine, the same one Uncle Tate threatens to set fire to if he finds it on her desk at Taylor Studios, Inc. where she and I pretend to do an actual job. I say an actual job because neither of us accomplish much music related work there, but they don't call it a blowjob for nothing and we've given our fair share of those at the office, so there's that. We all contribute our own skills to the team.

"Maybe you should put some sunscreen on" Bridget says as she removes her own top then rolls to her belly so the sun won't be in her eyes while she reads about Bash and the women he's never met. I know the article is fabricated because my uncle is the famous music producer, Tate Taylor. With him has come an extended family of rich and famous people that Bridget and I can never compare to. Like Bash Morrison. Bash Morrison is a Rockstar, married to a supermodel, and the long-lost brother of Damian and Drea Stone. Damian and Drea are Tate's cousins. This gives Bridget and I first-hand knowledge that Sebastian is a happily married man and father.

As Bridget opens the rag, I see the photoshopped picture of Bash with a woman that is clearly not his wife and mother of his children. I chuckle when I think how the tabloid has no idea what they're in for. It'll only be a matter of time before my uncle shuts down Bridget's favorite reading material. Chances are, Callan has already hacked into their system and caused mayhem.

Not wanting to burn my nipples off because I do so enjoy them being licked, I decide to listen to my sister and reach for the bottle of sunscreen. I squeeze a glop into my hand with an inappropriate thought about a man's ejaculation crossing my mind. I push that thought aside because it's one Courtney would have, not Adams. I need to remind myself that my plan is to have a ten-day man free vacation to clear my head before returning and facing the consequences of my decision to sign with Compatible Companions.

I raise my white covered hands to cup my breasts and begin to massage the creamy lotion into my skin. My nipples harden from muscle memory and I swear I can hear them telling me it's going to be a long ten days without the pleasure of a man's hands on them and other important parts of me.

But before I can reassure them that I'll make sure they get extra attention every morning in the shower, Bridget gains my attention by clearing her throat. I turn to smile at her because I assume that she knows where my thoughts have wandered, hers are usually right alongside mine. We might not be twins, but we have an eerie connection when it comes to our thoughts. "We're not alone" she says with a lift of her chin instead of the comment I expected, one about my nipples looking as if they'd just survived the world's biggest Bukkake.

Before you look that one up, I should warn you. You'll never be able to forget the things you'll see. Not judging, just saying. It isn't for everyone.

As I shield my eyes from the sun's glare, I turn my head in the direction of Bridget's chin lift to find the attention of a man built for sin and fun in the sun.

Fuck.

He was a man built for Courtney, but she wasn't here this week. She's tucked away in bad girl land while this perfect specimen of a man has found Adams. And Adams was a good girl who wouldn't know what to do with a man like him even if he came with an instruction manual.

Oh, shit! Well, now the thought of him coming is all I can think about.

This week is going to be harder than I thought now that my hope of it being man-free has been shot to hell.

As I think about how hard this vacation just became, I wonder how hard he can…Ugh!

Bridget interrupts the images forming in my mind. "Uh, you might want to stop tugging on your nipples, *Adams*." She stresses my name to remind me that I was acting like Courtney, not my new sexually innocent persona.

Then my eyes lock on the tall, tan man and I fight off the smirk forming on my lips. His hair is cropped tight to his head and light, and I can tell that he's a natural ginger. And everyone knows that gingers are sensitive, fiery creatures in bed, passionate and gratifying in their fucking of the women they hurl over their shoulders and toss onto the bed before slinking between their...

"Adams," Bridget admonishes a little louder this time. "Hands."

"Oh," I say as I let my lotion covered hands slide from my breasts. This is not good.

The man with the copper hair stands with a cocky lean to the right, his shoulder touching the pool house he must have just exited. He lowers his dark aviators and lifts a light brow as a smug smirk graces his lips. He doesn't even pretend to not be enjoying the show playing out before him.

This man has trouble written all over him and if Courtney were here, she'd had already been rubbing her slick hands down his bulging pecs until she was stroking his throbbing...

"Adams," my sister reminds me a third time. "You're Adams, remember? Stop touching yourself like that. He's watching you."

"Ugh! Fuck, I didn't think it would be so hard to be a good girl."

The man sends me another cocky smile, this one is filled with the confidence of a man that knows just how good he is in bed. My first instinct is to lick my lips and send him sex vibes. Looking at my sister, I remember that I'm not Courtney. Instead, I advert my gaze to the bottle of lotion that I try to shut. But it's slick and so are my hands, making capping it more difficult than one would have guessed. I try to close it, but I inadvertently fling it into the air. It lands at the end of my lounge chair in the grainy sand.

"Um," my sister clears her throat as I lean down to retrieve the bottle and distract myself from the presence of a man. "Adams" she says as a shadow falls over me. A shadow in the shape of a man with just the right amount of bulk on his body to be sexy as fuck.

My eyes start on the bottle of lotion and rake up the man's tight thighs. "Oh shit" I whisper.

Bridget lowers her magazine with a smile for the ginger that I can now see has the most perfect sun-induced highlights running through his hair that is trying to grow in. "Hey, I'm Br..." My elbow connects with my sister's left rib and she makes a sound like a cat being tossed into the ocean. "Oww, ugh, um...Maddie," she sputters. "My name's Maddie. This is..."

I interrupt. "Embarrassing. Did you enjoy the show that you were not invited to?" I ask as I demurely cover my breasts like the shy, inexperienced, innocent that Adams is."

My sister waves me off. "Don't listen to Adams. She's just cranky because you saw her without a top on."

I hide the smirk that tries to escape. My tits have been exposed for anyone to see since they hit C cup status in high school, and I figured out that they could lead the way into a reprieve from my thoughts.

"Adams? Your name is Adams?" he asks in a deep timbre, sounding confused by my male name.

I roll my eyes then huff and maneuver onto my belly to hide my breasts that Ginger's eyes haven't left.

"We're here on vacation" Bridget states.

"Vacation, huh? This isn't a resort. You know the owner or are you trespassing?"

"Who are you?" I ask then piece together that he must be the hired help. He came from the direction of the pool house, so that makes sense. "Do you work here?"

"Work..." he chuckles. "Yeah, sure. I work here. Can I get you anything?"

"I'd love a slushy drink with..."

I cut my clueless sister off. "Maddie, I don't think he's here to serve us drinks."

"You never know, try me" he tempts.

"See Ads," Bridget says, already creating a shortened version of my fake name. "Tell him what you want. Like I was saying, I'd love a slushy drink. Maybe mango flavored or pineapple. Heavy on the alcohol and I'm not picky which kind."

Gingy, (okay, maybe I was creating nonsense names as well, but, whateves) furrows his forehead and looks at my sister with a confused expression. "Slushy, you said?"

"Yes, you know, with ice and booze. A little fruit."

Gingersnap, (yup, I'm still at it) lifts a chin to me then says, "And you? You want your drink slutty, too?"

"Excuse me?"

Did I hear him right?

"Slushy," he repeats. "You know, your sister just explained that."

"Oh," I take a deep breath. With the blazing sun shining behind him, my breathing was unsteady. "Yeah, whatever. I don't care" I mutter as I place my head on my arms and pretend to be ready for a nap.

I crack an eye open to see the man has moved from the foot of my lounger to the side and from this closer advantage point, it's clear Gingerbread (I'm almost done) had definitely enjoyed the show I'd given him. I'm sure I'll be featuring in his one-man shower matinee after he delivers our drinks. "What?" I ask as he shifts left in his shorts.

"Nothing" he smirks as he shamelessly adjusts his junk again.

I try to remind myself that a man with an erection is unfamiliar to Adams and should be causing her to blush and look away.

I should look away but it's so hard. Yes, the pun is intended, and the junk is supersized. And hard. So obviously hard. Courtney should look away too because this week was planned out as a male-free zone. This guy is fucking my plans up big time.

A male clearing his throat jars my attention to the man before me that screams confidence. I had thought it was cockiness earlier, but on second examination, I'd say this is a man, not a college guy even though his boyish good looks say otherwise. I can tell that Ginger Root (okay, that's the last one, I swear.) here, is a man who is accustomed to being in charge, one who dominates every situation, knows what he wants from a woman and takes it without asking. But why does he have to be here of all places?

His eyes sparkle in my direction and I take note of their peculiar color. Green or blue, maybe brown or a combination of all three. I watch as he unabashedly allows his gaze to rake me from head to toe then back again while he emits a strangled groan and once again makes an adjustment in his shorts.

Christ, how big was this guy's dick?

His eyes lazily continue to roam over my body, and I react how I imagine Adams would. I shiver when his stare becomes too much to bear and my skin grows bumps as my exposed nipples pebble. I guess sinking into character is as easy as the actresses on screen make it appear. Look at me, I'm just another Raina Roman, actress-extraordinaire.

The copper headed god fights off his own grin when he notices the effects of his appreciation of my finer assets. "You sure you want that drink slushy?" he asks using the word my sister had. "It looked like you were already chilled."

I rub my arms as if I were back in my hometown and had just spent an hour out in the cold. "Why don't you let me worry about myself?" I ask, hoping that the sound of the surf can help to take the bite out of my tone. It's not his fault that he's fucking with my plans and making me have thoughts that I wasn't supposed to have here on this island.

But he's unaffected, his eyes never leave me while he holds his ground. And I hold my breath.

"Adams," I hear from my other side. It's a female voice, but in the moment, I couldn't care less who it was. Oh wait, it's my sister. That's right. We're on a private island with no men around to clear our heads and…but there is a man here. One who is all man. One who is looking as if he's going to cause a problem for me and my plans.

"Why don't we let the nice man get us our drinks?" Bridget asks.

The nice man? Is she losing her fucking mind, too? There are lots of ways I would describe this guy, nice isn't one of them.

"Elliot," he says. "My name is Elliot."

I laugh before I remember that I'm Adams and unsure of myself. "Mom was a child of the 80s, huh?" I ask with sass.

Elliot (yeah, that's not as fun as my plays on his red hair) shrugs a broad shoulder then as suddenly as he'd appeared, he turns and walks in the direction of the main house.

"What the fuck was that?" I ask my sister once he's out of ear shot.

"I don't know but you're screwed. There's no way you're going to survive ten days without fucking him."

"Me?" I ask. "What about you?"

Bridget sends me a look that silences me before she says two words. "Ace Lyons."

My slut of a sister agreed to this trip and my plans of reinvention because she has it bad for Ace and somehow (from my mother and aunt) she got it into her head that she needed to play hard to get. The idea of her withholding sex, from the guy that has already had her, not to mention me, in every position known to man already, is laughable.

And I had laughed. Then she'd admitted that coming with me for these ten days was the best chance she had to not sleep with Ace again until she'd made him see that she had more to offer than a vagina. Pointing out that she also had a mouth and an ass hadn't been well received at the time.

As I was about to admit to Bridget that Ace had it just as bad for her, my sister begins a flapping and coughing fit to alert me that Elliot (can we go back to Ginger?) has returned.

I straighten my back and roll my head from side to side to loosen my muscles from the tension this ginger (See? Much better, am I right?) is creating with his presence. I slowly turn to address him but when the intoxicating scent of his woodsy cologne fills my nostrils, I forget what I was about to say. After inhaling my fill, I stretch out my hand to accept the frosty mug filled with syrupy sweet goodness. I can only hope that it also includes lots and lots of alcohol. If I'm drunk, I can't be held responsible for my actions, right?

My lips surround the straw and I'm forced to fight off my urge to suck it like a thick dick and watch as Elliot's cock raises to greet me. Instead, I innocently place the straw in my mouth, letting it perch on my bottom lip before closing them to suck in the drink he's presented.

Elliot hands my sister hers then moans as he watches my lips purse and I begin to suck. Hmm...I guess even innocently drinking from a straw can hype up a virile man like him, then.

I make a cute slurping sound that the innocent Adams does not equate with sucking cock, Courtney, of course tries to guess what Elliot's heavy cock would feel like on her tongue. I clear my throat then moan in pleasure as the cold slush hits my mouth.

It's an interesting flavor. Maybe watermelon mixed with mango, definitely the right amount of alcohol and I suck half of it down before I remember it's cold and I'm going to suffer from a brain freeze if I don't slow down. Placing my tongue on the roof of my mouth to avoid a headache, I wait for the man who makes kickass drinks to say something. I raise an eyebrow then scrunch my forehead as a twinge of pain flows through it.

"Brain freeze?" he finally asks as his broad shadow covers me from the sun. I flick a hand at him, telling him to move out of my rays, he steps to the side and asks, "Is there anything else I can do for you?"

Well, that's a loaded question. Let's see. Courtney has a list at the ready. Neck licked in that spot right below her ear. Hands cupping her breasts while the rough pad on his thumbs hardened her nipples. A kiss to her mouth, one that forces her to open for him as he pulls her into his hard body so she can feel his growing thickness on her belly.

"Adams!" I hear my sister shout this time.

I look down and realize that I must have sat up to accept the drink and stayed like that with my breasts exposed while I drank my fill. Then, while picturing what Courtney wanted from Elliot, I must have returned to fondling my nipples.

"I can give you a hand with that if you need one or…"

"I doubt your employer would like that you're propositioning me."

"My employer?"

"Yes, your employer. I doubt he'd take kindly to what you're suggesting."

"Oh, what am I suggesting? I'm not suggesting anything, sweetheart. Those are your fingers flicking at those rosy, pink nipples, not mine."

"Oh," I sigh and let my hands fall. "I had an itch. Don't you have something else you need to be doing?"

I'd like to suggest that maybe removing his swim trunks and taking himself in hand for me to watch would be an excellent use of his time, but then I remember that I'm Adams, not Courtney, and I flop back down to cover my bare breasts and send him an annoyed stare. "What are you waiting for, then?"

Elliot chuckles and throws his head back, clearly finding something I'm missing as humorous. Then it dawns on me that he just got us drinks and he must be waiting for a tip. "I don't have anything on me. You'll have to wait for your tip."

I hear my sister choke on her drink and send her a look to kill. I turn back to Elliot who is still standing at the foot of my lounger, now staring at me with a huge smirk on his face.

"What?" I ask. "Is there something else or is this just about your tip?"

"Adams, with me, it'll always be about more than *just my tip*."

I let out a fake exasperated gasp as if his crude double entendre has offended me. And it should offend Adams. It's Courtney that wants to tell him that she couldn't agree more. With him, she'd never let it be about just the tip either. Courtney would beg for all (I'm just guessing here) ten inches of his thick cock.

"Well?" I ask as I clear my throat and shift around on my lounger to be sure my bikini bottoms are not revealing a big wet spot. "What do you need then?"

Elliot chuckles again. "Dinner. With you. Tonight, at the pool house. I'll cook."

"You'll…"

"Adams," my sister warns. "Remember we said we were going to spend this time together. Alone."

I wave her off. "Yeah, yeah…um."

Elliot smiles at my sister's pretend concern over my fake virginity being in jeopardy. Then he turns to Bridget and offers for her to join us. I whip my head around so fast, I'm sure I now need to be treated for whiplash. Bridget catches my eye and tries her best to come up with an excuse now that she realizes I'm throwing caution to the wind and fucking my plan for this week up.

I look back and forth between them as one side of Elliot's perfect mouth quirks upward. My eyes travel over his strong jaw covered in just the right amount of beard growth to make it functional in bed. At the thought of rubbing one out on his face, I clear my throat and pull both of their attentions back to me. Then, thankfully my sister squeals and Elliot's focus shifts to her.

"Oooo," Bridget moans. "Ohhhh, that feels…"

Elliot and I watch as my sister wiggles around in her seat with her phone vibrating and shaking her about. Christ, I guess holding out on Ace Lyons wasn't any easier for her than this situation with Elliot is proving to be for me.

"What are you…" Elliot begins to ask but is cut off at the sound of a seaplane approaching from above.

"Ace just texted me. He told me to look up. Holy shit!" she exclaims as she bounces to her feet, her breasts now directly in Elliot's line of vision. "He's here. That's him on the plane."

"What?"

"Ace," Bridget screams as she goes running, topless down the beach to meet the plane at the water line. "Ace!"

"Friend of hers?" Elliot asks.

I shrug because I can't talk. I need to concentrate on a plan. I can't have Ace Lyons getting off that seaplane and calling me by my name when he asks if we're up for a foursome.

Before I can formulate anything worth shit, because my mind stalls on what sex with Elliot would be like, my half-clothed sister and Ace are standing beside Elliot who is looking at Ace with a scowl.

"Monti," Ace greets with a sneer. "What the fuck are you looking at?"

"I've explained the female body to you already, Lyons. Those are called breasts, remember?"

"Monti?" I ask before Ace can respond. "As in full?"

"If you want to call anything about him, full," Ace snickers. "Because if what he's packing is full…"

Elliot laughs then the two men do that back-patting man hug thing. I guess that was friendly banter. I'll never understand the male species.

"When did you…" Ace begins to ask but I catch a look between he and Elliot, and he stops midsentence to look in my direction.

"*Maddie*," I stress my sister's fake name for the next ten days. "Maybe you should take your guest, Ace, is it, into the house and let him put his things away."

"Mad…"

Bless my sister's heart. She cuts Ace off as she wraps her legs around him, after mounting him like a koala, and seals her lips over his mouth. Thankfully, Ace appears to be in his usually horny mood, and never looks back. He walks in the direction of the house with my sister glued to the front of his body.

"That seat taken?" Elliot asks with a smile, knowing full well that it's just become vacant.

I lift my chin to indicate that he can sit if he wants. What choice do I have?

Without a reason to refuse him, Elliot takes the opportunity to sit beside me and stare.

My insides begin to melt under the heat of the sun, but more from Elliot's heated gaze.

"What?" I ask. "What?"

Elliot smiles. "Nothing. You just look nervous. If I were being nosy, I'd ask if maybe you and Ace had a thing going on behind your sister's back."

"I'm not nervous," I lie. "I'm lightheaded from the sun and that drink you gave me. I think you were trying to get me drunk. And I'm not sleeping with him."

Anymore, but I leave that out. And it hadn't been behind Bridget's back. If anyone was behind anyone, it was Ace behind me while…oh forget it. It's water under the bridge and not something I'm sharing with Elliot because I am Adams, a good girl.

"Now why would I need to do that?"

"Do what?"

"Get you drunk?"

"Oh. How would I know?" I ask. "Maybe you're an awful cook and you don't want me to realize how bad the meal you've offered is going to be."

Elliot smiles as he lazily places his arms behind his head and crosses his feet at the ankles. "So, you're coming?"

I choke on my own saliva. Dear God, was I? I mean, with him this close to me and heading into the third or fourth day without sex, one could never be sure.

"To dinner, I mean. Relax, Adams. You're way more tense than someone sitting on a lounge chair in paradise should ever be. Why is that? I'd say it was from lack of male attention and sexual experience, but someone who looks like you, isn't lacking for either, I'm sure."

He's right. I've had an abundance of male attention for years now. And yes, I'm aware that part of my issues stem from the lack of attention from one very important male. I'm not an idiot and I've been in therapy for years to address it. I'm also far from lacking in sexual experience, but I'm not me. Not for the next ten days. For now, I am Adams, sexually inexperienced Adams so I shrug and say, "How can you be so sure? Maybe there are circumstances about me that you couldn't possibly understand."

Elliot raises his eyebrow. "Are you telling me that guys don't fall all over you? Or," he clears his throat. "Shit! I'm sorry. Are you into girls?"

"What? No! I mean, there's nothing wrong with…" I shrug again. "No. I mean, yes. Ugh," I clear my throat. "No, guys don't usually fall all over me. I'm not a lesbian. And, yes, I'm telling you that maybe I am lacking in the male attention department."

Okay, so it would appear that we're now playing two truths and a lie. Want to make a guess?

Elliot laughs at my fake confession then stops when he catches my stare. "Oh," he says. "Um…"

"Listen," I halt him as a brilliant idea takes hold. "How about we agree to hang out without oversharing? I'm sure you'd lose your job if your boss found out that you were sniffing around me instead of doing your work. I won't say anything about our time together here on the island and you get to give me all the attention I need. Deal?"

Elliot sits quietly and studies me for longer than I'm comfortable with before he speaks. "I can spend time with you."

"Well, don't make it sound like a hardship" I scoff. Who does this fucking guy think he is?

Elliot laughs. "No hardship at all. Answer a question for me, though, okay?"

I nod.

"Are you a rule follower? Do you conform well with authority?"

Yeah, that about sums me up, pal. Not. But I can't say that because that does sum up who Adams is. Adams is a girl that has made it into her twenties with next to no sexual experiences because she's a good girl who does what she's told. Not like Courtney who does whatever she can to get a rise out of those around her.

"As long as I know what the rules are and I agree with them, I can follow them just fine."

As the sun begins it's decent, Elliot makes to stand with an explanation that he needs to start our meal preparations. Before leaving, he turns to me and says, "Beautiful."

"Yes," I agree. "The sun on this island is amazing."

"I was talking about you, Adams" he says then he turns and walks to the pool house. "See you in an hour" he yells with his back to me.

I am so fucked.

I stop myself from calling out to my sister just in time. My bare foot hits something soft on the floor and I look down to find Bridget's bikini bottoms wrapped around my big toe. I slow my gate and ease my steps as not to make any noise. But the house is ginormous, so it doesn't really matter. No one could hear me if I screamed. Which gets me to thinking about tonight at the pool house. Now, I know this week was supposed to be about changing my colors, but it's like that bear shitting in the woods. If no one hears what goes on between me and my very own gingerbread boy (yes, we are back to that), does it really count? I say no.

I'm only a step or two away from the door to my bedroom when I hear my sister call my name. "Court?"

"Oh, hey."

"Hey," she says. "Are you trying to sneak in like we used to do in high school?"

"No," I laugh. "I found your suit and figured it was best if I didn't disturb you guys."

I toss my sister her bottoms with a knowing smirk.

"Are you upset that we didn't ask you to..."

I hold my hands up in front of my chest. "No. I think we both know that part of our lives is behind us. I know you like him, and the way he looks at you..."

Bridget smiles from ear to ear. "I can't believe he came all this way because of me."

"I can."

"Yeah, he said you told him about this trip. He figured out where we were going."

I shrug. I had but I hadn't done it in hopes of Ace Lyons showing up to stake his claim on my sister. Honestly, that thought never crossed my mind. I didn't think he had it in him to even consider handing in his manwhore card yet. I just sort of figured it would have maybe prompted him to ask her out on a date or something small like that. I should have known that when it came to Ace Lyons, nothing was small.

"Well, whatever you said, it worked, so thanks."

"Sure. Is he staying until we go home?"

"Oh, shit. Oh, my God! I'm so sorry. I didn't even think about your man-free plan when I asked him to stay."

"It's fine," I lie. "I'm going to go to the pool house in about an hour so you guys will have the place to yourselves."

I smile and start for my room when my name pauses me again.

"Court?"

I turn to see what my sister wants now. "Yeah?" I ask.

"I asked Ace how he knew Elliot. All I was able to get out of him was through the military."

"The military? Elliot's in the military?"

"I don't know," Bridget says. "I tried to ask more questions, but Ace distracted me. I did make sure to warn him that he's not to tell Elliot our real names or anything about you."

"Thanks," I say as I turn the knob to my door and head inside.

After a shower and some primping, I step back into the main living area to find my sister still alone on the sofa.

"Hey, where's Ace?"

"Still sleeping. I wore him out" she giggles.

I laugh along with my sister. "So, no more changing colors for you, huh?"

"Well, not where having sex with Ace goes, but," she shrugs. "I'm going to try that monogamy thing Aunt Brook is always preaching about," Then she scans me from head to toe. "You look amazing. I don't think Elliot will be able to help himself. You're sticking to your plan?"

I smile. "I'm not fucking him if that's what you're asking."

"What?" Bridget screeches. "I thought for sure you'd reconsidered your plan as soon as the hot as sin man asked you to dinner. You understand that he wants to eat you, not a steak, right?"

"He's hot?" I ask. "I can't say that I noticed. The sun was in my eyes, so I couldn't see that well. For all I know, he could be covered in acne with crossed eyes."

She laughs out loud. "That's hysterical. Courtney Knight didn't notice how hot the muscular man in swim trunks and a tan was. He had facial hair, Court. Don't lie to me. You know exactly what he looks like."

"I don't want to talk about it."

"A-Are you," Bridget stutters. "Wait, you're nervous? About going to dinner with a guy? Jesus, you really did get into character for this vacation."

I slink down onto a soft cushion and rest my elbow on the armrest so it can help support my clogged-up head. My brain is swimming with ways this evening could go wrong.

My skirt billows before it settles on my legs. The dress I choose is ice blue and fits my body like a glove. The bodice pushes my breasts into the perfect position to bring attention to them. The waist cinches in to accentuate those breasts and highlight my flat stomach. The length is short enough that if I were to bend over the right way, Elliot would get a sneak peek at the goods. It was sexy but not slutty and in there began the crux of my nerves.

"You don't need to be nervous," my sister continues. "You look amazing. Scarlett's dress fits you perfectly."

I'd asked our new friend for a few of her things after Bridget and I decided this trip would be the catalyst for us changing our slutty ways. Scarlett is the furthest thing from a slut that I know. She's only ever slept with her boyfriend; a guy Bridget and I had given his first threesome to years before meeting Scarlett.

Yeah, that hadn't gone over well when it came out.

As I watch my sister cringe when she sits next to me and takes my hand in hers, I laugh. So much for her not spreading her legs. And then there was one. I guess that explains why Ace is in a sex-induced coma. He must have taken her hard in that glorious way he has. My sister is one lucky chick when it comes to her future sex life if she remains with Ace Lyons.

"I'm not worried about how I look," I state as Bridget plays with my long auburn hair, a color that could possibly be natural, but I've colored it so many different shades, who the hell knows. Even now, there are blonde chunks trying to grow out. "Maybe this whole thing was stupid, and I should go over there naked and just ride him like a wave."

Bridget chuckles. "I like what you did there…ride him like a wave. Hold still," she admonishes. "Let me put your hair up while you tell me what the problem is."

I nod because I know why she suggested it. Courtney doesn't wear her hair up. Not for the nights of unbridled passion she spends on her back or her knees. But Adams would for a sophisticated night like the one I had ahead of me.

I heave in a deep sigh. "Let's be honest, Bridge, I'm not going to pull this off. And I mean, why? Why can't I just do what I want? I'm not hurting anyone. I practice safe sex. I know it's not going anywhere and I'm honest with the guys. They know the score, and no one gets hurt."

"No one?" Bridget asks with a raised eyebrow for me. "And this was your idea in the first place. I didn't come up with this one, that's for sure."

A tear threatens to slip because I know she's referring to our mother being the injured party who has been through more than anyone should. Katrina Adams had made more mistakes with men than I have. Well, maybe not more, but definitely similar ones.

"I know. I know mom has had enough and she's worried that Bobby is about to run. I know why I told you I came up with this plan, but I have something else lined up for when we get home. I'll have enough money for us to move out and go back to school without asking them for a thing by the fall."

"What are you talking about?"

I shrug. "Nothing I can really share yet. Just let me handle it, okay? And who knows, maybe you'll be moving in with Ace."

Bridget laughs. "He's trying to figure out his feelings for me. He's nowhere close to being ready for us to live together."

"You'd be surprised. Some guys fall quick."

"Okay, Bailey Connors, let me know when your new book comes out and I can replace Raina Roman on the big screen when the movie version is released."

I laugh at her reference to our favorite author and actress then sigh and admit, "I've never had dinner with a guy and just talked. It's always been about innuendos that lead to me in his lap or him clearing the table and us fucking on it. I don't know how to be likeable or interesting. I only know how to be sexy."

"You've always been all three."

"I love you, but you only think that because you love me too."

Bridget shrugs. "Just sit across from him at the table and stay in your own seat. Enjoy that velvet voice of his. God, it was sexy, right?"

"I wouldn't say velvety but..."

"Liar. You should have seen the way you were squirming around on that lounge chair every time he spoke."

"Ugh" I sigh. "I'm fucked and that's the one thing I don't want to be tonight. I need to see this through before I go home and..." I stop myself before saying the words on the tip of my tongue.

"Just go over there and enjoy yourself. If you decide that you want to sleep with him, sleep with him. What's the big deal? Listen, when we get home, let's just try our best to relieve the stress from mom, okay? No more acting like spoiled toddlers. It's time we listened to Dr. Stevens and find our father."

And there goes that tear that wanted out.

I nod then heave in a breath to steady myself before I pat Bridget's knee and rise to my feet. "Don't wait up and don't do anything I wouldn't do with Ace" I smile.

"About you and Ace."

"Over. Water under the bridge. Forget it ever happened. I'm happy for you two."

And at that I head out the door to spend an evening with a man I plan to learn as little about as possible while also not fucking his sexy brains out.

6

"This is a horrible idea," I mutter to myself. "I can't believe this is my fucking life."

Then I hear my sister's voice in my head admonishing me and telling me to forget about everything and just enjoy my night. "What happens, happens" she'd say if she were out here on the beach with me instead of in bed with Ace Lyons who I'm sure was worshipping her body and promising to give her everything she's been waiting for. And good for her. She deserves that and so much more. The moon and stars, everything.

With a look down at my bare feet, I momentarily question if it's too casual of a look. But, I'm on an island in paradise. Was there even a dress code? I smooth down the skirt of my ice blue dress and take a healthy breath. As my steps pull me closer to the pool house, my heartbeat quickens until I'm placing a calming hand over my heart.

"What is wrong with you?" I ask myself aloud. "Pull it together."

With my mind in a whirlwind over what the night will hold, my nervousness turns to excitement and I remember who I am. I'm Courtney Knight, not Adams no last name. I'm self-confident and witty. I drip sex appeal and I have nothing to lose. I'm sexually experienced, not some virginal nitwit from the romance novels I read. I don't need a man to define me.

But isn't that how this all started? Haven't men, my biological father, my stepfather, and his best friend been doing just that all these years? As much as I hate to agree that my sister was right, I know it's time to start the healing process and the only way for that to happen is for me to confront them.

So no, I don't need a man to define me. What I need is a man's acceptance because that's what I was lacking in my youth. And that's what has me questioning this night. What if Elliot doesn't like the side of me that I'm about to present to him? The other side of me. Not the confident, sex kitten, but instead, the intelligent woman who has thoughts and ideas that do not only revolve around sex. It's ingrained in my psyche that sex is all I'm good for. My father left me and never looked back because I was an embarrassment. My first stepfather's best friend spent a year convincing me that I was a slut and had nothing but my body to offer a man. And I learned to believe him. Teaching myself new tricks might not be easy, but I'm determined to change.

I stop at the open wall of the living space that is the pool house and listen. A smile tugs at my lips when I hear what Elliot is singing as he prepares our meal. I think it's Kokomo, but he's so off tune and messing up the lyrics so badly, that I can't be sure. It makes me chuckle, but then I pull up short when I smell the sweet aroma of the flowers I see on the large table beside the open wall as I lean in to look around and see if Elliot is in sight. The flowers are beautiful and while I know they're not for me, they're in a vase and appear to match the décor of the space, a part of me momentarily wishes for that level of romance. Flowers, candy, bubble bathes by candlelight. All the things my Aunt Brook and Scarlett insist make the sex even better. I'm sure Bridget is luxuriating in many of them now with Ace Lyons and his three hundred sixty-degree turn about.

"Elliot?" I call. "Um, knock, knock."

I lean down to smell the beautiful bouquet of exotic fresh flowers then stand and marvel at the spectacular view of the surf and sand. Then I raise my head in awe of the man before me.

I lied to Bridget when I told her that the sun had been in my eyes and I wasn't sure if Elliot was even attractive. But, with him now standing in front of me, casually leaning against the wall, watching me, I lose my breath because I truly hadn't given him enough credit.

His chest is bare and exposed for my viewing pleasure. And it's not just muscular, it's sculpted into perfection with a smattering of light hair covering each bulging pec. As my eyes travel to his toned abdomen my insides turn to jelly when they land on that perfect male V that sinks into the low-slung pants resting on his hips. And his stomach? I'd call what I was looking at an eight pack at least, if not a full dozen.

"Amazing view isn't it" I hear him ask and can only guess he's referring to himself, because, yes, it is amazing. He must know that. He exudes confidence and cockiness; he must know how attractive he is.

"Um,"

When I stutter, he laughs and approaches me. "I was talking about the ocean," Then he shrugs. "Well, and the beautiful woman standing in my living room. You look flawless, Adams. I like your hair up like that."

Elliot leans down and places a gentle kiss to my cheek. His lips are plump and soft, my mind goes to thoughts of what they'd feel like on mine and my breathing hitches. "Th-thank you" I say as his finger toys with a strand of hair that must have slipped free on my walk over.

"Come in. Dinner is almost ready. Can I offer you a drink? Something slushy maybe" he teases.

"I limit my daily brain freezes to one" I quip. "But I could drink a glass of wine, if you have any."

Elliot nods. "Have a seat," he offers, lifting his chin in the direction of the sofa, I follow his gaze. "I'll join you with our wines."

I must have gotten lost in my thoughts of the handsome man I'm having dinner with because a clearing of a male throat alerts me to his presence a few moments later. Elliot is casually leaning against the wall again, the ocean breeze moving the curtains beside him about. Each hand is holding a fluted glass of wine.

"Do you always sneak up on people?" I ask. "I didn't hear you come back into the room."

"I've been known to surprise people with my presence," he answers. "And I enjoy watching you when your guard is down. I get the impression that you're trying your hardest to hide something from me. Why is that, Adams?"

His eyes do another sweep of my body but it's when they lock with mine that a rush of heat covers my cheeks. I get lost in his gaze and forget myself in their depth. Then he stalks in my direction and reaches out a hand to offer me my glass of wine. "Hope you like white, it goes with our meal," he says offering his other hand. "If not, I have red or even a sweet rose."

"White is fine," I say. "Thank you."

Leaving his previous question unanswered, I raise to my feet and allow him to lead me to the beach.

"Dinner has finished sooner than I thought. Let's sit so it doesn't spoil. We can talk over our meal."

"Sure. I can't wait to see if you're any good at this cooking thing. Or if you did in fact attempt to get me drunk so I wouldn't notice if you served up slop."

Elliot chuckles. "Oh, Adams, you're a breath of fresh air and…and I don't know what else, but definitely something."

I follow Elliot to the sandy beach outside his kitchen to find a small iron table with two chairs across from one another. The tabletop is set for two with a bucket of ice next to one padded chair and another bottle of wine chilling in the ice.

Elliot leads me to a chair and pulls it out for me to sit. I stop short for a moment to try to remember if a man has ever done this for me before. Maybe Bobby or Uncle Tate at some gala or event I'd attended with my parents, but never a man on a date.

There's one lone candle lit on the table and it flickers in the sea breeze as Elliot goes to his seat and sits down across from me. He reaches for my hand and this time, at his touch, I finally understand what I've felt each time our skin has met the other's.

Electricity. Sexual tension. Passion. Chemistry. All of it rolled together.

The powerful sensation shoots through my veins and it pulls my eyes up to his with a questioning look crossing my face.

A smile spreads across his and he confirms my thoughts. "That's called sexual tension, Adams. Chemistry. I'm not going to pretend; I'd rather forget about this meal and take you to my bed. I'm certain eating you would be better than the meal I've prepared" he leans back to assess my response to his bold proposition.

"Ell…"

Elliot smiles and holds up a hand. "I'm sorry. I shouldn't have been so forward with you. Where I get the impression that your lying to me about something, I'm also picking up on your reluctance with your sexual feelings. Am I wrong?"

"No," I admit, not sure if I'm being honest. I mean, I guess I am. I'm reluctant to submit to my sexual desires for him. Lord knows I want him and yet, I'm fighting it. "You're not wrong."

Elliot smiles with a nod then begins to pour himself more wine. I look down at my untouched glass then raise it to my lips with a moan of approval as the cool liquid enters my mouth. "Crisp" I state.

"You're enjoy the wine?" he asks with a disbelieving tone. "You don't look a day over drinking out of the standard college keg."

I laugh because again, he isn't wrong. "I'm twenty-one. Closer to twenty-two, actually. But I'm not in school right now. I'm going back in the fall. Maybe."

Elliot's eyes take a leisurely trip over my body once again and land on my breasts. I could call him out on it, but instead I watch his eyes dilate as I sit tall and wait for his gaze to return to mine. I lift my glass again and take a slow sip while I wait. When our eyes finally meet, he chuckles because he knows he's been caught.

"Definitely of age," he murmurs. "Thank God for that."

"Elliot, I…"

"I'll stop," he promises. "It's just been a while since a woman has caught my attention the way that you have. You've taken me completely by surprise, Adams. That doesn't happen to me. Ever."

I blush and take another sip of my wine before I return it to the table.

"Give me a minute to grab our plates," Elliot says before standing. "I'll be right back."

I sit and wait for his return and my mind rushes through several questions I'd love answers to, but I won't dare to ask him. Because asking him questions will mean that I'll also need to answer his, and I've no plans on sharing too much of the truth about myself. Why should I? Today is already coming to an end, that leaves nine more before Bridget and I leave this paradise behind and I once again become Courtney Knight. The girl who is scheduled to meet her Compatible Companion match on New Year's Eve and begin her year long contract with the man she's never met. Within a few weeks I'll be the whore my first stepfather's best friend predicted.

Elliot returns without my noticing once again. By the time I'm alerted to his presence, he's standing beside me with his glass in his hand waiting for me to respond so he can initiate a toast. When had he put our plates on the table?

"You get lost in your thoughts, Adams. I like a girl that has things to contemplate."

"Oh, um…yeah, sorry. I do tend to do that. It's not you, honestly. I'm not trying to be rude."

"No need to apologize," he states with a raise of his glass and a lift of his chiseled jaw. "To you, Adams, a beautiful woman with many thoughts. I look forward to getting to know you better. I'd love to understand what goes on in there" He taps my temple with his finger then plants a gentle kiss in its wake.

I take another small sip from my wine then place it back on the table. I look down at our plates and the aroma of our meal fills my nostrils. I inhale and give Elliot an appreciative moan.

"I hope you like fish. It's sort of the go to here on the island. It was all I had in a pinch."

"I love it. My mom is allergic and keeps warning my sister and I to be careful, but I'm fine eating it."

"The sauce should be spicier than I made this one. I wasn't sure how hot you like it, Adams. I didn't know how much you'd be able to handle."

I laugh to myself. If he only knew. I'd say having sex with two men and your sister would rank as hot as it gets on any guy's scale. Even this virile man's sitting across from me who exudes sex and sin.

"See, right there," he says pointing a finger at me. "What just floated through your mind?"

I clear my throat. "Nothing intelligent like you're imagining."

"You have no idea what I'm visualizing, Adams. No idea."

I blush again then lower my head. Good thing he has no idea what I'm thinking either.

"Eat, tell me if you like it."

I twirl a few strands of thick pasta around my fork, sure to collect a piece of shrimp with it. As Elliot sits across from me, his stare glued to my lips, I open my mouth and let my tongue peek out before I groan and take my forkful in. "Mmm," I hum. "Wow! That's amazing. Did you really make this?"

"I did. I'm glad you like it."

Elliot and I eat in silence for a few minutes as we watch the sun completely set into the ocean. I look up as the stars begin to glitter in the sky and I push my still half full plate away. "I'm stuffed," I state. "Thank you for dinner, that was really good."

"Better than slop?" he teases.

"Better than slop" I agree then my eyes meet Elliot's and he asks if I'd like to take a walk on the beach. Having eaten more than I ever have, I agree. A walk to help me digest my meal can't be a bad idea.

"Have you worked on the island long?" I ask without thinking as we walk along the edge of the surf. I want to know more about this man. If he turns it into a game of twenty questions, I can just avoid the ones I don't want to answer. I've grown to be a master at deflecting.

"My father knows the owner. He and his wife used to spend most of their time here, but since my parents became grandparents, they've been spending more time in the States with them."

"Oh, do you…"

Elliot laughs. "No, Adams. I don't have a child. My sister made our parents grandparents, not me."

Elliot casually reaches out for my hand and we walk in silence down at the water line. I screech every time the water hits my feet even though it's not chilly. When a huge wave threatens to reach mid-thigh, Elliot scoops me up and cradles me in his arms at the last second. "Elliot," I laugh. "Put me down."

He puts me back down and we continue to stroll down the beach, me dry, Elliot with pants wet to the crotch from splashing waves that I can't help but to stare at. What is it about men in loose gray sweatpants and no shirt or socks?

"Tell me something about you. We both have sisters. Any other siblings?"

That's a safe enough question so I answer honestly. But then I find myself unable to stop there and I share more information than I want to. I tell Elliot about my aunt and uncle, their twins, and the extended family that came along with them. I leave their names out. My guard is up even more now that he mentioned his father knowing Jonesie, the man that owns the island. Ace told Bridget that he knows Elliot from the military, maybe he was a military brat and that's how his dad and Jonesie are pals. Maybe he and Ace spent time on the same base as kids. I can't risk the Taylor name giving me away.

We continue down the shore hand in hand. Our conversation waning at times, but the silence is nice, not weird or awkward in any way. Elliot keeps a grasp on my hand with just the right amount of pressure to remind my body that he was all male. Then he pauses us, turns me to face him, and takes both of my hands in his. Sensing that he might be about to kiss me, I blurt, "Do you like living in the pool house?"

"I'm staying there, so I guess, yes," he responds then drops my hands and walks closer to the water, letting it come up to mid-calf.

I stand and watch his back, strong and broad, as it lifts and falls with his every breath. I feel like I got something wrong, overstepped or crossed some boarder we had silently created. "Elliot," I say, and he turns to face me.

"Adams?" he responds.

I approach him and apologize, adding that I think it's best for us not to share too much because our time is limited to the island and the clock is ticking. "Let's just enjoy each other until I leave. No more questions or sharing. Just...enjoying."

"What do you enjoy, Adams?" he asks as his eyes dilate and heat runs up my neck causing me to blush. Then a smirk covers his handsome face when he sees that reaction.

"I used to ski, that was fun. I like to shop. I danced when I was younger."

"Mmm hmmm," he hums.

"What's that?" I inquire. "That right there. Mmm hmmm? What does that mean?"

Elliot grabs me around my waist and hauls me into his strong arms, lifting me above the water. "Do you like to swim?"

I squeal. "You wouldn't dare. Put me down!"

"Do you like to swim, Adams, hmmm?" he asks again.

"Oh, my God! Stoooooop!" I shout as I become airborne.

I hit the water and sink under then resurface, sputtering, to find Elliot right there with me. His body heat emanating from his masculine form. He runs a hand through his tightly cut hair then brushes mine behind an ear. "I like you wet" he states with more meaning than Adams is supposed to understand. But when I stop to let myself relax, if for only a second, I know he's well aware of my arousal level.

"I want to kiss you, Adams."

Afraid to move, I look down. I feel his finger lift my chin then his hands tangle in my hair. As my eyes flutter closed, his soft lips brush over mine. Like the strong secure male that I knew he was from the moment I laid eyes on him, Elliot takes charge.

With a guttural groan, he pulls me into his body and deepens the kiss, his tongue running across my bottom lip before his teeth nip it. And I'm done. I let myself go and I sink into his embrace. I relax and let him claim my mouth, his tongue sweeping inside to taste me.

It's then that my mind begins to swim back over the years. All the men. My need for control while simultaneously seeking to be dominated. I sought out men who were everything I had wanted the first man in my life to be. I need a man that thrives on power and control, a man that wants to keep me safe and bring my life order and stability. All the things my father robbed me of when I was only a little girl. I've looked in too many places, all the wrong ones because here is the man that I've needed all along. Unfortunately, I've found him at a time that I can't have him because I'll belong to another man soon.

I sigh as Elliot's hands leave my waist, where they had traveled to pull me closer, and find my ass. He cups me and nudges me to lift my legs and wrap them around him. I do as he silently demands and realize, stupidly, that I'm acting as Courtney would. I pull back and clear my throat and Elliot meets my eyes.

What scares me most in his gaze is the undeniable electricity growing between us. Something I'm afraid I won't be able to leave behind on this island when I'm forced to return to my commitment to a man I've never met.

"Hey," Elliot says as one hand returns to my hair and he draws my attention to his lips. "You okay?"

I shouldn't melt at the sound of his deep gravely voice, but fuck if I don't. Adams wouldn't let her panties grow wet over a touch from a male, but I do. I shiver as panic rushes through me.

Elliot mistakes it for my being cold from the ocean. "You're cold," he says walking out of the water with me still wrapped around him at the waist. "I have clothes you can wear at the pool house."

He walks us to shore then places me on the sand and takes my hand to lead me back to his home.

When we get inside, I stand like the obedient child I had once been coerced into being, and I wait to be told to get changed into the clothes he offers me.

He gives me sweats and a t-shirt before grabbing pants for himself. He mentions a bathroom before leaving me to my privacy in what I assume is his bedroom, it's devoid of any personal touches, so I can't be sure, but his clothing is in the dresser, so I'm safe in my assumption.

I make my way into the attached bathroom and quickly dry myself with a plush towel as I remove my wet dress and undergarments. I hang them on a hook behind the door then straighten out my wild mane as best as I can before tugging his t-shirt over my head. His scent hits me instantly and I moan at the fragrance of him against my skin. I pull on the pants he left me and tie them as tightly as I can then roll them at the waist a few times to hopefully hold them in place. I'm without panties and the fact that Elliot hadn't grabbed boxers for himself either, isn't lost on me. Before exiting the bedroom to go in search of him, I pull his t-shirt over my nose and inhale one last time.

I find Elliot waiting for me on the sofa with a plate of the most decadent looking desserts I've ever seen. "Thought you might be pissed at me for tossing you into the ocean. Figured this would get me back on your good side."

"Were you ever on my good side?" I joke.

Elliot smiles and stands as I approach. He takes my hand and pulls me down to sit beside him. He's shirtless still, with loose black pants now that leave nothing to the imagination without boxers. I look down, unable to keep my eyes from checking his crotch. He follows my gaze and shifts as my stare hardens him and his erection begins to tent his pants.

"The mixed signals you send are fucking killing me, Adams," he groans as he shifts his dick again.

"I'm sorry. Maybe I should go."

"No. I'm a big boy. I can keep my dick in my pants. Well, until you leave. Then I plan on jacking off so hard I might not be able to use my hand tomorrow."

"Ell…" I begin but am silenced when his lips cover mine once more and he pulls me to straddle his lap.

He pulls back just as quickly, and I watch the colors dance around in his eyes. The blues, greens, and shades of brown mingling with desire. I feel his thick erection between us and I have all I can do not to reach down and free him from the confines of his pants. I wish I could sink to my knees on the floor before him and lick his shaft from root to tip before swallowing it whole. I'd take him to the back of my throat then add a hand to stimulate him until he came, his salty release filling my mouth.

"Adams," he questions. "Are you alright?"

I look down, unable to answer. Was I alright? I don't think so, but I can't tell him that. I can't tell him what I was thinking or that I'm not some innocent, sexually repressed virgin with no experience with men. I can't tell him that I need to return to the States and meet a man on New Year's Eve who I will spend a year pleasuring and allowing to take my body. I can't tell him I'm a whore. I can't tell him anything.

"I'm fine. But, um…my sister will probably be waiting up for me. I should go."

"You haven't had dessert yet."

"No, I haven't," I say meaning more than the delicious looking treats on the table. "That's why I should go now."

Elliot places me back on the floor and stands. He takes my hand in his and leads me to the open wall of his pool house. Before I know what hits me, his lips brush mine again and Elliot says, "Sleep well, Adams. I'll see you tomorrow. Just don't ask me to lift anything with my right hand."

And with that comment hanging in the air, he turns and walks back into his living quarters and I head back to the main house to sleep alone in his clothes.

7

I stumble into the main house like I've had too much to drink to find my sister and Ace looking like a romantic couple in love on the sofa. He's casually leaning back with his arms stretched out behind him and Bridget is snuggled around him with her head on his broad chest.

Ace eyes me as I plop down on a chair and huff. "Rough night, Court?"

I shoot my sister a look and she bats at Ace's chest, saying, "She wants to be called Adams while we're here."

"Yes, I picked up on that. Bridget, I'm sorry…wait, was it, Maddie? Mmm, yeah, Maddie you pointed that out earlier. But as I recall, you weren't cooperative in answering my question as to why. *Adams*, would you care to explain?"

"I-I…honestly, Ace, I don't owe you an explanation."

"Well, something's fishy with the two of you. You look…nervous. It's not a look I've seen on you before. What did Monti do to you over there?"

"I'm not nervous," I state. He's the second person who's said that to me tonight, though, so maybe I was. "And you and Elliot obviously know one another. Maybe I should be asking you questions, not the other way around."

"You're free to ask your lover anything you want, but it's not my place to answer anything."

"He's not my lover" I mumble, and Ace's eyes fly wide open then he laughs.

Ace falls into a fit of giggles fit for a pre-teen girl. "You cock-blocked the poor guy? Oh, that's classic, Cor…" he clears his throat. "Sorry, *Adams*. I think I see what's going on here. You, *Adams*, are some sort of sexually deprived innocent, not your usually sl…umph."

Well, that shut him up real quick and probably cock-blocked him for a day or two.

Ace sputters and coughs then looks to Bridget as his hands massage his sack that I just nailed spot on with a pillow. "What the fuck, Court? Jesus Christ!"

Bridget shrugs. "I warned you she was sensitive on the topic, Ace. And you'll be fine. I'll kiss it and make it better in a minute. Why don't you go to the bedroom and wait for me?"

Ace stands to leave then sends me an evil glare as he moans. He stops and turns back to face me to say, "Just be careful, okay. I'm not insinuating that he's dangerous, he's not or I'd had never let you go over there alone. But he is complicated. If you're trying to change or do…whatever," he waves a hand. "Monti might not be your best choice of men to help you out."

"This was supposed to be my vacation to turn over a new leaf" I say to Ace's retreating back.

He turns back toward me and smiles. "You don't need to change, sweetheart. Lots of us love you just the way you are."

Tears threaten to slip over as Ace disappears into one of the bedrooms and quietly closes the door.

"He's right, you know?" Bridget begins. "You don't need to change. You're hot, you're smart too, Court. Any guy would be proud to have you."

"Yeah, and I've lost count as to how many have," I shake my head. "No, I need to do this before we go back. I need to know that I can be more than sex to a man."

Bridget smiles sadly at me then stands to follow in Ace's wake. She stops to turn back and say, "It just takes finding the right one, Court."

"Is Ace your right one?"

"I don't know for sure yet, but I'd say there's a pretty good chance."

I nod and watch my sister walk down the hallway. As I'm about to sit down for a good cleansing cry, I hear my phone chirp on the coffee table where I must have left it earlier today. I jump at the sound, after only being here a few hours, it's blaring. There really is something to say about going off the grid.

I grab my phone from in front of where Ace had been sitting before I had needed to put him in his place. There's a strange number on the screen with a text.

Don't be upset. I couldn't help myself. You have my interest piqued and I knew I wouldn't last until morning.

Before I can think, let alone respond, my phone rings and I toss it into the air. Lucky for me it lands on the soft cushion of the sofa. I flip it over to see the same number that the text came in from.

I slide my finger across the screen and hold it up to my ear. "Um…hello?"

Then I hear his voice. Rough and gravely like he's been sleeping, but I know he hasn't been because I just left him only moments ago. "I have you on speaker," Elliot says with a smile I can't see but can hear in his voice. "I can't use either hand."

"I just left," I laugh. "How can your hands already hurt?"

Elliot doesn't answer. Instead he says, "Hi, Adams. You pissed that I swiped your phone and took your number earlier?"

I have no clue how or when he was able to accomplish the task, but I push that question to the back of my mind and let his deep, rough voice run over me.

"Um." Was I? "No. I...um, you could have just asked."

"Now where's the fun in that? And I like to have fun. Do you like fun, too?"

"Elliot, I should tell you that I'm not going to have sex with you then leave this island and never see you again. It's not who I...well, it's not who I want to be."

Elliot sighs into the line. "Yeah, that's what has me hooked. You're a walking contradiction and it's driving me wild after knowing you for a fucking minute and doing nothing more than kissing that mouth of yours."

I remember what his lips felt like on mine and I sink down onto the sofa and curl my legs under my body.

"I liked when you kissed my mouth."

Elliot chuckles. "I bet you did. So does that mean we can do more of that while you're here?"

"I guess" I say like a giddy schoolgirl with a huge smile on my face from ear to ear. What harm could it do? It's just a little making out.

"Maybe you would feel more comfortable if we established some ground rules for the next few days while you're here. I'd like to see you again, Adams."

"Oh, I don't..."

"I believe I've already inquired if you have a difficult time following rules. I'm beginning to think that's the case."

Bingo. Rule follower will never make its way onto my resume. It certainly isn't on my Compatible Companion's profile. But I was matched with a man who likes rules to be followed. Specifically, rules and boundaries he places regarding his sexual gratification.

"Did I lose you, Adams?" Elliot's voice brings me back.

"No, you haven't lost me." He also doesn't have me. He can't have me. As of New Year's Eve, I'll belong to another man for a year.

"Good to know," Elliot clears his throat. "So, I should let you get some sleep and I need to jerk off at least eight more times before I'll be able to get any, but I'd love to see you tomorrow."

I laugh at the absurdity of Elliot pleasuring himself eight more times, but then at the image it brings to mind, I add the idea to my own personal spank bank. Yes, girls have spank banks, too. I mean, right? Oh, whatever. When I hang up this call, I'm going to bed and getting myself off to thoughts of Elliot with his thick cock in his hand and I don't care what anyone thinks.

"Adams?" I hear him call. "Did I lose you this time?"

"No. I mean, sure, I'd love to see you tomorrow. When are you done with work?"

Elliot laughs. "I'm pretty open. Island life is sort of laid back with the working thing. How about a tour of the island? We can use the open-air jeep."

"Okay."

"See you around ten, then? Oh, and Adams, when you're in bed, playing with yourself to thoughts of me jerking off...I like long pulls to start, but when I finish, it's with my hand near the tip and my thumb rubbing the underside."

And then he's gone, and I'm left with the image of Elliot stroking his cock in my mind.

Bedtime.

8

My lips tug at the corners and I feel a smile play out on my face as I throw my phone down and head for a bottle of water. The house is quiet, Bridget and Ace probably sleeping off yet another sex high. I go to the kitchen to get what I need then return to my bedroom.

I notice that I left the curtains open and I imagine undressing in front of them while Elliot watches from his window. I leave the lights off and push open the slider. The curtains instantly billow out and a fragrant breeze enters my room. The beach air is warm, nothing like what I would be dealing with back home. Certainly nothing like the coldness of this time of year in Vermont where I had started out.

Far out on the beach, the water crashing sends a rumbling sound my way and I recall my time at the water's edge tonight with a man who intrigues me more than I thought possible. Usually, I meet a man, size him up for his worth in bed, complete the deed if he proves worthy, and move on. Gender role reversal at it's best.

But for some reason unknown, I can't seem to think of Elliot in only that one capacity.

I mean, don't get me wrong, he presents as a man who knows his way around a woman's body. I'm sure he'd be great in bed. It's just...my thoughts sway from the bedroom with him and I wonder what it would be like to have coffee together down by the water on a Sunday morning. Or a Saturday night at the movies. This is so foreign to me that I can't make heads or tails out of my feelings. I choose to return to my earlier thoughts of Elliot spying on me as I undress because I know how that scenario would play out. It's always safer when my vagina is involved, instead of my heart.

I pull my dress over my head and stand in front of the open space, the curtains moving in the slight breeze to my sides. I moan as my hands meet my breasts and lift them, my thumbs toying with the hard peaks of my nipples under the thin fabric of my bra. The sensation sends waves through my belly and I think I hear a male groan on the breeze.

I unhook the clasp between my breasts and allow my tits to fall out. They ache with their need for a man's caress, but for tonight, mine will have to do. I tweak and tug at my nipples until they're sore, the connection to pleasure from pain one that has always been strong for me during sex. It's not easy to find a male that understands that fine line and can keep my body teetering on it until I was begging for a sweet release. If I were to need to come up with a list of men that have done that for me, it would be two men deep. Ace Lyons and Callan Black.

With Ace now apparently a one-woman man and Callan a million miles away with his own issues, it's my own hand or...

Elliot.

I think about calling him. Telling him to look out his window and watch me. Take his cock in his hand and make himself climax to the sounds of mine. But I don't need to make that call. Within seconds of the idea crossing my mind, as if we're connected telepathically, my phone vibrates with a text from that same unknown number from before. I reach to grab it off the dresser and read the screen.

Lose the panties

Three simple words, no punctuation. Lose. The. Panties.

I remain rooted in place. Then my eyes slowly travel up to see if I can make him out in a window across the way, maybe standing in the sand. My eyes take a moment to adjust to the darkness, when they do, all I see is a brief movement. Nothing more than a shadow on the beach in front of the pool house.

Could that be Elliot? I don't know how he'd see me well enough from such a distance to know I was only wearing panties.

Put them on the lounger then go back to where you're standing and wait for my next direction. Let's test out my theory about your ability to follow directions.

Elliot decides to use punctuations this time as he delivers an order that sends shivers up my spine.

Follow my orders, Adams, or accept the consequences

He sends that next demand when I take too long to obey and the fact that he's in command of my every move, does something primal to my insides and my pussy quivers at the thought of what he could do to me if he were here instead of across the beach.

I don't know if it's my need to desperately have an orgasm, the fact that his command has gotten me to the edge, or my true self unable to stay tamed, but I do his bidding and slowly lower my panties down my legs. When they fall to my ankles, I reach down and grab them.

Are they wet? Smell them and tell me how sweet that pussy is

I gasp at his lude request but comply all the same.

My panties are soaked for him and have a faint smell of arousal, but I don't let that show on my face as I inhale them. I like the way this game is playing out, one-sided, Elliot giving orders, me doing his bidding after making him wait me out. I don't want it to end.

By the way, I like the wax job. My tongue will be able to slide over your slick flesh with ease

My legs go weak and I shiver. I place the panties on the lounger and back my way into my doorway. I don't turn around because I suspect, in that short time, he'd be able to snatch my panties like a ninja in the darkness.

Good girl. Now, show me how you touch yourself. Once your fingers are wet, taste them.

Holy fuck! It's not that his demand is something I've never heard before. It is. Many times over. What is it about a woman pleasuring herself then tasting her pussy off her fingers that makes a man insane?

I plan to comply as I've been. Mainly because I need to get myself off, but a little to hear him call me a good girl again. The sound of that on his lips, the way I imagine he'd say it, sends shivers straight to my core. So I slowly let my hand travel down my neck, my finger trailing across my heated skin. I let it linger between my breasts for a moment, then circle my nipple with it. My head falls back on a gasp as my nipple hardens. The other begs for the same attention and I flick that nipple a few times before I hear another incoming text.

Your nipples are very responsive. They'd be better served in my mouth, Adams. I don't like being denied things I desire.

My mouth gapes open at the thought of Elliot pleasuring my breasts, my hardened nipples. His tongue would swipe over one then the other, leaving them just wet enough that the breeze from the ocean would further harden them into tight buds that would make me insane with my need for release.

After I lick them, my teeth would bite down, and I'd pull. I'd tug at them until you were begging to come. Then I'd spank that ass for your impatience. Naughty girl

And that has me moving my hand further along down my body as quickly as I can.

I cup my pussy first, then let a finger slide inside. I audibly moan at the tight wetness before letting my finger slide out. I slowly raise it to my mouth and put it between my lips. As my taste hits my tongue, I let a smirk spread across my face, so Elliot will know.

That pussy is sweet as sugar, isn't it? When I get my mouth on you, I'm not stopping until I have you coming all over my face. Now, play with your clit and make yourself come for me. I want to watch as your climax takes over.

Fuck, yeah!

I let my thumb make a circle over my clit then add my other hand into the action to drive Elliot out of his mind. I open my pussy for better access to my clit and to allow him the visual of the rotation of my fingers.

Don't stop, Adams. I'm jerking off while watching you and I'm about to come.

I picture Elliot stroking his hard cock up and down, his head between my legs while I come on his face. He moans into my pussy as my release flows into his mouth and he comes with me. His cock spurts his climax onto my leg. It's hot and drips to coat my skin. Some lingers in his hand and he raises it to my mouth to clean.

I'm coming, Adams. Hard. Fuck!

I crash over the edge and come too, collapsing to the floor with a contented sigh. I allow my fingers to continue to stroke my slick flesh as I ride out my high.

You should sleep well now, good girl. See you in the morning

It takes me a few minutes to read his last text because I'm unable to move from the ball I've curled myself into on the floor. But he's right, I'm sated now, and I already feel sleep tugging me down.

I raise to my unsteady feet and make my way to the lounger to retrieve my panties. He didn't really mean to come over here and take them, right? Or did he? Because they're gone.

I stand and look out into the darkness while the sound of the crashing ocean surrounds me. A yawn has me returning inside to climb into bed with my phone in hand. I need to add him to my contacts.

Your pussy is the sweetest I've ever smelled. I can't wait to bury my face between your legs, Adams

Well, there's the answer to my question. My panties are across the beach in Elliot's hands and most likely covering his face.

With thoughts of Elliot sleeping with my panties, I fall into a contented slumber.

I wake the following morning feeling refreshed and ready to face my day. I stretch and yawn, then the events of the prior night resurface, and the battle in my head continues.

I'm supposed to see Elliot today. Certainly, after last night, he'll be expecting me to act as Courtney would, sexually aware and primed for a day of sex on the beach. Do I cave and give him that? Or do I hold firm to my plan and act as Adams? She'd be shy and embarrassed today by her uncharacteristically sexually bold and confident actions from last night. She's not a woman who knows how to take her pleasure into her own hands...literally. But she had last night while Elliot watched and had done the same.

The choice is taken from me as I make my way into the kitchen, rumpled from sleep, my hair a nightmare and not a stitch of make-up on my face, to find the man who stared in my dreams last night.

Elliot is standing, one hand casually in his cargo shorts, the other holding a steaming mug of coffee while he laughs at something Ace must have said. When he sees me, his eyes raise and lock with mine. A devilish smirk tugs at the corner of his lips and I can't help but to raise an eyebrow, daring him to say something about how we spent our night.

"Did you sleep well, Adams?" Elliot questions.

"Yes, *Adams*," Ace says stressing my fake name. "Did you sleep well? You look like you spent the night with a bunch of frat boys fucking the sh..."

Elliot interrupts Ace, clearly thinking his crude hypothesis would offend me, never thinking that scenario is one I would have actually experienced. He'd be wrong, I know my way around a frat house like it's the back of my hand. "I disagree. I think Adams looks adorable and refreshed."

"Thank you, Elliot. At least one of you has the manners of a grown man."

Ace laughs but before he can make another comment, Elliot removes his hand from his pocket and smiles at me when I see the blue lace of my panties poking out. So much for adult-like manners.

Ace says something that I don't hear while I mumble about needing a shower before our island tour. I rush back to my room before Elliot can notice that my cheeks have turned pink from my embarrassment.

9

As soon as I'm ready to leave my room and go in search of my island tour guide, I hear the blaring of a horn. I step out onto the sand and let my hand rub over the spot where I last saw my panties before they reappeared in Elliot's pocket in my kitchen.

Elliot is sitting in an open-air jeep with a smirk on his face. He knows where my panties were because, while I was recovering from my orgasm on the floor, he must have snuck up to the lounger to collect them. Where he acquired the skills needed to do that like a ninja in the night, I'll never guess. Oh, wait…the military thing that Ace mentioned. Hmmm…maybe I should have a chat with Elliot about his last job.

"You ready, good girl?" he asks with a laugh at what he obviously knows is a term that heats my libido.

"Mmm, hmmm" I mumble as I maneuver my way out onto the beach where he awaits.

As I approach the vehicle, that must be owned by his employer, Elliot hops out to help me climb in. I expect him to lend me a helping hand, but instead, I'm lifted into the jeep as if I weigh no more than the ocean air that surrounds us.

I hear a groan come from him and I look to see if he's hurt himself lifting me. I find him shifting what can only be described as a marvelously solid, thick and long erection. One that makes my mouth water and I'm forced to pull my eyes from his crotch and clear my throat.

His hand reaches out to tug on my hair. "Those are turning me the fuck on, Adams. I might need to call you a naughty girl instead."

"Elliot," I sigh as his hand continues to tug on my pigtails. I put my hair up today, so it wouldn't look like a rat's nest from the island wind in the open jeep. "I don't want to give you the wrong idea. I mean, last night was not like me. I don't usually…" I lie like it's my job.

"Oh, I'm sure you don't. But I seem to be able to get you to do my bidding fairly easy so…"

"Are you always this cocky?"

"Is it cockiness when it's the truth?" he asks as he climbs into the driver's seat. His green, brown eyes hold mine as he leans into my space and plants a friendly kiss to my cheek. "You look pretty this morning, Adams."

"Oh, thank you. You don't look so bad yourself."

Those eyes of his fill with a determined look. He wants to know something. I'm already beginning to understand his unspoken communication.

"What?" I ask.

"You seem surprised to hear that coming from me. I can't for the life of me imagine why that is. I'm sure you have men falling at your feet back home, wherever home is."

I shrug. His eyes remain locked to mine and his stare forces my eyes to my lap. I clear my throat. "I don't know. Guys don't usually say I'm pretty. Sexy, maybe, hot, but not pretty."

Elliot's neck straightens like a turtle's and his broad shoulders tense as he searches for a response. He growls when he apparently can't find one that he deems appropriate.

At the chance, I change the subject. "You like living on the island?" I inquire.

"What?" he asks. "I can't hear youuuuuuu" he yells as he hits the accelerator to end my line of questioning. We zoom off across the sand and Elliot laughs while I scream and hold onto the bar above my head for dear life.

"I hope you know how to drive this thing," I yell over the wind. "I can't believe your boss let's you take it out."

"I like taking it out," he quips. "In fact, I can take it out right now, if you'd like."

I roll my eyes. "I meant it's worth a shit load of money. I'm surprised they let you use it, is all."

"My boss, huh? Speaking of which, how did you say you knew the owner of the island?"

"Elliot," I say as his hand travels to my thigh. "I don't want to be rude. I'm having fun with you, but this week? It's about the unknown and being free for me. I have big changes coming my way when I return for the holidays and I just want this time on the island to be fun. No expectations, no information that could make this complicated. When I leave here, I need to leave myself behind and..." I break out into tears before I can finish, and Elliot stops the jeep and cuts the engine.

He turns his body to face mine and takes my hands in one of his, then the other lifts my chin when I lower my gaze to my lap again. "Hey, HEY," he repeats louder when I still don't make eye contact. "Adams, listen to me. We all have demons we're running from in our past and choices we've made for our futures that we might not like. I don't care to explain myself any more than you do. This week, it can be about us. Exploring each other for fun, having a good time. I'm not going to lie, I'd love for that to include having you in my bed, but my hand seems to be holding out okay even after last night."

We laugh together for a moment then Elliot's thumb wipes the tears from under my eyes.

"I'm sorry to be a downer. I promise, no more tears."

He tilts my head to allow himself the access he seeks, and I watch him. I stare at his plump lips as his tongue sneaks out to moisten them. "I'm going to kiss you now, Adams. Close your eyes," I try to defy him and keep my eyes open and locked to his, but he just chuckles and says, "Have it your way, bad girl."

Elliot's lips cover mine and my eyes are forced to flutter closed on a moan. I feel a hand move to the back of my neck to pull me in tighter to his kiss, then his other hand entwines in one of my pigtails and he groans from deep in his core. He holds me to him and kisses me like I've never been kissed before. With a passion I've longed for but never experienced.

My hands begin to rub at his strong chest, and I feel the twitching of the muscles underneath the shirt he's for once wearing. I let my hand cover his heart for a moment and pretend that's where I take up residence. I push him back as that thought flows through me. What the fuck was happening to me. "Elliot, I…"

"Shh," he demands. "Stop thinking and come here."

He pulls me across the seat with ease and places me on his lap where I straddle him. I feel his erection between us and he shifts me around until he's comfortable. I stare into his eyes and gnaw at my bottom lip. It's sore and bruised from his kiss and I love the twinge of pain.

"Relax," he says. "Fun, right? Let's just enjoy this. I get that you're skittish about sex, I'm not going to make you do anything you don't want to do. I just want to kiss you, okay? Can I kiss you again?"

I shake my head because I already crave his lips more than the air I need to survive. "Yes."

Elliot's tongue enters my mouth and my hands go to his face. I hold him to me as if my very existence depends on this kiss. My fingers feel the roughness of his stubble and I know how amazing it would feel against the inside of my thighs while he went down on me. His hands make their way to my hips and he slowly grinds me on his cock while he continues to explore my mouth.

We dry hump and make out like teenagers on a couch in their parent's finished basement.

Then, he groans and pulls back. "As amazing as that feels, I need to stop or I'm going to need a change of shorts. Jesus, you flip every switch I have, Adams. I haven't almost come in my pants since I was in high school. One make-out session with you and I'm ready to fucking go off like a rocket" he says.

He stills my hips and takes in a few calming breaths. I run my hands through my hair then climb back across the seat.

Elliot's head hits the back of the seat with a thud and he closes his eyes. When they reopen, he looks at me and smiles. "Let's finish the tour then we'll grab something to eat back at the house."

"We could watch a movie. In the summers, my sister and I would watch movies and eat green popsicles."

"Only the green ones?"

I shake my head, confused why that was a question. Of course, only the green ones. We had good taste in cuisine at a very young age.

Elliot laughs then pushes the button to start the engine.

We spend about an hour riding around. He drives into the water on my side and soaks me in the waves with a roaring laugh. I scream as the spray of the water hits me then lose myself in the chuckles I can't contain. It feels good to laugh and not worry about anything.

Elliot does that to me. Makes me forget.

By the time he's cutting the engine again, I'm relaxed and in the best mood of my life.

"You know what my favorite movie was?" I ask.

"I can only imagine" he says as he climbs out of the jeep and comes around to my side.

I jump out into his arms and he makes the sexiest harrumph sound, as if my weight were a strain to his bulging arms, but I know the bulging body part causing him to moan is much lower.

"Clue" I state.

"Clue? What, are you going to give me hints?"

"No, silly! Clue. Clue was my favorite movie. You know, like the board game?"

"You are amazing, Adams. Let's go" he says as he carries me inside the pool house.

He places me on my feet then tells me to get comfortable on the sofa while he grabs our lunch.

Elliot returns with a tray of wraps and side salads. His employer must keep one hell of a stocked kitchen.

"Hope you're hungry," Elliot says placing the tray down on the table in front of us. Then he reaches for the controller and scrolls through Netflix with a smirk until he finds the movie I requested.

"Netflix and chill, huh?" I say. "That's your game?"

"Are you offering, Adams?"

"Maybe I am."

Oh, shit. Why did I just say that? Ugh, I know exactly why I just said that. I said that because that's what I want. A movie that starts with a little snuggling, then adds a make-out session, that ends with me sucking his dick and getting fucked…good and hard over the arm of this sofa with my ass up in the air and…I clear my throat as Elliot smirks at me.

"You should really sell tickets to the show that plays in your head."

"Oh, I…no, I mean…"

Elliot chuckles and takes a bite from the wrap in his hand. "It's okay. You're not a booty call kind of girl. Don't ever sell yourself short like that. You deserve the moon and the stars, romance and champagne."

Wow! If he only knew what kind of girl I've been. Because yes, a booty call would sum me up in two short words. And when I return to the States and meet my Compatible Companion, I'll be a whore for the next year.

I shrug a shoulder in thought. Not much different than the last few years. Only, come December 31st of next year, I'll be a whole hell of a lot richer.

Elliot is staring at me again when I finally pull myself from my thoughts.

"That was some matinee, huh? You ready to watch the real movie or should I just keep watching yours play out behind your eyes?"

I roll my eyes to seem flirty and in no way freaked out by the idea that he can see into my soul. I'm beginning to think that I'd better monitor my inner thoughts and emotions around him as much as what comes out of my mouth. I'm not sure how, in only a few hours spent together, he's able to read me like an open book, but it would appear he's getting quite skilled at the task.

"Elliott, I'm only here for another nine days. We agreed to do this without any commitments, right? We can trust each other to leave whatever happens between us here and not need anything more, can't we?"

Elliot's hands find their way to my face and he pulls me toward him. My nipples perk up as I feel his warmth seep into me, and they harden into sensitive buds that desperately want his attention. He lowers his gaze to my lips when he pulls back then brings our foreheads together.

"Adams," he groans, his voice rumbling like thunder on a hot summer day, clashing with the elements. "You're beautiful," His fingers toy with my ponytails. "And sexy as fuck. I'll take anything you'll give me. Now, tell me your limits."

10

The sound of those words rolling off his tongue are words I've longed to hear from a strong and dominant male my whole life. Yet, I still ask, "Wh-what do you mean, my, my limits?"

Elliot's expression hardens for a moment before he can pull on the mask that then takes over. He shakes his head. "I told you that I won't push you into anything you're not comfortable with. You seem skittish around the topic of sex but then you respond to me perfectly in the moment and your body melts and sends me a much different message. So, when I ask you what your limits are, Adams, I'm asking you how far you'll let me take you...sexually."

"Oh."

A shiver runs through me at the thought of telling him the truth. Telling this perfect man that my hard limits would be few and far between. With him even less than usual. I want to admit to the need for pain with my pleasure, just the hint of it. I want to let him know that a good spanking from him would probably bring me to orgasm, I'm sure of it if he were to add the fact that it was a punishment for *his* naughty girl.

I raise my glass of lemonade to my lips and take a sip. Unfortunately, that's when Elliot chooses to ask, "Adams, are you still a virgin?"

I cough and sputter, choke really, until he's pounding on my back and saying something about knowing CPR if I need him to provide rescue breathing. After a moment, I settle and look into his eyes then my eyes drop to his lips and a fire runs through my veins. I mount him like a horse, legs wide open and wrapped around him, ready for the ride of a lifetime.

Elliot moans as our kiss heats, then he stands. He pulls back for just a second to meet my eyes and gain my permission. I shake my head and that's all the encouragement he needs. Elliot begins to walk us to his room.

He pauses again at the threshold, this time his eyes stay locked with mine and he quirks his head to the side in thought. "Was it enjoyable, Adams? Did you like having sex, like what the men did to you?"

I shrug. Had I? Honestly?

"Um, it's not like in the romance novels I read, but it's been okay, I guess."

Elliot laughs. "Just okay? And what you're looking for is a book boyfriend that says all the right things, touches you in all the right places, and has a thick twelve-inch cock?"

I stare at the man because, well, quite frankly, yes. That is exactly what I want, the unicorn of men.

Elliot laughs again then sighs and turns back to the main living space, his demeanor telling me he's about to completely change our plans. "Let's watch that movie you have me intrigued over then make out on the couch. If we end up back here later," he shrugs. "We'll talk about what it is you do like in bed."

"Wait, wait, wait" I stutter.

Elliot laughs. "What?"

"I thought we were going into the bedroom. You know, for sexy time?"

"Sexy time?" he asks, laughing again. "You're really something, aren't you, Adams?"

"I thought we promised our time here would stay here, so what's the harm, right?"

"We did. After your performance last night, I have a pretty good idea I know everything I need already, so let's take our time."

The way his voice sends electricity flowing through my body is scaring me and I know I should pull back. Things are happening with Elliot at a pace that's insane even in one of Bailey Connors' famous books turned into a movie starring Raina Roman. I want him like I've never wanted a man before. Not just his attention or the false validation I always seek from men, I want Elliot.

I. Want. Elliot.

Oh, fuck!

We return to the main living space and plop back down on the sofa. Elliot hits the play button and cues up our movie. We sit for the next ninety minutes and laugh at the corniness of the comedy while we nibble on our food. Elliot wraps a protective arm around the back of the sofa, and I sink into his chest as my eyes start to feel heavy when the ending credits begin to roll.

I yawn. Instinctively, Elliot lays me down and pulls me into his chest. "Shh, take a nap with me. The beach air tires you out. This is the first place I've been in a long time where I can truly relax, it seems to have the same effect on you."

I nod and begin to doze off. Elliot plants a gentle kiss to my lips and says, "Adams, I like you. I'm glad you decided to take this trip and walk into my life."

Without responding, I return his kiss. Our lips connect slowly as we're both fighting off sleep. Elliot lets his hands rest in the dip of my back, and he pulls me into his chest. I inhale the masculine scent of him and do my best to save it in my memory banks for when I'll be forced to cuddle up like this with another man. One I'll hardly know, one I might not like. Definitely one I won't have the same feelings for as I do Elliot.

We sleep peacefully for what must be hours because I'm awakened by Elliot to a darkened house, the orange glow of the sun setting is the only source of light.

"Hey, beautiful," he says with another swipe of his lips over mine. "Let's go watch the sun set. It's pretty amazing. Not as pretty as you, but a close second. Come on" he beckons with a teasing bump to my shoulder.

"A close second, huh?"

Elliot shrugs.

Out on the beach, he takes my hand and lowers me to his lap in the sand. "Adams, you don't need to tell me more about yourself than you want to, but I feel like you're struggling with something and could use a friend."

"Oh, we're friends now?"

"Yes. We are. At the very least. You know I want more; I've been clear about that."

Elliot shifts his erection under me to drive home that point, and I wish he was driving it home for real. Deep inside me at the same speed as a race car driver. Pounding me into...

"That mind gotcha again, didn't it, Beautiful?" Elliot reaches for my chin and forces our eyes to lock. "I mean it, Adams. I can be your friend. You can talk to me. No one gets that need more than I do, trust me."

I tilt my head as I contemplate that statement. Does Elliot need the same from me? I might not be able to tell him my whole truth, but I can certainly listen to his. Isn't that what this experiment is about? A real relationship. Getting to know the important stuff about a guy, not just their dick size. I mean, not that that's not important because anyone who tells you size doesn't matter, has a tiny dick and you should hightail it out of there pronto.

"I can be your friend," I say. "But that goes both ways. If you're going to listen to me, I get to hear your story, too. As much or as little as each of us want to share, right?"

Elliot nods with a smile. "If I only have you for a few days, I want to make the most out of our time. I want you to leave here ruined for all other men. That way you'll be receptive to me when I track you down."

"Elliot, I told you..."

"I know," he says. "I was kidding. What do you think I am? Some undercover spy with a team of detectives at my disposal?"

I laugh, but something about that comment tugs at a corner of my mind. Before I can let it play out and form into something I could hold on to, Elliot whispers into my ear and distracts me from my train of thought. "Watch the sun, it's about to disappear until tomorrow" he says then his tongue licks across the shell of my ear and sends a chill through my body.

A gasp escapes me as Elliot continues to let his tongue run the shell of my ear with a pained groan. He flicks at the sensitive flesh then nips my lobe with his teeth. White hot desire floods my system and I turn in his lap to straddle him.

His large hands travel to my waist and he begins the sweet movement of my body against his erection once again. "I might not stop this time, Adams. I might let you make me come in my shorts."

So much for talking.

"Jesus," I utter. "Elliot, I…"

His mouth crashes over mine to end my protest and I sink into the embrace. My hands go to his shoulders as I seek leverage to help him move my body up and down. Not that he needs it, he lifts and lowers me like I'm nothing more than a feather floating in the air.

"Adams, it's been a really long time since I've taken a woman," he admits, his breath heavy in my ear. "And you flip my switch, so it's not going to take much more than this to get me off, and embarrassingly quick. Tell me to stop if you don't want…"

It's my turn to silence him. I reach for the hem of my shirt and pull it over my head to expose my pink lace covered breasts. My nipples already peaking for him and Elliot groans again as he lowers his head in between them.

He pulls me into him, closer still, while he seductively licks at the tops of my breasts where they're exposed for him. "Take it off," he begs. "You're so fucking responsive, I bet I can make you come in your pants. Just from playing with these."

I pull in a deep breath because I bet he can, too. He'd be the first man to do it, but I don't doubt his skills or his power over me for even a hot minute.

I nod and stretch behind my back to unhook the clasp of my bra.

With my eyes locked on his, I watch the brown of his irises turn green then sparkle, the glint of the setting sun off the water creating the most beautiful color. The longer I look at him and he holds my gaze, the more I want to end this charade and free his erection, pull my shorts off and push my panties to the side. I yearn to let his cock slip inside and ride him until I feel the warm rush of his climax filling me.

"Stay with me," he admonishes. "Take it off and I'll make sure your mind is on nothing else but the pleasure I can give you."

I let my bra fall down my arms and Elliot, his eyes never leaving mine, slides it the rest of the way off and tosses it aside. I gasp as he finally lowers his gaze to take my half nakedness in. My nipples, hard peaks, begging for his attention, are aching with my desire.

"I've never seen more perfect nipples," he says as he lowers his head and gently flicks one with his tongue. "Tell me, Adams, how sensitive are they?"

Elliot bites down, not gently. My head falls back, my back arches and my hips continue their grind on his cock. I moan, and he knows my answer without me needing to say a word.

"That's a good girl. I love a woman who can accept pleasure with her pain. You deserve every second of what I'm about to do to you. Talk to me, baby. No being shy. Tell me when something is about to get you off or if you need more to get there."

I nod.

"You are my good girl, aren't you?"

"I'm a bad girl sometimes too, because I like it when you call me that."

Elliot sucks air in through his teeth at my admission, then says, "Good to know. We'll handle your naughty side another time."

Elliot lets me continue to rub myself on his erection and raises his hands to cup my breasts so his thumb can toy with the nipple his mouth can't. The rushing sound of blood in my ears blends with the crashing ocean waves as I approach my own breaking point. "That feels so good," I admit.

"You feel good in my arms. Every fucking thing about you feels fucking amazing."

I feel my inner walls clench tight in search of his cock. My pussy is seeking him out but coming up empty. But it's his next words that are what set off my internal detonation.

"Adams," he heaves. "You're going to make me come."

I hadn't realized just how fast and consistent I'd been grinding on his cock until then. My core tightens again at his admission and I feel him twitch in his shorts.

"Fuck!" he cries out then clamps down on my nipple with his teeth. "Come for me" he orders and without thought, my body obeys his command.

"Elliot!" I cry out as I crash under the waves of euphoric pleasure. I feel the tightening in his shorts then another twitch. Elliot's hands fly to my hips to help finish himself off. He finds the pace he needs quickly and calls out my name, as I did his, when his climax takes hold.

He's a sight to behold as he finds his release. His head falls back, and he shamelessly moans, pants, through each thrust of his hips with grunts. Then his mouth finds my neck and he nuzzles in while he finishes rubbing his orgasm out to completion. His mouth clamps over mine and his tongue seeks entry, he moans my name into my mouth on his final twitch. We kiss, our tongues dancing for a moment, then Elliot slightly pulls back to murmur praises on my lips, his mouth still on mine.

"I should go get cleaned up. It's getting dark, we should head inside. We can come back out with candles or…"

I silence him with another kiss then climb off his lap. "I should probably go. Tomorrow's another day."

I'm sure Elliot was able to see the quick beating of my heart as I run from him, leaving him alone on the beach with a sticky mess in his shorts.

I slowly run backward at first so I can see him for a few minutes more like this. He holds out a hand to me with a smirk on his face but never makes to chase after me. He knows that I desperately want everything about him. His intoxicating scent around me, his strong body looming over mine in that moment before penetration, his lips on every inch of my body. He doesn't need to chase me.

And I know if I give into my desires, Elliot will gladly take me right here in the sand.

But I can't let that happen. I made a promise to myself that I wouldn't, and I must remain strong. So instead of heading into a shower now with him to extricate the grains from my most private crevasses, I'm slipping into the dark house and trying to make my way to my room by running my hand along the wall. A wall with a bump in it that feels a whole lot like the curves of a man's chest. A man's chest that I have touched before but should not have my hands on now. Not now that the man is committing himself to my sister. "Ace!" I exclaim as I jump back. "What the fuck are you doing lurking around in the fucking dark? Christ, you fucking scared me!"

"Ah, now there's the Courtney we all know and love. Well, all of us except my boy, Monti. He's head over heels for some Adams imposter."

"How do you know Elliot, exactly?"

Ace smirks. I see it on his face as my eyes adjust to the darkness.

"Answer me," I demand with a hand going to my hip. "And why are you lurking around in the dark?"

Ace takes my hand. Correction, Ace *tries* to take my hand and tug me in the direction of the sofa, but I brush him off.

"What is your problem?" he asks. "We fucked, so what? Your sister was there, she was game, and it was before she and I…"

"What?" I ask. "Bridget and you what?"

"It was before we decided to be exclusive, okay? Your little fucking plan worked. I couldn't stand to have her away from me for two weeks with the possibility of her hooking up with some fucking douche on this island. I think I'm in love with her."

Ace plops down on the sofa and puts his head into his hands. "Fuck! Court, I love your sister and I'm scared to fucking death that I'll mess up and she'll leave me. I'm no good at just one woman. I've never had a girlfriend. Ever."

I sit next to the man that might someday be my extended family and take his hand in mine. "Look at me," I say. "Ace, look at me."

He finally draws his eyes up to mine and I can see the pain in his. He's being sincere. He really loves my sister and is legitimately afraid he's going to fuck it up with her before it even begins.

"I've been watching you and Bridget for a while. I knew you guys loved each other long before either of you did."

Ace raises an eyebrow.

"Do you realize that after the first time or two, you never touched me again?"

"What? Sure, I did. I mean, it's just the mechanics of being with more than one person. Maybe Callan was closer to you and he was already…"

I stop him with a smile. He knows he's caught. "It's okay. Bridget was the same. She never even looked Callan's way after that first time. It was like you two were in a bubble having sex next to Callan and I. He tried to reach out once to touch her, and you flicked his hand away. He knows too. We talked about it. It's why he's being more of a douche than I'm guessing he usually is. He's afraid that he's going to end up alone. The asshole even tried to talk me into an arrangement."

"I'm afraid to ask."

"You should be. He's a dick on a good day," I shrug. "I might have taken him up on it, though, but I can't now."

Ace kisses my knuckles and looks into my eyes. "Your sister is worried about you. Tell me what you're up to. Let me help you. If you're in some kind of trouble, I can…"

"I'm fine, it's nothing like that. Now, about Elliot. How do you know him?" I ask again.

"Your sister made me promise to keep your secrets from him. Why should I share his with you?"

"So he has secrets?"

"Don't we all?"

I guess Ace was right. I've been holding on to a whopper of one for years. One I've never even told my sister. One too embarrassing to admit even to my therapist.

I shrug. "I guess, but I like him. I wish things could be different. I'm happy for you and Bridge. But once I leave here, Elliot can't know how to find me."

"My lips are sealed, but don't be surprised if he finds another way."

Before I can ask what he means, my sister calls my name. "Court, is that you? How was the date?"

Bridget approaches Ace and I and he reaches out a hand and pulls my sister into his lap with a kiss going to her temple. "I missed you" Ace whispers into her ear, but I hear him and smile. I am truly happy for them. It was never meant to be anything more than a hot, good time between Ace and I. We shared sex with my sister and Callan, but Ace and Bridget had bonded.

"I'm tired. I'm going to head to bed. The date was fine, Bridge. I'll share details in the sun tomorrow. Have a good sleep, guys" I say as I leave the main living space and head to my room.

I leave the lights off when I enter in hopes of Elliot watching me from across the beach again, but my hopes of another together solo session are thwarted with his text.

Go to sleep, Adams. I'll see you on the beach in the morning

11

In my mind I understand that I'm on an island in paradise. I know I'm an adult, no longer a child in the cold climate of Vermont, but I feel a chill run through me as if I'm still there in the snow. I toss in my sleep as a dream takes hold.

I'm in my snowsuit, having just arrived home from a day skiing on the mountain with a friend. My mother's car isn't in the garage when I enter to make my way into the house. I cross my fingers in hopes that Bridget isn't with her because my stepfather's huge SUV isn't parked in its spot either, but my "Uncle" Jim's car is in the driveway, which means he's here. Alone.

I enter the house as quietly as I can. I take off my boots in the mudroom and throw my snowsuit on the floor in a heap. I make my way up to my room in my long underwear and thermal shirt. When I hear the clearing of his throat, I know I should have gone to Allison's house and called my mother for a ride home.

"Courtney," he says and even at my age, I hear the desire in his voice. "Come here."

"I need to start my homework," I lie, and he knows it. "I have a lot to do."

"Well," he says as his hand reaches for the clasp of his belt. "Now that will have to wait. You know I don't accept being lied to. Get in your room."

The tears start before the begging. Neither work.

His hand is on my arm, squeezing and tugging me along as his other hand pulls his belt free.

"Pull your pants down and be quiet. I'm not in the mood for the dramatics today. Your mother and sister should be home soon, and this punishment is going to take away from our time together."

"Where's Tom?" I ask.

He smirks. "At work. He won't be home until late. His assistant is helping him with a special assignment. It might take them all night."

"I don't want to…"

He pulls my chin close to his face and annunciates each word. "I. Said. Pull. Your. Pants. Down."

Crying, I obey and pull my long underwear to the floor.

"Don't be fucking cute, Courtney," he sneers. "Panties. Now."

"Please," I try to beg. "I really do have homework."

He chuckles. "Well, since you want to play school, hold onto your desk and shut your mouth. That second lie just earned you three more."

"Please, don't do this" I plead.

"Bend over your desk now, Courtney, and put your nose on it," he demands as he pushes me down on my desk then grabs my hands and places them over my head to force me to arch my back.

I try to plead with him again. I promise not to tell anyone; I even apologize for lying. None of it works.

"On your tip toes, don't come down until you're told."

Cooperatively getting into position is the primary act of submission to his spanking and this position elevates my ass that is about to be spanked and suffer penalty swats for every time a heel touches the floor.

"Uncle" Jim has the upper hand. He's an adult that I'm supposed to be respectful to. He's my stepfather's best friend, a guest in our home and my mother has told my sister and I to think of him as an authority figure while he's with us. The thought of my sister has me relinquishing my control and handing it over to him in hopes that he'll get his fill from me and leave her alone.

"A properly positioned bottom is fully exposed," he begins, and I shiver in disgust when I feel the rough skin of his hand brush across my ass. "Your cheeks are fully presented to me and split apart. Your rectum and vagina are fully visible, Courtney. You're completely helpless and exposed to me" he states. He always does it like that, using the medical terms like he's a doctor giving me an exam for my own good.

I gag and try my best to hold back the tears that fuel him.

Once positioned, I give up, relinquishing control to him, but I can still clench my cheeks together, mitigating the sting of a swat and the exposure while pissing him off.

His belt sounds worse than it actually is when it's swooshing through the air, and I try to remind myself of that before the first strike. He's always careful not to leave marks that will last very long, but they sting all the same upon contact and I cry out at the first.

"Owww," I cry. "Please. Aaa…"

"What do you say, Courtney?" he asks after the third strike. "Now, then we can finish up with my hand. Those were your extras."

"I won't lie to you again," I heave through sobs. "I'm sorry."

His hands tug at my hips to readjust me and he snickers when a heel touches down.

"At, at, at," he tsks. "Looks like you've earned another."

Snap.

That one stings worse than the last three and I scream then beg for it to be over. I promise to do anything he wants to not have to bear another swat.

"You'll take more and hold your pose. If you fall again, I'll keep tacking on more."

Hot tears fall from my eyes with each crack of the leather across my exposed bottom. The pain sears through me with the next snap of his wrist and both heels touch the floor.

"Uncle" Jim laughs. "You're lucky that ass is about to welt. Can't have you showing mommy that," He lifts my face, nods his head, then lifts his chin to my bed. "Behave yourself and I might not need to go in search of relief from your sister later tonight. Or your whore of a mother."

He grabs himself and my eyes lower and catch on the protrusion in the front of his pants. I've never told Bridget about Jim's behavior. I've never asked her if he's ever touched her the same way. He claims that he'll leave her alone if I do as he says. It's one of the reasons I don't tell my mother. Well, that and the fact that she's finally happy again with Tom. After my dad left us, she was miserable. I don't want to see her like that again.

Jim sits on my bed and waits for me to approach. When I don't, he snaps his fingers to hurry me along, saying, "We haven't much time and you've excited me. You'll need to fix that too once I'm done teaching your ass a lesson in respect."

"Please don't make me do that. I don't like…"

He pulls me down onto his lap and firmly grasp me around the waist, above my right hip with his left hand. I'm unable to squirm off his lap, I know, I've tried before. Then his left elbow is planted between my shoulder blades to hold my head and shoulders down. He raises his right knee slightly, turning my ass up further. Then he begins to paddle my sore ass with his hand.

Snap. Crack. Snap. Snap. Crack. Slap. Smack. Smack. Smack. Snap.

"Ten," I shout as I've been taught. "Sir."

I feel his erection bumping me from below as he continues to set fire to my ass with his rough palm. His hand is always worse than his belt because I never know when a finger will explore inside me. Or, maybe it isn't that it's worse, maybe it's just because it always comes after his belt and before the worst part of this whole thing.

When he finishes punishing me, he pushes me to my knees. I fall on the floor at his feet in a crying heap.

"Take it out and use your hand until you give me the relief I need from this," he demands while looking down at his crotch.

I do it the way he showed me, moving my hand up and down with a twist of my fist at the top. After a few strokes, I close my eyes at the sound of his groan to not have to watch.

"So beautiful. All you'll ever be good for, but beautiful all the same" he says as he tucks himself away.

I awake confused with a start when I feel my body being tugged toward a warm male one. I try to fight the intruder off, but he's so much stronger than me. I'm confused because "Uncle" Jim was always careful about getting caught so he never came into my bed at night.

Then I hear his raspy rumble of a voice trying to soothe me. "Adams, shhh," Elliot says. "It's me. You were having a nightmare. You're okay, baby. I'm here. I'm right here."

I fling off the sheet and push at Elliot until he lets me go. I flop to the floor in a heap of tears and sweat, my heart is pounding and I'm worried that he's heard too much.

"What were you dreaming about?" he asks. "I was going to surprise you with a midnight kiss when I heard you crying."

"I don't...I don't remember," I lie then wince when I remember what happens to little girls who lie. "I don't like surprises."

"You okay?" Elliot asks with a furrowing brow as I sit up and my eyes begin to focus in on him.

I shrug. "Can you, um...would you stay with me? Maybe just until I fall back to sleep."

"I'll do one better than that. Come on," he says. "You get the best night's sleep out on the beach. The waves will lull you right back to sleep."

"I don't..." But it's too late because Elliot has already lifted me into his strong arms and is walking out onto the sand. I place my head on his chest and feel safe with a man for the first time. I can't explain why. I don't know him. He's a stranger, and yet I know he'd never do anything to harm me.

He walks us down to the water's edge and turns to me as he places me on my feet. "Wait here. I'm just going to grab a beach blanket quickly. You're safe. The tide's going out, so we'll be fine here until morning."

"Elliot, I..."

"Be right back."

I huff in a sigh and plop down on the sand. My emotions are all over the place. I haven't had one of those nightmares in ages. I know it's stemming from Elliot's talk about me being a bad girl. The funny thing is, I've always liked a man with a touch of the BDSM bad boy in him, so why now with Elliot were these memories haunting me? And how was I going to fulfill a yearlong contract with a man, who by his profile, was definitely a Dominant who would expect my compliance?

I don't get the chance to let my thoughts solidify as Elliot returns with a blanket that he spreads out on the sand for us. He nods for me to climb on then he plops down next to me saying, "Come here, Adams. You can use me as a pillow. I'll keep you safe from whatever scared you."

"Elliot, we said..."

"I know. I'm not asking you to tell me if you don't want to. Shhh, close your eyes and go back to sleep."

I must have listened because the next thing I know, it's a bright sunny morning and Bridget and Ace are standing at the foot of our makeshift bed, Ace with a shit eating grin, my sister with her body dripping off his.

I clear my throat and feel Elliot shift next to me. He tugs my back into his front and spoons tighter around me as I feel his morning erection against my ass.

"Leave us alone," he mumbles. "It's the ass crack of dawn and I'm tired. Go away."

Ace kicks at Elliot's foot. "We're going out for a swim. Try to tame that down before we get back," he says. "You're still a fucking grouch in the morning."

Elliot groans and wraps his arms tighter around my middle when I try to move to sit up. "Just a few more minutes," he begs. "You doing better this morning?"

I laugh when he rolls me to my back and starts pretending to eat at my neck. "Yes, I'm fine."

"You're cute in the morning. I think I could wake up like this every day."

"We only have a week left."

"Then, let's make the most out of it" he says, staring at my lips before he covers my mouth with his.

Elliot takes my thoughts, words, and breath away. We don't come up for air until my sister and Ace return, wet from their swim. They shake the water off onto us and Elliot groans again. "Lyons, you're still a pain in the fucking ass, man."

I know I planned on remaining uncommitted to him, but I wanted to know more. "Let's all do something together today" I suggest in hopes of Ace slipping up and revealing something about the man who has me intrigued.

Bridget, loving the idea, smiles and agrees. "That sounds like fun. What should we do?"

"Well, I'm starving for starters," Elliot states. "So, breakfast first."

"Yes" Ace fist pumps the air. "You cooking?"

"Well, I'm certainly not eating any of the slop you'd make. Pool house in fifteen."

Ace picks Bridget up off her feet with a squeal and carries her into the main house, mumbling about taking a shower then meeting us for food.

"I should get a shower too" I say.

"Come to the pool house with me" Elliot suggests with an extended hand. "You can shower there."

"I don't have anything to wear."

Elliot shrugs. "There's extra clothes there for guests."

"Guests?" I ask.

Elliot laughs. "Do you see any other women around here, Adams? Did the green monster just come out to play?"

"I…"

Elliot laughs and picks me up, flinging me over his shoulder. "Let's go, jealous girl."

I shower while Elliot starts the cooking. The water feels amazing against my skin and my time with Elliot begins to take its toll. I had headed to my room last night in hopes of a repeat joint masturbation session, but that hadn't happened. Now, I was wound up tighter than I've ever been. How do people do this? How do new couples go about their daily lives sexually frustrated? Why, is a better question.

As the water beats down rhythmically on my protruding nipples, my mind remembers the erotic scent of Elliot's cologne, the rough timbre of his voice, and the feeling of his confident aura surrounding me. My core clenches in search of his thickness, begging me to give in to my desires and call him into the shower to help me relieve this ache and find a sweet release.

When I hear a rustling, I turn my head and see a shadow. "Elliot" I sigh.

"I'm sorry," he apologizes. "This is super creepy of me. I..I shouldn't have…"

I reach out a hand and Elliot accepts it in his. His other hand flips the snap on his shorts, allowing them to fall to the ground. He stands naked and proud in front of me, his full erection jutting out from his perfect body. It's the first time I'm seeing him naked and I'm in awe of his perfection.

"I won't touch you if you don't want me to. I just needed to see you. You're like a siren to my libido. I couldn't resist your call."

"I…I need you, too, Elliot. No sex, though, okay?"

Elliot nods. "Fuck," he says as his hand fists his cock at the base, and he begins to slowly stroke himself. His eyes gleam as they rake over my body and he groans from the pleasure, crippling me. "You're so fucking beautiful."

My sexual frustration reaches the pinnacle when Elliot licks his lips and his knees buckle under the strain of his impending climax. "I need…"

"Be patient," he warns. "I'll tell you when you can make yourself come for me."

His words send shivers through my system and my skin prickles.

"I'm ready now."

Elliot smiles. "I can see that. Those nipples are," he groans on an upstroke of his cock. "Fucking killing me. Touch your pussy, but no coming."

My pulse quickens at his demand, and I obey and run my hand down my tummy to the wet heat between my legs. Electricity courses through my system at Elliot's moans when my finger disappears inside. My knees buckle now as I call out his name. "Elliot."

Elliot's eyes sparkle with mischief and he moves closer to me. "Can I kiss you?"

I shake my head then tilt it to give him access. I feel his hand, the one not stroking his cock, run down the outside of my thigh. When it reaches my knee, he tugs and forces me to spread my legs for him. "Can I touch you?" he asks and again, I nod.

His thick finger brushes my sensitive skin and his eyes lock with mine when he finds my obvious arousal for him. "Fuck, Adams! Jesus, you're so goddamn wet," The velvety tone of his voice causes my eyes to flutter closed and my legs to spread further apart. With better access, Elliot slips a finger into my wet heat. "And so fucking tight. Baby?"

I moan. "It aches, my pussy, Elliot. Please, I need to come."

"That's a good girl. Tell me," he demands. "Tell me what you need. I'll give you everything, anything for you."

"I need you to make me come" I shamelessly ask again.

Elliot sends me a menacing look. "Do you? You're sure you want me to do it? You don't want me to just watch and jerk off to you getting yourself off?"

"Yes, no, I mean…I want to watch you while you touch me."

Elliot chuckles, his hand still making long slow pulls up and down his cock.

"You're big, it would feel so good to let you slide inside me."

"Yes, Adams, it would," Elliot says as he lets another finger join his first then begins to pump in and out of me. "But you're too close, and so am I. It would be over before it began. Come on my fingers," he demands. "This time. I'm about to shoot my load all over you."

"Elliot," I cry as he lets his cock go to lift one of my legs and places it on a ledge in the shower.

"Listen to the sound of my voice" he says close to my ear. "And do as I say. Relax and just feel. Feel my finger stroking the soft flesh inside your pussy," Elliot curls a finger and rubs my hot spot. "That right there? You like that, baby?"

I purr like a kitten laying out in the sun. "Yes, please."

"Your pussy is ready to come for me. Are you, Adams? Hmmm, are you ready to flood my hand with that sweet release?"

He switches angles and this thumb finds my clit. Pressing down then making circles, one, two…fuck.

"I'm coming," I announce as I see Elliot's other hand return to his cock. "I'm coming!"

Before I come down from my orgasm high, my body is being turned around to face the cool tile and my hands are being forced to the wall. "Don't move," Elliot warns. "I don't have a condom and I'm about to go off."

I feel my ass pulled back, his strong hands on my waist and I arch my back. His cock is there in the crease of my ass rubbing back and forth when I look over my shoulder as Elliot bends his knees and throws his head back. Then I feel the warmth of spurt after spurt of his hot release as he coats my back with his teeth gritted and grunts filling the air.

"Fucking Christ," he curses as he turns me back around to face him. Then he covers my mouth with his and sinks his hands into my hair. "That was…"

"Good."

"Yeah," he says. "That was good. We should get cleaned up now, though. Your sister and Ace are probably on their way over already."

"Or still in their shower doing that and more."

"More," Elliot says and lets it hang in the air. "Adams, we…"

"Only have a week. Don't," I warn. "I'm starving, let's shower and go eat."

And that's how we spend the next week. Elliot and I sleeping together down at the water's edge, waking up to have breakfast with my sister and Ace then spending the days with them sunning on the sand. Each night, we go our separate ways, Bridget and Ace making love for long hours into the night while Elliot and I avoid sharing too much information and engaging in sophomoric petting and fondling, never actually having sex.

The day the seaplane arrives, I fly off into the clear blue sky, and Elliot isn't there to see the tears that fall for what could have been between us. Ace assures me that Elliot wouldn't be there to say good-bye. He worked his magic somehow and Elliot told me the night before that he had to run a quick errand early that next morning for the owner of the island, still not knowing my connection with Jonesie. I promised to sleep in late and have breakfast with him when he returned.

It was sucky to lie to him like that and I regretted it before I even said the words. But I didn't have a choice. My time was up. Adams needed to make it back to the castle before the stroke of midnight when she'd become Courtney again.

On that seaplane, I think about what can never be while on my way back to New York City and a man I've never met before. A man that I have committed myself to for the next year. A man that stands in the way of my happiness with Elliot.

Good-bye, Adams.

Welcome home, Courtney. Time to be the whore "Uncle" Jim always knew you were.

12

I look out onto the freezing streets of New York as our limo flies along on its way to Stone Towers. Usually, I'd be excited for a New Year's Eve party at Damian's penthouse because it would provide me with numerous male opportunities for the evening. But not tonight. Tonight, my fate will be sealed at the stroke of midnight.

I'm meeting my Compatible Companion outside of the penthouse. He's already contacted me through the app and told me to be prepared to give him my undivided attention for the following week. When I told my sister that I was going to need her to cover for me for at least a week, she'd asked if I'd finally gave in and contacted Elliot.

I hadn't. I also hadn't answered any of his texts or messages either. It wouldn't have changed anything. There's nothing I can do for three hundred and sixty-five days and three hundred and sixty-five very long nights. Thankfully, he stopped trying to reach me.

"What's on your mind, honey?" I hear my mother ask.

"Nothing, mom. I was just watching the snow fall. It reminds me of Vermont."

I hear Bobby clear his throat. He's never been a fan of Tom and doesn't like when we bring up the only father we knew before him. What neither Bridget nor I have ever told him, is that he's the best dad we've ever had, he needn't be jealous.

Bobby Knight and my mother fell in love as teenagers but had gone their separate ways only to find one another again not long after my mom's marriage to Tom broke up. Bobby instantly took to my sister and I. Back then, I figured it wouldn't be long before he had an "Uncle" for us to meet, too.

That never happened. Well, Bobby has a ton of male friends, all which Bridget and I have met numerous times. None of them were like "Uncle" Jim, though, and Bobby will never know how much comfort I took in that. That's why I'm doing what I am tonight. I need to grow up and give him and my mother freedom to enjoy their lives together. I need to come to terms with what happened in my past and make a future for myself and Bridget so that they don't need to worry about us.

I saw the stress our behavior was starting to have on their marriage, and I knew if I didn't make the changes, Bobby would. My mother couldn't survive if she lost him. So, instead, I'm securing that she won't.

The limo pulls up in front of Stone Towers and Bobby opens the door for my mother to step out. When Bridget tries to exit the car, I tug on her hand. "Remember, I'm going to leave right before midnight, and you need to cover for me. Don't get all distracted with Ace. Tell mom and Bobby I went to spend the week with Scarlett at her school apartment. She knows to cover for me in case mom calls her looking for me. Tell them I'll be back in about a week."

"I don't like this, Court," my sister says. "Why can't you tell me what you're doing? I'm worried about you."

"I'll be fine," I say as I push her out of the car. "Act normal."

We ride up in the elevator, my sister bouncing on her toes over her night with Ace. He's working security at the party, so she came with us. He's promised her that as soon as the guests leave, he's all hers for the taking. I asked her how that was different than every other night since he showed up on the island. Bridget had just rolled her eyes at me.

Ace got pussy whipped quicker than I could have predicted. Take earlier today when we came over with our mom to help Sydney with a few last-minute things. He didn't even try to fool Callan into thinking my sister was just a piece of hot ass for him to toy with. Instead, he'd warned Callan that things had changed where both of us were concerned.

I hadn't corrected him, because he was right, they had changed. If it wasn't for my contract with Compatible Companions, I still wouldn't be giving it up to Callan Black or anyone else. My heart was captured on an island and there it will remain. I might be forced to give my match my body for the next year, but he can't make me give him my heart. It was no longer mine to give. It belonged to a man I might never see again.

"Can you two please try to be on your best behavior tonight and not embarrass your mother and I?" Bobby asks.

"Bobby," my mother says with a gentle hand going to his chest. "They don't mean to…"

"Stop making excuses for them, Trina. I asked them both about going back to school, they blew me off. I gave them a job, and what did they do?"

"Ace and I are a couple now, so how it started shouldn't matter" my sister says, her voice growing small as she lowers her chin to her chest.

Bobby rolls his eyes. "A relationship? How long will that last? Until the stroke of midnight when one or both of you find trouble together," he sends us a pointed glare. "Or alone. I've had enough and your mother shouldn't be made to deal with your immature antics."

"We've changed, I swear," Bridget says. "Seriously, Ace and I are exclusive. No more nonsense. You'll see."

"And what about you?" Bobby asks me. "Did you find Jesus on Jonesie's island, too?"

"Something like that" I mumble as the elevator deposits us into Damian and Sydney's foyer. Was Jesus a redhead? I add a foot stomp because old habits die hard then I turn and storm off while thoughts of the copper-haired god play around in my mind.

I'm annoyed at my parents. I'm pissed at Elliot for walking into my life and being perfect at a time when I couldn't have him. I'm mad at my sister and Ace for finding happiness and I hate myself for all of it.

Bridget follows me as I hear Bobby say, "Let them go. I've had more than enough of this shit. They're adults whether they act like it or not. This is our night to enjoy and I'm done letting them ruin things for you."

"Court, wait up" my sister calls out and I whirl around.

"Listen, I need a minute, okay? I can't think straight. I think I'm having a nervous breakdown."

"Tell me what's going on with you," she demands but then Ace appears and wraps his arms around her middle and sucks at her neck. "Stop" she giggles.

"Ace," I say in greeting. "Do me a favor?"

He looks up at me and nods. "Yeah."

"Look out for my sister."

Ace heaves in a deep sigh. "Courtney, Adams, whatever the fuck name you're using tonight, what the fuck are you getting yourself into?"

"Nothing, okay? I'm fine."

"You keep telling yourself that" Ace says.

I roll my eyes then hear the call to sit down for our meal. But I can't do it. I can't eat. I feel like I have a boulder in my throat already. I can't do this, any of it. I can't go through with this, this charade. I can't allow a man I don't know be my boyfriend for the next year. Go on dates with him, kiss him, sleep with him, whatever. I need to get out of here.

I turn and start to run, tears streaming down my face with an apology for my sister and a warning to let me go.

I run out of Damian's living space and thank the powers above that the elevator is open and waiting to take me to the lobby. I climb inside and watch Callan Black come into sight with his hands on his hips and a brow raised for me as the doors slide shut before he can stop me.

I pound on the lobby button and will the elevator to move faster. The stroke of midnight is approaching, and my match will be waiting for me on the street below soon. I don't want him to see me. Realistically, I know I could lie if he asked if I was Courtney. I could say, "No, my name is Adams."

I'd say that because that's who I wish I were. I was happy when I was Adams. I was with Elliot when I was Adams.

I remember being her and I remember the man she spent her week in the sun with. Elliot Montgomery, a ginger with a strong build and a face made for a model, all sharp edges and firm muscles. Elliot Montgomery was a vision to behold and one I will never forget.

I fling myself from the elevator and I'm crying so hard that I can barely see an inch in front of my face. I look side to side then locate the main doors and fly through them with my hair flying behind me and tears streaming down my face. As my feet hit the concrete sidewalk of the busy New York City street, I feel my right heel snag on a crack and snap off. I wait for the pain of my fall.

But it doesn't come. I remain upright and wobble. Then as I'm crashing to the ground, a strong hand is on my elbow. Then an arm comes around my middle.

"Careful," a deep, sexy, and familiar voice warns with a puff of breath into the cold air of the December evening. "You'll hurt yourself."

Elliot stands out in the freezing cold New York City night with his back against the wall of Stone Towers just like I'd first seen him standing with his back against the pool house.

"I'm good at doing that," I quip as I right myself then pull away from Elliot's grasp and wipe my tears. "Thanks."

Why was he here? Jesus fucking Christ, hadn't I told Ace not to get involved? I begged Bridget to make sure Ace never told Elliot who I really was or how to find me, yet here he is.

"Where are you rushing off to?" Elliot asks.

"Not off to anywhere, just avoiding where I was" I say.

I omit that I was also rushing from where I needed to be and that I was scheduled to meet my Compatible Companion match right here in this very spot, but that since meeting him, I was having second thoughts and I was actually running away.

"Ah," Elliot says. "Avoiding seems to be the theme for the night."

"You too?"

What the hell was he avoiding?

"Fuck, yeah!"

I can't help the coy smile as it spreads across my face or from saying, "Want to go hang out somewhere warmer and avoid our shit together?"

Elliot smiles then he laughs, "Netflix and chill? I'm not sure I've had the pleasure of a beautiful women offering me that yet."

A smirk pulls at the corner of his lips at the dig. I'd offered him Netflix and chill once, but he'd turned me down because it was the right thing to do at the time and he was being a gentleman.

"Have you been living under a rock?" I ask to be a bitch.

Elliot laughs. "Something like that."

"Well?" I prompt because if we're going to get out of here, we need to move along quickly, or I'll be leaving with a man I don't know instead of the man I want.

Elliot shakes his head and offers me his arm as the snow begins to fall, a flake landing on my nose. "I have a place we can use, Snowflake," he says as he kisses the flake off the tip of my nose. "If we can make it that far."

13

I gasp as Elliot opens the door to one of the nicest hotels in the city. It's a swanky place and people are milling about, waiting for midnight. My gate falters momentarily as I try to comprehend what he's even doing in New York, let alone a place like this. How in the world can someone who works as a groundskeeper on an island and lives in a pool house afford anything close to a place this expensive...even for a night?

As my brain is trying to do the math, he tugs me along past the registration desk and it hits me that maybe he isn't actually staying here. Maybe as we walked past, he decided the place looked as good as any to find a secluded spot to quench his thirst for what I hadn't given him on the island.

Then, the next thing I know, Elliot yanks open a door and pushes me inside. The space lights up when the sensors feel our presence and my eyes take a moment to adjust to their fluorescent assault. Elliot turns the lock, then turns toward me as I'm taking in our setting.

A bathroom. A bathroom in the lobby of The Stone Hotel. The. Stone. Hotel. Owned by Damian Stone, a man that is the cousin of my stepfather's best friend.

Has he lost his fucking mind? It will only be moments before we're arrested in a place like this. This isn't some random nightclub like the ones Callan and I fucked in. No, this place has cameras recording everything. This is not the kind of hotel where people go to fuck in the bathroom. And when they see what's going down in here, instead of the NYPD showing up, it'll be Mac with Ace and Callan breaking down the door.

Fuck me!

Wait, no.

I stare at him with my mouth agape and ask, "What the hell do you think you're doing?"

"What I should have done the minute I laid my eyes on you" he answers with frustration dripping off his words and his hand running over the top of his head. His hair looks longer somehow here in the city. On the island, it was barely visible, now it's growing, and he was for sure a ginger as a child. Now, copper colored hair is doing it's best to make its way into the world. Not usually my thing, but on Elliott, it's pushing my buttons.

His eyes bore into mine, his greenish brown orbs gleaming with lust and want, mine meeting his with confusion and need. I watch as his chest rises and falls, his breathing growing shallow along with mine. He looks like a caged animal just released back into the wild and I question if I'm nothing more to him than prey. A game. A conquest. My usual to men.

I don't get the chance to ask him exactly what it was that he wanted to do on the island because Elliot slams my back against the cold tiles of the bathroom wall and pulls my face into his grasp. He tilts my head and claims my mouth to silence my questions. I melt into his embrace and tilt my chin further to grant him the access he desperately desires. He groans into my mouth, his tongue making a sweep over mine, the rumble coming from deep in his core. "You taste like fucking sin, Adams. I have so many fucking questions for you and so many fucking things to say, but…"

"Just kiss me" I demand cutting him off.

"Oh, I plan on doing a whole hell of a lot more than that, baby."

Then his hunger for me overtakes his calm and Elliot becomes a ravenous man.

His hands make quick work at the zipper on my back and he pulls the front of my dress down to reveal my bare breasts, ones that he has used to make me come before. His thumb flicks the right, his fingers pinch the left, his touch familiar yet foreign, but one that knows what it's doing. He remembers how I like to be touched, what gets me off and it makes me wonder if he's thought about it since I left the island. Has Elliot laid in bed night after night replaying our time together while stroking himself to climax like I have?

Then Elliot sinks to his knees and says, "I should punish you first for running away from me without even saying good-bye."

All thoughts leave my mind as Elliot yanks my dress up to my waist.

"I couldn't, I didn't know…" I stammer.

"You're a very hard girl to find, Adams. Running into you like this was…"

"Wait? What? What do you mean running into me? Didn't Ace tell you…"

His fingers find their way into my panties and they pull, silencing me. The thin material gives way, snaps in his hands, and Elliot smirks as he lifts them to his face. I know what he's going to do before he does it and it ignites a boiling in my blood. My panties are soaked, they have been since the minute I saw him on the street. There's no hiding my desires for this man now.

With a deep inhale, he groans and my body trembles with my need for Elliot to be inside me. It's a stronger feeling than I've ever had. One I'm sure that will destroy me for all others. Especially the one that's probably waiting for me on the street where I found Elliot.

Fuck. My Compatible Companions match.

I hadn't meant to run off completely. I just needed time to think and have a good cry. Or maybe I was planning on standing my match up. Could I? I'm almost certain there was something in my contract that didn't allow for that type of behavior. That was why Damian lost his shit after purchasing the company only to find my name on the employee list. If there was a way for me to get out of the contract, I'm sure Damian would have made it happen already. I really should have read it better before signing it.

Elliot spins me around and our eyes catch in the mirrored wall above the sink. He forces my hands to the edge and angles my ass into just the right position for what he plans to do. "Watch," he commands. "Don't take your eyes from us. I'm going to fuck you the way you deserve to be taken. Rough and raw...primal. The way I thought about every night since I met you. Yes, Adams, while I jerked off."

I hiss when I feel his hands on my overheated skin.

"After," he shrugs. "I'll give you roses and champagne, and make sweet, slow love to you for hours. Because, Adams, you deserve that, too."

"Elliot, I..."

My words are halted at the sound of his zipper and our eyes catch in the mirror.

I watch as he frees his cock then reaches into his pants for a condom. He tears it with his teeth as my eyes catch my own reflection in the mirror. I look like a slut being taken in a public restroom, people just outside the door, listening to our every move. But then I catch Elliot's face as his eyes rake over me and I see myself as he does for the first time.

I'm not a slut. To him, I'm a princess. A woman he desires so desperately that he couldn't wait to get inside me so he's taking a risk by having me right here, right now.

"You're beautiful," he states. "I..fuck, baby..." he trails off as he sheaths himself with a pained groan. "I'm so fucking hard for you," Elliot pushes my legs apart with his knee and a demand, "Spread your legs for me."

Like Courtney, I obey. Like Adams, I do as well because she wants this just as much as Courtney.

"Elliot, I..." I attempt a second time.

"Shhh," he whispers close to my ear, the front of his body against the back of mine. "This time," he smirks at me in the mirror. "Yes, there will be more. This time is going to be what I just said, primal and raw. I'm going to fuck you hard and come deep inside your tight pussy while you coat my cock in your sweet release," he shrugs. "Later, it'll be gentle, but right now, I'm not capable of being gentle, Adams, so, only chance. Stop me now if this isn't what you want."

"I want you. Now, Elliot, please" I beg. No sense in fighting it any longer.

"Say it," he demands. "Tell me to fuck you."

"Yes! Fuck me," I cry out. "Please!"

"That's my naughty girl," he praises as he bends his knees and lines the head of his cock up to my entrance. "Now watch" he demands.

Elliot bunches the bottom of my dress around my waist and glances down. He takes his cock into his hand and holds it at the base. I watch as his head falls back when his thumb runs over the tip. Then he tugs my hair with the other hand and our eyes lock again in the mirror.

He lowers to plant a gentle kiss on my shoulder then rears back and plunges inside my wet heat. The force of his first thrust sends me into the edge of the sink, my grip faltering. I seek to gain purchase as he pulls out and slams back inside with a curse. "Fuck! Don't let go again," he warns. "I don't want to hurt you and I can't go at you any easier. I'm sorry, you have me out of my mind."

I feel stretched and full, a twinge of pain at his invasion, but I've never felt better in my life. It's as if Elliot is freeing me, taking everything from me, stripping me to my bare core and I let him expose all of me, my body, my heart, even my soul. I sink into the pleasure, the abyss and float above myself. Giving him what I've never been able to give another.

My trust.

I watch him take me in the mirror, pulling out to his tip on every slow exit stroke then slamming back in like a battering ram. His hands go to my waist and he adjusts me, pulls my ass up then back for his pleasure and he manages to sink in deeper still.

"So."

Trust.

"Fucking."

Thrust.

"Tight around my cock."

Thrust, thrust, thrust.

"You like that, Adams? Hmmm? Tell me that you like the way I'm fucking you."

"Yes, Elliot, please. So good. It feels so good."

"You want more, baby?"

"Oh, God, yes!"

"Then I want to hear you," he demands. "Beg me to fuck that tight pussy with my big cock. Say it."

His words stroke the desire catching fire deep inside of me as his flesh strokes mine and I feel my pussy tighten and clench around him. Elliot must feel it too because he quickly pulls out with a moan. "Tell me," he demands again. "You're about to make me come. So. Tell. Me. Now!"

"Fuck my tight pussy, Elliot," I scream, relenting and giving in to him, showing him who I really am. Courtney Knight. "Make me come on your huge cock. Oh, fuck…I'm…"

He continues to thrust in and out of me at a pace that can only be described as frantic.

My hair falls with my head between my shoulders, but Elliot won't accept that my gaze slips from us. He yanks my hair back and orders me to watch. "Watch while I fill that pussy with my come. Next time, it'll be without a condom. I don't like having anything between us and it won't happen this way again" he says.

Then Elliot seals my fate with a brisk slap to my ass, making me cry out his name as I come around him. "Elliot!"

"Yes! I'm coming" he says as he moves faster still, stretching me with each thrust into my body.

Elliot crashes down over me and roughly lifts my chin so his mouth can have mine. His tongue enters with a groan escaping both of us, my pussy clamping down to milk him with his final thrust. "Christ," he sighs. "That was…"

"Yeah," I sigh too. "That was…"

Elliot pulls out and turns me to face him. The scent of sex fills the air and I shyly lower my head to his chest and bury my face in my hands as the tears hit. He's quick to raise my chin and gently take my mouth. His lips gentle over mine say, "Adams, what am I going to do with you?"

"Elliot," I say. "We need to talk."

14

"Fix your dress and no more crying," he orders as he tears the condom off with another complaint over it and tosses it into the trash. "Fucking hate these things. Let's go."

"Go?" I ask as he tucks himself back into his pants. We can't just walk out of here together. I'm sure everyone in the lobby just heard us."

Elliot shrugs and lifts my dress to cover my breasts then signals for me to turn around so he can zip up my dress.

I let the hem of my dress fall and as I'm straightening it out, I watch Elliot in the mirror as he grabs my panties from the sink and places them into his pocket. I raise an eyebrow and he delivers a panty-soaking smirk. I guess it's a good thing that I don't have mine on. They'd had been incinerated if I had.

Elliot flicks the lock and opens the door with one hand while the other reaches for mine. He tugs me from the bathroom into the lobby where a man is standing, clearly waiting for us to exit. I pray for the ground to open and eat me alive. I mean, it's not having sex in a public bathroom that's causing me this embarrassment. I've done that more times than I care to remember. The last time not that long ago with Callan Black. So, it's not the fact that we're exiting a bathroom per se, it's where this public bathroom happens to be that's causing me the issue. Did I mention I'm in one of the most expensive hotels New York City has to offer and it's owned by Damian Stone? And that he knows my stepfather?

"Mr. Montgomery, sir," the man begins.

Ummm...sir? Wait, who? Christ, is Elliot's father here?

"I thought that was you when you entered" he clears his throat and looks me up and down.

Elliot snaps a finger to bring the man's eyes back on him. "Something you need from *me*, Scott? I'm over here."

"Oh, um...no, sir," he stutters. "My apologies. I just wanted to be sure everything was to your liking. You mentioned not returning until much later in the evening. I was just concerned, then I saw you with the lady and..."

A smile spreads across Elliot's face. "Everything was more than to my liking, Scott. Have a nice evening."

Elliot's hand tugs mine and he pulls me along to a private elevator as Scott calls out, "If you need anything, sir, don't hesitate to call down to the lobby."

"Elliot, wait," I say as I dig in my heels before he tugs me into the waiting elevator. "I don't understand."

"I haven't understood one single fucking thing since the day I saw you sitting on that lounge chair in the sun so welcome to the party, Adams."

"Wait," I try to demand yet again but Elliot continues his mission. "Where are we going?"

"To my room. I need to figure some shit out, but I can't be without you for another second so you're coming with me."

Elliot tugs me into the elevator and flashes a card across the panel. The box begins to ascend to the penthouse suite on the top floor.

"Are you fucking serious? How can you afford...oh, my god! You don't work on the island," I say. "Wait, you can't be the guy Bobby says owns it because he'd be like old, right? And married!"

Elliot laughs. "I'm not married. And I'm twenty-five, hardly a senior citizen."

The elevator chimes as the doors slide open to reveal the most exquisite ten-thousand-square-foot living space I have ever seen with views of Central Park and the city skyline before me. It feels as if the ceiling disappears into the sky, the sleek and modern design, crisp but inviting.

"Wowww!" I exclaim pulling the word into a long murmur. "This place is ridiculous. How can any one person afford this?"

Elliot shrugs. "I don't know."

"What do you mean, you don't know? I don't understand what..."

Elliot silences my questions with his mouth over mine. I open for him and groan when he presses his hard body against my soft one because he feels that good and I forget everything else when he's this close to me. His hands go to my ass and he pulls me in tight to his erection without apology. "I need you again. Now. Then we'll talk" he demands as he rubs my core against him.

"Elliot..."

"Shhh. The only thing we need to say right now is that we're clean and you use birth control."

"I...yes. I'm on the pill and I'm clean but..."

"I was just tested before we met. I haven't even considered touching anyone but you."

I nod because I know the feeling. I haven't been able to get Elliot out of my head either.

The next thing I know, he sweeps me up into his arms and is stomping through the penthouse in search of the master suite. With six to choose from, I can see why he hesitates at the first door. But then another thought enters my head. "What's the problem? Have you been here with someone else?"

Elliot chuckles. "No, Snowflake, I got here about an hour before running into you. I barely had time to put down my shit before I walked back out the door."

"But they knew you at the front desk."

Elliot shrugs. "It's their job to know their guests."

He plops me down on the plushily carpeted floor and begins to remove his coat and tie. I hadn't processed how he'd been dressed until now. He fucked me in the bathroom of The Stone Hotel in a suit with nothing more than his dick out while he'd had me completely exposed to him in that mirror.

Next, he empties his pockets onto the table. The keycard he used to gain access to this insanely expensive penthouse suite, a pack of gum that I now realize he'd chewed on the whole time he fucked me, and a strip of condoms. I raise an eyebrow at him. "New Year's Eve plans, huh?"

"Plans change, Snowflake."

"What's up with the new name?"

"You had a flake on your nose when we were outside," he shrugs. "I think it's cute."

Yeah, cute. At this point I'm reaching Cybil level with the number of identities I hold.

Elliot flings his tie to the table then begins to stalk toward me. He pauses when his phone begins to ring from the table and mine from my purse at the same moment. The ring tones the same.

The tone is the one that was set by Compatible Companions. The day I signed my contract, they asked for my phone and had one of their tech guys rig it to ring a specialized sound so that I would know it was them. After being assigned my match, I recall having a conversation about them calling me thirty minutes after our scheduled meet-up time to be sure I was comfortable. They had assured me that every one of their clients had been through a complete and rigorous screening and vetting process, but in the event of something going wrong, this was my safety call and my way out.

Elliot's eyes meet mine as we stand in the silence of the enormous space and listen to the exclusive ringtone we share.

How does he have the tone on his phone and why is his ringing at the same time as mine?

I reach for my phone, but Elliot is faster than I am. He takes it out of my purse and turns it over to reveal the symbol used by the company that employees me for the next year. I look up at the clock by the bed, it reads 12:31am.

He reaches for his own phone and tosses it down on the bed next to mine. Both lay there, screens facing up, ringing the same tone, with the same symbol on their screens.

"Well, Adams, I guess we really do need to talk."

"Elliot, I don't understand. Did you set me up?"

Elliot laughs then picks up his phone and swipes his finger across the screen with a nod for me to do the same.

"Elliot Montgomery," he says as I swipe my finger and clear my throat.

I hear the voice on the other line but I'm not listening. I'm focused on trying to hear what Elliot is saying so that maybe I can figure out what in the hell is going on.

"Yes," he says. "It's fine. Thank you. I'll be in touch."

I'm snapped to attention when I hear someone from Compatible Companions bark into my phone. "Courtney, I need you to tell me that you're good or use the safe word that was given to you. Do you remember it?"

Do I?

"Ah…um, yes. I, ah, I remember. But, it's not necessary. Everything is fine."

"Wonderful. Then as we told you at our last meeting, we don't need to speak again until your contract is ending, Miss Knight. You'll receive monthly pay outs in your checking account that you provided."

She hangs up before I can reply.

When I look up, I find Elliot's eyes on me, his lack of words filling me with worry and the air around us with a deafening silence. His stance is one of a man ready to explode. A fire has already been ignited and the flames are burning bright. If I don't speak, I'm afraid of what he might do. If I try to explain, I'm scared of his reaction all the same.

He isn't happy and it's the first time I've seen him filled with rage and directing it at me.

His jaw ticks and he cracks his neck on one side while we engage in a staring contest, the heat in the room rising as if we're still on the island instead of in a winter wonderland.

"Is Adams really your name?" he bluntly asks, and I shake my head.

This isn't how I'd spent our nights apart dreaming it would be if we were to ever meet again, and I want to fix this. But first, I need to understand what's happening.

"Shit," he whispers. "Did you come to the island because you knew I'd be there?"

"What? No! I didn't think anyone would be there," I admit as I begin to think he didn't either. "I had no idea who you were, I still don't."

I fling myself into a chair and Elliot lets out a strangled sigh. "It would appear, *Adams*, that I am the man who owns you for the next year."

My eyes lock with his. "Owns me? I don't…"

Elliot reaches into the drawer of the bedside table and retrieves a document that I recognize all too well. I have the same one in my purse. But to protect the client's identity, my copy lists him as nothing more than "client". My name and signature along with that of the company's representative is listed but Elliot wouldn't have known that Courtney Knight and Adams no last name were one in the same.

When Elliot plunks his down, I see not only mine but also his name on his documents. It's right there in ink above mine. It's the contract I was told I would match to mine to be sure the man I was scheduled to meet tonight would be who he said he was.

"Yes," he says looking down at my signature then back up to hold my gaze. "*Miss Knight*, I own you" he repeats while taking my chin between his thumb and fingers.

I remain silent for a moment as I process the situation. Elliot continues to stare into my eyes and a vein in his neck begins to pulse with his aggravation. Then he moves his eyes to my lips and tilts my chin. His lips brush over mine gently and he emits a groan before pulling back and heading across the room.

He clinks around in the liquor cabinet until he finds what he's looking for. He pours enough amber fluid into his tumbler that it sloshes over the side. I think about warning him not to make a mess in a place like this, but then I think better of opening my mouth. Why poke the bear that already seems ready to pounce?

Elliot gulps his drink in one take then slams his glass down on the table with a loud thud and a sigh. His body follows suit and crumbles into a chair as he demands, "Explain," His multi-colored eyes, greens, blues, and browns swirling together to create a color of their own unique shade, turn to a dark hue caused by the emotions threatening to burst from him as he bellows out the order again, only louder. "I said explain, Miss Knight. Do I need to repeat myself a third time?"

"Explain?" I question.

"Yes, explain, *Adams*. From the beginning and I suggest that it be without any more lies."

I heave in a deep sigh. My subterfuge was up, my luck had expired, and I knew if I wanted to have any kind of chance with this man, I had to do as he asked. Obviously, he notices that I'm questioning my thoughts, so Elliot takes the final decision from my hands. "Let me remind you, because I see that mind going, that by own you, *Adams*, that means you will do what I say. So, let me be very clear. I am seeking the truth, the whole truth devoid of bullshit. And," he points a finger in my direction. "If I suspect you're withholding or fabricating anything, a punishment of my choosing will follow."

"Elliot, I..."

"That seems to be about all you're capable of saying this evening, Miss Knight. My name is not what I'm seeking from you. Not yet anyway. I'd love to hear you shouting it out in ecstasy, but I'm afraid until we clear up our little mess, that won't be happening. But, as I just stated, if you're looking to get over my knee, feel free to throw the bullshit you're trying to come up with in your head around."

"I've only said your name because you keep cutting me off and you wouldn't spank me for..."

Elliot raises an eyebrow. "Try me."

I begin to pace the room while Elliot sits calmly like a king on his throne, me the jester sent to entertain him until I was no longer useful. Like every other guy before him. I turn my back on him and wipe a tear as it falls because I can't stand to think that I'm nothing more to him than a pussy to purchase for his pleasure, then I go for broke. "Adams was a clean slate; she didn't have demons from her past clunking around in her closet or a decision she made that she was already regretting about her future. I had the opportunity to completely reinvent myself, be someone so different from Courtney that even I wouldn't recognize her, and I took that chance" I say with a shrug.

"Courtney?" he whispers.

"Yeah, Courtney Adams Knight."

Not wanting to reveal too much, I shrug off the part of my story where my biological father leaves my mom, Bridget, and I for greater things. Bridget and I were young girls at the time. My mother then met, dated, and finally married Tom. Tom then cheated on her with anyone he could find, ultimately getting caught with his pants down with his assistant in his office. Literally. My mom and Bobby were finally reunited when my Aunt Brook and Uncle Tate were in California. Not long after, my mother entered her third union with Bobby and for the first time in my life, I know she's truly happy.

I'm still undecided just how far back in this tale of mine I'm planning on going with Elliot, so I say, "I made myself the kind of girl I wanted to be. The kind I should have been able to become."

And Adams was the perfect persona for that. My mom's last name, she was flawed like every normal person is, with rough edges around her exterior. But, unlike me, she didn't have ghosts in her past that she couldn't let anyone else know about.

Adams and Courtney were so very different from one another, but looking at it now, I question if either of them is truly who I am. Maybe I really am a clear combination of the two. Or completely out of my fucking mind.

I loved my time on the island with Elliot while I was Adams and he didn't question me, he accepted that was who I was. I went about without the pressure of my past on my shoulders, living life like I imagine others must be able to do without always looking back over those shoulders to see if their past was finally catching up with them. But all good things must come to an end, right? And now it was time to face my future. And my past.

I know I need to tell Elliot something, but I'm not sure how to begin or how much to say. Could I explain it all to him? If I were to, it would mean handing him my trust, a commodity I don't hand out. Ever. Not to any man, anyway. Not since my father took it and threw it in my face when I was too young to even understand. I hadn't learned my lesson with my dad and so I allowed my first stepfather to teach me that lesson in the worst of ways. I paid dearly for that mistake and never planned to do it again. But hadn't I already started to trust Elliot? Could I give him more?

"You deceived me. You lied" he states.

"Yes" I admit with my head hanging low in shame.

"Why?"

The heat of his stare bares down on me as I continue to pace the room until Elliot joins me. I hadn't even realized he'd gotten up until this very moment when I feel his hands on my arms. "Come sit down" he demands as he pulls me with him to the bed.

Elliot sits me down on the plush mattress and joins me. His hand goes to my thigh as he sits next to me and turns to face me. I decide in that moment that I'm not ready to hand over my secrets.

"It might be best to begin with that spanking" I say.

Elliot shifts next to me and the air clings to my skin, heavy with his arousal and my fears. I shiver when he rises and holds out a hand to me. "If that's how you want it, Ad…Courtney," he shrugs correcting himself. "Have it your way."

I force my body to stand and accept his hand. Then I watch him transform before my very eyes into the man I've been convinced I need. But now that I've seen the side of Elliot I had on the island, did I still yearn for the confident and aggressive sexual Dominant to take me and make me his, teach me how to be a good girl while loving that I was a slut? If he filled out his profile honestly, that's who he was, a sexual Dominant with dark desires and kinky tastes.

Elliot releases the buttons of his dress shirt one at a time and as slowly as he can before letting the garment fall to the ground. I marvel at the familiar sight of his chest and toned abdomen, a sigh escaping me, and Elliot allows a chuckle to escape him. It's the only thing that reminds me that he might not be doing this solely to cause me pain. "Enjoying yourself, *Miss Knight*?"

"Why do you keep calling me that? And I don't like you calling me Courtney, either."

"Why, because it's your name, isn't it? What would you like me to call you if not by your real name?"

"I don't know. I liked when you called me Adams" I say with an attitude I don't believe I have the strength for.

"Oh, *Adams*, that attitude is going to cost you dearly."

"You can't just spank me like a child. Do you even know what you're doing? I think there's classes you need to take or videos…"

I'm cut off when Elliot scoops me up into his arms and walks across the room to a piece of furniture, a bench, I hadn't noticed was there. He plops me back on my feet with one command. "Strip."

"What?"

"You heard me. I said to take off your clothes. Now, take them off. Everything."

Elliot flicks the button on his trousers while he waits, impatiently, for me to comply with his request. When I don't, he sends a quick smirk my way before adding, "We've both been tested and have the other's medical records, so the issue of safety and birth control is resolved. Now, there shouldn't be any reason for you to still have your clothes on unless you require my assistance to remove them. Do you need my help?"

I shake my head without removing my eyes from his and reach behind me for my zipper. Unable to reach it, I sigh and Elliot beckons me to turn around. Not knowing what else to do, I finally give in to the man that ignites something so primal in me, he elicits an organic reaction that's out of my control.

"Now that's my good girl. I'm glad to see you're giving up the rebellious attitude. This night might progress better than I anticipated."

"It's morning" I point out in my snarky voice laced with attitude.

Elliot smirks but I see his Adam's apple bob when he swallows what he'd like to say. By his expression, I'm guessing instead of what he was thinking, Elliot says, "Remove everything."

I do as he asks, and the task moves along quicker than it should have because I was already devoid of my panties, a theme when I'm around him.

"Lean over that bench," he commands with a flick of his chin. "And I'd suggest you hold on tight."

I'm hit with the familiar feelings that come when bending over to get into position for your ass to be spanked. The act of bending over alone, signals the beginning and builds anticipation. In my past, I anticipated the worst. Today, I'm anticipating something much different, but then as I go to lean down, I hear the snap of Elliot's belt breaking free from the loops in his pants. "I…I can't do this. I don't want you to hit me. I won't let you hurt me like that."

"I don't want to hurt you either, Adams," he admits and if he had used my real name, I might not have believed him or done as he was asking. But he'd called me Adams and I did believe him. In this moment, I believe he can be the man I need, so I bend my body over the bench and wait for the first sting of his belt. "Christ, why would you think I wanted to hurt you?"

I shrug while remaining in place and waiting for the first blow to be delivered.

I know I'm in the optimal position to be spanked because my ass is presented in a plump and relaxed manner. Well, as relaxed as it can be with the anticipation of Elliot possibly giving me everything I've been searching for and need from a man. Or destroying me with my past.

I lay my full weight across the bench, my feet hanging because I'm too short for them to reach the ground. My hands seek purchase and I grasp the legs of the bench so as not to topple off once his punishing blows begin. Unfortunately, I'm still in a position that offers little support for my upper body.

Elliot is standing and admiring the sight before him. "Having to assume this position is humiliating in its submission and rubs in the fact that you're about to be spanked. You've done it with grace and beauty.

That will be rewarded, Adams, but why do I get the sense that you've done this before?"

I slightly nod as I continue to anticipate the familiar sting of leather, but I don't give him any other answers. When the sting doesn't come, but instead a low rumble from Elliot's chest, I sigh as his hand gently runs down one of my thighs. Then I feel him tug my hair from out of my face and wrap it in something to keep it from falling forward again. "So fucking beautiful" he praises.

I heave in a gulp of air, still waiting for that sting, the one that will remind me of my stepfather's best friend. When it still doesn't come, I chance a look at Elliot over my shoulder and realize his belt isn't in his hand. He doesn't have plans to silence me with it. But I'm not prepared for what he does have in mind. Because the pain of his belt, I'd know how to handle. But what Elliot begins to do is the opposite and that I don't know how to process.

His body is pressing into mine as he leans over me and I feel his solid erection press against my thigh. It has me questioning whether I'd be better off with his belt. This is leading toward the direction of high emotional stakes and I'm not ready for the fall-out from that. Elliot plants kisses on my shoulder then moves to my neck. "The way you smell right here," he hums. "The only place you smell better is between your legs."

I moan as his hand cups my pussy with his words then gasp when a thick finger enters me and swirls around my entrance on its exiting to collect my arousal and bring it to my clit.

"Jesus," Elliot groans. "You're so fucking wet."

"Elliot" I begin but I'm silenced when I feel the loss of his body's heat as he stands back again. Then I feel the first slap of his big palm across my over-heated, exposed flesh and I jerk forward.

"Didn't listen when I said to hold tight. You'll need to learn to obey me, Adams, or this perfect fucking ass of yours is going to remain sore."

Slap.

The sound echoes in the large expanse of the room. It's a familiar noise but the emotions running through me are completely foreign.

Slap.

My teeth gnash and I grind them, my jaw already aching from the tension. I sigh and turn to relax into the blows. I know fighting them won't help any.

Slap.

My knuckles turn white as I hold on tightly so as not to be catapulted off the bench by his harsh assault to my now very sore and I'm sure bright red ass.

Slap.

The tears begin to flow then, and I don't even attempt to hold them back. But they're not tears of pain. Well, not physical, anyway. Years of pent-up anguish release in this moment and I don't hold back. I let the tears fall to the ground in huge plops as the memories go with them. Every slap Elliot delivers to my ass morphs into Jim's from years ago. But I accept them, because I own and control them this time. It's cathartic, healing, and I have no clue if Elliot has any idea what's he's doing for me or not, but I will never be able to thank him enough.

Elliot delivers so many blows that I lose count and just as I'm sinking into the sensations and processing what Jim had done to me all those years ago, he switches gears without warning. He begins to add teasing into the mix, and it brings about a whole new set of emotions. Jim was an asshole and a pervert, but he rarely touched me in a sexual way. He usually spanked me until he was close to climaxing, threw me on my knees, and jerked off. Most times, he finished in his hand, it was few and far between that I'd have any evidence left on me.

But Elliot is using this spanking to excite me and it's working.

Between his sharp blows, I begin to feel his probing finger at my entrance. He never lets it sink back in; he circles then withdraws to spank me again. As I sink back into the blows, he changes gears again and I feel his thumb press down on my clit. He continues alternating between blows and stimulating me until I'm a mess of tears and mucus, rubbing myself on his legs for release as my arousal and groans fill the air.

My emotions are raw and on the surface. I can no longer hold back. I let my tears turn to audible cries. I let my silent moans morph into pleas for release. And I let my memories release into the thought of the future this man can give to me if I can only just open myself up to him.

Elliot goes on for minutes, maybe hours in this way, passion emanating from his every blow. I don't know how long it lasts because I've lost all sense of time. But then as my climax is approaching, his questioning begins, and I'm forced to face this experience as my punishment not only for my past but also for my lies.

"What the fuck were you thinking joining a company that gives you to someone?"

Slap.

"Answer me."

Crack. Slap. Slap. Crack. Crack. Crack.

I heave in a gulp of air and try to speak through my tears and sobs. "I don't know."

"Wrong answer," he states as he rains down countless slaps of his hand on my aching flesh, none of them hard enough to do any physical damage but the illusion of it is enough to work its magic. "Try again."

"I'm not who you think I am. I'm not a good girl like Adams. I'm not the girl you met on the island," I admit with a cry as he lands another blow on my ass. "I'm a slut who lets guys use my body to help me forget my past."

Elliot immediately stops the punishment he'd been so enjoying, and I feel his body freeze next to me, his erection deflates against my leg and I realize I just blurted out the truth. My world swirls and goes dark as I feel my heartrate increase.

The next thing I know, I'm wrapped in a sheet in Elliot's arms on the soft bed and he's making calming, soothing sounds as his hands rub gentle circles on my back and hip. "Baby, shhh," he coos. "You're okay. Talk to me. I'm right here. I didn't mean to scare you. Did I hurt you?"

I hear sounds. I'm not sure what they are. A cat meowing in pain, maybe. It's raw and anguished and it takes me some time to realize that it's coming from me. The room blurs again, and I do my best to fight off the darkness but it's so tempting that I struggle to remain alert. Elliot pulls me on top of his body and wraps me in his arms. I place my head on his chest, over his heart and when I decide to align mine with his, I find it already matches.

We match. He's my match. My Compatible Companion. If I believed in the concept of soul mates, I'd say I found mine, but...

The memories of my past and the last few minutes with Elliot swirl together and confuse me. I was afraid of being spanked as a child because I knew it was wrong of me to let my stepfather's best friend do that. He told me that I couldn't help myself because it was all that I was good for. That I was a slut and a whore in the making. It scared me because I knew he was right, but more so because I knew what came next. He never penetrated me, but he always found his pleasure.

I feel the pounding in my head and the soreness of my ass. But the feeling that's different this time is the aching between my legs. The need for Elliot to fill me with himself and take that ache away was never there with my "Uncle" Jim. What he'd done to me never aroused me. What Elliot just did, is driving me out of my mind like no one has ever been able to do before.

Sure, I've let a few guys try their best to spank me and get me to this point. I always knew on some level that all the therapy in the world wouldn't help. I always knew this was what I needed. So, I had let men try their best. They all failed. Until now.

Stupid me, I thought it was their lack of skill. Apparently, it was me. All I needed was the emotional connection to a man. A man that could rip me open with his skilled hands. Now, I can only hope that Elliot can put me back together again, too.

He remains silent and waits me out. My breathing evens and echoes his as I settle into his embrace. The scent of his cologne mixes with his male hormones and fills my nostrils, easing me into a restful state, lulling me to sleep.

I awake with a startle only moments later and Elliot shushes me again. His hands go to the sides of my face and he pulls my lips to his. "Tell me where on earth you got the idea that you were a slut?"

I cuddle closer to him for the strength I need for my confession. I don't want to leave the warmth and safety of his arms, but I know he needs to see my face when I say this. I know I need to look into his eyes and gauge his reaction when he hears me. "I signed with Compatible Companions for a few reasons other than my impulsivity issues. None of them make me look good."

"Continue" he says without emotion.

"My mother needs my sister and I to grow up and get out of her marriage. My second stepfather is about to jump ship, and I can't say I blame him. If that happens, because of us, my mom will be devastated, and I can't be responsible for her misery any longer. Her first and second marriages ended because of me, I can't watch it happen again."

"I'm sure you're wrong, Adams. Were you a child when your parents split up and she remarried, when her second marriage ended?"

I shrug. I should have been. I was by chronological age. By sexual experience, I was ahead of my years when Tom left and took "Uncle" Jim with him.

"Adams," he prompts. "Were you a child?"

"By age, yeah. But I was far from innocent when Tom left, and I did end her marriages."

Elliot raises an eyebrow then changes his line of questioning when he sees that I'm not ready to head down that path. "Okay, what about this marriage? What do you think you've done this time?"

"Like I said, I'm not who I led you to believe I am. My sister told me that it was a crazy idea, on the island," I say as explanation. "I mean, I've been fucking guys for attention since I was fourteen," I shrug. "But with you, it was different. What we shared made something happen inside here," I point to my chest. "But I had to keep with my plan. Bobby has reached his breaking point and I know it's only a matter of time before he leaves my mom, so I cried over you as I snuck off the island and every night I've spent alone since. I don't want my mom to have to cry over Bobby like that. They're meant to be together. They dated in high school then went different ways. She married my dad who turned out to be an asshole. After that, she dated and remarried my stepfather who was worse.

By the time she and Bobby reunited, Bridget and I were on the road to becoming a case study in daddy issues."

"I don't understand what that has to do with joining Compatible Companions."

"I need the money. I figured I was fucking every guy I went on a date with or met in a bar for free," Again I shrug. "Why not get paid. Sex was always a means to an end for me until…" I clear my throat.

"Until" he prompts.

"Until I met you."

Elliot gently kisses my temple. "I'm still so confused. Did you come up with this Adams idea on the spot when we met or…"

"No. I decided that Bridget and I would take Bobby up on the island trip to give him and my mother time to be alone. And I needed time to think. I knew when I returned that I was facing a year long relationship with someone I didn't know, love, or had even met. After the year, I knew I'd have enough money for Bridget and me to go back to school and get our own place. We need to stop expecting Bobby to support us and pick up the pieces."

"Your parents struggle financially?"

I laugh. "No. Bobby's rich as fuck. It's not about the money per se."

Elliot shrugs as if he understands. "My father isn't going to be thrilled with me when he finds out that I left my job."

"On the island?"

Elliot laughs. "No, Adams, you weren't the only one lying when we met. However, mine was a lie of omission. You seemed to think I was the hired help, I let you believe that."

I raise a questioning eyebrow and let that sink in. "You're my match?" I ask. "Wait, so, why did you join Compatible Companions?"

"For sex," he states with no apologies. "And I didn't join as much as I was asked. I have particular tastes when it comes to fucking. I'm not in a place where I can muster up the energy to elicit it on my own and have my needs met. When the opportunity arose, it seemed like the best option."

I'm not sure what to say to that so I remain silent.

"Yeah, it makes me look pretty bad, too, huh?"

"No worse than me, I guess."

Elliot laughs at that then gently brushes his lips against mine. "After I met you, things changed. I wasn't sure what the hell I was going to do with my match."

"But you went to meet her?"

Elliot shrugs. "I guess. I was supposed to be up in the penthouse of the building you flew out of. The owner was having a party I was supposed to be at with my parents. Then I was supposed to meet my match outside, well you, I guess, on the street at midnight. I never did make it up to the party. Obviously."

"Wait…a party in the penthouse of Stone Towers? At Damian Stone's?"

"Yeah, you know who he is?"

"Oh, my God! That's where I was. My stepfather is Bobby Knight. His best friend is Damian's cousin that is married to my aunt. How do you know Damian?"

"Let's just say we have similar tastes and my father is tight with his brother-in-law."

"Mac? Wait…holy fuck! Is your dad one of those hot old guys that was in the military with Mac?"

"The leader of the pack."

"Wow! So, are you…" I pause and let a few things take root in my head. His hair shaved tight to his head, the stealth spying on me, the morning I woke to find him covered in sweat next to me having what I thought was a nightmare at the time. Now, I'm starting to question if it was a flashback. PTSD? Then Ace knowing him from the military. "Are you in the military, too?"

"Nope. Left. Daddy is going to flip his shit. I'm sure he already knows. Mac and crew told him the minute he walked into that party, no doubt."

"I never knew you made this much money in the military, maybe I should have looked into joining with them instead of Compatible Companions."

Elliot lets out a huge laugh. "You're not really equipped to be military, baby. And you don't make shit doing your standard jobs."

"So how did you pay to join Compatible Companions and for me?"

"In cash," he laughs. "From what we'll call side jobs. The policy, don't ask, don't tell, is really not about who you're fucking as much as who you're working for."

My insides bubble, they grow hot at the thought of Elliot as a secret agent or a SEAL. Maybe one of those guys in camo that lurk in the desert just waiting to save a girl in distress then take her under them and fuck her into…

"That mind of yours again," he says. "I need a camera in there."

I giggle then startle when Elliot's phone rings.

He stretches to see the screen and winces. "My dad, right on time."

He silences his phone and flings it back down.

"You're not going to answer him?"

"I'm not going to answer him. Not now, anyway, it's the middle of the fucking night. I'll deal with him in the morning. Right now, we need to figure this out. Our contracts…Adams, I own you for a year. We've met and came into this room. It's a binding agreement that we can't get out of."

I nod. I hadn't read all the fine print. I'd meant to while lying in the sun but Elliot's presence on the island had distracted me from everything else but him. I recall seeing something about a place, and once entering it, being unable to back out. I guess they had a few exits built into the arrangement, but it seems like Elliot and I have crossed into the land of no looking back.

"Do you understand what I mean by the fact that I own you? Did you read my requirements?"

I widen my eyes but don't answer because, no, I hadn't read through that either. The guy they gave me was my match. The company claims to have a ninety-nine percent success rate, so I figured if they matched me with him, we'd be compatible. Jesus, I mean, it's the name of the company, right?

"You didn't read the contract you signed? You have no idea what you've agreed to do for a year? Fucking Christ, Adams! What if I'd been…" Instead of completing his statement, he crushes his lips to mine and takes my mouth. I open for him and moan when his tongue runs over mine. He pulls back and catches my eye then brings our foreheads together before pushing me to arm's distance. "Adams, I don't think that spanking was sufficient for what you've done."

16

"Come," he demands. One word then a raise of his brow when I don't move. A smile crosses his face and Elliot lets out a tiny chuckle. "Adams, I suggest you read every word of that contract. But, first, we have a punishment to get to. Now, I said, come."

He stretches out a hand and this time I move and clasp mine in his.

He leads me to the door of another room in the suite and stops before swiping his card in front of a sensor.

"I think we need to amend our contract just a bit. We'll discuss it after I show you what you so callously agreed to do without reading the fine print."

He lets the door swing open and sweeps his arm for me to enter first. The room is dark, and it takes a moment for my eyes to begin to adjust.

"You asked how I knew Damian Stone. Are you familiar with The Society?"

"I've heard the rumors."

Elliot laughs. "About his BDSM club?"

I nod my head as the room slowly begins to light. It's easy on the eyes, more of a warm glow than illumination.

"My tastes, the ones I said were like his, Adams? I'm a sexual Dominant. I need control and I like to deliver a little pain with my pleasure. I belong to his organization; it's how I came into Compatible Companions."

"He recently bought the company out. When he found my name on the list of employees, he flipped out and threatened to tell my parents."

Elliot shrugs. "He can't. He's too much by the book. Now that I'm thinking about it," Elliot laughs, his head going back at the neck. "The son of a bitch set us up."

"What?"

"He came to me. He knew I was back in the States and in need of…a distraction. He fucking played me. I'll put money on the fact that he contacted me the minute he found out about you and set this up. He couldn't break your contract and he can't tell your parents. But he could manipulate the system to work in his favor. Pair me, a guy he knows and can be in contact with, with you so he'll know you're safe."

"But you paid…"

Elliot shakes his head. "I paid only after arguing with him. He also insisted on a private agreement between us stating that if I were to end up with the woman that he paired me with, I'd accept the money back as our wedding gift."

"He's such an asshole. Wait until I tell my aunt what he's done. She's going to kick his ass. Or Sydney will."

Elliot shakes his head again. "You can't. You need to abide by the contract and so do I. One year," Elliot shrugs. "Then, who knows? Maybe we'll get the world's most expensive wedding gift."

That stops me dead in my tracks and I begin to stutter about the absurdity of the institution of marriage. I've watched what it did to my mother who spent her whole life striving for the kind of romance her sister had and falling into relationship after relationship and marriages just for the sake of having a man. I wouldn't become my mother. Ever. Marriage might be for many women; it wasn't an option for me.

Elliot watches me falter and lets me off the hook. "Now, speaking of that contract you signed. I believe I brought you in here for a reason. That bench was vanilla, Adams. This room is more aligned with my darker tastes."

My eyes begin to finally scan the room. Oh, holy mother of…sweet baby Jesus, it's the Holy Grail. A real-life, Mr. CG red room of pain. Or pleasure. I hope. Only this room is gray which brings a smile to my face. Fitting, isn't it?

Elliot untucks the sheet that he'd wrapped around me from under my arms and lets it fall away, puddle to the floor at my feet. His gaze is intense and fixed on me, it shifts between my eyes and lips, never going to my exposed breasts that are aching for his attention or my bare pussy that wants nothing more than to be filled with him. He moans when he finally lets his eyes scan me from head to toe and the sound sends shock waves through my system. My skin heats then goose bumps break out as my nipples painfully harden and I groan along with him.

Elliot raises a hand to gently lift one breast. He lowers his head and takes my nipple into his mouth. I arch my back when he clasps that nipple in between his teeth and pulls back. "Aaa..Oh!"

"You like that?" he asks. "You were so responsive on the island. I knew you shared my tastes. Let's find out just how much and how many, shall we?"

He smirks as my core tightens and my insides turn to goo at the promise of finally meeting a man that pushes every one of my hot buttons and, praise the stars above, is a trained Dom who must know how to do this correctly. Thankfully, for once in my life, things appear to be going my way.

Once the popular book about that millionaire hit the shelves, then Bailey Connors exploded on the scene, every guy that painted their bedroom red thought they knew how to use a flogger. They didn't.

Elliot? Yeah, Elliot appears to know exactly what he's doing, so I nod. I mean, I've signed the contract, what choice did I have anyway? I might as well see where this can go and being with him is hardly the hardship that I pictured being with my Compatible Companion would be.

He lowers to my other nipple and his skillfully trained lips and teeth begin their job. He licks and flicks with his tongue, his other hand still holding my breast up, his thumb circling that nipple still wet from his mouth.

"I have rules you'll need to understand, agree to, and follow. If you fuck up, and you will," he says with an evil grin. "I will punish you. It's simple behavior modification, really. You do what I ask, I give you pleasure. You disobey me, well…we'll see how much pain you actually enjoy."

"I've read all of Bailey Connors' books and saw the movies. I can take pain, but I've read some other pretty freaky things. Not that I'm judging, I mean, whatever. If people like it," I shrug. "It's none of my business, but I'm not letting you use one of those electricity wands or piss on me. Just putting that out there now."

Elliot laughs from the pit of his belly. "I'm afraid to ask where this knowledge of my sexual preferences has come from."

"PornHub, mainly."

Elliot laughs again. "I see. Well, *Miss Knight*, I can assure you that I've been potty trained since I was a toddler and I'm a good boy who only goes pee-pee in the potty."

That makes me laugh too. Momentarily. But then his tongue runs the shell of my ear and a shiver runs through me. My core liquifies and my knees weaken.

It's early morning and his stubble is already growing in. It's rough on my neck and sends chills to my pussy. I want to feel those prickers on the insides of my sensitive thighs while he rests his head there and toys with my slick folds.

Elliot chuckles. "I'm going to have my work cut out for me to get you into subspace. You spend a lot of time in your head, don't you? I need to know you're with me. I'm going to explain my needs and I need you to respond with a yes, Elliot. Understand?"

"Not Sir?"

Elliot shifts the erection trapped in his pants. "We'll get to that later. Right now, listen and stay with me. Say yes if you agree and understand, and no if you don't."

"Okay" I sigh as his hands circle my waist and he pulls my body into his. I feel his hardness against my belly, and I reach down to cup him.

He's hot, I can feel the warmth of his arousal through his pants. He groans then pulls back, saying, "Rule one, I will touch you where, when, and how I want. At all times. Do you understand? I'll expect your hands all over me too."

I nod then find myself being spun around and thrown over Elliot's legs as he falls into a chair with me on his lap.

Elliot plops down with good posture in the armless chair, his knees together and jostles me until I'm lying face down across his lap, my head to the left and my feet to the right. I'm so far over his lap that my ass is conveniently located directly over his right thigh. Elliot shifts me slightly so that my head and shoulders are angled down, and my knees are tucked down out of his way. This position gives him total access to my presented ass. I feel his strong palm press against the back of my head and swats to my thighs to encourage my cooperation. "Spread your knees apart and arch your lower back for me" he demands.

I know as I obey that I'm fully exposing my sex. A groan from him along with a swipe of a thick finger through my slick folds proves me right.

Because I'm fairy-sized, my toes are hoisted off the ground by a few inches with my full weight resting on Elliot's lap. My mind returns to my past and the warning "Uncle" Jim used to give about my heels never touching down. I clear my throat at the memory and Elliot checks in with a questioning glance. He readjusts the ponytail holder to secure the fly-away hairs allowing him to see my every emotion play out on my face.

"Use your hands to hold the legs of the chair. If your hands fly back during your spanking, I'll pin them to your back," he warns. "Now, be a good girl and take your punishment. Do you understand?"

Elliot slightly shifts my upper body to the right to give himself a fuller swing and be able to deliver a stronger swat.

Slap.

"Hey!" I say as I try to get up. His big palm presses me back down.

"Let's try that again. I said, do you understand, and you say…"

"That fucking hur…awwww!" I yell when the second blow comes.

"Adams, I can slap this ass all morning. I asked you a question. How were you told you were to respond?"

Self-preservation finally hits and I obey his commands. "Yes or no."

"Good girl" he praises and his large palm cups and rubs my sore ass then a thick finger again explores just a tad lower. It doesn't sink inside, just swirls around my entrance to collect my arousal. When he feels my wetness, Elliot groans then circles a few rounds over my clit.

I sigh and sink back into his lap, relaxing and grasping the legs of the chair once more while thinking that his spanking is over. But I'm wrong.

"I need control at all times, Adams, not just when we fuck. At. All. Times. I can be a difficult man and I need to know that you'll cooperate. Do you think you'll be able to relinquish control to me?"

"I don't think I follow rules very well."

Slap. Smack. Slap. Slap, Slap.

"I can see that," Elliot says. "Now, let's try that again. Do you think you can follow *my* rules?"

"Yes," I say to save my ass and because I want it to be true.

"Are you just saying that to save your ass?"

"Yes."

Elliot laughs. "Well, at least I know my next request can be accomplished. I need the truth from you, Adams. No more lying to me. I won't stand for it and if it happens again, you won't sit for a fucking week. So, can you promise me that you'll always be truthful?"

"I'll try...awww. Christ! Sorry. Jesus, you're really serious about this, huh?"

"You're talking and thinking way too much. What should you say?"

"Yes. Yes, I'll try to always tell you the truth."

Slap.

"Not try, sweetheart. You will. Say it."

Elliot's finger returns to its earlier explorations. This time he allows it to sink inside and curl. He finds my hot spot and rubs as his calloused thumb finds my clit and presses down.

"You'll learn to orgasm on my command and hold off when I demand. Do you think you can handle that?"

"I don't...don't spank me," I beg. "I'll try, but I'm being honest. I don't know if that's possible."

Elliot smiles. "Mmm, hmmm. Watch." Elliot removes his finger then plunges back in with two. "Come for me, baby. Come on my hand."

If it wasn't happening to me, I'd be laughing at the dramatics, but here I am coming on his command and thrashing over his legs as my orgasm hits and runs through my body with each pump of his fingers. It's a reaction I thought only possible in books or fabricated on film.

"That's my girl. Now, I suspect holding one off is going to prove more challenging for you. We'll work up to that. Back to my tastes. Yes or no, nothing else. Have you ever had your nipples clamped?"

"No."

"Been tied up tightly so you couldn't move while being fucked however the guy wanted to take you?"

"Yes and no."

"Elaborate."

"I've tried bondage. It didn't do what I thought it would for me. I didn't like or hate it."

"When done properly, you'll like it. What did you expect it to do? You may speak freely."

Elliot's hands leisurely rub circles on my ass and the backs of my thighs while I explain that I wanted the bondage to make me feel safe, grounded, and to help clear the noise in my head. Elliot raises an eyebrow, doesn't say much more than he can do that and more for me before he asks his next question. "Hot wax, ice, dildos and vibrators?"

"Um, never used wax or ice but I'd be open to them. I've used the others alone, no one ever asked to use them with me, but I'd like to try them with you."

"Okay, good to know. You can continue to answer in sentences," Elliot says as he sits me up and cradles me in his lap. "See how much nicer this can be if you cooperate and don't need punishment?"

I nod and Elliot chuckles. "You're a brat, I can see. That's going to keep you over my knee, Snowflake."

I shrug. It's not a bad place to be. Especially when his fingers go exploring and make me come on demand. I'm kind of hoping we can try that again soon.

"Have you ever had a threesome?"

I laugh aloud. "Are you kidding me?"

"No, I'm dead fucking serious. Do I need to toss you back over my knee and ask that again to get the answer I'm seeking?"

"No. I mean, no to the over your knee for the answer. Yes, to the threesomes."

Elliot's jaw ticks and a vein in his forehead begins to visibly throb. Then he releases a pent-up growl. "I asked about a singular experience. You answered in plural form. Explain."

"Do I have to?"

"Of course not. You can keep quiet and we'll have our first lesson on delayed gratification as means of punishment."

"Huh?"

Elliot smiles then stands with me in his arms. He walks to the bed and places me on my back. "Don't move," he demands.

He reaches down and pulls a chain with a cuff from under the bed and claps it to my ankle. It's soft inside and he tugs to be sure it's tight and going to hold me in place. "You okay with this?"

I nod.

"Words. I need to always hear your permission. Are you okay with this?"

"Yes."

Elliot reaches down three more times and secures each of my limbs, being sure that I'm immobilized and spread wide open for him.

"How many threesomes have you had?" he questions now that I'm at his mercy.

"I have no idea" I honestly answer but Elliot appears unhappy with my response or my honesty. Maybe both.

He growls then smirks as he glances down at my bare pussy. A chill runs through me as he lowers his body and settles between my legs. "Wrong answer," he states. "Let's see how long it takes to get the correct one."

Elliot reaches out a single finger. His pointer one. That stupid children's song comes to mind and I can tell you where Pointer is right now, the thick and skillful fucker. He's gently rubbing up and down on my clit. Making slow passes that are not hard enough to do much, but present enough to cause a building inside me. One I'll need taken care of very soon if he doesn't stop.

"Anytime you're ready to fix your answer, I'll either stop what I'm doing or make it more of what you need. Depending on what that answer might be, that is."

I heave in a deep sigh because the light touch to my most sensitive, nerve-laden area is now starting to create a deep burning in my loins and I need relief for the ache. "A lot," I finally admit. "Most with Bridget."

Elliot furrows his brow. "Honesty will get you a small reward. But the truth pisses me off all the same. What the fuck do you mean a lot?"

I try to shrug but remember that I can't move enough to complete the action. "I don't know. Like I said, my sister and I..."

He interrupts me. "Wait, you have another sister?"

"No, Bridget. You met her on the..." Oh shit! I remember now that I never told him about her fake name.

Elliot sits back as an evil smile spreads across his handsome face. "Another lie, Adams? You've been a very naughty girl, haven't you? I was just about to suck this sweet little clit into my mouth and watch you explode. Now," he shrugs. "Oh, baby, now I can't do that."

"No!" I protest. "Yes, yes you can! Just...Oh, fuck, Elliot!"

Elliot lowers his mouth to my core and his tongue snakes out to swirl around my clit. I can feel the stubble covering his jaw scraping across my skin and abrading it. I'll have stubble burn in no time, but I try my best to lean into his embrace all the same.

But he's careful, too fucking careful if you want my opinion, and he doesn't apply pressure. I feel the barest of sweeps around my hardened bud and only know that Elliot is there by the low grumbling and praise coming from him. All spoken directly into my pussy. "I've been waiting for my first taste of this sweetness. Your pussy tastes so fucking good. Wish I could eat you properly, but you've been a very bad girl, Adams. A." Lick. "Very." Swipe. "Bad." Suck. "Girl." Swirl. "Mmm…"

Elliot continues with the swooshes and swirls, never giving me enough pressure or continuing the same motion for long enough to push me over the edge. When he feels my body tightening to prepare for the detonation anyway, he pulls back with a chuckle.

Fucking bastard!

"Oh, Snowflake, I should have started out by telling you that your orgasms would all be mine and upon my request. That was close and would have costed your perfect ass dearly."

"I don't care," I pant. "Do whatever you want, just please make me come, Elliot. Please" I cry. Real tears of frustration fall from my eyes. And I expect them to work because they usually do, but Elliot just keeps right on laughing. If he weren't so sexy, I'd liken him to that psycho doll with red hair from that scary movie. I'm sure that would earn me a swat or two. Maybe even enough to make me sneak in a tiny, little quake of an orgasm.

"Not working with me, Adams. Stop being a brat and accept your consequences like a big girl. Then, maybe we can see about getting you a nice orgasm."

I growl in frustration. I want to throw myself off this bed and delve my fingers deep inside my pussy until I come while Elliot watches like he had in the shadows on the island. That would show him. My orgasms are all his? Fuck him!

"Wishing you had a few fingers free, huh, Snowflake?"

"Ugh. Elliot, come on" I plead.

"Hmmm, not a bad idea. I'd love to come on that hot pussy of yours. But…we haven't taught you your lesson yet, have we?"

"Fucking masochist!"

Elliot smiles at me then lowers his lips to my mouth. He nips my bottom lip then lets me taste myself on his. "Not in the slightest and never with you," he says. "Now, relax and cooperate. Give into me and give me what I need, and I'll return the favor three-fold."

I cry. Long and hard before I finally give in. And Elliot sits and watches, the whole time silent. His hand remains on my belly offering me strength and support, but he doesn't speak.

"My sister's name is Bridget," I say as I finally relent and give into his demands. "Her and I both started having sex around fourteen. I started a few weeks before her, told her it was good and that she'd like it. By senior year, we were bored with it because it was no longer getting us the attention it had been or that we were seeking. We raised the bar and started fucking guys together. Most recently, we started having group sex together."

"Ace?"

I nod. "And his friend, Callan."

"Fucking Black!"

"You know him, too? How? Oh, my god! That's right, the military?"

Elliot nods but offers nothing else in return on the topic. Instead he lowers to whisper in my ear while his hand begins to roam. "Let me be very clear about something, Adams. I paid very well for you. You are mine. This pussy," he cups my heat in his strong hand and lets a finger slip inside. "This hot, tight, delicious, fucking pussy," he praises as he pumps that finger. "Is mine. All fucking mine. I don't share, you will not go near another man for a year. Especially not Callan motherfucking Black. Are we clear?"

He fucks me with his thick finger until I'm panting and shaking my head to agree with his request. It's the only part of my body I can move, and it frustrates me as I seek out my release. I want to thrash around on the bed and use my body to demand that he make me come, but I can't move. Instead, I'm forced to lay here and accept what he gives me or what he doesn't.

Elliot pulls back again just as I'm about to come around his finger. "I suspect the reasons for your behavior are going to take me some time to get out of you. I'll accept that for now. We need to build trust and I respect that. I'm fine putting in the hard work to earn yours."

He stands from the bed and my eyes travel with him to watch as he lowers his pants.

"I'm going to fuck you now and you will not come until you're told. Do you understand?"

"Yes. Please."

"Good girl," he says as he climbs back onto the bed, between my spread legs. "I like you spread open for me like this. I'm not going to last long."

Elliot pushes into me with such force, the bed bangs into the wall.

"Fuck, yeah," he growls on the second thrust. "So wet. So fucking good without anything between us. I'm going to fill this pussy with my come, Adams."

I lose count of the number of thrusts it takes for him to get to the pinnacle of his pleasure, but his earlier statement of not lasting long was bullshit because he's held me on the brink for what feels like hours by the time his grunts increase and he's ready to come.

He finally rears back then lowers to claim my mouth. "You're about to make me come, Snowflake."

"Yes" I sigh because I'm right there with him.

But then he pulls out and I feel the loss instantly. Before I can protest, he whispers into my ear. "Come for me" he demands as he grips the headboard and without guiding his erection back into me, he sinks deep with a strangled growl as he empties himself inside me.

I come with him as he demanded. Hard. Around him as his hips continue to move and he rides out his pleasure. His cock pumping me through each spasm as I ride out my own.

17

I must have fallen asleep because Elliot is kissing my ear and neck to wake me from my slumber. "Wake up my lucky girl" he coos.

I wonder what it is that is making me lucky and *his* girl. I like the sound of both, the latter the most. I still groan and try to shoo his advances away.

Elliot scoffs and reminds me that I'm his to do with as he wishes and that if I didn't want to cooperate, we could have another punishment session instead of what he had planned. "I have many ways to punish you, Adams. Would you like me to show you another one of them now?"

"Nope," I sass. "I'm good."

"That mouth," he complains with a smile. "You hungry?"

I lift a shoulder then stretch the rest of my muscles that ached from my restraints and the force of the climax Elliot had elicited earlier. "I could eat."

"Mmm, me too, baby," he says with a smile. "But I have all year for that."

"Elliot, we should…"

"Talk?"

"Yes."

"About what, Snowflake?" Elliot reaches for my hand and pulls me to stand beside the bed. He's dressed in loose fitting lounge pants with his chest and feet bare and I'm as naked as the day I was born. Feeling self-conscience over that, I wrap my arms around my breasts.

"No, no, no," he admonishes. "You look amazing. Don't ever cover yourself. I just might have you remain naked for the next three hundred sixty-four days."

"Elliot, you can't expect me to…"

"Oh, but I can. Remember, Adams? I own you. I can expect you to be naked all day, every day. I can punish you for no good reason, just because I like seeing your ass glowing red under my hand. And I can fuck you any way and as often as my heart desires."

Elliot's hands reach around me and cup my ass. He pulls me into his tight body then grinds his erection into my belly. "I *can* punish you for no reason, unfortunately we haven't worked through the actual offenses you truly need punishment for yet, so those will need to be addressed first before we can move on to the fun stuff."

I frown and Elliot kisses the tip of my nose.

"I think we might begin with the fact that you seem to tend to lie about your name and the names of your family members. I'm wondering who else in your life you've lied to me about."

I roll my eyes and try to wiggle out of his hold. If he finds out about Callan Black and I, I have a feeling he'll be spank my ass red kind of mad. I guess that's something I'll just have to do my best to keep from him for as long as I can.

Elliot is quick as fire when I wiggle, and he leans into my space and clasps my earlobe in his teeth and pulls. I feel his erection throb as he groans and shifts me in his lap. My stomach picks the perfect time to rumble from lack of food and it saves me from my impending punishment.

"As much as I can be a dick, I don't like the thought of you hungry. Come," he commands. "I'll feed you before we resolve your tendency to lie to me. Or, on second thought, maybe we'll combine the two."

Elliot grabs a few things from the closet and tosses them into a black bag before I have the chance to see what they are. He takes me by the hand, and I pull back. "Wait," I ask. "I'm still naked. Where are we going?"

"Yes, and plan to stay that way until we leave this suite."

"What? Wait, you're wearing clothes. Why am I naked?"

"Because I like you naked and I paid a shit ton of fucking money to do with you whatever it is I please, remember?"

"Yeah, but…I mean, isn't that more of a suggestion and not like a rule?"

"No," Elliot states. "It's a rule. Come, I'll make sure the kitchen is warm, you won't be cold."

Without further explanation, he leads me into the eating area of the suite that is larger than most gourmet home kitchens. I try to object along the way, but Elliot ignores my complaints. I do catch him mumbling about regretting not grabbing a gag. That shuts me up for the time being.

When we make it to the kitchen, he pulls out a chair and taps it with his foot, saying, "Need to be sure this is nice and sturdy for what I have in mind."

"Um…okay?" I say but it comes out as more of a question.

"Sit and get comfy," he commands. "I need to check the heat and get a few things."

"I'll be quiet. You don't need to get a gag."

Elliot laughs. "Not just for your silence, but okay. This time."

I sit and watch as he moves around the space before returning to where I sit. Naked. Elliot's eyes scan my body before he leans down into my space, his hands going to the arms of the chair before his mouth covers mine. I open for him and feel his lips curl into a satisfied smile. His tongue runs along my bottom lip then his teeth nip me. My hands raise to his head and Elliot groans when my nails rake his scalp.

"I'd love to let you use those hands on me, but I have other plans for you. Now, be a good girl," he says. "And hold still."

Elliot reaches to the floor and opens the bag that he had dropped at my feet. He removes a long black rope, pulling it to test for its strength.

"What are you…"

"Shhh, no questions."

Elliot gets to work on my wrists and secures one then the other to the arms of the chair. The rope is tight but not painful. I try to tug and test the limits and Elliot leans down once more and takes my mouth. He pulls back and says, "Sink into the security it can bring you. You know I'm not going to hurt you, you're safe. Enjoy that."

I'd ask what he meant had I not already noticed my heartrate settle. Elliot was taking everything from me and in total control. He was giving me the freedom to release it all to him and relax, enjoy the sensations without a concern.

I feel his hands lift my breasts and his thumbs harden my nipples. "There you go," he soothes when they peak for him. "Give me your trust, baby."

I nod my head and then tilt my chin in search of another kiss. Elliot smiles and takes my mouth once more with a moan.

He pulls back before I'd like but then his hands make me forget. They travel down my body as he lowers to his knees in front of me, his big body spreading them open. He reaches back into the bag and takes out another strand of black rope. This one, he wraps around my ankles, securing them to the legs of the chair so that I am bound tight with my legs opened wide.

"So fucking perfect," he praises. "Just one more thing and then we'll be ready for your punishment."

"My," I stutter. "Wait, I thought you'd forgotten…"

"Never. You were a bad girl, Adams. I can't very well accept that behavior from you and expect you to respect me, now can I?"

"Sure you can."

Elliot laughs. "Not the way I roll, baby. Now, I'd say hold still, but…" He lets his words trail off as he retrieves a thick, black blindfold from his bag. He moves behind me and covers my eyes. The room goes dark and I jolt at the realization that I am bound naked to a chair with my eyes covered, at the mercy of a man I hardly know.

"Relax," he commands. "I'm going to kill two birds with one stone. I'm going to take care of your hunger while punishing you. Are you ready, Snowflake?"

I don't answer because I don't know how. Am I ready? I've no idea what he has planned so I don't know if it's something I want to be ready for. He says this is a punishment, so I'm inclined to tell him I'm not ready for that. But, it's Elliot and even his torture is sweet.

"That mind of yours," he scoffs. "Let go. Stop thinking and just feel. Listen to my voice and give all your worries over to me. I've got you."

I heave in a deep breath and nod.

"Excellent," he praises. "We'll begin now."

I feel the loss of Elliot's presence by my side, the heat of his arousal momentarily absent as I hear him pad across the room. I try to remember what the space looks like to determine where he's gone off to, but I can't pull up the image in my mind. I hear doors opening and closing, possibly cabinets or the refrigerator, maybe the freezer.

I sit immobilized and wait for his return.

Elliot's hands wrap around my throat as he comes to stand behind me. He leans down to whisper into my ear with a gentle squeeze of his hands. "When I tell you to open for me, you will obey, understand?"

He uses his grasp on my throat to nod my head for me.

"You will do as you're told without question or complaint or this punishment will go on longer. Now, let me remind you that it is a punishment. I've no plans on hurting you, but a punishment isn't about pleasure. Well, not yours anyway. I plan to enjoy myself immensely."

I swallow hard as Elliot releases the pressure on my throat then demands that I open my mouth. I do as he commands while I try to process the taste and texture of the item he works onto the tip of my tongue. It's cool and smooth, tasteless.

"Pull your tongue into your mouth and eat that" he demands as I hear him retrieving more.

I bite down on what I figure out is a black olive, the kind that Bridget and I used to put on our fingers and pop into our mouths when we were kids.

I hear Elliot chuckle. "Raina and I used to pop them off our fingers, too."

"How do you always know what I'm thinking?"

"It's my responsibility to know what you're thinking."

"What?"

"I own you. You're mine. I'll explain the finer points of being a Dom later, but one of the big things is that I'm always in tune with your thoughts and feelings."

"Oh," I sigh. "Okay. Um, is Raina your sister?"

"Yup, but you're not supposed to be asking questions or talking," he scolds. "Now, shh and open for me again."

This time he puts the olive on my tongue with a command for me to leave it there with my mouth open. Just when I'm about to close my lips so as not to drool, he steals it from the tip of my tongue with a chuckle and a moan as he eats it.

Next, I feel something brush across my lips. Kind of like hair tickling me. Elliot makes a few swipes then it's gone, replaced by his finger running over my lips. I instinctively lick my lips and scream out as the hotness enters my mouth. When I do, Elliot inserts his finger and demands that I suck the buffalo wing sauce from it.

For a little pay back, I suck his finger as I would his cock, my tongue swirling as I moan, then sucking it in between my hollowed cheeks.

"Naughty girl," he laughs as I gasp for relief from the burning sensation filling my mouth and covering my lips. "That was celery first. Here, have a bite, it'll help with the heat."

I chomp down on the crunchy stalk and sigh at the relief. I run my tongue over my lips to send some their way as well. When I do, Elliot's tongue joins mine and tangles with me in a dance of seduction. He pulls back to confirm I don't have any food allergies.

"You mentioned your mom being allergic to seafood, but you're good, right?"

"Yes. I'm getting smelly fish next, huh?"

Elliot laughs. "You're never going to learn, are you?" he asks as I feel a thick finger swipe through my wet folds. "I'm giving you *finger* foods, Adams," he states as his finger delves inside my wet heat and begins to pump. "You like *finger* foods, don't you?"

I heave in a breath as Elliot's second finger joins the first. He pumps them, his thumb making a round at my clit then pressing down as his fingers curl up.

"I like *fingering* you," he crudely states. "I love feeling your pussy wet on my fingers." Elliot extracts his fingers and I groan at their loss then at the sound of him moaning because I know why he's made that sound when he says, "Your pussy tastes so sweet, I think I need more of a taste."

I feel myself falling backward but I don't flinch. I know Elliot is there and he's got me. He tips my chair so he can have better access to my center. I feel the swipe of his tongue as he runs it up from my entrance to my clit. "Fuck," I moan. "Elliot...."

"What? Remember, this is a punishment," he says as his mouth leaves my pussy. "This is what I meant about killing two birds. This part is going to be uncomfortable at best. I'm going to keep feeding you, but I'm also going to take you to the brink of explosion over and over. This is going to be your first lesson in delayed gratification."

"Nooooo!" I cry. "Fuck, Elliot, come on. It hurts, please I need to come."

Elliot laughs as he returns his mouth to my pussy and sucks my clit between his lips, his tongue flicking at my tight bud. He stays between my legs, his tongue inside me, swirling around and fucking me, but never doing enough to make me come, until I finally relax and give my pleasure over to him. There's nothing else I can do. I'm in his hands. He's in control, the puppet master to my marionette.

Just as I'm about to sigh in relief, knowing the first spasm of orgasm is right there, he pulls back and praises my efforts. "You're learning quickly to give yourself over to me. That's what you need to do. Always. Relax like that. Let me give you your pleasure, stop trying to demand or force it."

I groan in frustration. "Then why the fuck didn't you let me come?"

Elliot laughs. "Because of that right there. That fucking mouth and attitude are going to ruin more orgasms for you than you can ever imagine. Now, back to your meal."

"No, wait, I'm sorry. Please. I promise I won't say another word. I'll be a good girl, just let me come this one time."

"Not how this works, sweetheart. Relax and open that mouth" he demands as he lowers my chair to the floor and stands.

I do his bidding because, let's face it, if I don't, I'll never get to come.

He uses a gentle finger under my chin to tilt my head back with another demand for me to open for him. Then I feel the slimy raw oyster slip down my throat.

"Ugh, ick," I gag and sputter. "No more of those."

Elliot laughs. "Okay. No more," he says then I hear him slurp one down. "But that only means more for me." Another slurp. "And you know what they say about oysters and a man's libido."

"Good" I say under my breath.

Elliot chuckles then tells me to open again, this time I obey with a yawn.

"Tired?" he asks. "I would imagine so, it's mid-afternoon and you've barely slept."

"I'm okay."

"Good girl. Let's wash that oyster taste out of your mouth then."

Elliot offers me a bubbling champagne that he lets slide into my mouth. Then by the third gulp, he spills it down my neck and lets it coat my heated skin. His tongue following in its wake all the way to my stomach where he makes a few rounds of my belly button at the same speed his finger begins the rounds on my clit.

My body tightens instantly, and I know I only need a few more rotations to solidify my climax. I try to remain as still as I can so Elliot will miss the signs of my impending release and let me come. Too bad for me, he's a master at this delayed gratification shit.

He chuckles when he pulls off me just as I'm about to explode a second time.

"Nooooo," I cry out. "Fuck!"

"Bad girl," he says. "Trying to trick me. That's going to cost you another. Open again, this time just stick out your tongue."

I cry real tears, but I do as he says and let my tongue snake out. He must free his cock then because I hear his strangled groan with the fabric of his pants moving. Then there's something sweet and sticky on my tongue, pooling and running down my chin to my body. He squeezes more of the liquid over my skin and rubs it in with his hands before telling me to swallow.

It's honey. Sticky and sweet and his hands are massaging it into my flesh, running over every inch of my body.

"Open again," he demands and adds another drop to my tongue before feeding me his length. "Suck my cock until I tell you to stop."

I moan at his masculine taste and at the first exit of his cock when he drops more honey into my mouth then again when he pulls out to add some to his dick. He moans and grunts through my ministrations and the sounds coming from him are ramping me back up to the brink of an orgasm.

"I was going to stop you, but I'm so fucking close and this feels too fucking good to pass up. Make me come in your mouth, baby" he demands with a loud grunt as his hips pick up speed and he helps me take him to the finish line.

I feel him twitch, then his body tenses and he pulls back just a tad before thrusting back in hard. He pulls out again and lets more honey drip into my mouth, this time with his warning, "You're going to make me come. Swallow it all" he demands.

He fills my mouth and his climax mixes with the honey, thick and sweet, savory and gooey as it slides down my throat.

"Fuck," he sighs as he begins to soften in my mouth. "Lick. Clean me off like a good girl."

I do as he asks again then tense when his finger enters me. He swirls it in my excitement and praises my arousal. But, like every time before, he removes that finger just when I'm about to shatter around him.

"Your pussy is sweeter than honey. Time for dessert now" he says.

"What? Haven't you had your fun torturing me?"

"Yes, but now I'm going to make you my dessert."

I taste the maraschino cherries with syrup next as they drip off a spoon and land on my out stretched tongue. Elliot is sure to be messy and lets them drip down my chin. His mouth nips at me, then he sucks the juice off my face before lowering to my neck where he sucks so hard, I'm sure to have a mark like a teenager with her first boyfriend.

He continues to lick off the syrup from my face as he messily feeds me more. Then I feel the spoon go to my nipple and leave a trail there, too.

"This is going to feel wet and cold," he warns as he squeezes something over my body. "It's watermelon," he says. "Open."

He places a rung-out piece on my tongue then delves in with his own to steal it.

"Hey," I complain. "I love watermelon."

"And pineapple?" he asks as he places a sugar-coated slice in my mouth. So sweet that it could only be imported fresh from an island like the one we had met on.

"Yes" I sigh with another yawn that I try to stifle but Elliot catches it.

"We need to finish up and get you cleaned up for bed. You need a nap."

"Mmm" I hum thinking that I'm finally going to get my orgasm then Elliot will carry me into the bathroom and run me a warm tub to soak in before drying me off and snuggling around me in bed for a late afternoon nap.

His laugh from behind me and the light returning to my eyes brings me out of my head as he removes the blindfold. "Not exactly what you're thinking, Snowflake."

My eyes begin to adjust as he walks to the freezer and turns to smirk at me over his shoulder. "I know you haven't tried ice, so I think I'll save that as a reward for another time. Let's give something a little," he smirks at me again. "Thicker a try. You like thick, don't you, baby?"

"Not really sure," I taunt him, suddenly feeling brazen. Maybe it's because he basically just told me, my idea of an orgasm is probably not how this is going to end for me. "It's been ages since I've had anything *thick*" I add just to be a dick.

Elliot lets out a loud laugh that rumbles through the air. "Such a fucking brat."

He retrieves a small pint of ice cream then opens a drawer and grabs a spoon. He heads in my direction, where I still sit restrained in the chair with my legs spread wide for him, a sticky, trembling mess.

He pops the lid with his eyes holding mine then slowly sinks to his knees between my legs. He puts the spoon on the table and warms the ice cream between his hands to soften it enough to be able to scoop some out. Once confident that he can get a glob, he reaches for the spoon and sticks it into the container. "This is going to be cold, baby. Colder than the watermelon. But you liked that, so take a deep breath and tell me why I'm punishing you again."

The spoon is freezing as he runs the smooth back of it from my ankle to my knee. It's devoid of the sugary treat, Elliot ate that glob, but still feels sticky against my over-heated and already sugar-coated skin. When he reaches my knee, he bends and kisses it like I'm a child with a boo-boo.

"Elliot," I beg.

He laughs, obviously having no plans to relieve my aching pussy anytime soon. Instead, he puts the spoon back into the carton and runs it up from my other ankle to that knee. He plants a kiss there as well.

"What's your favorite flavor?" he asks.

"I don't know. Um, maybe strawberry."

"You're in luck" he says placing the filled spoon in my mouth. "And so am I. It just so happens that strawberry flavored pussy is my favorite."

I groan because I know this is going to play out much like the other courses. Elliot has no plans on letting me come any time soon, if ever.

He fills the spoon again and starts for my mouth with it. Then he pulls back at the last second and kisses me instead. While he does, he lets the spoon make an ice cream trail down my neck and around a hardened nipple.

I shiver at the sensation. It's cold, the spoon smooth then Elliot's tongue makes a round over my areola and his teeth nip and tug on my nipple. I cry out as my head falls back. "Please" I beg, my ass squirming on the chair.

"While we're on the topic of favorites," he says as he lets another glob of the cold dessert fall on the other nipple before he takes the first into his mouth with a low groan. "I know your favorite ridiculous movie, what about a real one?"

"Elliot, I can't think with you…shit!" Elliot makes another trail of ice cream on my belly, his tongue circling then delving into my belly button again. "Oh, my God!"

He smiles at me as he lets a huge glob fall on my mound. I hiss at the coldness then screech at the warmth of his mouth as he clasps, open-mouthed over my pussy. He groans into me and mumbles something about his favorite flavor as he moves his head from side to side. His tongue comes to the party and licks at the cold treat, up and down my slit until I'm panting with a need to come so strong, I feel tears stinging my eyes. I want to lower my hands to his hair and hold his head to me. I want to use his face to make myself come.

But I can't do that because he has me restrained in this fucking chair. So, instead, I'm forced to accept his torture until he's ready to bring me pleasure.

"Want another taste?" he asks as he grabs another spoonful. Only this time, he drops the ice cream on the tip of his erection. "You said strawberry was your favorite."

And if it hadn't been, it'd sure as hell be now.

Elliot leans closer to me, lowering the pint and the spoon to the table to take the back of my neck into one of his palms, his other grasps the base of his cock as he feeds it to me with the demand, "Open." Just the one word and it sends shivers through my system.

I suck his dick again, but only for a moment then he retreats and in one quick motion moves my chair. He tips the front legs up and props the chair against the table. "I'm going to fuck you now, Adams. You may not come unless you're told. Understand?"

"Elliot, please. No. I'm going to come the second you…Ohhh!"

Elliot slams into me and I feel my chair tilt a fraction further onto the table.

"This."

Hard thrust.

"Is."

Slow retreat through my swelled folds.

"For."

Deep thrust back inside. I stretch to accommodate his size and moan at the pinch of pain.

"Me."

Slow pull out and a thumb presses down on my clit.

"You will not come."

Thrust. Retreat. Thrust. Retreat.

Sobs and pleas follow, and Elliot continues to fuck me at a pace that is making it difficult for me to think.

"Adams," he scolds and brings my focus to my body just in the nick of time. "Hold off. I mean it."

"I…oh, my God! I don't know if I…"

"I'm going to fill that fucking pussy with my come again. Fuckkkk…coming!" he grunts as he empties inside of me. I feel his warm release and the throbbing of his cock.

Then the sobs and tears really hit. I can't control my emotions or frustration and I cry and scream, cursing him as he grinds into me to rub out the last of his seed deep inside my body. Using me as a vessel for his pleasure while leaving me aching and on the blink of insanity.

"Time for that bath you were thinking about," he says as he exits my body and rights my chair. He bends to release my legs first as he says, "Then we can sleep the rest of the day away. That might not be as easy for you, though."

"What? What the fuck does that mean? Are you seriously not going to make me come?"

Elliot shrugs. "Delayed gratification, sweetheart. Learn your lesson and don't lie to me again."

I mumble about not giving a shit what he says and that I'll just make myself come as soon as he falls asleep as he tugs me along into the master suite.

Elliot laughs loudly in the cool space of the bathroom. "Not my first time, baby. You'll be sleeping, well, tossing and turning, more like it, with your hands secured behind your back."

18

Before we made it into the bathroom, Elliot made us an actual meal and insisted that I eat every bite. Then he had bathed me like I had imagined he would, joining me in the large bubbling tub overfilled with hot water and scented bubbles. He'd cuddled me, then carried me to the master bedroom where he cuffed my wrists together behind my back and plunked me down on the bed. He spooned behind me and threw the covers over us. The bastard was sleeping in minutes.

Easy for him after the three orgasms he'd had. Yeah, he'd had another in the bathtub while I stroked his length with soap. But I was frustrated, and sleep took awhile to finally find me.

Not sure when it had, but I must have surrendered to the Sand Man a few hours ago because as I awake now, my eyes are gritty, and my body is still strung so tight I feel like I might bust at the seams.

I seemed to have wiggled myself around in my sleep and I'm now facing Elliot. He's still sound asleep so I maneuver a few more twists until I'm in the position I need. Elliot sighs but doesn't wake as I fit his thick thigh between my legs for friction. All I need is a few rubs against my clit and I'll be flying off into space like a jet.

One rub. Oh…so fucking good.

Mmm, another heats up my blood and I feel my clit throb.

Just a few more and…

"Adams?" Elliot asks with his eyes still shut tight. "What are you doing?"

I cuddle closer to him and sigh at the warmth of his body next to mine. He smells like the bubbles from our bath which wasn't masculine in any way but mixed with his phenomes is now a very manly scent and it's making me need him in a way that scares me.

"You're awake?"

"Yes, why are you mounting my leg like a dog on a fire hydrant?"

"Elliot, I…I need…"

"You need to come?" he asks. "I'm sure you do. Now, be a good girl and ask me nicely and let's see if I can help you."

"What? I asked a hundred times before."

"Would you like to argue, or would you like me to make you come so hard you lose control of your senses for a good two minutes?"

I heave in a defeated sigh. "Elliot, will you please make me come?" I ask as sweet as sugar and plant a gentle kiss to the tip of his nose.

Elliot reaches under the mattress on his side of the bed for the key to unlock my cuffs and frees my wrists. He rubs them to be sure the circulation returns quickly then plants a wet kiss with a tongue flick or two on my pulse point. "With pleasure, sweetheart. You did well during our last session."

Elliot lays me back and takes my mouth as he climbs on top of me. I feel his heavy erection on my belly and reach for it with my newly freed hand. He's warm and solid and groans into my mouth when I lower that hand to cup and tug on his sack, my finger toying with the sensitive skin of his taint.

"I thought you were desperate to climax? Keep that up and I'm going to have a hard time letting you go first."

I peck at his lips with a smacking sound then smile when he returns the kiss to the tip of my nose before he begins his descent under the covers. His warm, wet tongue makes a path down my stomach to my thigh. Then his fingers are on my sex, spreading me wide. His nose runs up my slit and he inhales my scent. The lude act almost sending me into an orgasm.

He licks at my slit and circles my clit before blowing a cool rush of air along the same path. I shiver at the sensation and reach down under the covers to find his head. I kick at the sheet because I need to watch him, see his head between my legs while I scratch at his scalp and ride his face into a climax that he promised would make me lose my mind.

I moan and the thrashing soon follows as Elliot's tongue works its magic on my pussy. Long licks up before circling and then flicks on the way back down. I know I'm done and need to beg for my orgasm when his tongue rims my ass on a down stroke.

"Elliot, I'm going to come."

"Not until you're told, baby. Hold off for me. This is going to blow your mind."

I pant and groan as my nails scrap at his scalp, my grip pulling his head into me so I can use his face fir my pleasure. My hips begin to pump then I remember what he said about letting him make me come instead of demanding it or seeking it for myself. I relax and sigh. I lay back and give myself and my pleasure over to Elliot.

He smiles into my pussy then pulls back to praise me. "Such a good girl. That's it. Let me take you there."

Elliot returns his mouth to my core and adds two fingers to the mix. They pump while he licks and sucks. Then, with one final command mumbled into my pussy, "Come for me, Adams. Come all over my face." I shatter, seeing stars behind my clenched eyes.

My climax hits me head on. Warmth spreads throughout my body and my back arches off the bed as my legs clamp shut, trapping Elliot between them. He blows on my clit at each spasm and I watch as he stares at my pussy when I come for him. Then, with a smirk and one more flick of his tongue on my clit, I scream out and my body seizes. I float high up into the air and disappear into darkness that feels so good I don't ever want to return.

I'm warm and loose, every muscle worn out and aching but in the best of ways. I feel Elliot's warm breath on my sex, his fingers still inside me, no longer moving. He gently kisses my clit one more time to wring out the last of my twitches before slowly drawing his fingers out and swirling my arousal around my clit.

"I can't…oh, my God!"

"One more," he demands. "Take it. And give me what I want. And what I want is for you to come again for me."

I didn't think it possible, but with how many times he'd held me off, I'd say he still owes me another dozen to break even.

Elliot climbs up my body and thrusts deep inside then takes my mouth with a pained groan. "So fucking tight, baby. Fuck, your pussy squeezes me just right. Give me a minute to get there with you, then I want you coming all over my cock while I fill this pussy again."

"Elliot," I sigh as he picks up the pace he likes, one I'm quickly growing to enjoy as well.

"Just a few more…" he grunts. "Oh, fuck. Gonna come. You there?"

"Yes, Oh, fuck…Elliot, yes."

"Come for me, Adams."

We come together filling the air with the poignant scent of sex and moans of the depraved.

Elliot collapses on top of me but makes no move to exit my body. Instead, he rolls us so I'm on top and pulls my hair back to hold at the nape of my neck. Then he pulls me down for a heated kiss.

As he pulls back to break our embrace, he lets his softening cock slide from my body. He rolls me to his side and his hand goes into my hair on the side of my face. "So precious," he praises. "We have a lot to discuss. Are you feeling up to that now or would you like to eat first? I did a shit job of giving you much nutrition yesterday."

"I could eat," I say. "Let me just get dressed and…"

"Adams," he scolds. "I wasn't joking around. The heat is on tropic levels, so you'll be more than comfortable as you are."

"It's not all about the temperature, Elliot."

He shrugs but ignores my desire for clothing.

"Come, we'll talk in the kitchen while I make you a proper meal. You like eggs?"

"Yeah," I relent and let him lead me back to the kitchen where I expect to find the mess we made a few hours ago. When we enter the space, it's spic and span. "What? How did you…"

"I didn't. This suite comes with complete luxury services. I told them I'd be doing most of the cooking though because I do enjoy it."

"Oh, so someone was in here while we were sleeping? Cleaning up the mess we made while mixing food with sex?"

"Are you embarrassed, Adams?"

Was I?

I shake my head. "I don't know. It's all just a lot to take in."

"Sit," he nods at the island. "We'll talk while I cook. Scrambled okay with you?"

"Yeah, fine."

I sit on the high chair at the island and glance over at the table. The chair, that he'd fucked me in and had left propped up the way it had been when he'd thrusted into me to find his own pleasure while denying mine, was now righted and pushed in at the table.

"Did you like playing with food?" he asks.

"Um...yeah. It would have been better if you'd let me come."

Elliot chuckles. "Yeah, the part when I got to was pretty great. Well, for me," he shrugs. "Hope it taught you a lesson about lying."

Elliot stands in front of me, bends and takes a nipple between his teeth and gently nips. He tugs slightly with a groan then plants a kiss to my abused peak. He turns and starts the food preparations without further conversation.

I clear my throat to regain an ounce of my composure. I don't seem to be able to keep it for long when I'm with him, so I figure I better get right to the chase. "What do you want to talk about first? How we're going to tell Damian to fuck off with his contract or..."

Elliot turns and glares at me. I stop mid-thought as he approaches me again. He lowers to lick my neck and a moan, more like a purr, escapes me as I lean my head back to give him better access. "We're not telling Damian a damn fucking thing" he states then moves back to my nipples. His tongue flicking one then the other until I'm squirming on my chair.

I finally manage to speak when he once again pulls back. "I thought you wanted to discuss our situation," I shrug. "But fine, how about the weather? It's predicted to snow pretty bad later today."

Elliot chuckles with his back to me as he whips up some magical culinary concoction at the counter then comes back to the island to cook it in front of me like he's a red-headed chef at Beni-Fucking-Hanas! The aromas momentarily distracting me. "Mmm," I moan. "Smells so good."

"Maybe I'll let you eat it off a plate. Would you like that?"

I heave in a gulp of air. I've watched enough porn to know that some asshole Doms like their women to act as animals, forced to eat food from their feet on the floor. If Elliot thinks for one minute that I'm going to...

He breaks into my thoughts with a hand on the nape of my neck. He tugs me closer to his body then covers my mouth with his. "That imagination of yours needs to be utilized for good. You're wasting an untapped talent and causing your mind to work overtime."

I stare at him, unable to speak. How did he know I had an interest in storytelling in some form? When I return to school, I'm undecided if I want to focus on creative writing or filmmaking.

Elliot plates the delicious smelling eggs he's made, yellow and creamy with just the right ratio of ingredients. He pushes a plate my way then makes a heaping one for himself. "I was going to suggest that we talk about my rules for the next year."

"I thought you'd want to go to Damian and tell him this was bullshit. I'm sure there's something in our contracts about manipulation on the company's part."

Elliot shrugs. "I have no intention of letting you out of your contract. Now, my rules."

"Elliot, I..."

"Rule one," he interrupts me yet again. "We covered the lying, correct? No more, unless you want to spend the next year standing up with a bright red ass."

I let a forkful of eggs melt on my tongue and my eyes involuntarily slide closed. "Mmm."

"Rule two," he smirks then swallows a mouthful of crispy bacon. "We don't tell anyone about Compatible Companions. We follow the rules of the contract," he shrugs. "It'll be easier than we thought. Your sister and Ace already know about us from the island. We tell them we reconnected and are dating. You'll be on my arm in public like a princess and naked for me in private like a whore. But make no mistake, the only one who will ever see you as such will be me. That side of you is all mine now."

My mouth gapes open.

Elliot's finger lifts my chin to bring my lips together before coming to stop on them. "Suck," he demands.

I slightly part my lips and allow his thick finger access. I taste a mix of myself and Elliot on my tongue as his growing erection tents his pants.

"Rule three," he says with his finger still in my mouth. "You'll allow me to push your sexual limits and you'll share every one of your fantasies with me. I'll make them all come true."

"Oh," I sigh, and Elliot removes his finger then adjusts his dick in his pants.

"We agreed to not share anything personal on the island. Rule four, you'll now tell me every detail about you. I don't expect it all today, but you will tell me everything."

"Elliot, please, that's not fair."

"Life isn't fair," he smiles. "But I'm not a total asshole. Well," he laughs with a shoulder raise. "Not all the time. So, if you're not ready to talk about something, you can ask for a pass. You will not lie and there might be times when you're not granted that pass. We'll work that out as we go along. Moving on."

"What? Wait..."

Elliot raises an eyebrow while shoveling more food into his mouth. "Eat up, princess, you're going to need your strength for my next lesson."

I roll my eyes and take another forkful of eggs.

"Rule five," he continues. "You're mine. You will not be with another man unless it's orchestrated by me."

I snap my head up at him. "I thought you..."

"Relax. The chance is slim to none, but I suspect you have some sexual shit to work out. I'm just keeping the door open. As I said, you're mine. You will remain faithful to me, and I'll respect you in the same way. The whore part is only for our bedroom, for play, but I'll treat you like a princess always."

"Our bedroom? We're a couple, then?"

"Yes. I thought that was clear when you signed on the line. Oh, wait, that's right, you didn't read a damn thing you were signing. I'm still not done punishing your ass for that one."

I take a sip of the freshly squeezed orange juice while I watch the pulse in Elliot's neck throb with annoyance.

"We'll remain here for the week then you'll move in with me."

"Move in with you? Where in the contract..."

"Page eight."

"Oh. I don't think I can, I mean, my sister and..."

"Rule six, you will not argue with me. I'll hear your opinion on topics and give them my consideration, but you will respect my final decisions and not disobey them. Understand?"

I mumble, "Dick" under my breath or so I think. Elliot apparently has supersonic hearing and pushes his plate back.

"Stand" he demands.

"Elliot, I..."

"Unless you're about to say that you were unable to hear me and ask for me to repeat my request, you should not be talking. And, by the way, I heard you perfectly. Stand. Now, Adams."

I sigh and push back my chair. Elliot tugs it further away then pushes his large palm into my back. The island's tile is cool against my breasts and I turn my head to the side. It's cool on my cheek too.

His large hand holds me down, but I feel safe. I know I could tell him to stop, unlike when "Uncle" Jim gave me no choice. With Elliot, I could say that I didn't want him to spank me, but it would be a lie.

I hear him rumbling around for something in a drawer with his other hand and wonder what he could possibly be looking for moments before he was going to spank me.

"This should be perfect," he says. "Now, let's practice you counting through it this time. We'll go with ten if you can be a good girl and stay nice and still for me."

I feel the first sting of the spatula on my right side. "One" I say with bravado but then the second slap of the hard-plastic lands in the exact same spot and I huff out, "Two." The next three strikes to my right cause me to tear up. My voice, when I count, sounds meek, nothing like the strong girl Courtney is.

Elliot's palm rubs across my right cheek. It feels like it's on fire and the roughness of his hand adds to my discomfort while the gentleness of his touch soothes me.

"You're learning fast. Five more. Count the same then we'll be done."

I don't tell him this isn't a new lesson for me. I learned how to count through a spanking many years ago.

I feel his thick finger explore between my legs instead of the sting that I expect on my left side. Elliot hisses in air when I coat his finger with my excitement and I momentarily wonder if it should embarrass me. It doesn't. If anything, it excites me more and my wetness increases.

"I think someone enjoys being disciplined."

I know enough not to speak. I learned that lesson early in life in a situation disturbingly similar, yet lightyears apart. Elliot isn't doing any of this to humiliate or hurt me. If anything, if I'm being honest, every supposed punishment he's rained down on me has ended in immense pleasure. If his finger continues what it's doing now in between my folds, this round will be no different.

Then I feel the sting to the left side of my ass and it's hard enough to bring new tears to my eyes. "Six" I cry out then heave in a deep breath. Before I can process anything, I feel the last of the cracks and finish counting through sobs.

"You're perfect," Elliot says as he lifts my right leg at the knee and places it on a chair. "I'm going to fuck you now," he says. "Hold onto the island. And don't forget to ask for your orgasm."

"Elliot," I scream out his name as he sinks deep inside my wet heat. He sinks into the root and groans as he fills me. I hear words coming from him. All praise, but I feel soft and floaty, like I'm in another world. A warm place where Elliot is everything there is and the only thing I need.

My climax climbs quickly and sneaks up on me. It crashes over me without my seeking permission. Elliot hisses when he feels me tighten around him and he increases his thrusts. "You're making me come" he announces as he empties himself inside of me. He leans down over my body and kisses my cheek, pulls my hair out of my face, and whispers into my ear.

I lose it. Complete sobbing ensues. I'm a mess as I collapse to a puddle on the floor as soon as he pulls out, but Elliot doesn't miss a beat and I'm hulled into his lap.

"Shhh," he soothes. "You're okay, baby. Relax. I'm right here. I've got you. You're crashing from the endorphins. It's called subspace and bottoming out. Just breathe and listen to my voice. You're exhausted and wrung out; you'll be okay in a few minutes. Don't be scared, I'm right here."

I try to focus on his words, the timbre of his voice, but I can't form a thought.

"You don't need to cry, Adams. I felt that orgasm coming on long before I allowed it to happen without my permission. I'm not mad."

I heave and sob. Those were the words that I had needed. When I grew to be the kind of girl that need approval from a man to orgasm, I'd love to know, but here we are. I need Elliot to reassure me that I make him happy, that he's proud of me. That he wants me even when I screw up. Maybe even that he loves me or can over time.

As that thought begins to take root, I try to hold on to it. I've needed approval from a man for a very long time. It was just now, that I felt safe with Elliot, that I was beginning to see what it was I've been seeking in the countless faceless men I had allowed to use me. It wasn't attention after all. Maybe it was approval.

Elliot spends the week spoiling me like a princess while simultaneously treating me like a whore and the contrast is more pleasing than it should be. Cathartic in a way I couldn't find before. He alternates between ripping my guts out and making me confess to things even I hadn't thought were important, to lathering me in attention and what feels an awful lot like love.

He never uses the word nor do I let it slip from my lips even though I suspect we're both falling deep. He praises my every accomplishment in my sexual training which still makes me chuckle. Who would have thought that I had anything to learn in that area? But Elliot has shown me how amazing it could and should be.

Elliot is patient with me, and he's spent the last week teaching me how to fully enter an altered state of consciousness. It brings me reductions in pain, feelings of floating and peacefulness, increases my mindfulness and even distorts time. I'm open to experiences in a different way now. I'm less neurotic about my past even though Elliot still has no idea why I was in such desperate need of male attention. I'm less sensitive to rejection and more securely attached because of him. Because of his love and patience. He doesn't have to say the words to me, I know how I feel, and I know he feels the same.

My concern is that all of that is about to end.

The week in the penthouse goes by fast and it's one of the best of my life. Elliot makes me remain naked and by the second day, I don't miss my clothes. Especially when he's naked with me. He never leaves the suite; he spends the entire week wringing orgasms from my twisting body. He's done things to me that I didn't know existed, things I never would have sought out for pleasure. But with Elliot, each experience was better than the last and by today, my body is spent.

I'll be sad to leave our cocoon. Elliot has insisted that I move in with him, so I know we'll form another, but he still hasn't answered my question about his job and his secrecy is starting to weigh heavy on my mind.

I hear my phone chirp. I've had it off since the night we arrived, and our phones began to ring with the same tone. But we're leaving in a few hours, so I had plugged it in to charge. It must have turned on.

I walk to check out who it is and hear the shower cut off. My screen shows Bridget's name and a ridiculous picture of Ace sucking half of her cheek into his mouth.

"Hey Bridge," I say in greeting. "Is everything okay?"

"Oh, my God! Where are you? I have called you a hundred times. Even Ace has been worried. I know you said…"

"Calm down. There was a change in plans. I've been with Elliot. I'm here in the city."

"WHAT?" she screeches as Elliot enters the bedroom with a raised eyebrow when he finds me talking on my phone. We'd agreed to remain in our bubble until we left today.

He stalks toward me in a towel, still wet from his shower. Then he casual lets the towel fall, his erection hard and pointing in my direction. He takes his dick in his hand and leisurely provides it with long strokes of his fist.

"Bridge, I…um, I need to go. I'll call…"

Elliot's gaze holds mine as he takes my phone from me and tosses it on the bed.

"I didn't hang up," I say. "She'll hear every…"

"Hang up before I fuck your sister while you listen," Elliot warns Bridget while holding my stare. A moment later his cock sinks in deep and it's my turn to scream.

19

Elliot ushers me into the back of a limo and ignores my questioning over its necessity if we're remaining in the city. I'm moving in with him for the next three hundred fifty-eight days. I can't think what will come after that.

The limo slows to a stop and I look up at a very familiar building. "What are we doing here?"

"The scene of the crime?" he asks as he opens his door and climbs out in front of Stone Towers. "I have an apartment here."

"You have got to be fucking kidding me. I can't stay here with you."

"Nope, not kidding. Damian's a smart man, Snowflake. He offered me the place as a signing bonus. Now, it's obvious it was to keep an eye on us. And, yes you will live here with me. Rule six, remember? No arguing."

"Yeah, well I say we give Damian an eyeful then."

Elliot laughs. "I love that spunky fire you've got in your belly. Maybe I was wrong, maybe you would have done just fine for yourself on the frontlines."

I wiggle my manicured nails at him. "I'm not so sure."

"Come on," he says as his hand warms the dip in my back. "Let's have a look at the place. My brother-in-law won't shut up about his handiwork."

"What?"

"My brother-in-law and Damian have been tight for years. He was the general contractor on the build."

"Oh, my God! It's like seven freaking degrees of separation with you. Pete Roman is your brother-in-law? Your sister is Raina! That Raina? As in my favorite actress that stars in all of Bailey Connnors' books come to life, Raina? Holy fucking shit, dude…I can't even right now!"

"Ah, yup" Elliot says as he waves at Pedro from the front desk as if the fact that his sister is *the* Raina Roman means nothing at all. Christ.

Pedro, the poor man looks at me with the most confused expression on his face. I've met him a handful of times with my mother or Aunt Brook, I've even been here a few times with Sydney. Tate and Bobby have brought me here, too.

Fuck! Uncle Tate and Bobby will see me here. Over the course of the year, our worlds are sure to collide. But wasn't that what Elliot said he wanted? We're to act as if this relationship we're in is normal, as if we met on Jonesie's island and reconnected once back in New York.

Poor Pedro. You should see his expression. I'm sure he's trying to figure out how we've managed to walk through the door together and in obviously more than mere friendship with the way Elliot's drawn me tight to his body.

"Hey, man. You know Ad…Courtney Knight, right?"

"Yes, sir. Of course," Pedro says with a smile for me. "How are you Miss Courtney?"

"Hey, Pedro. I'm fine. You?"

"You didn't look so fine the other night. You'd let me know if you needed anything?"

Elliot chuckles. "Pedro, I'm sure you realize I can get a woman without kidnapping her and bringing her here where she has just as much family ties as I do."

Pedro growls under his breath. "Damian said you'd be arriving today, but he didn't mention you'd have Miss Knight with you," he clears his throat. "1-A is ready. Your brother-in-law sent you a package and," he clears his throat again. "Mr. Taylor wishes to speak with you once you're settled."

"Uncle Tate knows about…"

"That you'll be staying with me? Of course, sweetheart. Now," Elliot commands. "Let's head up. Pedro, man, thanks for everything. If we need anything…"

"Just holler" he says with annoyance dripping off his words.

I smile at Pedro and allow Elliot to lead me to the elevator for the quick one flight ride up.

Apartment 1-A has a history. I know the story from overhearing my mother and aunt talking with Sydney before they had thought Bridget and I were old enough to be privy to the debauchery Damian was involved in. If they had only knew.

Damian Stone is my Uncle Tate's cousin, but Tate being an only child, Damian was more like a brother to him. Damian was also a sexual Dominant and multi-zillionaire. In his younger days he had slept with his college professor only to find out years later that he was in love with her daughter. He married Sydney Cooper and ended his New York City rein as the most sought-after bachelor and sexual expert. He's now a family man with a hoard of kids, the girls just as sassy as their mother, the boys exuding testosterone before they're old enough to produce the hormone.

Apartment 1-A was once used by Damian as a place to house his submissives where he could keep a close watch on them. The place was equipped with the best high-tech security and surveillance his money could buy. Years ago, Sydney had agreed to be his sub and used the apartment for a very short time. After Damian fell hard for her, he moved her into the penthouse and the rest is history.

And now it's where I'll live for the next year. With a man who has yet to share anything more than general information about himself, but one I already know has stolen my heart.

This situation really couldn't get much worse or so I thought as Elliot opens the door and ushers me inside.

There stands Damian Stone and my Uncle Tate. So much for leaving a package.

"Elliot," Damian greets us with a hand extending to him and leaning in to peck my cheek. "You're looking as beautiful as ever, Courtney. Elliot seems to suit you."

"Speaking of which, young lady," Uncle Tate begins to scold me. "Have a seat. You have a lot of explaining to do."

I grimace as Uncle Tate takes me from Elliot's hold and leads me into the main living space and deposits me on the sofa.

"Imagine my surprise when Damian pulled me aside on New Year's Eve to inform me of this latest stunt of yours. If your aunt and mother found out that I…"

"What?" I screech. "No! Uncle Tate, please," I change to begging real quick. "You can't tell them. Damian, tell him. It's breaking confidentiality or something, right?"

Damian shrugs as Uncle Tate smirks at me. "I don't work for him. What I overhear at a party and then babble in my sleep to my wife can't be construed…"

It's Elliot's turn to break into the conversation with his hand extended to Uncle Tate. "Hey, man, ease up on my girl. I get it. I wasn't thrilled about any of this either," He turns to Damian. "Speaking of which…"

Damian rolls his eyes. "Don't start with me, Montgomery. Getting your brother-in-law involved wasn't really what I was looking to deal with right now either."

Elliot's expression softens and he looks deeply into Damian's eyes. "You doing okay, man? I heard about your troubles. My team…"

"Yeah. I'm fine," Damian interrupts. "Better now, actually. But this shit was the last thing I needed to be dealing with."

"I get you, not my fault though."

"No, it's not," Damian says then turns back to me. "It's hers. But by the look of you two, it makes you responsible."

"What the fuck were you thinking becoming a fucking prostitute when Bobby gives you everything you want?" Uncle Tate blurts.

"Hey!" Damian scolds. "I don't hire prostitutes. Compatible Companions is an upscale, exclusive dating site for people with similar needs and desires."

Uncle Tate rolls his eyes.

"Don't," Damian warns with a hand going to Elliot's shoulder who had considered lunging into Uncle Tate's space.

Elliot holds back but glares Uncle Tate's way. "Call her that again and I'm kicking your fucking ass. Got it?"

Damian smirks at Elliot then makes eye contact with my uncle and says. "See, I'm as good at this matchmaking shit as our wives."

"Yeah, you've been pussy-whipped for so long now, it's like you have one."

Damian laughs. "You still have me beat by twenty-five years. You probably should look into vaginal rejuvenation, dude."

Elliot and I turn heads back and forth between the good-natured bickering of Damian and my uncle then return to staring at one another. I'm not about to interrupt the insane banter because I know I'm going to be put right back into the hot seat and I'm not sure I know how to wiggle my way out of it this time.

"Okay, boys," Elliot chuckles. "Let's break this up and say our peace so Adams and I can get settled in."

"Adams?" Uncle Tate asks then rolls his eyes again. Didn't Carol warn him as a child that if he does that too much, his eyes will stay that way? Maybe I should point that out.

"Uncle Tate, didn't…" Or maybe not.

His hand goes up and silences me. "*Adams*," he says with sarcasm dripping off my mother's last name, his wife's too. "Is there any good reason why I should stick my neck out there for you with my wife and my best friend not to mention your mother?"

"Sounds more like it's your dick you should be worried about" Damian laughs then stops when Uncle Tate glares his way. "With Brook anyway."

"Yeah, Syd will love it when Brook calls her and fills her in on your involvement. I just went along with this shit. You're paying her to be a…"

"Don't say it!" Damian and Elliot demand in unison.

"I'm not a prostitute," I finally find the courage to whisper and defend myself. "And I had my reasons, none of which are any of your business. Any of you."

Elliot's head snaps my way and a warning crosses his face. It's one both Damian and Uncle Tate also catch.

"Okay," Elliot begins. "Nice of you both to stop by for this little chat but the welcome committee can go home now."

Damian pushes Uncle Tate in the direction of the door. "We'll talk about this more later," he says to Elliot then whispers something I'm not able to hear. Uncle Tate appears to hear this comment though, and Damian pushes him out the door scoffing over it.

"Well, that little family reunion was a good time. Now, what was it you were saying about your reasons for joining Compatible Companions not being any of my business? Oh, and before you answer that, I should probably tell you that Damian had the extra bedroom converted to my specifications. Care to have the conversation in there?"

"Your specifications?" I ask, my voice shaking but heavy with arousal.

"Yes," Elliot says as his hand grasps the nape of my neck and tugs my head back. My neck exposed, he leans down and licks behind my ear before tugging the lobe between his teeth. "I wasn't planning on that being the first room I took you in," he shrugs. "But I guess it's as good as any."

"Wait," my hand goes to his chest. "Can we talk first?"

Elliot sighs. "Of course. I've been waiting for you to ask to speak freely. Whatever you want to say, I'll listen, and we'll discuss. This won't add to your punishment. But, Adams, you are getting your ass lit up at some point soon for that comment in front of them. There's no getting out of that."

I heave in a deep sigh. With the promise of his punishment lingering in the air, I'm not sure I want to waste another second with conversation. But there are things that need to be said. Things I need to ask.

"I don't know anything about you and I'm afraid the things about me that you know, do not put me in the best light. I'd like to explain a few things before…"

"Come here" he demands and pulls me into his arms.

Elliot kisses my temple then settles on the sofa with me in his lap.

"This place is really nice, by the way."

Elliot chuckles. "It should be. The rent is insane."

"He's charging you after everything that he…"

"No," Elliot laughs. "My brother-in-law told me about this place years ago. Damian isn't collecting a dime on this place this year."

"Oh."

"Talk, Adams. Tell me what you need to say."

I take a cleansing breath and bite the bullet. "I'm not a whore. I didn't sign up with Compatible Companions because I enjoyed the idea of selling my body to a stranger. Damian's right, it's not like that. You understand?"

"I never thought that was your motivation and yes, I completely understand."

"Why did you agree to it? I mean, I guess I get the no commitment prostitute thing in a way. But, why did you accept Damian's offer? Have you paid a woman for sex before?"

Elliot snuggles me into his chest then kisses the tip of my nose. He murmurs, "Snowflake, there's a lot you can't possibly understand about me yet."

"What does that mean?" I ask.

Elliot heaves in a deep sigh and adjusts me in his lap, his growing erection seeking my attention.

"It's a different world overseas. A lot of guys are lonely and desperate for the distraction. But, no, I've never paid for sex before. I watched a few too many of my men going to the medic for rashes and shit after a night of paid fun."

I gag and possibly puke just a little in my mouth.

Elliot goes on to explain the hardships of military life, finally admitting that had been the career path he was on until recently. He talks about the hot days in the sun, his skin feeling like it was roasting off his bones and I make a crack about his fair ginger skin that earns me a good rib tickling. I tell him about how when I first met him, I had made up a bunch of ginger related names for him. He makes me promise to use a few in bed later.

Elliot shares the exploits of his buddies who had found themselves without female companionship and an itch they didn't want to keep scratching with their own hands. They'd go into the city limits and spend an hour or two in an establishment where not much was off limits. Elliot says he never went, for a few reasons. He claims the main one is that he couldn't get past the fact that the girls were most likely there because they didn't have any other options. It's not like someone wakes up one day and thinks, "Hey, today is the day I'm going to sell my body to a stranger for fun." The fact that some of them might have been underage was another biggie for him. Then he tells me about Raina and how having a sister made him more protective over women. He also mentions that his work in the military focuses on saving women sold into sex trafficking and not wanting to be a hypocrite.

"Those girls are someone's sisters or daughters, maybe even someone's wife," he shakes his head. "I just couldn't do that."

"So you went without hooking up with a girl for how long?"

"Well, wait a minute. I never said I didn't hook up while in active duty. There are women in the military now, you know?"

"Oh."

Elliot tilts his head, an inquisitive look on his face. He points at mine. "That right there, what's going on?"

"Nothing," I bat his hand away. "Nothing's going on."

"You're jealous."

I shrug. "I don't love thinking about you with another woman. I don't know if I'd go to jealous, though. I mean, I..."

"You're jealous."

"You want to hear about the," I pretend to count on my fingers. "Forty-eight guys I've been with?"

"That's your actual number or..." he seethes.

I laugh. "Jealousy is a bitch, huh?"

"Are you looking to add to the spanking you're getting as soon as you stop avoiding what you wanted to tell me?"

I growl then think about his offer. I lift a shoulder. "Maybe" I say with a smirk.

"Tell me what you started out wanting to talk about."

I figure what the hell and go for broke. "My dad leaving us when Bridget and I were little fucked me up a bit. He's never tried to reach out to us, never gave my mother a dime. Until Bobby, things were tight."

"How old were you? Do you remember him?"

"Not really. I mean, I have this picture in my head of what he looks like but it's most likely from an actual picture. Not that my mom kept any of those around for long. When he left, she took down every family picture he was in. She started dating right away and was re-married not long after."

"I can't believe your uncle and his group of friends let your father get away with not supporting you."

I shrug. "I guess Uncle Tate was younger back then and didn't have the resources he does now. He's always been good to us. He thinks of my mom as a sister. I know he gave her money over the years."

"Mmm, maybe I have the resources he didn't."

"No! Elliot, no! Promise me you're not going to open a can of worms. Please, let it go. I need to move past it. And," I clear my throat. "I think my issues stem more from my first stepfather."

"Did he fucking touch you?" Elliot roars, takes me off his lap, and places me on the sofa so that he can stalk around the room like a caged animal.

"No. This is difficult. I've never told anyone about this. Not even my mom or sister. My therapists never even got it out of me."

"Courtney," he demands. My real name crossing his lips tells me he's serious and about to lose his shit. "Tell me what your stepfather fucking did."

"It was his best friend. We called him Uncle Jim."

"How old were you?"

I lift my shoulder again. "I'm not sure. Maybe twelve when I met him. He came to live with us a year later."

"He raped you?"

"No. I mean, there were things, but he never had intercourse with me."

Elliot's skin is as red as I imagine it might have been while stationed in a desert. He circles around the room, unable to stay still while he tries to process the information. "Things?" he asks. "What things, Adams?"

"He got off on spanking me. When the fun of that wore off, he added his belt. When he didn't get caught and I stayed quiet, he threw in a little touching. He made me," I clear my throat because I can't say the words. "He made me, um, help him finish."

Elliot pulls me to my feet and takes my face in his hands. "And you let me," he blows air between his teeth. "Why did you let me do that to you?"

Elliot's hands shoot to the top of his head and I can tell that he wishes his hair was longer so that he'd have something to tug and yank at.

"It's different with you. I've been coming to terms with what happened and understanding my needs better. I started thinking that I needed a strong man, a Dominant to help my healing. I tried light BDSM stuff with other guys. They just didn't know what they were doing enough to see what I needed. It was just hot sex to them. It made it worse and started a cycle. The slutty behavior got me attention from my mother and Bobby, and I used that to my advantage. Bridget saw what worked for me and followed suit."

"You need to feel safe. You want to know that someone is in control and protecting you because you couldn't protect yourself when that motherfucker was raping you."

"He didn't…"

"He touched you without permission. He used his power over you and forced you to provide him sexual relief. You were a fucking child, Adams. In my world that's fucking rape and he needs to fucking pay for what he did to you."

I shake my head. "I guess."

"You guess? Adams, don't even tell me that you think you asked for it."

I shake my head again. "No. I know that I didn't. But I also didn't do anything to stop it because I was afraid that he'd…"

"You thought he'd go after your sister next."

"Yeah," I whisper. "He threatened me with her and my mother all the time. He told me I had to be a good girl and take it. If I didn't, he said he'd make them. He told me it was my fault that he was aroused, and I had to take care of it for him and if I didn't, he said they'd pay the price for my disobedience."

"You are going to tell me this son of a bitch's name and the last place you know he lived. And when I find him, I'm going to rip his dick off and shove it down his motherfucking throat."

"Elliot, I don't want to think about him. I joined Compatible Companions because I was in search of a strong Dominant. It was my main requirement for a match. I never thought I would also find someone that I…" I pause and look up at him.

"What? That you what, Adams?"

"Someone that I could also fall in love with."

Elliot pulls me to his body with his hands tangling in my hair. His mouth crashes over mine and I open for him with a moan.

"I'm going to take you to bed and make love to you. I'm going to show you that you're safe with me and no one will ever harm you again."

"Take me to the other room first," I request. "Show me your world without holding back."

Elliot looks into my eyes and momentarily contemplates what to do. His eyes roam my face then, when he sees what I need, he nods. "Okay. But first you need tell me your safe word."

20

The room I'm led to is off the main living space, a spare bedroom usually, but in its current state, it's a room built for sex and pleasure. And pain. Sweet mind-numbing pain that will make me forget my past and morph into the sweetest of pleasures when brought on by the hands of the man who currently has a one in the dip of my back.

Elliot guides me to a softly padded chair and sits me down with an examining eye. "At any point you need this to stop," he instructs. "You'll use the safe word you've picked. Tell it to me now."

"Um," I think for a minute. "Blizzard" I say using my Compatible Companion safe word.

"Explain" Elliot demands as he kneels at my feet and begins to remove my shoes. His strong fingers kneed my arch and I groan at the pleasure of the simple act.

"I grew up in Vermont. That was where I lived with my stepfather and his friend."

"Uncle Jim?"

"Yeah."

"Okay. If you need this to stop, Adams, use it. If I hear the words, "no" or "stop", they'll be ignored, and I'll assume you just need a deep breath. If you need me to slow down but not stop, use yellow, understand?"

I nod. This is happening too fast for me to process but at the same time, I already have the feeling of weightlessness. I'm starting to float, and my limbs are warm. My mind is turning to liquid and everything except Elliot is going away.

"This is going to get intense," he warns. "I've only tapped the surface with you. I'm considering a blindfold again, but something is telling me you need to process this with all of your senses."

"Thank you."

Elliot's hands skim up to my waist and he tugs at my pants. I raise my hips to allow him to pull them down. Once my feet are cleared, he pushes back. His hand goes behind his neck and he tugs his shirt over his head.

I sit and watch as he kicks off his shoes then returns to my clothes. His hands reach for the hem of my shirt and I lift my arms overhead, allowing him to pull my shirt off. I sit exposed in my bra and panties, a shiver running through me as his hands skim over my flesh.

Elliot's eyes dilate and he steps back to examine me. "Adams, you must know how absolutely amazing you are. I understand your feelings better now, and you need to understand that I'm going to do my best to show you how deserving you are of so much more than you've ever expected."

I suck in as much air as my lungs will hold and a tear slips down my face.

"Shhh," Elliot soothes as he offers me his hand and leads me to the bed that's positioned in a far corner of the room. Its bedding is a cool blue, not what I would have expected in a BDSM room, but it's exactly what I need. "Lie down and relax."

Elliot cradles me in his arms then lowers me to the silky sheets, laying me on my back with a gentle sweep of his lips across mine.

"Bondage is about me taking control and you letting go of yours...for me."

I nod at him as my eyes focus on his and in them, I begin to see something there that I hadn't noticed before. Love, admiration, respect, or concern? Maybe all the above.

Elliot leans down and kisses me again, this time deepening it with his tongue seeking entry. His hands tangle into my wild mane of brown and tug my face closer to his. He tilts my head to gain the access he seeks. I open for him and moan at the first swipe of his tongue across mine. Then he pulls back and adjusts his hard cock in his pants.

"I'm going to render you with a feeling of complete helplessness. You need to surrender all your trust to me. I can and will do as I wish to this perfect fucking body of yours. Tell me your pussy is mine, Adams."

"Yours. My pussy. Yours" I babble as I begin to float higher into the stratosphere.

"Stay with me until I tell you to let go" he demands, and I try my best to shake off the feeling of complete relaxation tugging me under.

Elliot plants a calming palm to my lower abdomen while reaching under the bed for something with his other hand. Within moments, I find my ankle secured in a softly lined leather cuff like the one he used at the hotel.

"That was easy for you to offer me, wasn't it?" he asks as I feel the softness enclose around my other ankle. "You've been giving that pussy away much too freely. Let's try something a little harder this time, shall we? Tell me I have your trust" he demands.

"Trust you" I murmur as I glance down at my wide-open legs, my ankles now held captive by a spreader bar.

Elliot plants yet another sweet kiss to my lips then asks for my heart.

His hands wrap around my forearm and he brings my pulse point to his lips. He licks at my wrist then kisses the beating of my blood flowing through my body. "Tell me I'm in here" he says bending down to secure my wrist to the bed and kissing my heart.

I hiss and arch my back into his embrace while I confirm his place in my heart. "Yes. You're in my heart. Elliot…"

"Shh, easy," he soothes. "Hold still. One more wrist to cuff. You're doing well."

My remaining limb gets pulls tightly to the bed and I'm rendered immobilized for his pleasure once again.

"Adams," he says, snapping me out of my dreamlike haze. "I need your soul. Do you feel me in your bones, everywhere? Just me? All me, Adams, everywhere."

"Oh," I sigh as Elliot clasps his mouth around a nipple to wet it. He pulls back and blows then licks a circle around my areola. "I...fuck! Yes, Elliot, yes. You. Everywhere. Please."

Elliot smiles and leans down for another kiss. This time his finger and thumb clasp around my hard nipple and he pinches tightly as he takes my mouth.

I arch into his embrace as much as my restraints allow and promise my love. "Love. I...Elliot."

"Shh," he calms me again. "I know. I heard you before and I feel the same way, baby. You have everything from me that I've just asked from you. Now, let the cuffs and the bar do their work. Let them give you the emotional release they're meant to.

"They're calming, restful" I admit. "I like when you use them."

Elliot smiles. "I caught on last time, Snowflake."

I smile at him, my eyes feeling heavy.

"Bondage reminds you of my ownership of your body, your heart, and soul. Your love, Adams. It's all mine and this reminds you that you're safe with me. Allowing me this, tells me your feelings more than any three words ever could. Me binding you, asking for that trust, should tell you more than me saying the words, too."

I sigh at the mention of the concept of love that I have never had from a man before. Well, Bobby told Bridget and I he loved us like his own flesh and blood when he asked my mom to marry him and again at their wedding, but never has a man alluded to loving me in this way.

I lay here bound, completely at Elliot's mercy, while knowing this is how I will remain until he decides to release me.

"I'll let you slip eventually, but for now I didn't blindfold you because I want those eyes. You'll have limited mobility for this session with your legs spread so I can see that pussy, lick it when I want, finger you, smell your arousal."

I hiss again at the vulgarity of his statement but also because it causes my arousal to pool between my legs and I feel myself grow slick.

"When I'm finished with this," he shrugs. "We'll see what we get up to next."

Elliot pulls up a chair and sinks into it, pulling it close to the foot of the bed and propping his ankles between my spread legs.

"What are you…" I begin to ask.

"Shh," he scolds. "No questions. I'm sitting here enjoying the view, Adams. Your pussy is mine to enjoy, correct? That also means visually."

"Yes," I say. "I…Elliot, I'm…I don't know how I feel about this."

Being this open and exposed to him is difficult. I trust him to know what I need and, in the end, give me the greatest pleasures I've ever known. But, laying here like this, my emotions are as exposed as my pussy and it's hard to handle.

Elliot makes a sound between a chuckle and a groan then I hear him shift in his seat before I feel his hands surround my ankles. His touch eases me.

"Explain. Do you feel exposed?"

"Yes, but I feel safe with you. I'm a little lightheaded, floaty kind of."

"That's to be expected. You're learning to let yourself go. It's called sinking. Subspace is different for everyone, but it sounds to me like you're starting to get there."

"Oh. Okay" I sigh as his hands continue to massage my lower legs, never coming close to my pleasure center but ramping me up all the same.

"Your orgasm is a privilege I allow you to have when I wish for you to have it. When you signed that contract, Adams, you gave up the right to have them without my permission. This might be turning into a different relationship, then either of us planned, when we signed that document, but giving me power over your pleasure isn't negotiable. We're going to start this with a lesson in orgasm control. I'm going to suspend you in a high state of sexual arousal for as long as it pleases me, but trust that I will not push you past what you can physically handle. It's called edging," Elliot explains while he strokes his hands up my calves. "You're not going to like this at first, but trust me, it'll end with your pleasure. This time."

Elliot's hands disappear and I hear him rummaging around under the bed once more. When he returns to his chair, I feel the soft, firm plastic of what can only be a dildo molded from his cock; solid, long, and enticingly thick. He follows the previous path of his hands and rubs the toy up and down my legs, dragging it over my heating flesh.

"This toy will become your favorite, most sought-after and your biggest fear all at the same time."

"Elliot," I beg. "I don't know if I can do this. Maybe we should just fuck and get off then…"

Elliot laughs. "I'm going to train you over the next twelve months to give yourself small orgasms, gentle releases that don't quench your ache for my cock. You'll learn that you need this," he says cupping his crotch and rubbing it for relief. "To explode and feel satisfied."

"I already feel like that. I need you now, Elliot."

He smiles and plants a sweet kiss to my nose.

"You think that now, but I want your body to need nothing more than my voice to respond."

His voice is nice, deep and masculine with the right amount of edge to it, like he'd been sleeping and had just rolled out of bed after hours of pleasing a woman, me, with his hard dick. Raspy and raw, his voice. I'm pretty sure my body was already capable to responding to it exactly the way he wants it to.

I feel the Elliot-size dildo travel to the apex of my thighs and begin to acquaint itself with my most intimate parts. I'm forced to arch my back and hiss in a gulp of air when Elliot lets the bulbous head enter me.

He swirls it in circles, stretching me while I feel the roughness of his tongue on my inner thigh. "I'm going to sit in that chair at the foot of the bed where I can see your pussy with this cock in it. Just like mine. I'm going to sit there and watch you struggle not to come. I'll be able to see every pulse of that pussy and smell you, so don't think you'll fool me, baby. Now, let's turn this on nice and low so the fun can begin. Don't come until you're told" he warns.

Elliot pushes the dildo inside me a few more notches and turns the speed to a low simmer before sitting back in his chair to watch me make myself come.

"Move your hips," he instructs. "Thrust on it like it's my cock."

I do as he says without thought and I'm fucking the damn thing before he's had time to back away.

He chuckles and calls me a minx when he delivers a gentle slap to my thigh.

Elliot comes to stand beside the bed, to my side so that I can see him. He leans down into my space and demands my eyes. "Don't be scared," he states. "Trust me?"

I nod but I'm apprehensive as to where this is heading.

"Eyes on mine, don't close them and don't break our connection."

I nod again, words impossible for me in the moment.

Then I feel Elliot's right hand as it reaches down to my clit while his left wraps around my throat. I lean into both, moaning and shamelessly pumping my hips up and down on the toy. The pressure on my throat begins to make me slightly lightheaded, floatier than I already was. Then the rough pad of Elliot's thick thumb rubs against my clit, so firm it makes my pussy tighten around his toy. My core clenches in search of him. This toy might be similar in size, but it's no comparison to the pleasure of having Elliot's warm pulsing cock in my body.

But as he releases my throat and reaches down to move the dildo in and out of me, it becomes harder to hold back. I begin to feel the muscles in my legs shake with my effort to delay my orgasm that is brewing deep inside me. I moan, I whimper, and I beg. "Please, Elliot. Fuck! I need to come."

His hands pull away, leaving my clit and the dildo. I'm without stimulation, only the feeling of fullness from the toy inside me keeps my blood at a low simmer. "No," Elliot reprimands. "Your orgasms belong to me. I decide when you come, if you come. That's a lesson you'll be well-served to learn now."

I gasp for air and try to calm my racing pulse, regain control over my body that almost betrayed me.

"Now, I'm going to sit in my seat and enjoy the sight of you and your aroused pussy."

I groan as I lose sight of him. I hear him sigh as he settles into his seat then I feel his legs meet the space on the bed between mine once more and I know he's sitting back. I know he's looking at my dildo filled pussy, dripping with my arousal.

I picture him, bare chest heaving, his strong palm stroking his tented pants for comfort.

I feel exposed with his inquisitive eyes watching me while I can hear the rustle of his hand stroking his cock through his pants and I know I've pictured the scene accurately. I stop my hips from gyrating against his toy.

"Don't stop on my account, Snowflake, I love seeing you fuck yourself. Knowing you won't receive satisfaction but working your hardest anyway? It pleases me. You're so fucking hot held in this state of arousal and your pussy looks so fucking good. I can't wait to lick it, taste you."

"Please" I beg.

"Shh, not yet. Listen to my voice," he orders with a stroke of his finger down the arch of my foot. I shiver then smile as he does it again to playfully tickle me. The combination of sex and playfulness hitting me in the chest. "Naughty girl," he teases. "You like how full it feels? Hmm, how arousing the vibrations are?"

"I wish it were you inside me."

"That's my good girl. That's right, your pleasure is mine. I can make you feel better than any toy, every man. Tell me."

"Yes. You. Better. Elliot, please, fuck me."

Elliot chuckles. "Not yet, baby. I'm enjoying myself just like this for now. I'm going to make you entertain me and beg for what you want. What is it you want again? Hmmm? My cock? Say it" he demands.

"I want your cock, Elliot, please," I beg as my hips begin to undulate on the toy again. "Please, please touch me."

Elliot leans forward and I feel his hands run over my body, my legs and up to my belly. I relax as his touch creates a tingling around my clit that starts to build, while a heat in my pussy makes me moan and press against my restraints.

"Getting close?" he asks.

I feel my orgasm approaching, but the dildo brings on the build slower than Elliot's cock. It's tiptoeing up on me instead of hitting me head on like a freight train without breaks. It's still hard to hold back, but for Elliot I'll do my best to hold off. I'll clench my internal muscles until I have his permission.

"Please," I beg for that permission. I moan and whimper, "Please, Elliot. Elliot, please let me come for you."

I feel his hand on the dildo then the vibrations disappear, and I groan with frustration. He turns off the toy, taking away my only means of reaching a climax. I whine and arch my hips in his direction, panting and shaking with my need to come.

"Breathe," he commands. "Then we'll start again once you're under control."

I heave in air and feel the tears begin to flow down my cheeks. Tears of frustration at his denial, tears from years of searching for a man that could control my pleasure like he is, and tears for what the future can be.

Elliot turns the toy back on and raises the setting to medium. It's my go to speed that can make me come in under three minutes when alone. I moan when I feel the wet moistness of his tongue swipe a circle around my engorged clit. With one more skillful lick of his, I know I can find my release. "Fucking Jesus," I curse. "Yessssss…"

But then his tongue leaves with my orgasm and I begin to incoherently babble nonsensical words as he removes the toy from my body. Words that make no sense together, but all requesting his fingers, his tongue, his cock. Him.

Elliot snickers in my ear as his heavy and comforting body covers mine. "You should see your pussy. It's so pink, red almost. Your lips are swollen and puffy, and your tight little clit is exposed and begging me to feast on it. You taste amazing. See?" he asks as he covers my mouth with his and I taste myself on his lips.

I pull his bottom lip in between mine and suck my flavor off. Elliot's strangled groan fills the air as his hips push his erection into my belly.

"Want to fuck that pussy so fucking hard" he says as his fingers enter me. He pumps them as hard as he claims he wants his cock to.

It doesn't take much to get me to the edge this third time, but Elliot pulls back after only a handful of finger thrusts into my wet heat. Each one filling the room with the sound of my wetness.

He stills his fingers but leaves them inside me and I lose my shit. Completely. Lose. My. Shit.

I scream and cry, try my hardest to thrash on the bed. But while held down, I'm unable to move as I'd like.

Elliot leans down to take my lips with his. His tongue enters my mouth and I feel him flick at my clit with his thumb. He only gives me a few swipes and I sob when he pulls back. Long and loud sobs filled with frustration and pain. "No!" I scream out. "Yellow! Please, Elliot, no more. I can't…"

He frees my wrists and kisses my lips once more. "Okay, shh," he calms me with gentle strokes to my head. "Stay here," he laughs when he glances down at my ankles still shackled to the spreaderbar. "Let me get you some water. We'll take a break, then we can finish up when you're ready for more."

"I…Elliot, no, I mean, I need…"

But he just smiles at me, adjusts the hard-on in his pants like it's not torturing him, and leaves to get me a fucking bottle of water when what I need is an orgasm.

Elliot returns to find me a pissed off mess with tears streaking down my face. He says, "Good girl. I thought you would have gotten yourself off once I left," Then he shrugs. "I was kind of looking forward to punishing you for it."

"What the fuck?" I seethe having not thought of that myself.

Elliot smiles. "You could have gotten yourself off, but you didn't because you want to please me. You also know I can give it to you so much better than you can give it to yourself."

Elliot hands me the bottle of water then accepts it in return when I'm done. He gulps down the rest before removing the spreaderbar with a kiss to each sore ankle.

"Better?"

"What? No. We're not done, are we? I didn't come. Elliot, you're still hard. Have sex with me" I beg.

He smirks at my offer. Fucking smirks.

"I have a question for you. Which do you want more, my orgasm or yours?" he asks.

"I…um," I stutter for a moment then let his question settle. I ponder the choice, but once I think it through, my answer becomes clear. "Yours," I say. Because if I'm being honest, watching his might be enough to make mine happen too. Or maybe I truly just want to see him happy and sated.

What the hell is wrong with me?

Apparently, Elliot has driven me out of my mind with the numerous orgasms he's denied me. Well, I hope he's happy now, he's got a year with a crazy person ahead of him.

"Good answer," he says with a smile and a kiss to my lips. "Such a good girl."

"Elliot, I've changed my mind," I say. "Can't we talk about this?"

He laughs as he stands and frees his cock then drops his pants and kicks them off before sitting back down in his chair.

I go to move, scurry toward him but his commanding voice halts my movements and I remain at the head of the bed. "Touch yourself for me," he commands. "While I watch and jerk myself off."

I raise an eyebrow.

"Are you challenging me?" he asks.

"No," I say with a gulp. The last thing I want to do right now is earn myself another missed orgasm. "No, I just thought you'd rather come inside me than in your own hand."

"Who said I was coming in my hand?"

"Oh."

"Fuck yourself while I watch. Make me have no choice but to pound into that pussy so hard my cock explodes."

"Elliot" I sigh as I allow my right hand to slide down my belly then into my pussy.

"Mmm," he moans. "Use your fingers to spread your pussy open."

I do as he asks, my wetness coating my fingers before they've even slid inside.

"You're so fucking wet," he praises. "Lick those fingers for me."

My fingers taste salty as they enter my mouth and I suck at them, my eyes never leaving his.

He nods after a moment and I remove my fingers from my mouth and return them to my sex. I press and rub at my clit, but I'm careful not to come until Elliot allows it. It's all so overwhelming, the build-up, the holding back, the admissions of our feelings without using the word love but both knowing it's only a matter of time. But that was hours ago and I've yet to process our words. I know as soon as this session is over, we'll need to talk about them. But right now, my poor, overstimulated pussy is all I can think about.

Then I hear Elliot's groan of pleasure and my focus changes. I focus on him. On him stroking his cock and moaning in pleasure, the sound deep and masculine. I want him to come. I want to watch him come, knowing I'm the one that aroused him.

"That looks so fucking hot, baby. Keep fingering that tight pussy for me. Hold the vibe on your clit."

I whimper, knowing how much harder that will make my task. Holding back might be impossible with Elliot jerking off while watching me, my fingers inside my pussy, and vibrations pressing down on my clit. But I do as he asks. I place just the tip of it at the center of my pleasure. And I hold it in place with my left hand while three fingers from my right become a horrible substitution for Elliot's thickness.

I hear him growl on an upstroke of this cock and my pussy clenches around my fingers. "I'm going to come" I warn.

"Not yet," he demands. "Take your fingers out, leave the toy on your clit."

"I'll still come," I plead. "Please."

"Okay, turn it off, give it to me" he says.

I press the button on the toy and hand it over to Elliot.

He raises it to his nose and inhales my scent. The sight alone almost makes me come without stimulation. Then he lets his tongue slowly snake out of his mouth and he licks the vibe. Licks my wetness from the toy. When my flavor hits his mouth, he groans, opens wide and sucks the toy in as deep as he can. He pulls it out with a smirk in my direction. "I don't know how you girls suck dick," he says. "But I couldn't resist the taste of your pussy."

I'm speechless and ready to go off like a rocket. I never would have guessed that sight would have ramped me up to the brink of insanity, but holy motherfucking hotness!

"Actually," he says. "I think I need more."

Elliot pounces on the bed by my side then pulls me on top of him. He turns my body so I'm facing his feet and positions my pussy over his mouth. With strong hands to my ass, he pulls me onto his face with a satisfied moan. His mouth covers my core and his tongue enters me as I suck his cock into my mouth.

I suck eagerly at him as his tongue fucks my pussy. When his fingers open me and he latches onto my clit, I see stars and reach for him with my fist, using it to pump in time with my lips.

I take Elliot to the back of my throat and greedily swallow.

"Fuck, Adams," he cries out into my pussy. "You're going to make me come in your mouth."

When Elliot suckles harder on my swollen clit then slides two fingers inside with his command for me to beg, I moan and hum around him. I relax and let my body feel the sensations, hoping that this time I'll have his permission to orgasm.

His fingers fuck me, curling up to press on my clit from the inside while his tongue sucks on the outside.

I'm so close to the edge. I pant as I suck him deep and feel him swell in my mouth. Knowing his climax is only moments away, I shamelessly hump his face and beg for my release. "Please, may I come for you?" I ask.

Elliot groans deeply and grows harder as he raises his hips, his cock forcing its way back into my warm mouth.

My hips shake with my determination to hold off until told, and I squeeze my thighs around his face.

Elliot speeds up the rotation of his tongue around my clit and demands, "Ask me again like a good girl."

"Fuck," I cry out as I feel the heat of my impending orgasm radiate to my limbs. "Please, let me come for you."

"Again," he demands. "Tell me who's orgasm it is."

"Yours" I mumble around his thick cock.

"I'm coming," he howls. "Tell me who makes you come."

"You" I cry as he thrusts up into my mouth one last time and explodes. And I come too. Hard. Each spasm jerking my body on top of his.

My pussy clenches over and over as if there's no end in sight to the immense pleasure pulsating through my body. I clench around his fingers and trap his head between my legs while I ride out my release.

Once I still, Elliot shifts us and cuddles me to his side. I look into his eyes and see his emotions there. His care, his control, his desire for my happiness, and I see his love. I grow stiff at the thought of what that means. Of what our future year will hold.

"What is it?" he asks. "Are you bottoming out again?"

"No. I don't know. Yeah, maybe. I was just thinking that the look in your eyes…"

"What?"

"I don't know," I whisper. "More than I expected."

Elliot kisses me with the love I just saw in his eyes. "Good. You need to start expecting more. It's what you deserve."

21

A banging sound wakes me from the warm comfort of sleep in Elliot's arms. "What the hell is that noise? What time is it?" I ask, my voice sounding like rocks rubbing together.

Elliot smiles at me. Obviously, he's been awake and watching me sleep. I wipe at my face to make sure I wasn't drooling.

I wasn't…thankfully.

"You don't drool in your sleep. You snore like a fucking bear, but…aww," he laughs then pulls me under him and nuzzles into my neck.

"Elliot," I scream as I laugh too. "I think someone's at the door."

"It's my sister. She texted me an hour ago."

"Your sister?"

"My sister."

"Are you going to answer it?"

Before he responds, I have my answer.

A deep male voice calls out, "El, your sister is in the apartment. Put some fucking clothes on, man. I can't hold her back much longer."

"Who the hell is that?"

"Pete."

"Pete?"

"Mmm," Elliot moans as he thrusts his erection into my belly. "Pete. My brother-in-law."

"How did he get in here?"

"He knows the code. Remember, he's the one that helped with the design of the apartment."

"Idiot," a female voice yells from outside the door. "I know you're in there. And don't think that Pete didn't explain why you're in the spare room and not the master. Get out here, or I'm coming in. He knows the code for that door, too."

"Fucking Christ" Elliot swears. "Will she ever drop that fucking nickname. One dumb-ass in the fourth grade and I'm still dealing with it."

I laugh then jump up to get dressed when his sister yells, "I'm not fucking around, Elliot. Now!"

"Alright, alright," Elliot yells back. "Calm the fuck down, princess. We'll be out in a minute."

I hear his brother-in-law laugh then choke through the door. His laughter apparently earning him an elbow in the gut from his spunky wife.

"I can't go out there looking like this. They'll know what we've been doing in here and…"

Elliot laughs and gathers me into his arms, still naked, his erection presses into my belly. "Snowflake, they already know what we've been doing in here. They've been doing the same shit since college. I endured a year of listening to it every night through my wall. So," he shrugs and pulls at the bed sheet to wrap around his waist. "Fuck them. Their turn. Let's go."

"No, no..." I begin to protest but then the door opens, and I'm silenced, my mouth hanging open on my last word and my ass hanging out under Elliot's shirt. It was the first one I had found on the ground and tossed over my head.

Standing there in the threshold is one of the most beautiful women I have ever seen, and I recognize her instantly. "Oh, my God! Raina Roman really is your sister."

"Yeah, the pain in the fucking ass really is. Did you think I was lying about that?"

And out from behind the door comes a stunning man with dark hair. "Watch it, pretty boy," he warns in jest. Elliot smirks at him then shakes his hand and brings him in for a man hug. "You look good."

"Yeah, you like the sheet or the hard-on, which is doing it for you?"

"Elliot Montgomery," Raina scolds. "Don't be an asshole."

Elliot smiles warmly at the model turned actress then allows her to kiss his stubble covered jaw.

"You do look good. Possibly better than I've ever seen you. And don't make a comment about it being from the obvious abundance of sex you've been having."

I heave in a mouthful of air. Holy shit! Raina Roman is privy to my sex life. Double holy shit! I'm fucking Raina Roman's brother.

Elliot pulls me in tight and plants a sweet kiss to my temple then whispers, "Yup, you're fucking the one and only brother of Raina Montgomery Roman."

"Why do you do that?" Pete asks. "You know the name thing is a sore spot," Pete nods at Elliot and they share a knowing glance. "You're still a fucking troublemaker. Now, introduce us before I let your sister slap you. This is the most excitement she's had all week."

"Not my fault her husband is old and boring as fuck these days."

Pete smacks Elliot in the back of the head then man hugs him. "I missed your wise-ass mouth, asshole. Now introduce us."

"Can I get pants on first or you're that excited about the prospect of my dick falling out?"

Pete rolls his eyes and wraps an arm around his wife's waist. "Let's give them a minute, princess."

Raina growls but allows her husband to lead her back into the main living space.

"I...What just happened?" I ask.

"My sister blew in like the tornado she's always been," Elliot says. "We don't have a choice now. Get clothes on and let's go deal with her so they'll leave, and we can get back to bed."

I laugh. "Bed? We've done nothing but have sex since we got here."

"And?"

"Elliot!"

"Okay, okay, come on. My sister is really a great person. I'm just giving her and Pete a hard time. I was going to ask them over this week to meet you. They've never met anyone I was with before."

"Oh."

Elliot and I throw on whatever items of our clothing that are necessary and that we're able to find scattered on the floor then head out for him to formally introduce me to his sister and brother-in-law. I find myself wrapped up in Raina Roman's arms moments after clearing the bedroom door.

"Rain, this is Adams, my girlfriend. Adams, that's my sister koala-ing you," Elliot says then tugs at his sister. "Ease up on my girl. You're overwhelming her."

"Sorry," Raina apologizes. "It's just, we've never seen Elliot with anyone. Not even a date. The fact that you're his girlfriend is just...Wow!"

"Okay, that's enough. Behave or I'm having your husband take you home...to Florida."

Raina smacks Elliot's chest then his cheek before she tightly hugs him, and plants kisses on every area of his face. "We're leaving tomorrow," she sadly states. "Unless..."

"Nope," Elliot teases. "Tomorrow is perfect. Keep those plans."

Raina sends her brother a scowl and in it I see the spitting imagine of Elliot. How I had missed that before is anyone's guess. "That doesn't leave us any time to get to know each other. Maybe you guys can come to dinner with us? Mom and dad are going to be there. You should have heard mom when she found out that dad had..."

"Raina" Pete scolds and a look of warning sets in on his handsome face.

"That dad had what?" Elliot asks but Raina remains silent. "Are you fucking kidding me, man?" Elliot asks Pete. "He went to Stone, didn't he? Told him I needed to get laid? What a fucking asshole. Christ!"

"Wait, what?" I finally utter my first words in front of the actress I have obsessed over for years and the sister of my...wait. Did Elliot call me his girlfriend?

"Oh," Raina says. "Um, sorry. I didn't mean to start a thing. It's nothing. Forget I brought it up."

"She knows, Raina. Adams is my match."

"Oh," Raina says. "I thought you said…"

"That she's my girlfriend? Yeah. It's complicated. We met before New Year's Eve. And let me just say that for a company that is supposed to be confidential, a hell of a lot of people seem to fucking know my business. And be involved in it."

"Dad was only trying to help, Idiot," Raina offers. "He's worried about you."

"Yeah, well, I'm fine. And let's drop the nickname."

"Are you?" Pete asks. "Are you fine?"

"Yes. I am," Elliot says as he sits on the sofa and pulls me into his lap. "Now drop it."

Raina sits across from us and Pete joins her on the sofa.

"So," Elliot says. "Mom found out that dad hired me a prostitute. That's fucking classic" he laughs.

So much for the euphoria of him calling me his girlfriend. I suck in a breath and struggle to get to my feet. Elliot instantly catches his error and wraps a strong arm around my waist. "I'm sorry, baby. I didn't mean for that to come out like that."

"No," I state. "You're right. Your father went to Damian to set you up with a whore," My voice begins to shake, and the tears start to flow. "I'm sorry," I apologize to Raina and Pete. "You must think horrible things of me."

"Frist," Elliot scolds, halting my attempt to leave his lap. "You're not a fucking whore. Secondly, neither of them is in any position to pass judgment. And finally, I could give a flying fuck what anyone thinks. How we feel, that's all that matters in this situation. Your reasons are no one's concern but ours."

Raina smiles at her husband then raises off the sofa and approaches us. Elliot stands in my defense before his sister has a chance to lash out at me with her words. But instead of shooting venom my way, Raina bends down and hugs me. "Welcome to the family. I've always wanted a sister."

"What?"

Raina shrugs. "It's so beyond clear that my brother loves you. I'm sure that's going to send him into a tailspin, but it's a fact. He can deny it all he wants. It's all I need to know. If he loves you, we all love you."

"Oh…um…" I remain speechless and immobile as Elliot continues to rub soothing circles on my back and I note he never once corrected or scolded his sister for her comment.

Instead, Elliot smiles at his sister and pulls her in for a hug then says, "Thank you for making this more than awkward. We're not ready to share everything yet, but she's not a whore. Her reasons for joining are complicated and something we need to work out on our own. I'll talk to mom and dad tomorrow. Are they going back to Florida with you?"

"Yes," Pete says. "You should both come, too. We're only there until April then we're going to visit Amanda and Justin in Maine."

"Maybe in a few weeks. We'll see," Elliot casually answers. "Things are working out for Amanda, it seems."

Pete smiles. "Yeah, Justin is cool, and TJ loves him. They're all happy."

"As happy as you can be in Maine in the winter," Raina scoffs. "I refuse to go there until it'll be in the double digits."

"Princess" Elliot says under with breath with a cough and a smirk.

"Okay, well, maybe we should leave you two alone to work things out," Raina suggests. "Come to Florida soon. Then if you're not too much of a pussy, you could always come to Maine, too. Amanda would love to see you. And we can get to know Adams."

"My name is Courtney. Adams is kind of a nickname" I whisper.

Raina winks at her brother then takes her husband by the hand. "See you soon, Idiot."

They're gone before I can say good-bye and Elliot can complain about his nickname.

"Well, that went well, huh?" I tease.

"Yeah, really well, smartass," Elliot yawns and stretches. "I need to get back into my routine tomorrow. This lazy shit is catching up with me."

I let my eyes roam over the tight muscles covering his stomach and laugh. "Yeah, you're turning into a real slob."

Elliot lunges at me and I take off running behind the kitchen island.

"You'll only make it worse for yourself if you run, Adams. You know I'm going to catch you. Might as well present your ass now and I'll promise not to light it up too bad."

"Fuck, no!" I screech as he lunges at me again. "I'll take my chances."

Elliot smirks and lifts his chin, telling me to give it my best effort. I know as well as he does, he's going to catch me. I know because I'm going to let him. Then I'm going to bend over and take my punishment like a good girl. My three orgasms too, thank you very much.

Unfortunately, while I'm thinking about those orgasms, my mind grows a little hazy and Elliot manages to get the upper hand.

He boxes me into the island, his strong arms on either side of my body. He leans in and captures my mouth. "You're lucky that I'm starving and feeling like a fucking recluse. Let's go eat. I think the anticipation of the punishment you'll have waiting for you when we get back will be fun, don't you?"

22

"When you said you wanted to go get food, I have to admit," I giggle. "Not what I pictured" I say as I dump my fries out of their packaging.

"What? You got a problem with the Arches?"

"Not at all. Actually, I'm a bit of a fast food junky."

That makes him laugh. "Really? With a body like yours? I don't believe that for a hot minute, you little liar" Elliot says then pops a chicken nugget into his mouth with a grin.

I suck in my breath. "I'm not a liar," I state. "And your body is ridiculous. No way you eat like this often."

Elliot quirks an eyebrow.

"And okay, I know what that look is about. I might have told you a lie or two, but I'm serious about my junk food."

Elliot plucks a fry from the wrapper laid out in front of me. I like to unwrap my burger and spread out it's wrapper then empty my fries onto it. He snags my sweet and sour sauce too, then winces as he dips the fry into it. "Ketchup should be the only condiment used on fries. This right here, sacrilege."

I roll my eyes. "Over dramatic much?"

"Not me" Elliot says then points his finger in my direction.

"Me?" I chuckle. "You almost cried when they told you they were out of the toy you wanted."

"Hey," he scolds. "Don't fuck with my Lego Batman."

"I wondered if you were him when my panties went missing that night on the island."

Elliot laughs. "Not Batman, Snowflake, just know how to get what I want when I want it."

"What did you do in the military?"

"Kill people with my bat wings," he deadpans. "I wrapped them up in them until they stopped struggling."

"You're insane."

"Little bit. Yup" he laughs then takes a huge bite of his multi-patty burger and buns.

I take a bite of my own single patty and say, "Too bad I didn't know Batman when I was growing up."

Elliot reaches across the table to wipe a spot of ketchup from the corner of my mouth. He pops his finger into his to clean off the red sweetness then tilts his head a tweak to study me.

I feel the heat of his glance and know that he wants me to talk. "What? Sharing time?" I ask.

"I'd say well past."

I heave in a deep sigh and close my eyes. My hands push my remaining food to the center of the table, and I lean back in my chair and protectively fold my arms over my chest. "My mom married my father when she was young, too young," I shrug as I begin my story. "She wanted what her sister had. She didn't get it."

My mother, Katrina Adams grew up as the middle child. My Aunt Brook is only slightly older than her and my Uncle Michael is not younger by much. Early on in their lives, their roles in the family were created. Michael was the baby and the only boy. He was spoiled and my mother had been jealous of him since the day he arrived in their family. By the time he was in high school, Uncle Michael had a flare for the arts and being flamboyantly dramatic. Oh, and gay. That earned him even more attention for a while, but in the end, it ultimately formed a rift between him and my grandparents.

My Aunt Brook was and still is my mom's closest confidant. They're a lot like Bridget and me. My mother has always been happy for her sister, but that never changed the fact that she also wanted what she had. And who wouldn't? Brook had fallen in love early, the way only young girls do in books created for pre-teens, and she and my Uncle Tate remained together. Sure, they've had struggles, but they've also always had the other by their side to weather them.

My mother always came up just that side of short when it came to comparing herself to my aunt. They look almost identical, but my Aunt Brook has that special something that just sets her apart from everyone else in a crowd. They were both cheerleaders in high school. But where my mom made the team each year, my aunt was on Varsity as a freshmen and captain by her second year. Then she went on to cheer for the best team in D1 college history. They both danced, too. My mom can still move on the dancefloor, but my Aunt Brook is a world-famous choreographer.

When it came to love, that's where my mother's need to have what her sister did took hold. As a pre-teen, she'd watched my mother fall in love with the most gorgeous boy at school, with long dark hair that used to flop in his face. My Uncle Tate had been shy despite those good looks, and the way my mother and aunt tell the story, it drove the girls wild and they all wanted to be the first to garner the attention of the three-sport athlete and star on every team he played.

Tate Taylor had first set eyes on my aunt at a dance and the rest was history.

My mother dated Bobby in secret for a stent, but they'd gone their separate ways when he graduated from high school and she remained in the same small Connecticut town where we live now. My mother then spent years feeling as though she'd let the man, she was destined to be with get away. Instead of reconnecting with Bobby Knight, she'd sought solace in any man she could. So, while Bobby was living the high-life by Tate's side, dating models and actresses, my mother settled into a loveless marriage to an asshole who turned out to be my father.

Kyle Collins was an established man of business when my mother's path crossed his. They'd engaged in a whirlwind romance, him sweeping her off her feet. But Kyle was a wolf in sheep's clothing, a fact my mother wouldn't discover until she was sitting at home, alone, with two little girls and he was gone.

They divorced by the time I was four and I never saw or heard from my biological father again.

My mother dated various men for the next few years. She kept them out of our home and away from Bridget and I, so at the time, we just thought she was going to scrapbooking classes like all the other moms.

Then, I must have been about eight, when she introduced us to Tom Walker. Tom was kind and friendly, Bridget and I instantly liked him. So, when my mother told us that he'd be moving into our home, we were thrilled to finally be getting a daddy like all our friends had.

He went to work every day, where he put in excessively long hours, and traveled a lot for business. But when he was here, Tom took us to ski lessons and played with us in the snow. We had family movie nights and birthday parties. For a few years, things were ideal.

And then his best friend, Jim, had fallen on hard times and needed a place to stay.

"You realize, that as Batman, I have the powers to find him, right?" Elliot says as he holds the apartment door open for me. "I mean, if what I'm about to do to you doesn't get me the answers I want, that is."

"Elliot," I sigh. "Leave it, okay. I don't know where Jim is and it's water under the bridge."

"What if there were others?" he questions. "If someone right now is living through what you did?"

I heave in another gulp of air because that thought crosses my mind every day and sickens me. "I'm sorry for that. Truly. I don't want to think about anyone dealing with that, but…"

"But what?"

"But I don't want to deal with it either. Please, let this go."

Elliot tosses his wallet and the rest of the items he'd had in his coat pocket onto the island in the kitchen as the warm glow of the sensory light begins to illuminate the space. "Fine," he relents. "For now. But if you don't come to the decision to make the right choice on your own, my hand will be forced. And reddening your ass."

"Elliot, I…"

"Dropped," he promises. "Like I said, for now. You want to watch a movie or…" Elliot is interrupted by my phone. I glance at the screen and see my sister's picture. "Get that," he says. "I'm going to head to the gym. I need to get back on track. We'll figure out our plans for later when I get back."

He kisses my temple then retreats to the bedroom to get changed.

I swipe my finger across the screen to hear my sister crying. I can't make out a word she's saying and try my best to calm her down. She sighs and I manage to piece together a few words as Elliot strolls through the apartment and sends me a curious glance. He mouths, "Everything okay?"

I shake my head then whisper, "Probably her first fight with Ace. Go. I'll fill you in when you get back."

Elliot kisses me on the lips then gently closes the door behind him.

"Bridge," I try to soothe. "Honey, shh, tell me what the hell you're talking about. I can barely understand you. Is Ace there?"

"Brother." Gulp. "Maine. Ace doesn't know."

"What are you talking about? Does Ace have a brother in Maine? Why does that matter?"

Then the call drops, and the line goes dead. I wait a few minutes to see if she'll call me back. I know I have excellent service in the apartment, it must be where she is that isn't so great. No sense in me calling her back if she's still in a dead zone. But after not hearing from her after fifteen minutes, I send her a text that goes unanswered. Then, ten more minutes pass, and I leave her a voicemail that doesn't get returned.

By the time Elliot is walking back in the door, my phone is dying and in need of a charge. He instantly reads my emotions that must be written all over my face.

He comes to sit next to me on the sofa and removes the phone from my hand. He glances down at the screen and asks, his voice rough, his breathing still heavy from working out, "Was that your sister that called when I was leaving? Did you talk to her this whole time?"

"Yes, it was Bridget. No, I only talked to her for a few minutes. You're all sweaty."

"I know," he says, lifting his arm to smell underneath then nuzzling my face into the spot where I can smell his scent mixed with his bodywash, deodorant, and cologne. I can't help but to inhale as he chuckles. "I need a shower. You okay? Want to join me?"

"Nah, you go ahead. I'm going to plug my phone in and see if my sister calls me back. I think she and Ace are fighting over his brother in Maine."

"Ace doesn't have a brother," Elliot states. "Only a much older sister who helped his parents spoil the shit out of him which is one of the reasons why he's a fucking dick most days."

I smile and kiss Elliot on the lips before he stands.

"If you change your mind, I'll be naked and wet in the shower."

"Pussy tease" I say.

23

I must have fallen asleep after plugging my phone in to charge because I'm startled awake to find the master bedroom dark and Elliot holding a gun, I never knew he had, to a man's temple. As my eyes adjust, I also begin to make out that man's voice. He coughs and sputters, but it's clearly Ace Lyons.

"Elliot" I scream before he shoots his friend.

He whips his head in my direction then returns his attention to Ace. Ace shoves Elliot off him and collapses to the floor to regain his breath. Elliot had had a hand on his gun, but the other was apparently crushing Ace's windpipe.

"Fuck, man!" Ace coughs.

"What the fuck are you doing breaking in here in the middle of the motherfucking night?" Elliot asks then turns to scold me. "Get under the fucking covers. He doesn't need a reminder."

I heave in a shocked breath. Elliot catches his error and winces at his own abrupt comment. "I'm sorry," he apologizes as he comes to sit next to me and pull me into his arms. He's covered in a sheen of sweat. "I shouldn't have said that. This fucking asshole has me riled up."

"When did you get a gun?"

Elliot laughs. "Christmas. When I was sixteen."

"Oh."

"Adams, listen…"

Ace breaks into our conversation. "Sorry to break up your walk down memory-fucking-lane, but I can't find Bridget."

"What?" I push to get out of Elliot's hold, not caring if I'm covered or exposed to both men now standing in my bedroom, "What do you mean, you don't know where my sister is?"

Ace huffs in a sigh. "I tried calling and texting both of you a million fucking times. I figured he had you tied up, literally, and that you guys were fucking each other's brains out and didn't want to stop to answer me. That's why I came over."

"And broke in?" Elliot asks with annoyance in his voice.

"I know the code."

"Why is there even a code if everyone that knows Stone also knows the fucking code?"

"Can we get back to my girl, please?" Ace asks. "I pulled her phone records when I couldn't track her on it…because it's off, and you were her last call. Hours ago."

I collapse down to the bed. "She was crying. I couldn't understand her. Something about you having a brother in Maine that you didn't know about."

"I don't have a brother and I've never been to Maine."

"That's what I told her" Elliot says as he sits then readjusts the sheet wrapped around me before pulling me into his lap.

Ace falls into a chair and his head goes into his hands. "Do you think she has someone else? You know, like in Maine?"

I look to Elliot who shrugs his shoulder. "Ace," I begin. "You and Elliot go into the kitchen and get a beer or something. Let me get dressed then we'll figure this out. Bridget can be...flighty, but I'm sure it's nothing like that."

Ace nods. "Okay. Callan is on his way over too. I called him. I'm sorry, I didn't know what else to do" he says with a slight cringe in my direction.

I heave in a deep sigh. Elliot seems to be able to handle Ace and the fact that we fucked. But I suspect a lot of that is because he's with my sister. Now, Callan Black was a whole different ball of wax. A smart-ass ball of wax with a chip on his shoulder and a mouth to boot. Callan will sense Elliot's displeasure over our past and use it to cause trouble. Plus, the fact that we're in the past might still be a sore spot with him. If Callan had had what he thought was his way, we'd be in the present. Well, that is until he'd see another girl that caught his eye because Callan Black is in no way shape or form ready to commit to one woman. He only thinks he is. He has no fucking clue.

Elliot and Ace head into the main living space, leaving me alone to get dressed while I worry over what in the hell my sister has truly gotten herself into. This is what happens when I leave her alone for ten minutes.

I head into what will be mine and Elliot's bedroom for the next year and realize that I don't have clothes or any of my belongings with me. I had planned to meet my match out on the street in front of Stone Towers, spend the night with him, then meet up with my sister in secret to retrieve the bag I had waiting in my closet back in Connecticut. That never happened. So now I stand and spin around in this new space wondering what in the hell I'm going to wear.

I walk into the huge walk-in closet and find it split in half. One half has men's clothing, the other half is equipped with every item I could possibly need for the foreseeable future. I check the tags and find they're all in my size and style. Did Elliot do this? If he did, he must have done it from the hotel. He couldn't have known my style beforehand. My size, sure, I'd had to supply that on my application, but my style, that's another thing.

I sense Elliot standing behind me and turn to see him leaning up against the door jam with a smirk. "I hope you like everything, if not, we can go shopping."

"No, it's…it's perfect. How did you…?"

"I arranged it once we came up for air at the hotel. I figured you'd need something to wear when you left the apartment. Those few things you had with you in that mammoth bag of yours won't last you a year."

"So, you're still expecting me to walk around naked when we're alone?"

Elliot smiles. "Kind of hoping you'll want to, but," he shrugs. "We've gone over this. You signed the contract. That means you're mine and you've agreed to…"

"I know what I agreed to. Well," I backpedal. "I mean, I know what you've told me."

Elliot growls. "Before I take you over my knee again about how fucking stupid that was of you to sign that contract without reading it, we should probably get out there and deal with whatever in the hell your sister has pulled. I'm guessing you and she share your," he clears his throat. "Impulsivity issues?"

"Bridget isn't usually as *spontaneous*," I stress the better term for our personality flaw. "But this thing with Ace has her, I don't know, but she's different in some way. I have no idea what she's involved in, but I know it's not another guy. She thinks Ace is her reason, the one to make her change, to be a better person."

"Yeah? How about you? Do you have a reason?" Elliot asks as he approaches me and wraps me up in his arms.

"I might" I say through a giggle as he nuzzles my neck.

"Get dressed," he orders. "Callan is here and already mouthing off about where your sister might be and what she might be doing. I need to get back out there before those two go at it and bust up the place."

"Elliot," I stop him. "Try not to let what Callan says get to you. He can be an asshole and he and I…well," I shyly look at Elliot. "We have a history and I'm pretty sure he's going to use that to get a rise out of you."

"I can handle Black. Get dressed, Snowflake."

Elliot leaves and I hop into the shower then get dressed and follow in his wake. I find the three men taking up more space in the living area with their personalities than their huge bodies.

"She's not fucking someone in Maine, you motherfucker. Why would she go all the way there to get laid? We're in fucking New York. Have you seen her? She could get laid two seconds after walking out the door."

"Speaking of getting laid," Callan says with a chin lift to me. "How's it going, sweetheart?"

I plaster on a sweet smile and ignore his comment. "Hey, Cal, what's up?"

Callan looks down into his lap and adjusts himself. "Now that you're in the room…"

"Knock it the fuck off, asshole," Elliot warns. "I told you, I'm not putting up with you disrespecting my girl."

Callan smirks and laughs with his head falling back on his shoulder. "Good luck with that, man. Now, if we're going to deal with the little runaway, let's get on it. I got shit to do."

"Shit to do?" Elliot asks. "What shit?"

"A blonde I left at my place. You know, shit" he says while sending a smirk in my direction.

Elliot shakes his head then takes control of the room, giving orders and moving about. "Black, when you're done being a douche, track her phone again. If it gets turned back on, we'll get a location. Then snag her records, past calls, texts, ins and outs. Maybe she's used it since calling Adams earlier."

I stand with my mouth open and my newly donned fresh panties getting wet while I watch him. He's strong and sexy, in control and commanding. Then he turns to me. "Time to meet your parents, Snowflake."

"Wait, what?"

"I want to speak to them in person. Feel them out before we tell them that Bridget is MIA."

"I don't…what are we going to tell them?"

Elliot smiles at me then with a nod of his chiseled chin, he dismisses Ace and Callan. After the door closes, Elliot addresses me. "I've been waiting on this one. I'm not accepting no or an argument, just so we're clear. I own you for the year and you'll do as I say. If you want to find your sister quickly, I suggest you cooperate, and we head to your parent's now. If you want to fight me on this, we can spend the next hour modifying your behavior before we leave, but the outcome will be the same. Well, accept your ass."

"What are you talking about?"

"We're going to tell your parents the truth. Our version of it, anyway. We met on the island and reconnected here. You'll be staying with me here in the city to be closer to school."

"School?" I ask. "What the fuck are you talking about, school? I told you, I dropped out."

"Yes, and I secured you a spot in the English department," he shrugs. "If you decide to head more into the media and film side, we'll adjust your curriculum."

"I don't even know what you're saying right now."

Elliot sits me down on the sofa and plops next to me. He takes my hands into his and strokes his thumb over my beating pulse at my wrist. It instantly settles me, but my agitation quickly returns when he says, "I called in a favor. Stone fucking owes me. His mother-in-law was a professor. She made a few calls. You start at NYU in two weeks."

"What?" I screech. "I can't pay that tuition."

"You're not," Elliot states with a smirk. "I am. End of discussion. Let's go. I called for a car to take us to Connecticut."

I refuse to stand, and Elliot raises an eyebrow at my challenge.

"Adams, do you really want to introduce me to your parents and explain why you can't sit down at the same time? It'll barely be ten in the morning when we get there. Don't you think that seems unreasonable?"

I roll my eyes which turns out to be a bad decision.

"Did you just roll your eyes at me? Stand up, Adams," he orders. "Last chance," I hold my ground and Elliot chuckles. "Fine," he says. "Have it your way. Just remember when your mother offers you a hard chair to sit on at the kitchen table, why you're uncomfortable."

He reaches for my arms and pulls me to stand while simultaneously turning my back to him. In one more smooth movement, he has my pants and panties on the ground and my shirt hiked up over my boobs.

"Bend down and hold your ankles," he orders while his strong palm forces me into position from its place in the small of my back. "Don't let go or we'll start back at one."

It's the classic naughty schoolgirl paddling position he contorts me into where the student stands clear of things so she can't reach out and hold onto them. Her feet, like mine, are shoulder width apart.

Elliot kicks at my feet slightly to get them spread further to his liking. "Stay still and not a word. You brought this one on with your challenging behavior and that eye rolling shit that you seem to think is cute. We'll see how cute you think it is in ten minutes" he states.

"Elliot," I attempt but quiet when he reaches for a magazine on the table. He rolls it then smirks at me.

"Count, Adams" he demands.

Leaving my knees and back straight, I'm bent over grasping my ankles with both hands with my ass up in the air. Elliot stands facing my left side, far enough away so that the magazine will barely reach my right cheek. I smirk to myself when I think about sitting at my mother's table on my right side and winning this round of our game.

Unfortunately, Elliot knows what the fuck he's doing, and adjusts his stance to ensure that both cheeks will be struck at the same time. "Had you there for a second, didn't I, baby?" he laughs.

Bastard.

It can't be possible to more fully expose my ass than in this position and Elliot adds insult to injure with his next comment.

"When I told you to bend over and grab your ankles, you listened like a good girl. You'll get a reward for that later. It's not easy for you to relinquish control," I feel his palm brush across my ass. "Especially when you know that I intend to thoroughly smack it. So, not only did you present your ass to me, you will continue to stick it up and out as far as you can throughout your spanking like a good girl," Elliot makes one final adjustment to my position, angling me to spread my ass cheeks and expose my tight entrance and pussy to him. Then he orders, "Count."

I hear the swoosh of the magazine as it moves through the air. Before it makes contact with my body, I manage a gulp of air. Then I feel the first swat and obey his orders. "One," I state then add, "I'm sorry."

"Tell me why" he says as he delivers the next couple of swats.

I count to five and explain my apology was for misbehaving.

Elliot finishes with the last half of the swats to my ass then pulls me upright saying, "I need to fuck you," while he tugs my shirt over my head, somehow managing to take my bra with it. "Now!"

I try my best to lift his shirt over his head, pausing to nuzzle into his chest, but I'm so much smaller than him, that Elliot needs to remove the garment. I kneel as he pushes at my shoulders, kissing each of his nipples on my way down. I look up at him from under my eyelashes, into his eyes as I unbutton his pants, my fingers slightly shaky, then slide my hand into the waistband. I smile at the silkiness of his hardening cock straining against his pants. I pull them out and over his erection, freeing him as Elliot's hands gather my hair and sweep it back off my face so that he can watch as my lips fall open and I take him into the wet heat of my mouth.

"I love your mouth, Adams. You suck my cock so fucking well, it would be a shame to let that talent go to waste. Your apology is accepted. Don't let it happen again."

I chuckle and smile up at him before I begin to lick my way up his shaft from the base to the tip, circling his head with my tongue to collect the moisture pooling there. "We'll see" I say in yet another struggle of power. One I know that will end in my pleasure. Eventually.

"Fuck" he groans as his head falls back.

My lips close around his cock and I close my eyes at his masculine taste. I bob my head back and forth slowly at first, sucking firmly, as my hand slides down to his base. It's a stroke I repeat over and over, only down, never up, to keep him on the edge. "Careful," he warns. "You're toying with me. You know that's playing with fire, Adams. We need to get to your parents. If I need to punish you again, that might not happen."

Instead of backing down, I pull him in deeper, enjoying the feel of him in my mouth. I moan as his hips push forward, sending his cock to the back of my throat. "That's a good girl," he praises when I look up at his face tight with his restraint. "But only a few more strokes."

I flick the tip of my tongue and press gently against the spot under the head of his cock where it meets his shaft and I smile around him when I feel his legs tremble. Up and down, my cheeks hollow as I suckle his cock, my hand pushing down on every other stroke.

Elliot finally reaches his breaking point and growls, pushing me off his erection and laying me on my back on the hard floor of the apartment. He's on top of me and thrusting inside me before I have time to react. I cry out and wrap my legs around his slim waist. "Elliot, so good."

"I know, baby. You're so tight around me. Love this pussy," he says then leans down to take my mouth. He pulls back and whispers. "Always."

Then he raises my arms and holds my wrists together above my head. Our eyes lock as his hips find their pace and in them, I see what I've grown accustomed to, control and safety, love and respect. Rationally, I know that he's not trying to be a dick and make me do something because of that stupid contract. He's pushing me to return to school and study something that interests me because he knows it's what's best of me, it's what I need to do. But we're going to battle over that tuition payment and who's footing the bill. Later. But there's still a part of me that's growing uneasy with his reminders about the fact that he "owns" me.

As Elliot pumps his cock in and out of me, I thrust my hips up to meet his, crying out when the head of his cock rubs against my most sensitive spot. "I want to come, Elliot."

He pulls back, lifting my legs up, then slams back in. "I know you do, baby, but you know our rules. You will not come until I do. This is still a punishment for that behavior you can't seem to help."

I groan in protest. I want to come. Now. But Elliot knows it'll be better for me, stronger if I hold off and I love that he knows my body better than even I do. It's not all about his control when he's like this. He can pretend it is all he wants; I see through him like a wall of glass.

I feel every slide through my slick folds as his thrusts increase, his cock reaching every sensitive place inside me, pressing back and forth, sheathed in my tight heat.

"Touch yourself," he orders. "Rub your clit while I fuck you."

I don't hesitate to follow that command.

I rub at my clit as Elliot looks down, a growl escaping him and causing him to push in harder. He leans forward to lick my neck then he bites my lobe with a smile. I cry out and arch my back as my limbs begin to warm with my impending release. "I'm close already."

"I know, baby. Me, too. Fuck, you feel so good."

I feel my orgasm building, sense his as well. My pussy tightens around Elliot's shaft and he twitches, hardens further, then pushes in deep and holds still. "Fuck, I'm about to come."

"Please," I beg for his release. "I want your come, Elliot. Pull out, come on me. Mark me as yours. I'm yours."

He growls deep from within his chest and increases the force of his thrusts. "Don't stop touching yourself. Tell me what you want again."

"I want your come. All over me. I want you to come, Elliot."

A strangled moan escapes him as his thrusts increase even more. "Beg for it," he demands. "I'm right there."

"Please," I plead. "Pull out and come all over me."

"Yeah," he howls. "Then you'll make that pussy come for me, won't you, baby?"

"Yes, please. Now, Elliot. I can't hold off much longer."

My body shakes from holding back and waiting for his approval, and my begging starts catching with sobs from the effort.

Elliot growls on his final thrust then pulls out and takes his cock into his fist. It doesn't take much, just a few strokes, before the first burst of his hot release hits my flesh. Then another, and another, covering me in spurt after spurt, warm on my chest, my neck, my belly and I can't hold back another moment. "I'm coming" I say.

"Yes," he moans while still pumping his cock. "Come for me, Adams."

24

"Courtney," my mother admonishes. "Sit, baby. You're being rude hovering over your guest."

Elliot smirks and pushes his chair out slightly to offer me his lap. "Yes, Courtney," he says with mirth in his voice. "Sit down."

Bobby sends Elliot a look of parental concern and confusion. He's never seen me with a man before. Well, that isn't entirely true. He'd caught my sister and I with Ace and Callan on my desk, but that was a different situation than me sitting here in the kitchen of our family home with a man who clearly is making his intentions, where I'm concerned, well understood as he pulls me into his lap and gently kisses my temple.

"The two of you met on the island, spent, what, ten days together and have now decided to live together?" Bobby asks with a scoff. "This is what you were referring to on New Year's Eve as your changes?"

At the mention of the night I was supposed to meet my Compatible Companion match, before I knew it was him, Elliot stiffens under me then regains his composure to answer for me. "That and the fact she's been accepted into the English department at NYU."

Bobby's eyes widen as he looks to my mom for answers. She shrugs. "I didn't know you'd applied to go back to school. Honey, NYU...Wow! That's great."

"And expensive," Bobby interjects. "Don't get me wrong, I'll pay if you're serious, Courtney. But your track record isn't..."

"Her tuition is taken care of" Elliot states, causing Bobby's eyebrows to disappear into his receding hairline.

"Courtney?" My mother questions. "What's this about? You know we'll pay for..."

"Mrs. Knight," Elliot interrupts. "With all due respect, it's already taken care of. Ad...Courtney will live with me. It makes sense as I'm in the city and closer than if she were to remain here. That will save the room and board fees and her classes for this semester have already been paid in full."

Bobby and my mother make eye contact then Bobby speaks up. "Elliot," he begins. "You seem like a very nice guy. I know your father; he's always spoken kindly of you. But I also understand that there might be some reasons for me to be concerned about my daughter being in a relationship with you. One, with all due respect to you," Bobby echoes Elliot's early words to my mom. "That already appears to be very one-sided."

I suck in air through my teeth at Bobby referring to me as his daughter. Sure, he's done it before, but now, hearing him say that, it hits home. I've always been so focused on my feelings of abandonment left over from my biological father's exit, that I never stopped to think about what my behavior might have been doing to him. I'd always just assumed he'd be like my dad or Tom. I never considered that my behavior was also hurting him.

Bobby Knight walked into my life when I was a pre-teen, angry and seeking attention. He didn't for one-minute bat an eyelash at my sassy attitude. Instead, he'd stepped up to the plate and thought of me and Bridget as his own.

A memory comes to mind of our time in California when my Aunt Brook was pregnant and living there with Uncle Tate. Bobby and my mother must have just begun dating. I'm not even sure if it was official back then. I think the only reason that Bridget and I met him so quickly was because he had been my Uncle Tate's best friend since they were kids and it was more as if he were there with our family as Uncle Tate's friend, not my mother's new love interest. Or old love interest, as I later discovered.

On that trip, I remember Bobby playing with Bridget and I in the ocean and taking us for ice cream. I never once felt like he was doing it to impress my mother or because he felt that he had to because we were her kids. Most of that trip, we spent together doing fun things. I remember a few nights where Bridget and I hung out with Uncle Tate and Aunt Brook. It isn't until now that I piece together what my mother and Bobby had probably been doing on those few occasions.

I shiver at the thought.

Ick!

Then I remember being with them when my aunt had the twins. Bobby had been there for my mother when she thought her only sister wasn't going to survive. I have a picture in my head of my mom in his lap. He'd caught sight of me and Bridget and had shifted my mom to make room for us.

One day, not long after the twins were born healthy and my Aunt Brook arrived home from the hospital, she and my mom had told us a fairy tale about a man and a woman who had fallen in love but hadn't known it at first. They told us that it took them a long time to figure it out. I remember thinking it was a magical story, one I wished to have for myself as a young girl just starting to have an interest in the male species, all sexual at the time, but be that as it may. Looking back now, I shiver because it was clearly the story of my mother and Bobby.

Not long after, they were married, and Bridget and I went on our slutty dating spree that lasted close to a decade.

Turning my attention back to Bobby and my mom, I start to realize how much I might have gotten things wrong. Bobby doesn't look like a man preparing to leave my mother any time soon, regardless of the stressors my sister and I put on their marriage. No, Bobby Knight looks perfectly content in his role as husband and father as he gets my mom a drink and slides the same flavored iced tea that I love in front of me.

"I'd offer you a beer but it's barely noon," he says. "Fuck it! I might need one too, beer, then?"

"Sure," Elliot says. "And you've no reason for concern. Anything my father may have told you, is neither here nor there in my relationship with your daughter. So, are we good with Ad…Courtney living with me and going to school or not? But I must tell you, good or not, it won't change anything. I'd like to have your blessing, but without it, things will still proceed as planned."

"Why do you slip up every time you try to say her name?" my mom asks before Bobby can explode on Elliot over his curt response.

Elliot smirks. "She's a devilish minx, this one of yours, isn't she?" he asks. "Seems like she had it in her pretty little head that she needed an alias while on vacation to reinvent herself. She told me her name was Adams and it stuck. I call her Snowflake, too, but that's a different story."

"Reinvent?" my mother questions. "Why would you need to do that?"

"She got it in her head that she wasn't who or what you wanted her to be, that she should be a better person. I've explained her self-worth and that I happen to enjoy her as she is. Well, the man-crazy part aside. Those days have come to a screeching halt. She'll only be crazy over me moving forward."

Bobby smiles and I know in that moment that he's been won over and is already warming to the idea of Elliot and me together. "We're good," Bobby says. "Sounds like you've got her number and I must admit; I haven't seen her looking quite so balanced or compliant…ever."

Elliot smirks at me and lets his hand gently pat my ass in the sorest of spots. The flash of discomfort bordering on pain sends a signal to my pussy to flood my panties and I shift in his lap. Elliot stills me at the waist and whispers into my ear. "Not looking to sport a hard-on in front of your parents. Stop squirming on my dick."

"Oh" I sigh, and my mother catches my eye and sends me her own smirk.

Yuck! Jesus, could she even know what I'm doing to Elliot?

Pushing that thought aside, I clear my throat. "Um," I begin. "We came over for another reason."

My mother and Bobby sit, expecting me to tell them I'm pregnant or carrying a contagious STD, with bated breathes.

"I'm not pregnant," I blurt. "I mean, well we've been…" I cough as I hear Elliot groan. "No, I'm not. I guess there could be a chance, but…"

"Snowflake," Elliot suggests. "Why don't you tell them about your sister and why we came to Connecticut today."

Bobby growls and sends him a glare. "Yes, Courtney, do tell us what your sister has gotten up to?"

25

After spilling my guts to my parents about Ace and Bridget's budding romance, which they had already known about, and filling them in on her odd phone call, Elliot and I make it to the car without further discussing his earlier conversation with Bobby.

Elliot turns down Bobby's offer to call Mac, saying Ace had already filled him in and he's working with them. I promise to call my mother as soon as I know anything but reassure her that Bridget is most likely fine and just running wild with a crazy notion about Ace Lyons in her head.

Elliot escorts me to the car with a strong hand in the dip of my back. He leans down and whispers in my ear. "Good girl waiting until we're alone. We'll address your issue in the car."

The driver steps out and opens the backdoor for us. As soon as the car door closes, it's on.

Elliot knows I'm fuming over something as I haul my ass to the opposite side of the car. He might not know which comment I'm taking issue with, but he knows he's done or said something during the hour at my parents that now has me in a snit. He pulls me back to his side and holds me tightly to his body.

"I said I'd hear you out and I will, but I'll do it with you touching me. No exceptions. Now explain your issues with whatever it is I might have said or done that you didn't care for. You were fine one minute then it was like a switch went off."

I huff, "Fine, ugh! Whateves, Elliot," I raise my voice to a near screech. "I know absolutely nothing about you. Not one fucking thing about your time overseas, your military job, your friends...Not. One. Fucking. Thing! Bobby seems to know things from your dad. I'm completely clueless when it comes to you."

He goes to speak but I'm on a roll and cut him off. "And furthermore," I say and pointedly roll my eyes in his direction when he smirks at my gumption to put him in his place. "Bobby has no reason for concern? Anything your dad said about you, is neither here nor there in our relationship? What the fuck is that?"

Again, before he can answer, I continue, a woman on a mission. "And, what the fuck was that caveman bullshit about not caring if Bobby was okay with this or not? God, you're such an asshole."

Elliot smirks and tries to respond, but again, just as his mouth begins to move and he starts to speak, I continue with my rant. "I'm a, how did you phrase that? Hmm? I believe it was a devilish minx. What is that, a fucking cat? A play on the word pussy? Is that all I am to you, hmm...pussy?"

Elliot scowls at me then manages to settle his internal beast and explain, "I think you're thinking of a lynx. They're in the cat family. A minx is a cunning, flirtatious girl. Really, Adams, for someone in the English department at NYU, I'd expect…"

"Oh, no you did not!" I interrupt again as I hear the driver chuckle and Elliot slides up the privacy divider. Then he reaches for me, but I pull away with a huff. "Stop!" I demand. "You're not going to avoid this with sex. And you are so not pulling the Dom/sub card either."

"Okay," he tries to calm me. "Okay, fine. We'll start with the issue of your idea that you know nothing about me. What do you wish to know?"

"I don't know specifically. Anything, I guess."

"You can be rather infuriating, you know that, right?"

I send him one of my famous million-watt smiles. "Mmm Hmmm. How about your childhood. What was it like to be Raina Montgomery's little brother?"

"Annoying," he states as he pulls me onto his lap. "Before she became a legit model and actress, she was a pain in my ass drama queen. The summer we moved to Florida; she became obsessed with Pete. They had this group of friends that were together all the time. The guys were always cool to me, but the girls used to try to do anything they could to embarrass me. Being a young teen around a group of hot college chicks, it didn't take much. I spent most of the summer alone jerking off in the bathroom."

I laugh at his admittance of self-love then wet my lips with my tongue as I let that image take root in my mind. A young Elliot with his head thrown back as he came into his fist…

Elliot laughs. "Calm down. I wasn't what you see here today, Snowflake. It took me a few years to grow into my body. High school was rough at best."

"Oh yeah, I'm so sure. I doubt you were ever lacking for female attention" I scoff.

"I was," he says. "It wasn't until I," he sighs. "I can't tell you much about my time in the military, you understand that, right?"

"No! I don't."

"Adams, I worked special ops stuff, it's not even on their books. My job didn't exist in anyone's eyes except for my team's. Everything I saw, everything I did is confidential for good reasons. And trust me, none of it is anything you want or need to hear."

"Did you kill people? Can I ask that?"

"Yes, you can ask that and yes, a lot. Bad people, a few good that were in the wrong place at the wrong time. Those casualties are what keep me up at night."

"Are you still working for the people who know you exist?"

Elliot shrugs. "It's complicated. Let's not worry about that. It's a bridge we can cross if and when the time comes, okay?"

"I guess if that's my only choice."

"With this, it is. I'm sorry. It has to be that way."

I huff, not liking his answer but understanding that he really isn't at liberty to share the information with me. What he can share is the answer to my next question though. "Sexual history then. You know mine, let's hear yours."

Elliot lets his hand creep up my thigh, but I halt his advances. He sighs. "Fine. What do you want to know?"

"Age of lost virginity. Name of the girl. It was a girl, right? I mean, no judgement. Love is love and all that."

"Adams," Elliot laughs. "Your mind."

"Yeah, yeah, I'll be a great writer. Whatever, Romeo. Spill."

"I had a major crush on one of my sister's best friends in Florida that summer. She dated Pete's friend, Todd. He tragically died a few years ago from a brain tumor. Like I already told you, I spent that summer jacking off. When school started up, I was the new kid. For the most part, that blew. But with a few of the girls, it was awesome. I was the new guy, the one no one knew or had dated before. A few of them wanted to be the first to try out the new ginger, which reminds me," Elliot says. "You mentioned creating nicknames for me in your head. Those would be…"

"Nope, not now. Age you lost it."

"Fifteen."

"Girl's name, Gingerbread Boy?"

"Gingerbread…" Elliot laughs from the pit of his belly. "Amy. She was in my math class. A few months younger than me. I can't believe you thought of me as a fucking animated cookie."

"Details about this Amy chick."

"Adams, really? It was a lifetime ago. I don't remember…"

"De. Tails, Chucky."

"Chucky? The demented doll? Are you kidding me, Adams, do you think that little of me?"

When I don't answer he smirks. "Fine," he sighs as we cross over from Connecticut into New York. "I asked her out. We went to the beach and sat on a blanket. I kissed her and she let me feel her up. I figured, what the hell and went for broke. I shoved my hand into her panties and finally understood why I always heard Pete saying something was so wet through my wall. That made me want to throw up a little in my mouth, then when she returned the gesture and started jacking me off, I really thought I was going to lose my cookies. Yeah, they were ginger snaps" he says, and I smirk behind a hand.

Elliot continues. "I reached into my pants for the condom I asked Pete for and put it on. She laid on her back, I climbed on top of her and finished after three strokes. She was embarrassed that she let me fuck her on the first date and unsatisfied, I'm sure. I was mortified that I had finished that fast. I spent that summer listening to Pete go at my sister for hours, so I knew it was pathetic to come in less time than it took to actually get the condom on."

"When did you become…you?"

"Not overnight," Elliot states with a laugh. "I dated a bit after that throughout high school. Used girls to fuck but never had a girlfriend. I went into the service from there and fucked around with girls on the base. A few of them were younger, stationed there with their families. Ace and Callan got caught so many times with their pants down that it became a going joke. I was smart enough to not get caught with my dick in my commanding officer's wife or daughter. Having my father be who he is, I didn't have the leeway that Lyons and Black had."

"They were special unit, too?"

"Yup. After training, we stayed together. They were both pretty pissed off when I was put in charge. Of course, they both bitched that it was only because of my father."

"Was it?"

Elliot shrugs. "It didn't hurt that Dave Montgomery had trained more men in the unit than not. They all watched me grow up and that carried a lot of weight. Ace and Callan are also loaded guns so…"

The sun sets as we hit the FDR and I rest my head on Elliot's shoulder. "I'm worried about my sister" I state.

"Ace will figure it out. I'll call Mac when we get home and see what's going on. It's odd I haven't heard from any of them."

I shrug and close my eyes to catch a few winks before we reach Stone Towers.

Elliot must have carried me inside because I wake to a dark room and it takes me a few moments to acclimate to my new setting and remember where I am. I turn toward his side of the bed. Funny how after only a few days, we have our own sides. I find his cold and empty. I reach for his pillow and draw it into my face to inhale the scent of the cologne he's left behind.

"I love watching you sleep," he says. "And the fact that you seek me out the second you awake, and that you crave my scent? Jesus, Adams, you have no idea what you do to me."

"Elliot," I sigh. "Why aren't you in bed? What time is it?"

"It's early," he states looking at his cell. "Nine-ish. You fell asleep in the car and didn't wake up even when I undressed you. You were exhausted and needed your rest."

I look down to find myself naked. "Mmm, hmm, is that all you did?"

Elliott laughs then sends me an evil grin before licking his lips. "I might have allowed myself a little taste."

I open my mouth wide in exasperation. Fake albeit, but whatever. "Elliot!" I scold.

"I have some good news. You might want to let me share that before your mouth gets you in trouble. You know, the withholding of an orgasm for three hours kind of trouble."

I quickly shut my mouth and smile pretty at the man who holds so much power over me, it should be scary. And it would be if he were using that power for the bad kind of control. I never understood the girls who changed their hair style for a boyfriend or dropped their friends because a guy was jealous of their need for girl time. That's not what Elliot does. The control he has over me sends us both to the height of our sexual pleasure and lets us soar through the universe together.

"I see that naughty gleam in your eyes. If you want to play, just ask. You don't need to act up and obtain a punishment, just ask me if you want to try something. I promise, I'll always be game. But, honestly, you really do want to hear what I need to say first."

I quirk an eyebrow at him. "Okay, make it quick."

Elliot laughs again. "Bridget is in the living room. I'd say she's sitting down, but Ace made sure that wouldn't be possible. At least not for the rest of the night. I called Bobby to let him know she was okay."

"Oh. My. God!" I scream and leap from the bed. Elliot grabs me around the waist only a moment before I plow through the door. Naked.

"Whoa, whoa, whoa, not so fast, Snowflake. The guys are out there, too. Put some fucking clothes on."

"Oh, sorry. Impulsive."

"I've noticed."

I throw on a pair of soft shorts and a tank. Elliot groans. "You need a bra, sweetheart. Or a sweatshirt."

I roll my eyes. "It's nothing that they haven't…"

"Don't remind me. I slammed Black into the door only an hour ago after he made a similar comment."

"Elliot, about…"

"Later. Get dressed. Your sister has news that she needs to share with you. I'm not quite sure how you're going to respond and I'd rather you be dressed appropriately."

"Oh?"

Elliot doesn't say anything more. Instead, he hands me a bra from the drawer on the top right. Again, funny how we already have settled into our own sides. He motions with his finger for me to spin around. I remove my tank top and twirl so Elliot can don my undergarment.

"Something is very wrong with this picture," he quips as he secures my breasts into the bra.

"You can play with them as soon as I'm done talking to Bridget."

Elliot nods and I finish getting dressed. He takes my hand and leads me into the living room where I find Ace and Callan sprawled out on our sofa and my sister standing next to them. Elliot wasn't shitting me about her ass, I guess.

"Told you," he whispers into my ear. "And you have me thinking up all sorts of ideas for playing with you later."

I moan then remember that I had been worried over my sister and I run to envelope her in my arms.

"I'm going to hug you first, then I'm going to slap the shit out of you."

"Ah, Ace kind of took care of that part already" Bridget chuckles then rubs at her sore bottom.

"Damn straight. And when we get home, you'll be getting round two."

"Oh," my sister purrs. "I can talk to Court later, let's go home now."

"Not so fast," I scold. "Elliot says you need to talk to me. What the hell were you crying about and where were you?"

"Court, I think you should sit down."

I look at Elliot who nods and then plops down on the sofa opposite where Ace and Callan have grown comfortable and pulls me onto his lap.

"Is everything okay?" I ask. "Is someone dying? Shit, is it me?"

"I explained that you can't die from missing my dick already, sweetheart," Callan purrs, his voice velvety smooth. "And anytime you need it good, you know where to…"

Elliot tosses me to the sofa, lunges at Callan and throws him into a chokehold. "Warned you not to be a fucking douche to my girl." he seethes.

"Elliot!" I screech as Callan elbows him in the ribs and the two collapse to the floor in a heap with Ace standing over them laughing.

"Stop them" I scream, but Ace shrugs nonchalantly and rides it out.

It doesn't take them long to come up for air, Callan sputtering that Elliot needs to calm the fuck down. Elliot spits back a comment that he's a motherfucker or something along those lines. I've stopped listening to them because Bridget just blurting something to get them to stop. Something that sounded a lot like…

"We have a brother in Maine."

"What?" I ask as I turn toward her. "What do you mean? Who has a brother in Maine?"

I feel Elliot return to my side with a groan as he rubs his ribs. "Sit down, Adams," he instructs and takes me back into his lap.

"What the fuck is she talking about?"

"I got a call the other day from a strange number," Bridget begins. "When I answered, it was a guy."

"She's learning that lesson when we get home" Ace mumbles and Callan makes another off-color comment that I don't bother to pay attention to.

"A guy?" I ask.

"Yeah, he asked if I was the daughter of Kyle Collins. I hadn't heard his name in so long, I almost said no."

I suck in a deep breath at the sound of my biological father's name. She's right, it's one neither of us have heard in years. One we certainly never speak.

"Who? Was it him?"

"Dad? No," Bridget says. "He said he was his son and in New York. He said he wanted to meet me. He asked if I could spare an hour."

"And instead of telling me," Ace begins while shaking out his hand, the one obviously sore from slapping my sister's ass. "She went to meet a strange man in a coffee shop...alone."

"He's not a stranger, Ace," Bridget explains. "I've told you, he's our brother."

"Wait," I say. "I don't understand."

Bridget explains the course of events that occurred while we were trying to locate her. She had apparently hung up on the guy at first then, while crying hysterically over what she initially thought was a mean prank, called me. Then a text had gone through and she'd decided to turn her phone off to think.

"He texted me an address," she says. "I wasn't sure what to do. I needed to think so I hung up on you and turned my phone off. I didn't want him to reach out again until I had figured out what was happening."

Ace growls. "That's where she should have called me, but whatever."

Bridget smiles at Ace. "I said I was sorry. I wasn't thinking."

"Obviously."

"Wait, finish about this guy," I demand. "Did you go meet him?"

"She sure as fuck did," Callan interjects. "Has the ass to prove it too. And I don't mean in the good, been fucked up there, kind of way."

Now it's Ace's turn to go a round with Callan. One would think he'd learn, but nope.

Bridget ignores them and continues to explain that the text asked her to meet up in a coffee shop uptown and she finally decided to go.

"Was it, was it...our brother?" I stutter.

Bridget shakes her head in the positive.

"How can this be? We don't have a brother!"

"Uh, we kind of do, Court."

If I weren't already in Elliot's lap, I'd had collapsed onto the floor. Even now, I feel my body shaking and I'm starting to float off. As things begin to dim, Elliot's strong grip on my arms and his jostling of my body keep me alert enough to sigh and ask, "Does mom know?"

"About me finding out? No, I don't think so. The guys told Bobby and Mom that I had been with some friends and we were playing a juvenile prank on you. Of course, that was accepted without question."

Ace laughs and kisses my sister while he whispers something into her ear that makes her blush then return his smile.

"I'm confused," I sputter as tears threaten to escape. "How old is he?"

"He's in his thirties, Court. He lives in Falls Village, Maine and is married to a woman named Mallory."

"I...wait, thirty? How?" I stutter again, sounding like a moron who can't hold an idea in her head long enough to figure it out. "That would mean he was born before mom married our father."

"Yeah, about that."

"Oh, my God! I don't know if I can take anymore right now," I admit then ask, "What?"

"So, here's the thing," my sister begins. "Kyle, our dad, was married to someone else before mom. He had a son, Joey, before they split up and he met mom."

"Ugh! Does mom know about him?"

Bridget shrugs. "There's more."

"Jesus Christ, did we sleep with him?" I ask as a shiver runs through my body and Ace and Elliot growl in unison.

"Ah," Bridget moans. "I don't think so. I didn't recognize him, but I mean..."

Ace cuts her off. "Your ass is still sore," he warns. "You really think you should finish that sentence?"

"Oh, um...yeah, probably not. Anyway, Court, he's like thirty something but his sisters are younger. Dad has two other daughters."

I suck in a breath. "I need to lay down."

Elliot plumps a pillow and rests my head on it as Bridget continues to talk. She says things like, "Left his wife for mom but went back to her." I don't move as she explains that Kyle Collins, our father had obviously had a wife and a son, left them for my mother who then conceived us, only for Kyle to leave her and return to his first wife and father two more daughters.

"Joey wants to meet you. Our sisters don't know yet, but he said they'll want to meet us, too someday."

"I...this is all happening way too fast. I-I need to think."

"Joey is leaving in the morning. He was here for a business meeting and took a chance contacting me. He seemed preoccupied with something going on back home," My sister speculates. "He mentioned things being strained with his wife."

"Oh, I...um, I'm not sue if I can meet him just yet."

Bridget shrugs. "He's pretty cool. He looks nothing like us, so I guess he looks like dad."

"Dad" I say letting the word I don't say much fill the air.

Callan breaks the moment when he announces his departure. "If you don't need me to break into his bank account or run a background check, I'm out. Call me if anything else comes up. If I don't answer, assume my dick is already up and once something," he coughs. "i.e., my dick, comes, I'll call you back."

"You're such an asshole" I mutter as Elliot strolls in his direction and tugs him along to the door.

They must talk for a moment, Elliot probably telling Callan he can do whatever he'd like with his dick as long as he keeps it far away from me. Then he's back by my side.

"You should eat something," he says. "Name your meal and I'll whip it up."

I catch my sister's eye and raise an eyebrow. "Our fav?" I ask.

"Sure," she says. "So, you're not mad at me, too?"

"Oh, I think Ace gave you exactly what you deserved, but nope," I say. "Not mad. But if you ever scare me like that again, I'll tell him to add on ten from me."

"How do you...Oh!"

"Yeah, Elliot's pretty kinky, too."

Elliot laughs at my description of his sexual preferences. "Okay, baby, that's enough. What'll it be from the kitchen. What's this *fav* you speak of?"

In unison, Bridget and I say, "Tomato soup with grilled cheese."

That gains us a smile from Elliot and a head nodding in agreeance from Ace. "Soup and sandwich, coming right up" Elliot promises as he disappears into the kitchen area to scrounge up the ingredients he needs.

"I just assumed you were going to open a can of Campbell's and slap some Velveeta between Wonder bread" Bridget says as Ace takes our plates, rinses them in the sink then starts to load the dishwasher.

Elliot scoffs at the idea and says, "Not the way I roll in the kitchen, ladies."

My sister yawns and Ace comments about the time, saying he should get her home to bed. She blushes, knowing he has no intentions of letting her go to sleep anytime soon.

"Think about Joey, okay?" Bridget requests. "And call me in the morning."

"Will do. I promise."

I kiss my sister on the cheek then Ace and I share a moment of uncomfortable leaning in to say good-bye. We don't know if we should hug, kiss on the cheek, shake hands. Finally, I pull him in for a hug and kiss his cheek. I whisper, "Take care of her. She's putting up a brave front. It's what she does."

He nods then extends a hand to Elliot. They shake then man hug before Ace takes my sister home.

Elliot murmurs something soothing into my ear, something about how strong and beautiful I am. And then I'm in his arms and being carried back to our room. He puts me down in our bed and starts to remove my clothing. But it's not sexual like it usually is. Instead, it's as if he's changing a child into their jammies for bed and an image of Kyle Collins pops into my mind. That's something that hasn't happened in years.

I must have been three or four years old, not long before he walked out of my life for good. We're in my bedroom with the pink walls and roses stenciled around the headboard of my bed. I'm wearing a headband with hearts bobbing around and my favorite Little Mermaid pajamas. My dad tucks me under the blankets and kisses the top of my head. He sighs and says, "I wish things could be different" then huffs. "Life can take turns you don't expect and get messed up."

"I wish things were different, too, daddy. I wish I were a mermaid with shiny scales and a tail. Feet are dumb. I want to swim under the sea."

My dad laughs sadly. "I'm sorry. We can't always have everything we want, princess. Remember that. And remember, even though some things can't be changed, some can. Life is too short to waste, but," he huffs. "I can't win in this. Someone is going to get hurt anyway this plays out. I'm sorry. Remember, I'm so, so sorry."

"That mind again. What are you thinking about?" Elliot asks as he pulls my back to his front in a spooning position.

"I don't remember much about my dad, but I remember a night, not long before he left us, he was tucking me in at bedtime, and we talked. He said something about being sorry and not being able to change things. I'm not really sure, it's kind of a fuzzy memory."

"Do you think your mother knew about his first family or that he went back to them?"

"I don't know, maybe. She never talked about him after he left. Like I said, I don't even really remember what he looks like."

"You should call her," Elliot suggests. "Your mother. You and Bridget need to tell her about your brother. Invite her over tomorrow for lunch. I'll even make you something special."

I laugh. "Oh yeah?"

"Anything you want, Snowflake."

I nod and send my mom a text asking her to come to Stone Towers for lunch and informing her that my chef of a boyfriend will be making us a spread to die for. Then I turn around to face Elliot who had been reading over my shoulder and laughs over my menu choices.

"Thank you," I say after reading her response text. "She's heading in for noon. Can you text Ace and ask him to tell Bridget while I run to the bathroom? Meet you back here in five?"

"You got it. But Adams?"

"Yeah?"

"You wanted to play earlier? Experiment a little?"

"Oh, um…"

Elliot laughs at my response, the little shutter he watches run through me, then he kisses my nose and says. "I'll expect you in the guest room in a minute. And Adams?"

I clear my throat and swallow heavy this time because the husky timbre of his voice lets me know he means business. "Yeah?" I ask with my lust filled voice.

"Be ready for me."

26

I enter the guest room cautiously to find it empty except for a small piece of paper I immediately notice on the bed. I finger it before picking it up to read. I'm drawing this out. The anticipation, the building of sexual tension, is like aloe to a sunburn. My skin soaks up the soothing gel, but my body is still overheating, and I find that I enjoy the warmth.

With the note I find a set of makeup brushes from my favorite cosmetic company and laugh to myself. Is he planning on giving me a makeover before we have sex? I mean, he did use the term "play." Maybe growing up with a model turned actress sister, Elliot is more in touch with his feminine side than I'd realized. Maybe he's so secure in his manhood, that playing beauty school comes like second nature to him and I'm about to get my lashes curled instead of my toes.

But then I read the note and...oh!

Adams...You said you wanted to play. What better way to start with such a beautiful woman than with brush play? These tools are made for women to make themselves up. You don't need them for that. You're perfection as is. But I don't want them to go to waste, so I hope you're ready to play.

Remove all your clothes and lay on the bed. On your stomach, head to the left facing the wall with your eyes closed. Keep them closed and don't move until I give you your next direction.

Practice saying your safe word in your head, Adams. You just might need it this time.

I've always loved everything there is about makeup. The color palettes, the shades of eyeliner and blush, the textures of the brushes and sponges. Everything. But I have a feeling in the pit of my stomach as I remove my clothing and lay down to wait for Elliot's next direction that he's going to make me have much different feelings for those brushes.

I hear him enter and pull air through his teeth when he sees me laying on the bed. I'm on my belly with my feet pointed in the direction of the door, so that when he entered the room, I know the first thing he saw was my exposed sex. It's exposed because, even though he hadn't requested my legs already be spread for him, they are. Wide.

My hands are clasped and in the dip of my back, my head is turned to the wall like he asked. My eyes flutter closed as I hear him enter and I know a smirk crosses his face at my minor defiance.

"I picture you and your sister getting into your mom's or aunt's makeup as little girls. I see you with red lipstick on all around your mouth" he laughs.

I don't respond. He hasn't told me I could. When I don't, he rewards my quiet obedience with a gentle brush of his palm across my shoulders.

"I'm sure you loved playing with pretty things. Makeup and high heels," he chuckles. "After what I have planned, though, applying makeup will never be the same. Are you ready to play, Snowflake?"

I moan. His voice, it does something magical to me. I'm floating and warm, comfortable and content. For now. I know once his hands, his fingers, his tongue start to tease me, I'll be in for hours of frustration, but for now, I sigh.

"These are lined so they won't hurt your wrists," he says as I feel him place handcuffs on me. "You'll keep them in the dip of your back, Adams. It'll help you arch your back for me."

I don't respond. I let the cool silk of the padding inside the cuffs take me away. The clinking of the metal on the outside ignites a pinch of fear and sends it running through my veins.

"That's a good girl. I've got you," Elliot soothes. "Remember, all your trust."

I take a deep breath and sink into the mattress. "Elliot," I murmur.

He responds by giving me a warning. "Ready?"

I wasn't. Not for this.

Elliot grabs each of my ankles and in one fast jerk of his arms, I'm flipped over onto my back, hands cuffed together in the small dip under me now.

"Eyes stay closed until you're told," he warns. "And no squirming while I take care of these legs. I like the way you were spread wide for me," he praises. "Let's keep them that way."

I feel the same silky coolness surround one than the other ankle as he shackles me to the bed, spread-eagle.

"It's lucky for you that you keep this pretty little pussy waxed bare," he says. "If not, we would have needed to begin with that task."

The thought of him grooming me, waxing my pussy muddles my mind and takes away my remaining inhibitions. I'll try to remember to cancel my appointment next week. I'm sure Elliot will add pleasure to the painful task instead of Olga, who rips the hair from my body with her strong hands and barely a warning to grip the table before she pulls the fabric from both sides. At. The. Same. Time.

Once he has me bound to the bed, he orders my eyes open. "I want you to watch," he says. "It might be difficult to keep your eyes open at times. Try your best. This is your first time, so you won't be punished for closing them. But try your best to watch what I'm going to do to your pussy."

"Elliot," I sigh again. I'm not able to come up with more than his name.

"Yes, Snowflake?"

"I don't know if…"

Elliot smiles. "Shh. I know. Trust, though, remember? You'll do fine."

I nod.

"Good girl. Now, as I said, you'll be able to arch into my touch in this position. That's why your arms are free. But, being behind your back as they are, you won't be able to push my touch away, even when it becomes too much. With your legs attached to the bed, well, you won't be able to squirm away, either. Or close them."

"Yes," I hiss, ready for him to stop talking and touch me already. "Please."

Elliot reaches for the set of make-up brushes and pulls them from their protective packaging. He makes a show of examining each one, running the bristles on his hand then smiling at me as if he knows what each texture is about to do to my helpless body.

"Want to feel, sweetheart?" he asks.

I slightly nod. I know the size, shape, and texture of each luxurious brush. Well, I know what they feel like on my face. Now, how they'll feel on my pussy might be a different story.

"Let's see if I remember how these all work," Elliot says. "Which comes first? Raina used to practice her make-up on me, so you have her to thank for this."

I moan when I feel the densely packed synthetic bristles of the foundation brush slide across the inside of one thigh.

Holy fuck! Yeah, that's not the way it feels on my face.

I shiver.

Elliot's fingers begin to run over the skin on my thighs and down to my calves. He murmurs praise for me with each stroke before leaning down and planting a gentle kiss to the instep of one then the other foot. His tongue snakes out and he trails it up one leg and I'm already finding it challenging to keep my eyes open and watch him. But I also can't look away.

God, he's beautiful. Especially when he's between my legs.

He smirks at me, right before I think he's going to swirl his tongue around my pussy, he smirks, the bastard! Then he pulls back and gently uses his fingertips on my sex instead. Light fluttery touches that feel nice, but ones that will only frustrate me in the long run.

"I think I remember that this one goes first, right? You use it to put on that goopy shit."

I nod then smile because this brand, this high-end brush is designed to mimic the application of your finger and I'd love his finger right where he's heading with the brush right about now. "Yes, it's called foundation."

Then I nearly jump out of my skin at the first taste of what Elliot calls brush play. Jesus Christ!

The tapered-dome shape of the brush, the one that fits any angle of the face, also fits every angle of my pussy. The stiffness of the brush as he toys with my clit to harden it, makes me moan, throaty little sounds that have Elliot rubbing at the erection in his pants.

"You like this one?" he asks. "The way it flicks at your clit making it pop. It's so hard right now, baby," he praises then lowers to gently kiss me there, pulling my clit into his mouth to add moisture to this new brand of tortured pleasure.

"Elliot" I groan.

"Just getting started, baby," he says. "Relax into this. Let's try another. This one is for the powder stuff, isn't it?"

"Oh, God!"

When the fluffy, natural-hairs brush down my pussy with whisper-soft strokes, my legs shake, twitching with my growing arousal. I can already feel the fire inside me kindling, wanting to burn like a wildfire in the dry forest. But there's nothing dry about me. My pussy is primed already and dripping for him.

Moans and pants, throaty sounds fill the air. Mine and Elliot's. I look down between my legs where his face is mere inches from my core and see that he's released his cock and is stroking himself. The look on his face is primal and I giggle when I remember liking him to the crazy red-headed doll from the horror movie of my youth. "Fuck, Elliot. Please."

He chuckles. "You'll get it soon, Adams. Be a good girl and be patient. What had you laughing?"

"The red-headed doll from the horror movie. When we first met…"

"Ah, back to the ginger nicknames?"

"Yeah, but let's not talk about…holy shit!" I cry out and arch my body up to try to get him to apply deeper pressure and set me off. It doesn't work.

Instead, Elliot continues with the down strokes of the soft bristles over my clit and down my slit, never up, only the one direction. Down. Down. Down.

Jesus, I want to scream at him. Beg him with all that I have to make him stop. To force him to let me come then fill me with his cock that he's still stroking in one hand.

Knowing what I'm seeking, Elliot holds the soft powder brush on my clit and presses down. The pressure is perfect, if only he'd keep it like this for a few more seconds. But he pulls back every time I throb, and my orgasm tries to take root. Every raise of my hips and acceleration of my breathing has him delaying my release.

He makes tiny strokes up and down, flicks more like it and I'm a mess of yelps and groans. My body is covered in a sheen of sweat and strung so tightly I feel as if I could orgasm on demand. I'm sure of it, actually.

Then his side to side brush strokes begin and I'm lost in another world. A world where only Elliot's deep voice exists, his hands bring me to the pinnacle of pleasure, and his kisses are my substance, nourishing me.

Until he removes the brush and I'm forced to cry. Tears fall as I beg him to return it. Beg him to make me come then fill me with his cock.

"Say it again," he orders.

"I want you to fuck me. I need to feel you inside me. Want to feel you come in my pussy."

"Mmm, me too, Snowflake. In good time, though. The longer you can hold out, the better it'll be. Trust me?"

I groan as Elliot returns to the back and forth strokes like he's painting a landscape but then he switches to a circular motion. Around and around in circles he proceeds, and I feel my pussy clench in search of his thick cock. "I need you now" I plead.

But instead of giving me what I crave, what I'm begging for, he continues with the torture of the brush. Light strokes going up and down and they make me cry as I feel my pussy grow wetter. He taps my clit with the brush, the bristles wet from my excitement coating them. Then he plunges the brush inside me to further coat it in my wetness and the tease angers my pussy. It thought it was getting the firm thick shaft it's grown to enjoy, instead it only had a moment of pressure when he pushed the tip of the brush in, then nothing.

"Elliot" I say his name for what must be the millionth time in this session alone.

"What is it, Adams?" he asks but doesn't wait for an answer because the fucking ginger (yes, I might be back to that) knows exactly what it is. "Your pussy is so plump and ready," he states as he runs the bristles down one then up the other side of my sex. "But the light touch of the brush can't push you over the cliff, can it? Its torture being made to hold back, isn't it?"

I cry, thrash on the bed, beg him to let me come. But nothing works. The deranged leprechaun (maybe the nicknames only happen when he pisses me off) between my legs, spreads me open to expose my bundle of nerves.

I'm breathing heavy now, so close.

The bristles dip back inside me and twist, gets pulled out and twirls. Goes back inside and twirls then gets pulled out again to twist. It coats me in my wetness as Elliot rubs it over my tight bud.

I'm groaning in agony. I need to come so badly when I finally hear the words I've been waiting for.

"Come for me, Adams" Elliot orders as he lowers his mouth to my pussy, and I break. I shatter into a million pieces but every lick, each stroke of his strong tongue through my slick folds puts me back together. Heals me.

Elliot doesn't waste time removing my restraints before he thrusts his cock into me. He pushes into the root in one forceful thrust, knowing I was primed and ready to accept him.

"I want you to come again. This time with me, baby. Can you do that?" he asks as his fingers flick at my clit that hasn't even recovered from orgasm number one yet.

"Oh, fuck, Elliot. Jesus!"

"I know. I'm about to fucking come, too. This pussy is so tight, so perfect."

He thrusts and pulls back, groans and sinks in deeper. When he leans down and takes my mouth, I'm done. I come. Again. Then again as Elliot fills me with his own hot release, his hands in my hair as he grinds out the last of his orgasm.

"Better when I make you wait, isn't it?"

I growl at him because even though he is right about that, I don't want this waiting shit to become a thing. I like my orgasms when I want them.

"I know you'd like to control when you orgasm, Adams, but that's not how this is going to work. For the next year, your orgasms are all mine and I'll decide when they occur or don't."

For some reason that statement, the comment about our contract doesn't sit well with me. I know he's told me time and again that I'm his, he owns me, I signed on the dotted line, blah, blah, blah, but for some reason, this time, I don't like it.

"Because you own me" I state, not liking this arrangement as much as I had a few hours ago.

27

The following day greets me with a feeling of unease that I can't seem to shake. Last night had been great. I mean, the sex with the BDSM element Elliot brings to it is always hot and satisfying, but I can't get past his laissez faire attitude about our relationship status. I know it's only been a second over a week, but I'm falling hard for him and I thought this thing between us meant the same to him. The fact that he feels the need to still stress his ownership over me, no longer bodes well.

But I push my concerns to the back of my mind and let him pull me into his side when we open the door of 1-A in Stone Towers to my mother and Bridget. Elliot planting a gentle kiss to my temple as he invites them in and asks my sister where Ace is.

"He's upstairs with Callan. He said to send you up to Damian's once you're done cooking."

"I'm sure that's not how he worded it" Elliot scoffs as he leads us over to the kitchen island and starts putting out the spread of food that the three of us won't come close to making a dent in. When I had mentioned that earlier, Elliot said he'd eat the leftovers for dinner.

"He may have used other words" my sister says with a smile for my boyfriend.

Boyfriend.

Is Elliot my boyfriend? I'm growing more confused and apprehensive with each passing day.

Once the food is set before us, Elliot gives me a smoldering kiss on my lips, apologizes to my mother and sister for the PDA, then promises to give us enough girl time before he returns. "Walk me to the door, Snowflake."

Bridget cat calls as we retreat for a moment of privacy.

At the door, Elliot opens it and pulls me into the hallway. "If you need me, text and I'll be back in a second. You can do this. Talk to them" he encourages me.

Last night he convinced me that telling them about what "Uncle" Jim had done was a good idea. Today, I'm not so sure. "I don't know, Elliot. I might just wait on that. I mean, with Joey showing up and everything. Don't you think that's enough?"

"I think you need closure and to be validated. I think what's best for you is to tell them what happened to you."

I sigh. "I'll see how it goes, okay?"

"Good girl," he praises with a kiss. "And when they leave, I'll run you a hot bath and give you a full body massage."

"Mmm," I purr. "And what might that lead to?"

Elliot tugs at my bottom lip with his teeth then slaps my ass. "That'll be up to you, Adams."

I nod and wave as he walks to the elevator then I head back inside to find my mom and sister moaning over the goodness that is Elliot's cooking.

"Oh. My. God!" my sister says. "He's hot, great in bed, and he cooks like this. Remind me why you're not already married?"

"Because we've been together for a hot minute and…I don't know, he can also be an asshole."

"What's the matter, honey?" my mother asks. "The other day at the house, you were head over heels. Has something changed?"

"No, ma. It's just what I said. We're early days, okay?"

My sister holds her hands in front of her body and agrees. "I'm in the same spot with Ace. I get it. I'm sorry, I shouldn't have said anything."

Then it's my turn to apologize and explain why I always have such an adverse reaction to the institution of marriage. "Actually, that's kind of why I wanted to talk to you both today. My reaction when you mentioned marriage."

"Oh," my mother says with surprise. "Courtney, did Elliot ask you to marry him?"

"No," I state with a sigh then suggest we eat. I'm stalling but they're so looking forward to tasting Elliot's treats that they let it go.

I push food around on my plate while they eat their fill then complain about feeling bloated and needing to get in a few extra workouts this coming week to combat the amount they consumed.

"Let's go talk in the living room," I suggest. "It's more comfortable on the sofa."

My mother giggles. "You should ask Sydney about that sofa."

"Ugh," I gag. "Seriously? Her and Damian?"

"Yup, pretty much every surface of this apartment."

After that information, I perch with my ass barely touching the fabric of the chair while my mother and Bridget sink into the plush sofa with smiles as they wiggle their asses around.

"So," my mom begins. "What is this all about if not marrying that amazing man you found in paradise?"

I heave in a deep sigh. "It's not easy. This isn't something I really want to be talking about, but I need to get it out."

"Holy fuck!" my sister exclaims. "You're fucking pregnant, aren't you? Or, shit, do you have herpes or something?"

"What? Dear God, no!"

"Well, I mean…"

"What is that supposed to mean? Like you weren't as slutty as me, Bridge? You know what, fuck off."

"Okayyy" my mother says. "Why don't we step back and…"

I sigh a deep breath in and release it. "I'm not pregnant," I state with a glare for my sister. "And I don't have a fucking venereal disease."

"Okay, why don't you start at the beginning and explain what it is that you do want to talk about?"

"It's about when we were kids in Vermont."

My mother sucks in air then rises to her feet to pace the room.

"Mom, sit down, you're making me more nervous."

"I'm sorry, it's just not really a time I like to discuss."

"Yeah, that's part of the issue," I state. "Maybe instead of me starting, you should start at the true beginning. Like what happened with you and Bobby when you were kids? Why didn't you stay together? Then dad…I mean, he was…"

Bridget sends me a panicked expression. "Court, don't make mom talk about something she doesn't want to."

"No," my mom says. "I should have explained things a long time ago to you girls. I wanted to, but Bobby thought it would make things worse. You two were running wild already and he thought that you would respect him even less."

I quirk an eyebrow as my mom wrings her hands and starts at the real beginning.

"It was my sophomore year, Brook's last year of high school," she says with a far-off look crossing her pretty face. "Even though we're only a bit over a year apart, the way our birthdays fell separated us in school further. Not like you girls."

Bridget and I are only fourteen months apart and were back to back in school growing up.

"It was like I had just seen Bobby for the first time, even though I'd known him for a few years by then. I was head over heels in love with him, but I made him swear never to tell your aunt and uncle about us. I knew Brook would be pissed at me and she'd never let me near her friends again if she found out."

Bridget and I sit silent as we listen to our mother tell us how she'd kissed Bobby for the first time and how he'd been with Aunt Brook's best friend, Asia at the time.

It was the annual car wash for their school and Aunt Brook and Uncle Tate signed up to go with Bobby and Asia, but my grandmother made my aunt take my mom with them, too. Within an hour, Asia abruptly left, pissed off again at Bobby for something he'd said or done.

"Aunt Brook and I got soaking wet and some boys started trouble with Uncle Tate and Bobby."

I roll my eyes over the immaturity of my aunt and uncle during their youth. Then I chuckle because if a man commented today, about a wet t-shirt Aunt Brook was sporting, Uncle Tate would still flip his shit.

"We went back to our house and your aunt and uncle went upstairs to get changed," she says that last part with air quotes and Bridget and I both regurgitate some of our lunch.

"Uck," Bridget gags. "Mom, please."

"Oh, but it was okay for Bobby to find you two having sex on your desk?"

"Moving on. This isn't about us, right, Court? Continue, ma."

My mother chuckles then continues with a clearing of her throat. "Anyway, as I was saying, Bobby and I were left alone. He was upset over Asia; I was just trying to make him feel better."

"Oh God," I sigh and cover my ears. I look to my sister and she's doing the same while getting into the fetal position.

"He leaned over and kissed me on the lips. It was just a friendly kiss. At first," my mother smirks at us. "Well, until his tongue entered my mouth, that is."

"Eww...gross, I've heard enough" my sister screeches and I keep my ears covered.

"Your aunt said the same thing when she found out."

My mother just has to throw in the fact that Bobby was a great kisser, way better than any of the other boys she'd kissed before. "This powerful feeling came over me when his hands grabbed my face. I was instantly in love" she admits.

"Hmmm," I sigh. "That issue might run in the family then."

Bridget agrees but before my mother can turn the tables, I demand that she finish explaining what happened that made her and Bobby part ways.

She tells us that she and Bobby had kissed a few more times during that school year, but it wasn't until the night of the prom when things really heated up.

During the months leading up to the prom, Bobby and Asia brook up and Asia had met a guy from the local college and asked him to go to the prom with her leaving Bobby without a date. After my grandmother had flipped out about Tate and Brook having sex on prom night, they talked Bobby into taking my mom, supposedly as just friends.

"Your grandmother was so oblivious. She was thrilled to have me tagging along with your aunt that she agreed to let me stay out all night."

Like my own prom, theirs was boring, too. It wasn't until the after party that the fun kicked in.

"I lost my virginity to Bobby that night."

"What?" Bridget screeches again then starts bouncing up and down on the sofa like this is the best love story she's ever heard. I have to admit, it's kind of pulling at my heart strings now, too.

"We got drunk…"

"Bobby got you drunk so you'd fuck…um, have sex with him?" I ask.

"No, we got drunk, but he didn't get me drunk, we were just hanging out and drinking with our friends. We ended up in a room together at the end of the night. I thought we'd go to sleep. But then Bobby kissed me, and we started making out. We were on the bed and Bobby kind of pulled me on top of him. I was able to feel his," she clears her throat. "Excitement, if you know what I mean."

"Yeah, we get it, ma. Can you maybe leave out the sex parts?"

My mother laughs. "What, you don't want to hear how I let him put his hand up my shirt and then I undid his shorts?"

"No!" Bridget says. "Nobody wants to hear that."

"So what happened?" I ask.

"What?" my mom questions. "After, I undid his shorts or why we didn't end up together back then?"

"Why you didn't end up together" Bridget and I rush to say in unison.

My mom giggles then grows somber at the thought of what happened all those years ago.

"I was in love with him. Even as a teenager," she begins then shrugs a slender shoulder. "But sometimes love just isn't enough."

I watch as my mother speaks about her past and question if my love for Elliot is enough. She shares Bobby's past with his ex-girlfriend. I'd had no idea that Bobby had gotten her pregnant in high school, nor that she had an abortion that caused the beginning of the end for them. Bobby has always spoken about wanting children and how thankful he was when Bridget and I came into his life. I always called bullshit on that, I guess I was wrong.

"Bobby was not in a very good place when he was leaving for college. I don't know if you girls are aware, but Uncle Tate and Bobby lost two of their best friends in high school in a drunk driving accident."

"Oh, um…no," Bridget says. "I didn't know. That's terrible."

My mom nods. "Yeah, it effected the whole town. Bobby and Tate took it hard. Uncle Tate reacted immediately; Bobby didn't show signs of its effect until years later. Leaving for school…I don't know, it kind of screwed his head up for a while."

Bridget and I listen quietly as my mother tells us about the day Bobby came to say good-bye to her. He waited, until my grandparents were sleeping and my aunt was already at her own school, to toss a few rocks at my mom's window.

It makes me smirk. I never thought of her as a teenager engaging in typical behavior like Bridget and I took to the umpteenth thousand degree. I guess all those antics my sister and I pulled, where we thought her and Bobby had no clue what we were doing, weren't so secret after all.

My mom ran to her window, worried my grandparents would wake up and catch the boy she loved throwing rocks at her house. She laughed when she saw him standing on the front lawn with another handful of stones at the ready. "Hey," she called out before he tossed them and hit her through her now open window.

"Get your perfect ass down here and say good-bye to me," he ordered.

My mother quietly snuck through her house and out the front door while she figured her parents obliviously slept. But now that I'm aware of my own mom's behavior and figure she'd known more than Bridget and I thought, I wonder if her parents had been on to her all along.

Bobby was waiting for her in his car. As soon as she got in, he pounced on her and took her mouth in a hungry kiss. "I'm going to miss you, Trina."

"Me too," she sighed. "I hate that you're all leaving me behind."

"You'll forget all about me in no time. You're the hottest girl in school, the guys have been foaming at the mouth to get near you. With Tate and I gone, it won't take them more than a day to attack."

"What?" she laughed.

"Yeah, you didn't know that? Tate and I have held them back. Now, all bets are off. Promise me you won't fall for any of their shit."

But she had. She had because Bobby Knight had left for school the following day and broke her heart. He hadn't called her, like he promised. Hadn't written to her either. But she had heard the rumors of him with an abundance of girls. By the time he'd come home for the holidays, my mother had hardened her heart and opened her legs for half of the male student body at her school. Not really what either Bridget or I wanted to hear, but to lighten the mood, I said, "Like mother, like daughters, I guess."

My mom shoots me a glare then continues to explain that Bobby had been outraged when he'd arrived home to the rumors of her promiscuous ways. She'd called him out on his own appalling behavior, and they'd fought. His argument of making poor decisions and trying to deal with the loss of a child he'd never get to know, hadn't flown with her. The nail in the coffin of their secret romance was Asia. She'd been over before returning to her own school after the holidays and told my mom and aunt that Bobby and she had hooked up a few times while they were home. She told them that his head was messed up over some girl he thought he loved, and he'd gone to her for comfort. Stupid, he knew, but he told Asia he didn't know where else to turn.

My mom listened quietly as Asia explained Bobby's turmoil over their secret love affair and his heartbreak over Asia's abortion. None of it excused his behavior and when he went to see her again, late that night, she'd told him to go fuck himself and every girl on his campus, if there were any left that he hadn't gotten around to fucking yet.

With her heart in pieces and her self-esteem back in the gutter, my mom spent her last year in high school much like my sister and I had. She was forced to walk in the shadow of my aunt, a person she never felt she could compete with.

"Your aunt and uncle had the love story of the century and I had a secret romance with a guy who forgot about me five minutes after leaving town."

"But I thought he loved you?"

"He did," my mom says sadly. "But he was young and dumb and made horrible choices. I was equally was young and stupid and did the same. By the time he pulled his shit together, I was gone. I went to school and met your father."

"What?" I ask. "Bobby tried to get back together with you when you were with Kyle?"

"Yes. It wasn't pretty. Bobby showed up on campus drunk and making a scene at my house. He professed his feelings, but your father intervened. I barely made eye contact with Bobby that night. The next day, I accepted your father's offer of marriage and the rest is a clusterfuck in the history books."

"Did you know Kyle was married before you?"

My mother's eyes shoot to mine. "Wh-what are you talking about? How do you know about..."

"You knew."

My mother shakes her head. "He was my professor. Only a few years older than me, it was his first year in his first teaching job."

"But you knew he was married?"

"Yes. I'm not proud of my choice to ignore that and have a relationship with him regardless."

"Do you also know that he went back to his wife after leaving us?"

"I do."

I'm trying my best not to flip my shit with my mother so instead I yell at the only other person in the room. "And you have nothing to say about this?"

Bridget turns to me and shrugs a shoulder as a tear escapes and runs down her cheek. "He has other children," she states. "You knew we had siblings?"

"Children? No, I mean…"

"Joey contacted Bridget. They've met," my mother's eyes fly to my sister and her hand covers her mouth. "He told her that after Kyle returned to his family, he and his mother had other children. How do you not know that?"

My mom shrugs. "When he left, I was in a bad place. You girls were too young to remember. Uncle Tate and Aunt Brook took you for a while and paid for me to…take a break."

"You had a nervous breakdown." It's more of a statement than a question.

"I remember them coming to Vermont and staying with us. I never realized how long" Bridget says.

"Wait a minute," I say. "Bobby was there, too, wasn't he? Holy shit. Bobby took care of you, didn't he?"

My mother shakes her head as she cries. "Yes."

"Then how in the hell did you end up with fucking Tom?"

My mother stands and paces the room. "Uncle Tate paid your father to disappear. He told him if he ever contacted any of us again, he'd have him fired. His wife never knew about any of us. I mean, she knew he'd met someone else, but…"

"Wait a minute," Bridget interjects. "Joey grew up in Maine. Did dad not live with them?"

"He took the teaching job, but Joey's mom didn't want to relocate in the event he wasn't happy. He needed to teach for at least three years before being given any kind of job security. They decided that he'd live in Vermont and visit them on weekends and school breaks."

"That's just fucked up and a recipe for disaster," I state. "Obviously."

"What made him go back?"

"He had his reasons. But after he left, I cleared the house of any reminders of him. You girls were young enough that your memories of him would fade."

"Yeah, thanks for that," I sneer. "Neither of us were effected in any way because we felt abandoned by the first male figure in our lives."

"I'm sorry. I'm so sorry," my mother sobs. "Tate and Bobby swooped in and handled things while I wasn't able. Your aunt took care of you girls and Bobby stayed with me until I was able to function on my own."

"Okay, so again, why the fuck did you not end up with him then?"

"I turned him down."

"What?"

I'm now fuming over this ridiculous turn of events that has fucked up my entire life. Had my mother not turned down Bobby Knight, she'd had been with him and never would have met Tom. I never would have had to live with "Uncle" Jim and his shit.

"Why?' I ask, this time raising my voice to screech level. "Why in the fuck would you do that?"

My mother sits back down on the sofa and looks small and broken and I momentarily feel bad for her. "I couldn't do that to him. I couldn't strap him with a broken woman. He deserved better than that. Better than me. I was always the girl in Brook's shadows, I had to find who I was and get stronger. I needed to do that on my own. Prove that I was worthy of love from a man, not just sex."

My sister chokes and sends me a knowing glance. "Like mother, like daughter, like you said, huh, Court?"

"What?" my mother asks. "What is that supposed to mean?"

"Nothing. This isn't about me. This is about you and the fact that you turned Bobby Knight down and ruined my life."

"What are you talking about? Ruined *your* life? You hadn't even remembered any of this until now."

"No, I hadn't, but you know what I do remember? I remember "Uncle" Jim teaching me a lesson with my pants down over his knee."

My mother's eyes fly wide open and lock on mine again.

"What?" my sister asks.

I nod and share my embarrassing story with my mother and sister for the first time as they listen dumbfounded. They ask questions and tell me that they had no idea any of it had happened. We cry together. Then my mother losses her shit and says she's telling Bobby and having him sick Mac and his team on Tom and Jim.

"You know where he is?"

My mother nods. "Jim? Not personally, but I know where Tom is."

I make eye contact with Bridget and we silently speak to the other. Our connection is almost like that of twins. Our eyes tell each other that Ace and Elliot will be the first in line with their fists ready for battle. I doubt Bobby would be far behind.

After begging my mother to keep her silence until I can think for a day or two, Bridget and I walk her to her car and say our good-byes. She apologizes twenty more times, as she had done when I first shared my past, then cried again before taking off to head back to Connecticut.

"I'm ready to meet him" I state.

"Who?"

"Our brother. Call him, tell him we'll be there by morning."

"By morning?"

"Yes, we'll wait for the guys to be fast asleep in sex stupors then we'll sneak off. Your car's in the city, right?"

"Yeah, but Ace and Elliot…"

"There's something I need to tell you. You can't tell anyone. We'll talk on the drive. But I need you to trust me until then and not let on to Ace. Let me work out the details and I'll text you. Call Joey and set up a place for us to stay."

"I don't know about this," my sister says. "The guys are going to lose it."

I shrug. "Let me handle them. I need this, Bridge. Trust me on this one. I need space from Elliot to gain perceptive. You'll understand once I explain. Going to Maine and spending time with Joey, getting to know him and maybe the others, it might help me figure my shit out, okay?"

"Okay. I'll knock Ace out with sex so I can sneak away and call Joey then we'll leave. Just remember, when Ace and Elliot catch up to us, because they are going to find us, you're taking the punishment for the both of us."

28

Elliot wraps me in his arms for as long as the minutes he'd been gone. "Are you sure you're not ready to talk to me about it, baby?"

"I already told you, there's nothing else to say."

"Mmm hmmm" Elliot sighs because, rightly so, he doesn't believe me.

"Honestly, Elliott, what more do you want me to say? I told my mother and Bridge about Jim. They were both shocked and upset. I feel better at least knowing that neither of them had a clue. If they had, and hadn't helped me, that'd be a different story. We cried with my mom over her and Bobby, but that's ended well so there's nothing there to continue to cry over. It's all in the past."

"In the past" Elliot says, not sounding for one minute like he means or believes those words.

"Elliot," I warn. "You're not still making a thing over Jim, are you?"

Elliot growls at his name and changes the subject when my stomach growls. "You're hungry. You want me to whip you up something? I'm good with the leftovers, but I can make you something fresh. You women eat like birds."

I laugh at that because my mother and sister had housed that food. It's just that Elliot made enough for an army of men. Probably what he's used to, instead of three women, one of which, me, didn't touch a thing.

"I'm good with the leftovers too."

"Because you were too nervous to eat and didn't touch a thing, am I right?"

"Maybe, wiseass."

Elliot raises his brow. "Careful, sassy mouth."

I join him in laughing then agree to a plate of leftovers.

"Elliot, can I ask you something?"

"Anything."

"Can we…um, I kind of want to play after."

"Play?" he asks with a grin. "What, like Clue?"

I tilt my head and smirk at him. "No, not like Clue."

Elliot leans into my space and takes my chin in his thumb and finger. "Don't ever hesitate to ask me for what you need. Sexually or otherwise. And don't be shy about your sexual desires. Tell me what you want, and I'll make it better than you're imagining. Unless you want to be surprised, then…"

"I know what I want."

"That's my good girl. Of course, you do. Tell me."

"I'm not so sure you're going to go for this idea."

"Try me."

Elliot has no clue that I'm asking to have things played out like this because I need to wipe him out as much as possible so his Spidey-senses will be dulled, and I can sneak out of here and meet Bridget. Not that what I'm proposing isn't something that I want to do. It'll be hot. Sex with Elliot always is. Watching him relinquish control and come undone for me, that's going to be heady.

It doesn't take much convincing. Elliot says that as a reward for my openness, he'll play along. So here I am, after showering together, shoving whatever I can find in a bag and hiding it in the closet for as soon as he falls asleep, waiting to seduce him.

I send Bridget a quick text telling her I should be good to go by shortly after midnight. Then I remind her to delete our texts. The last thing I need is her to be the one to end up in the sex stupor with Ace reading our strand and warning Elliot before I'm even out the door.

"In here, Snowflake or would you like me in the playroom, Mistress?" Elliot asks with a sly grin, playing along with my need to be the one in control for this session.

"Ha, ha, that smart mouth is going to be a problem tonight, I see."

"Do what I do," he shrugs then changes his voice to a fake pleading. "Oh, but please don't make me eat your pussy for hours. That will be such torture."

I send him a glare with a hand on a hip. "Behave. I need this tonight. I was always the one in control, but I felt nothing. Not good, not bad, just…nothing. The handful of guys that tried to have the lead or play the BDSM game, didn't have a clue what they were doing. Ace," I clear my throat at the mention of his friend and my sister's boyfriend. "Um, Ace seemed like he knew how to control a woman. But he really only wanted my sister. Then Callan…"

Elliot growls. "You don't need to explain how they are in bed. I've seen them in action."

"What?"

"Another time, Adams. My dick is hard just thinking about your plans. Do you really want to talk about other men?"

"No."

"Good, here or the playroom?"

"Here" I say because I need him to pass out and stay asleep until I'm out of the building and on my way to Maine.

Elliot smirks his devious red-headed grin and stands in front of me. "Have at it, sweetheart. Give me your best."

I smile and nod then smirk my own grin to myself. As many times as I told him about my slutty past, Elliot doesn't seem to process what that level of experience has done for me. Maybe it's because he's used to me relaxing, submitting, and giving myself completely over to him. He doesn't think I have it in me to work his ass...well, more like his dick, over.

Elliot is in for the surprise of his life!

I gently place my hands on his shoulders and stretch up on my toes. This dominating thing does work much better when you're the bigger party, but whateves. I'm committed to seeing this through, if for no other reason than to wipe that look off his smug face, the arrogant asshole.

Then I remember that I have a lot more at stake here than that. I need this to work.

I kiss the tip of his perfect nose, the one that remains perfect after being broke a few times. The imperfection of it is what makes it just right.

"I'm only going to take control for a bit, Elliot, now be a good boy. If you can manage to behave and do what you're told, I might let you have your way with me after I'm done. That's if you're still able to...function," I laugh. "But if you don't obey me, well..." I leave the threat hanging in the air. "Now, get naked. Slowly while I watch."

Elliot raises an eyebrow and smirks as he reaches behind his head and makes a huge showing of stretching. He slowly reveals each ripple on his toned stomach one speed bump muscle at a time. He grasps his shirt at the nape of his neck and tugs it clear off his body. A man removing his shirt like this, and with his eyes glued to mine...hottest fucking sight ever.

Elliot smiles and runs his hand over his head.

"Your hair is growing in. Are you going to cut it into a style or..."

"Free balling it is usually my style. You're stalling."

I nod because that style sounds about right. Very Elliot Montgomery. "Oh, Elliot, just wait. Get your pants off."

"As you wish, Mistress."

Wiseass.

Elliot hooks his thumbs into the waistband of his track pants and makes another show of lowering them. Pulling them first over his erection to free himself with a groan. Of course he was commando. I'm not sure the man owns more than a pair of underwear.

His hand instinctively goes to his cock and he begins to stroke himself. The look of surprise on his face is one for the records when I roughly slap that hand away and reprimand him for his naughty behavior. "Don't make that mistake again," I warn. "You'll touch yourself only when told."

A smile morphs his face and he looks down as his cock bounces, throbbing for friction it's not going to see any time soon.

"Lie on the bed" I order then head into the closet to his Dom bag and retrieve a black leather blindfold. It's one I haven't seen before. Does the man receive a box a month of sex toys like my sister and I do of books?

As I approach the bed, I marvel at the majestic man lying in wake for me. He's perfection personified and I can't let this opportunity go to waste. Elliot needs to hear how I feel in this moment just like I need to hear it from him when he has me laid out and vulnerable. I lean down and take his lips with a purr escaping, tell him how I love the taste of his lips, then secure the leather blindfold to the back of his head.

He sighs and I visually see the tension leaving his body. His muscles go lax and his breathing evens out.

"That's a good boy," I praise and capture his lips again. "Open for me" I demand and push my tongue inside. Elliot's hips raise of their own volition and I use both hands to push them back down. I feel him smile into my kiss. It earns him a nip and tug to his plump bottom lip.

Elliot groans as I pull away.

"You're so fucking sexy, Elliot," I praise. "I love those divots right here, this male V" I say as I let my tongue explore the spots I praise.

His breathing begins to quicken and his cock bounces again, seeking out relief. It's a beautiful cock and I compliment it next, telling him how thick it is and how I love to run my tongue up the vein on the side.

"Do that now" he begs, his voice husky and desperate.

I chuckle. "Not just yet. First, let's talk about a few rules."

Elliot accepts with a nod and a deep sigh.

"I'm not going to tie you down. Instead, you're going to remain still and listen to what you're told."

As much as bondage lets the acting sub understand who is in control, releasing control and obeying what you're told, when you have the option not to, seems somehow more submissive.

"Roll over and you're not allowed to move without permission, understand?"

"Yes" he says, his voice sounding softer, sexy as fuck with the raspiness of an aroused male.

"It won't be easy, Elliot," I warn. "I'm going to tease and sensually pleasure you. But don't look for an orgasm any time soon. If you're close, you'd better warn me. You will not come without my asking for it, yes?"

"Yes, Adams."

"Good boy. Now, over" I demand and Elliot flips to his belly as I scoot back into the closet and drag his Dom bag back out with me. I reach inside again and this time I pull out a paddle. I place it on the bed with a thud so that he'll know exactly what he has in store.

"Are you sure you know what you're doing?" he asks, nerves on the edge of his voice. "Don't fucking graze my balls with that thing."

I hadn't planned on delivering my first blow without warning or preparing him, but after that little demand of his...

Smack.

My hand slaps his ass. Hard.

"Shh," I demand. "I'll graze your balls every time if I so wish and you'll thank me after every single one. Yes?"

Elliot moans as my hand cups him between his shoulder width legs and squeezes just shy of painfully.

"Yes, I'm sorry."

I think he might just be playing along with me, not actually this easy to overpower, but then again, his body language is speaking for itself. Elliot is a strong man, always in control. This might possibly be the first time anyone has ever allowed him to give up the power and control and just relax. Accept pleasure, albeit mixed with a twinge of pain.

He needs some tender loving care before I bring out the big guns, so I trail my fingers, just the tips then my nails, across his body. Elliot's breathing increases and he moves his hips in a rhythm to gain friction from the bed.

"I wouldn't dry hump the bed, Elliot," I warn. "Remember, if you come, you're going to be in trouble."

He chuckles at my warning and the fact that I would accuse him of coming from a few seconds of dry humping a mattress.

We'll see.

I reach for the massage oil and rub it in my hands. I begin with his broad shoulders and he groans as I begin to release the years of pent up tension he's holding there. Until this very moment I hadn't realized just how tightly strung he was. It makes me question why. What is he dealing with that I don't know? All the more reason for me to have a little space to figure things out and gain some perspective.

I circle the many fading scars on his arms and back, focusing on one I have always wanted to ask him about, clearly a bullet wound. "What happened?"

Elliot groans. "Don't stop Ads, feels so good, baby," he begs. "Took a bullet in duty."

I suck in my breath because the thought of Elliot being shot freaks me out.

"I'm fine," he explains. "Flesh wound because Lyons and Black got their asses into deep shit, their dicks were buried deeper, by the way, inside the pussies of two commanding officers. I had to save their fucking asses. They, of course, didn't end up with a bullet in them, but..."

I feel him growing tense again from the talk of his time in the trenches, so I shift gears and compliment his body again. "I love your arms. It's called arm porn and you could be a star."

That earns me a deep laugh and his renewed relaxation.

"You're adorable and way too good for my ego."

I shrug. "Want a full body massage?"

"Does it come with a happy ending?"

I wish I knew because in a moment like this, I'd say that Elliot and I definitely have one waiting. But...then he'll bark some order at me, reminding me this is just some yearlong contract we're fulfilling, even if we've both admitted to having feelings for the other, and then I'm not so sure. Before falling for him, I wouldn't have questioned the intentions of any man I was with. But that was because my heart was never in the equation. Now that it is, I need to protect it. If all this is to Elliot is some game, some contract he agreed to for a year of free sex and a way to keep his father off his back, then New Year's Eve is going to gut me. But I will walk away.

I'll never become my mother from her younger years.

The man I'm with needs to love and respect me. It's taken me until now to get to that space in my head, but now that I'm here, there's no turning back. My leaving in a few hours should teach Elliot a lesson and snap him out of his Dom macho bullshit. If not, Damian and Compatible Companions can shove their contract and their money up their asses.

I have two weeks before classes start to get Elliot to confess his true feelings and decide if he wants an equal partner that can be kinky as fuck in the bedroom and work his cock over the way I'm about to or not. If he chooses or not, then he can ask the company for a replacement. And fuck right off.

When I hear Elliot moan, I'm snapped out of my head. I realize I've been massaging him like an expert Swedish woman delivering a deep tissue massage. I guess I was rubbing my frustration out on him, literally. He seems to be enjoying it though, so I finish up with his legs then resume my original plan.

Elliot remains laying face-down on the bed, face pressed to the mattress. I nudge him to raise his hips so that I can shove a pillow under them. "Now," I warn. "No humping the pillow. We wouldn't want you to come and never get to the good parts, would we?"

"Coming is the best part, baby" he quips.

I laugh. He does have a point.

"In good time. Isn't that what you always tell me?"

"Much more fun that way."

I growl and tap his hips again, prompting him to shift so I can arrange the pillow the way I need it. "Mmm, well, it's my way tonight. Deal."

His hips and bottom are now elevated on a few pillows and his balls look heavy as they hang from his body. He gasps when I run a fingernail across them. "Jesus" he moans.

I spank him a few times and enjoy each flinch, each time he clenches his tight ass. After I've turned his bottom a nice shade of red and he's breathing heavy and thrusting his hips just slightly, thinking I don't notice, I add a little more massage oil to my palms and sooth his abused flesh with it.

Big circles over each side. Then smaller, until I'm only trailing my finger across his skin. When I trace his slit with it, Elliot groans. "Fuck, Adams, I..."

"Shh, it's okay. Relax. If you want me to stop, just tell me."

Elliot nods but makes no attempt to halt my finger's exploration. With the massage oil coating my skin, it slides between his cheeks with ease. Up and down until I find his entrance and circle it. "Have you ever..."

"No, but that feels way too fucking good to ask you to stop. Go easy, though?"

"Course. Yellow if I need to slow down, red for me to stop, right?"

Elliot moans.

"Words" I demand like he's done to me numerous times when I've been unable to speak.

"Yeah," he breathes. "Yellow and red. We're good. Ahh. Holy fuck!" he moans.

I smile to myself I've never done this to a man before, anyone for that matter. The thought never would have crossed my mind, but enough men have had their fun with me like this, so I know how it feels. If done properly, anal play can be amazing. Too bad, most of my experiences were painful and awkward. It wasn't until Callan Black showed me the pleasures of the dark side that I knew it could feel good.

Pushing all thoughts of Callan and the men that came before Elliot out of my mind, I focus on the responses of his body to guide me. He's relaxed and panting now, he's enjoying the stimulation to his anus, so I decide to increase the pressure and push in...just the tip. It reminds me of one of the first quips he said on the island. What was it? With him, it would always be about more than just the tip?

"You want more? You told me once, with you, it would always be about more than just the tip."

I let my finger sink in to the first knuckle and Elliot grips the sheet in his hands while a low rumbling growl escapes him.

"Okay?"

"Amazing," he sighs. "Keep going."

I let the massage oil dribble down his crack, the lubrication of it allows my finger to make its way in to the next knuckle. Elliot tenses then heaves in a deep breath and settles into the pleasure that follows the first shock of the invasion.

"I'm going to move my finger now," I state as I begin to let it slip out. "In," I push back inside his dark cavern. "And out," I pull out. "Until you can't take anymore."

"Fuckkkkk!"

I continue to move my finger in a slow rhythm until he's accustomed to the new sensation of fullness coursing through his most private of spots. Then I let my other hand join in the fun. I trail a finger gently to his heavy balls and begin to massage his taint with my thumb.

"Yes!" he cries out as his hips thrust, rubbing his dick into the pillow. "So good, Adams. I can come like this."

A wicked laugh escapes me. "I'm sure you'd like to, but no one has said you can, so..."

"I might not be able to..."

"Hold your load? No, you'll hold off for me. You wouldn't want to be denied my pussy for the rest of the night now, would you?"

Elliot emits a growl followed by a moan of deep frustration and I know it's time to remove my finger and move on or he's not going to hold off and our night's fun isn't going to provide the result I need.

I lean down and whisper how much I enjoy playing with his ass, how much it turns me on, and how I'd like to do it again, but for now, we need to move on.

Elliot protests and begs me to continue, to make him come, then do it again during round two.

I laugh. Silly ginger, treats are for later. Now is the time to suffer through a little orgasm control in a nice teasing session like he so enjoys doing to me. Payback is a bitch and her name is Adams. "Roll over and lay on the bed on your back," I demand. "Let me see how hard you are for me."

Elliot flips faster than I thought possible and instantly, without being told, places his hands under his head and says, "I'll keep them here."

"Good boy," I praise as I claim his mouth. He tastes like sin and, dare I say, love. The trust he just gave me to do what I just did was probably big for him. "You took that well."

"That was...we're definitely doing that again."

I laugh. "We'll see" I say, noncommittedly as I begin to trace my fingertips everywhere but where he wants them.

I blow chilly air onto his genitals and smile when they tighten closer to his body.

"So full and heavy baby," he sighs. "Need to fucking come soon, they're killing me."

I laugh again. "Are you fourteen? You're really going to try to cry blue balls to me?"

"Yes!" he states. "They fucking hurt. Please."

I chuckle. His balls do look heavy and I'm sure they're uncomfortable, but he's a strong man. I know he can take a little more, so I use gentle, light touches on his erogenous zones to keep him extremely aroused without gratification. I stroke the insides of his thighs, I lick around his nipples, and even once up that vein in his cock I love so much. Then I decide to take this edging to the next level. "I expect you to tell me when you're getting close to orgasm. If you don't, I'll make sure you don't come at all the next round."

A groan from Elliot with a nod of his head is all I need to start working his cock. I use my hands, both wrapped around his thick shaft, one atop the other, while I stroke him up and down. The massage oil allowing me a smooth glide while I hold him firmly. "So thick," I compliment him. "I love the way your cock feels inside my tight pussy. Fills me up so perfectly."

"Adams," he warns. "Baby, fuck...I'm getting there."

I slow my strokes to a snail's pace and Elliot groans in protest then his entire body jerks when my thumb brushes around the head of his cock. I rub it back and forth on the underside, his favorite spot, the spot that pushes him over the edge. But I don't let him fall. I wait until he's moaning and thrusting into my hand, then I pull my hand away and watch.

His head thrashes side to side, his hips thrust as his cock seeks friction from anywhere. Without it, his orgasm begins to subside as his cock bounces on his toned stomach and a pool of pre-come puddles into his belly button.

"That was close, Elliot. Now, try to behave" I admonish.

This round, I get comfy on the bed and take him into my warm mouth. I take him once again to the edge of an orgasm, my tongue swirling on each up stroke, teeth nipping, cheeks hollowing with my deep suction. But then, like with my hand, I pull back before he gets too close.

"Fuck," he cries. "I can't hold off much longer, Ads. That was...I was right there."

"I can see that," I state in a wickedly evil tone and grasp his balls in my palm. When he groans, I tug then let my nails gently run across the puckered skin. Elliot shivers and raises his hips to me. "These are so heavy, you were right, baby. So full of all that come that I won't let out."

"Please. Fuck, Adams, I need to shoot my load. Please" he begs.

I torture him time and time again, switching between a hand job and sucking him off, but I never let him get to the pinnacle of his pleasure. His cock is angry, dripping from the tip and bouncing on his belly. Elliot thrashes around but he never reaches for his cock to get himself off. He remains on his back, hands clasped behind his head.

I know he's almost to that magical point of no return when he pants and makes that sexy sound of his. It's a groan mixed with a growl. He'll only require a couple light strokes to get him near the edge this time, and I enjoy torturing him with the anticipation of his pleasure.

"You'll come when I decide you can. Maybe we should call it a night and I should deny your orgasm altogether. Maybe I won't let you come until tomorrow."

"No fucking way," Elliot protests. "I can't stay like this."

"Or maybe we should move into intercourse. You want to feel the tight walls of my hot pussy around this?" I ask as I grasp his cock again and gently stroke.

"Yes, please. I need to fuck you so fucking bad."

I laugh. "Not just yet. I think first, maybe I need to come. You're not to get off until you're told, understand?" I ask as I stand and remove my clothes then return to the bed and position myself on top of him, my pussy hovering over his face while I face his lower half.

"Jesus fucking Christ!" he mumbles as I lower to cover his face with my core.

He doesn't hesitate to devour my pussy. Knowing the pressure and speed I like; Elliot goes at me like a starving man having his first meal in months. I grind my hips onto his face to help myself get there quickly. This might be about withholding his pleasure, but it's not about waiting on mine.

"I'm going to come quick," I warn. "Make me come on your face, Elliot."

Elliot had left his hands behind his head like a good boy until now, so I don't scold him when his fingers touch my pussy to open me for better access. His tongue runs my slit then sinks inside and moves in and out, fucking me until I'm moving my hips, riding his tongue. Knowing that I'm close, he pulls back and clasps his mouth onto my clit and sucks until I shatter and explode while hovering on his face.

Elliot groans through my orgasm and the vibrations keep the spasms coming. By the time my body settles, and I go to shift, I'm worried I may have suffocated him.

Elliot heaves in a deep breath as I move down his body and grasp his ankles for leverage.

"I won't be able to hold off once I feel your wet pussy around me, Adams. I need to fucking come right now."

"I know, no holding off."

I lower my pussy to his cock and grasp it at the base, easing it in. With the length and girth of Elliot, there's no other way. He slides in easily enough after the last hour of my own excitement followed by a mind-blowing orgasm and we both release a satisfied sigh when he settles in to the root.

"Tight and wet, so fucking hot, Adams. This sight," he laughs. "Fuckkkkk! Watching you ride my cock like this, is enough to make me come."

I lay flat on his body; my hands grasping his ankles for purchase and grind my hips as I fuck him. Elliot returns his hands to their original spot behind his head and relaxes in to watch the show playing out right in front of his eyes.

"Your pussy looks so fucking good. Your dripping down my cock and swallowing it up. Shit, fucking amazing."

I fuck him like that for a few minutes, grinding back and forth, until I feel him throb. His cock hardens and he emits a guttural moan. I know he's close, but I'm not ready just yet to let him come, so I climb off just as his breathing hits panting level.

"Nooo," he protests. "Adams!" he bellows.

I laugh a little as I reposition myself, knowing this will either take him into heaven or end with his orgasm being denied. And I can't deny him because I need him to explode so hard that he finds the deepest sleep he can. I need him sleeping like a baby when I grab my stuff and sneak out. So, I tease him to ramp him up, but I have no intentions of not letting him come.

"I'm going to ride your long cock, up and down, you're getting ten strokes," I warn. "If you don't come by then," I shrug. "You'll be going to sleep tonight with a hard-on and your dick slowly dripping your release."

"Fuck, no! I'll come within five strokes the way your pussy fucks me, Snowflake. Now, you've had your fun. Make us both come. Now! Or I'm going to flip you over, spank the shit out of that ass for the last hour of torture, then fuck you into the mattress."

With the command in his voice ramping my pussy back up to the pinnacle, I stand on the bed, feet shoulder width apart, Elliot's body between them.

"Oh shit!" he smiles. "Yeah, baby. That's my girl. Ride my cock until I fucking come so deep inside you, it won't drip out for a fucking week."

I lower to his body, my hand on his base again to guide him back inside. I don't go to my knees though, I squat. Perching on my feet, I slide to his base then raise to the tip.

"Five at the most, you want to count, or should I?"

"You" I demand.

I sink back down then back up and smirk when Elliot says, "Two."

"Just the tip?" I tease and clench my pussy tight around him.

Elliot hisses. "All of it. About to fucking come" he grunts, and I can tell it's taking every ounce of his restraint to not thrust and take over.

I sink back down and stay still while Elliot tries to moderate his breathing to hold off until I'm with him.

"Hurry up," he demands. "I'm done."

I grind front and back to rub one out and it doesn't take long for me to knock on the door of my second orgasm. "I'm going to come."

"Fuck me hard, Adams. I'm going too."

I raise up and down, I think Elliot keeps counting, but who the fuck knows because all I can hear is the blood rushing through my ears as my orgasm rips through my body. Then Elliot's animalistic grunts turn to moans, deep and pained until he roars and explodes inside me.

"Nine!" he screams. His face contorts into a painful grimace then a satisfied smile breaks across his face as his body twitches and he comes, his cock spurting and throbbing deep inside me, filling me with his hot release.

When he catches his breath, he reaches for my hips and pulls me down to his body then turns me around. "That was the best fucking orgasm of my life. Get back on me, I need to come again. Easy this time, though."

I know how sensitive his cock is after an orgasm, so I smile and consider torturing him more, but then I change my mind for my own comfort. My pussy is sore from the fucking it just gave out. I know a slow, sensual orgasm will feel much better than another like the last.

Elliot sits up and sink his hands into my hair and pulls me to his lips with another moan and a raise of his hips. I feel his cock twitch and harden before it's had a chance to grow flaccid. We kiss and I feel the love from his mouth, his tongue. It comes from his heart and I know I'll need to remember this moment in the days to come.

"Elliot," I sigh into the kiss. "That was…"

"So good," he says, his lips on mine. "That I'll let you do that to me anytime you want."

"Mmm," I sigh as he slowly rocks my hips on his cock, tilts his hips so his tip runs across that most sensitive spot inside me.

"One more, baby then we'll sleep until next week. Nice and easy this time. Make love to me."

A tear slips down my cheek and Elliot reaches up and swipes it away. He's never said that to me before. Does he mean it? Make love. Share our bodies while we share our hearts, our souls?

"Elliot, I-I…"

"Shh, one day at a time. I'm trying here, Adams. Really, I am, baby, but I got shit going on in my head too that I don't understand. We have a year to figure it out, though, alright? Let's just enjoy ourselves for now. You're mine and that's all that matters."

And there it is again. The contract. The fact that he owns me. But then we make love slowly and come together with our lips on one another's and I'm more confused than ever.

"I'm tired" I state as he slips from my body, his dick finally content enough to grow flaccid.

"Me too," he chuckles. "You wore me out. You're a real hard-ass when you want to be. Let's grab a quick shower then crash. I'll make you breakfast in the morning then maybe we can go ice skating or some other romantic shit in the snow."

I nod, knowing I'll be in the snow alright. Just not in New York. And Elliot isn't going to be having a fun romantic day tomorrow. He's going to wake up pissed and ready to spank my ass red.

29

"When do you think they'll figure out where we are?" Bridget asks.

I shrug noncommittedly because I'm not sure how to answer my sister. She's looking to be comforted because she knows that Elliot and Ace are going to show up mad as hornets with Callan throwing gas on their bee nests. I'm pretty sure the guys are going to figure out we're missing five minutes after opening their eyes. After my sister's previous disappearance, I'm guessing Callan will have our location on lockdown before we even arrive in Maine.

"Let's not worry about that yet, Bridge. They're going to be pissed, there's nothing we can do about it now. But honestly, Elliot can suck a dick and fuck off."

My sister side eyes me then asks, "Did something happen between you and Elliot? I know mom asked you, but you never really said much."

I remain silent for a few minutes pondering if I should tell her. I know I'm not supposed to tell anyone about Compatible Companions or our contract, but this is my sister we're talking about here and I need someone else's perspective on the situation, so I heave in a deep sigh and turn to face the window for my embarrassing confession. Unable to see the expression on my sister's face I admit, "I'm his hired whore."

Thinking I'm being overdramatic, Bridget, with her hand on my leg, laughs and says, "Just because you broke down and are fucking him, doesn't make you his whore."

Oh, if she only knew.

"Well, he paid a company a shit ton of money to have me for the next year. Damian claims it'll be our wedding gift, but…"

"I don't know what you're saying right now. Did Elliot ask you to marry him?"

"No."

"Does this have something to do with that club of Damian's they all belong to then?"

"The Society?" I ask. "I mean, no but kind of, I guess. Who belongs?"

"Only confusing me more, sis. But all of them. Callan, Elliot, Ace."

I heave in another deep breath and go for broke. "Yeah, well, that makes sense. So here's the deal. You can never, and I mean *never* tell anyone. Not Ace when the shit hits the fan, definitely not mom or Bobby, and when you see Damian or Syd," I pull in a breath. "You can't even look at him weird. Understand?"

"No, not at all, but tell me."

"Damian bought out this app company that matches people up with similar interests."

"Oh, that's cool. Like a dating site?"

"Sort of. It's called Compatible Companions, it's more than a dating site, though, Bridge."

My sister glances in my direction before returning her eyes to the highway we're soaring down. I turn in my seat to face my sister even though she's concentrating on the road. "Okay, listen, don't flip out."

Bridget sends me a glare then looks back out the windshield. "Okayyy."

"I joined the company before I knew Damian was involved and set up a profile. I wanted the money so we didn't need to bother mom and Bobby for it and could go back to school and try this time. Get out of their house and their way so Bobby wouldn't bail on mom."

"Bobby's not bailing on mom."

"Yeah, I've sort of figured that out now," I take a sip from my dragon fruit water and clear my throat. "But I had already signed the year-long contract by then. It's ironclad and I can't get out of it. When Damian saw my name in the system, he flipped the fuck out on me then went behind my back and set me up with my match."

"So you're dating Elliot because he's your match?"

"Sort of."

"Did you know that on the island? Were you lying to me that whole time?"

"I never lied to you, Bridge. And no, that was an amazing coincidence on the island. I was scheduled to meet my match outside of Stone Towers at the stroke of midnight on New Year's Eve. When I went out there, I was early and thought about running. I mean, what was Damian honestly going to do, charge me the twenty-thousand-dollar penalty?"

"What?" Bridget chokes.

"Yeah, it's an expensive app."

Bridget laughs. "I'd say. I'm still lost. So, you joined this dating site, that's not a dating site and Damian matched you and Elliot?"

"It's a companion site. Elliot signed my contract, so he *owns* me for a year. Damian asked him to do it because he trusts him and knows I'll at least be safe with him. He couldn't let me out of the contract, even though he wanted to. This was the best he could come up with on short notice. The contract is pretty clear about what Elliot wants and what I agreed to. We live together and I promise to be faithful and obey his sexual desires. I must accept the consequences if I disobey him. Everyone's contract is different to fit their sexual desires, mine was written for a woman who wanted to submit and be controlled by a powerful, dominant man."

Bridget looks at me with a raised eyebrow. "You could have just joined The Society and asked to train as a sub, you know? Ace and I are in a program they offer there."

"Really?" I ask. "Hmm, a program?"

"Later. Finish your story. I still don't get why you thought you needed to…oh! The Jim thing?" she asks as recognition dawns.

"Kind of. It's been fucking with my head for years. Kyle leaving, Tom and Jim, then in my head I lumped Bobby with them and panicked that he was about to bolt on mom. I couldn't watch her fall apart again. The coping mechanism I developed, the guys, Bridget, it wasn't working for me anymore and I needed to make a change."

"Okay, so you joined this company then we went to the island and you fell for Elliot. You came back and found out that a computer system, I'm guessing its success rate is up there, matched the two of you. So what's the problem?"

"Elliot. I'm in love with him."

"And…"

"And he *owns* me for a year. He's mentioned it one too many times lately. I mean, I get we need to play along in public and all, but not in private, you know?"

Bridget shakes her head but never turns to look at me. "Ace is a Dom, too, Court. We might not belong to that app, but he likes to be the one in control."

"I get that. That's fine, if Elliot was just being all Dom-like, fine. It's the ownership thing that's getting to me. He doesn't need to bring up the contract and the fact that he's the boss of me all the time."

Bridget chuckles.

"What?"

"He's giving you exactly what you asked for when you signed up with the company."

"What? No! I mean…" I sigh. "Oh, fuck. Christ, I'm fucked up in the head, huh?"

"Nah, but you need to figure shit out and quick because I give them until nightfall to be in Maine."

"I don't like the ownership shit anymore, that's all, okay? My feelings for Elliot are growing and turning into…more and I don't like that he's still acting like all we are is a year-long game to him."

"Tell him that. But I don't think that's how he feels. I think he's trying to give you what you asked for. Ace says that he's never seen Elliot happier or with a woman for more than a quick fuck."

I send her a warning glance.

"Sorry," my sister apologizes. "But Ace said that Elliot must really like you."

"Really *like* me? What are we, in middle school?"

"I don't know, you know what I mean. Maybe being away for a bit is a good idea. Clear your head and figure it out. I can call Ace when we get to the bed and breakfast and explain. See if he can hold Elliot off."

I lift my chin at my sister. "I'll turn our phones on and see if they've woken up yet."

Big mistake.

Gingerbread Man: *WTF?*

Gingerbread Man: *Where the fuck are you?*

Gingerbread Man: *I swear to fucking God, Adams, your ass…*

Gingerbread Man: *Not answering me? Guess what, sweetheart? Callan has you two on lockdown. Get ready! Warn the flight risk with you that her man is as pissed off as I am.*

Gingerbread Man: *You're making this so much worse on yourself and your ass by ignoring me.*

Gingerbread Man: *I have my bag with me, want to know what's in there?*

I smile at first because I forgot that I had him saved in my phone as "Gingerbread Man". Then I read the messages and a frown covers my face. Of course Callan already found us. Not sure how when our phones are off. But then a thought crosses my mind. "Hey, um, Bridge…how many bags did you bring?"

"Ah, my Kate Spade, a bag with my toiletries, and then the one large rolling suitcase. Why?"

"Could Ace have planted a bug somewhere to track you?"

"What?"

"Well, we're moving, and our phones are off. We haven't used our credit cards or stopped anywhere. How else would they already know where we are?" I look around for a minute. "Where are we?"

"Just crossed over into New Hampshire like three seconds ago."

"Shit!" I swear as I see that Elliot's texts began not ten minutes after we pulled out of the parking garage of Stone Towers. Which means, going by the time of the text when he stated they already knew where we were, they've been tracking us since we hit I-95. So, if my calculations are correct, Elliot, Ace, and Callan are somewhere in Massachusetts by now.

I reach for my sister's Kate Spade and start rummaging through it.

"What are you looking for? I have gum in the glove compartment."

I don't answer her until I find what is in a zippered pocket she never uses or looks inside. "A-Ha!" I exclaim.

"What?"

"Ace bugged your bag."

"He did what?"

"He planted a device to track you. I'm sure he did it after your first escape, well, really your second if you count the island thing. Wow, you really are a flight risk."

"Me? The first and third were your fault."

I shrug. "Yeah, well...semantics."

My phone scares the shit out of me when it rings, and I toss it into the air. "Fuck!" I reach between the seats to fish it out then hit the silence button without checking the screen to see who it is. I know it's Elliot by our shared Compatible Companions ringtone. That's confirmed a second later when my sister's phone, that I turned on not a minute before, starts its own annoying shrill.

"That's Ace's ringtone," she states. "Maybe we should just turn around."

"No! We're going to Joey's," I state with confidence I don't feel. "We're a bit ahead of them. If you'd drive a little faster, we might be able to get to the bed and breakfast and talk the owners into not telling them we're there."

I roll down the window as my sister says, "You think they'll let that stop them?"

I toss the tracking device out the window and smirk at my sister. "Nope. But that just made them finding us a little bit harder though. Now, step on it, Thelma."

"Didn't that end with them both dying or something?"

30

We pull into the city limits of Falls Village, Maine just as the sleepy town is waking up for breakfast. Falls Village is at the epitome of your upscale New England town and where my newfound half-brother resides with his wife. My sister spends the trip filling me in on Joey and Mallory and the quaint town they're living in. It has under five thousand year-round residents, but many affluent New Yorkers come to spend their extended weekends and escape into nature here. Hopefully my sister and I will be able to avoid three specific New Yorkers for a day or two.

Bridget tells me all about Falls Village. It's located on the coast, a picturesque harbor town for art lovers, foodies, and charm seekers. It was once a small fishing village, but now it's the go-to summer retreat for city dwellers looking for soft, sandy beaches. Thankfully, it's January and only the year-round residents, like Joey and Mallory, are here. Unfortunately, in a small town like this, our presence is going to be known immediately. And those three huge men that are trailing our asses, won't go unnoticed for long, especially if they roll into town with their guns blazing. By guns, I mean those arms of theirs, and I smile when I remember telling Elliot that his fell into the category of arm porn.

Once Elliot, Ace, and Callan arrive, it won't be more than a day before we're the talk of the town. Bridget and I consider warning Joey, but my sister suggests that we wait and see how things play out first. She mentions that Joey seemed distracted when she spoke to him about this trip. He mentioned something about he and Mallory arguing but when Bridget told him we didn't have to come; Joey had said it wasn't a big deal and told us to get there as quickly as possible. He said he was looking forward to meeting me and didn't want to wait any longer.

Now, as my sister pulls the car into our bed and breakfast, I wonder how sane of an idea this really is. The house is amazing, sure, but maybe bringing my shit to a brother I've never met, isn't something I should be doing. Maybe he has his own shit to deal with and the last thing he needs is another sister bugging him with her drama.

The bed and breakfast has cute dormers and is surrounded by water on three sides. There are four acres of land, a deep-water dock, boats and wildlife, and views for days of what I can only predict will be spectacular sunrises and sunsets. But its best feature is the view of the nearby Lighthouse. I squeal and bounce on the balls of my feet as we exit the car and head up the front wrap-around porch.

"Joey just texted me that he'll be here any minute. He said Mallory couldn't make it though."

"Oh, that's too bad," I say. "I was looking forward to meeting her."

"Yeah, something seems off with them. He changed every time her name came up when we were out for coffee in the city."

"Hmm, maybe relationship issues are genetic."

"Relationships are hard for everyone, Court."

I shrug as we enter the living room/lobby with our bags in tow and make our way into the house.

A sweet older woman comes from a door that must lead into the kitchen. She's wearing an old-school apron and wipes her flour covered hands on the front before calling to who must be her husband slumped over sleeping in an armchair. "Henry," she scolds. "Oh dear, wake up, our guests are here and we've lots to do before we can head out."

"Head out?" Bridget asks.

"Well, yes, dear," the woman says then extends her hand remembering her New England manners. "I'm Betty, that's my husband, Henry. We own the place. I'm guessing you two are Courtney and Bridget, right?"

"Yes," I say. "I'm Courtney."

"Joey told us all about you. If it had been anyone else asking to stay, we'd had said no as we were heading out of town."

"Going to the son's for the storm" Henry reports.

"Storm?"

"Horrible Nor'easter coming in later tonight," Henry shares. "But Joey vouched for you two, so you're okay to stay as long as you need. Joey's a good boy. That Mallory," Betty tsks. "Anyway, I've stocked the fridge and put some meals in the freezer for you."

"How long are you going to be gone?" I ask. "What if someone else shows up wanting to stay?"

Henry and Betty have a great laugh over that one.

"House is not getting rented during a Nor'easter, that's for sure," Henry states. "We were shocked when Joey called and woke us in the middle of the night. But you girls will be fine here, don't you worry your pretty little heads over anything. Plow guy will be along, and Joey will check in. His best friend lives right next door. Name's Justin. He's got himself a new girlfriend, real sweetie that one. And her little boy, T.J, he's a character. They'll watch out for you."

"Oh, yeah, okay" I state with a glare to my sister and a wave for the elderly couple.

Without anyone at the front desk, this can go one of two ways. One, the guys won't be able to get...yeah, change that. This can only go one way. The guys will be barging in as soon as they arrive.

We spend the next hour avoiding the inevitable by keeping our phones turned off while we wait for Joey to arrive and Betty and Henry to hightail it out of snow country.

Bridget and I settle into the two adjoining bedrooms and plan to sleep with the door open because even as adults, in a big old empty house, we're babies. That leaves the master bedroom on the main floor empty and the two other additional rooms to rent on the top level. Before they leave, Henry and Betty give us a tour and tell us everything they can think of about the house and what to do in cases of emergencies. Then they leave out the front door and wave to a man pulling into the circular driveway.

"That's Joey!" my sister says as she jumps up and down like a child seeing Santa at the mall for the first time. "Joey!" she calls. "Joey's here!"

I watch as she runs down the front steps and lets the handsome man, who's image brings back memories in my head, hug her tightly in his arms while he kisses her cheek then sets her down and turns his attention onto me. I hiss in air at his stare because, I may not have seen Kyle Collins in years, but I knew I was looking at his clone. Actually, Kyle was probably not much older than Joey is now last time I saw him.

Joey approaches me slowly with an extended hand and his deep timbre says, "Hey little sis, what's the matter, not going to hug your big brother?"

"Oh, ah..um..." I stutter as Joey lifts me into his arms while my sister squeals in delight.

Someone must suggest getting out of the cold because the next thing I know, we're inside the warm living space seated on the plush sofa with coffees in hand and Joey is talking about our sisters and how they won't be able to meet us until the storm blows through.

"They're dying to meet you two but with school and everything..."

I interrupt to ask, "How old are they?"

"Jordon is nineteen and Jenny is eighteen."

"Oh, your mom liked the J names, huh?"

Joey giggles. "I guess. Jenny is finishing high school in a few months and Jordon just went back to Bowdoin a few days ago."

"Have you told your parents yet?"

"Uh," Joey glances at Bridget and they share a moment. "Bridget and I spoke about waiting until you were ready for our dad to know first, but, um...yeah, sorry. I told them."

"You look like him."

Bridget's head spins to me. "You remember what dad looks like?"

I nod and point at Joey. "Exactly like that."

Joey nods. "Yeah, I get that a lot, but I'm nothing like him. I swear. Mallory and I..." He cringes when he says his wife's name and trails off. I make a little mental note to find out why everyone, even her husband, appears to have a bad taste in their mouth after saying her name.

"Where is Mallory?"

"Oh," Joey stalls for an answer. "She's not here right now."

Bridget and I nod, not wanting to pry into something Joey clearly doesn't want to divulge.

"So," Joey says. "Bridget told me that you have a boyfriend. What's his name?"

"Elliot," I shrug. "But it's complicated."

A strange scowl crosses Joey's features and he asks, "Elliot? Oh, ah, yeah well, if he needs your big brother to kick his ass, you let me know."

Bridget and I laugh. I mean, Joey is a big guy, looks like he takes care of himself and works out, but Elliot? Elliot looks like a trained killing machine in comparison.

"I'll let you know."

"The guys didn't want to come with you and meet me?"

"Work," I blurt. "They'll try to join us in a few days if we decide to stay longer."

We spend the next hour or so sharing tidbits about our lives before Joey glances at his vibrating phone and stands, saying, "That's Mallory, she's not going to make it home with the storm and all, but I'd better head on home before the roads get any worse. You girls sure you don't want to come with me? We've got the space."

"Nah," I say. I've picked up on something between Joey and his wife and the last thing I want is to be involved in any more relationship drama. "We'll be fine here. We've no reason to leave, no place to go. The kitchen is stocked, and we have heat. We'll just hunker down and play games until the storm passes. Maybe we'll come by for dinner once we can get out, okay?"

"Yeah, yeah, sure," Joey says with his hand going to the nape of his neck like I remember Kyle doing when he was agitated with something. Usually Bridget and I or our mom. "Call me if you need anything. I told Justin to watch out for you guys. I can't wait for you to meet him."

I nod and stand to walk to the door with Joey and Bridget. Joey pulls us each in for a group hug then kisses each of us on our temples before jumping down the stairs and sliding in the snow all the way to his car.

We stand at the door and wave until he's out of sight, then Bridget and I head back inside to hang out and watch the snow fall as we wait for Ace, Callan, and Elliot to arrive.

After a day of playing games and sitting by the window, Bridget and I get the house locked up for the night. She locks the front door and double checks the back while I make my way around the bottom level, turning off the main lights but leaving on a few in case we should need to see in the dark.

I didn't realize how tired I was until my head hits the pillow of the king-sized bed in my room and I conk out. Lack of sleep the night prior and traveling finally takes its toll and I'm in dreamland before I know it.

In my dreams, Elliot is there and we're playing in the snow, having a snowball fight. The cold flakes fall on my nose and he runs and tackles me, taking me to the ground while protecting my fall with his big body and nuzzling my neck. We hear a crashing sound from afar and laugh when we see a heap of snow fall from the roof where I'd been standing before he'd chased me further into the yard.

Then I feel the weight of his heavy body on mine and I realize my dream feels too real to only be in my head. As I begin to process that I'm being held down in real-time, I struggle to free myself of my attacker.

I kick at the big body perched on mine. Just before my brain tells me to scream, to call out to Bridget for help or to warn her to get out of the house, my mouth is covered, and I lock eyes with my assailant.

Very familiar eyes.

"Shh, don't flip the fuck out, Adams. It's me. I'll let you go as soon as I know you're calm and awake. Look at me, baby. It's me."

I shake my head and Elliot eases his weight from my body then removes his hand from my mouth as I hear the door between my room and Bridget's close, then the click of the lock fills the air. And my eyes widen in fear for my sister as Elliot smirks at me. "Ace is not any happier than I am. Your flight-risk sister is about to get her ass lite up. I certainly hope it's warranted, and this little trip isn't your doing," he shrugs. "Either way, I'm spanking you too."

"What if it is? My fault, I mean. What if it was my idea?"

Elliot smirks again then says, "Ever have angry sex, Adams?" he asks as the sound of a bed in the next room hitting the wall fills our ears. "Sounds like your sister is having the experience right now. Angry sex can be hot. Fast, passionate, rough."

With every husky word of that description, my pussy gets wetter and my mind starts to soften on Elliot. Maybe I was overreacting to the whole contract thing. I mean, he must care about me to come all this way in a blizzard.

"No," I say with a shiver and sassiness dripping off the one syllable word. "I have not had angry sex, but I am pissed off at you, so…"

"It makes orgasm denial feel like a massage, sweetheart" he says as he blows into his hands then scoots me over to climb under the blankets. "It's freezing in this house. Did you turn the heat down before going to bed?"

"No, maybe Bridget did."

Elliot reaches down with one hand and releases his belt, the clink of the metal a threat and a promise rolled together. "You already being naked helps move things along," he says while holding my arms in place above my head with his other hand. "I'm going to get off so fucking hard in that pussy."

I don't know why or how but I grow a pair of lady balls and state, "It was me. It was my idea, my plan to leave."

"You can't save your sister's ass, Snowflake. By the sounds of that bed, Ace has about three strokes left in him."

"That has nothing to do with it. I told her to call Joey and be ready to leave once I fucked you into a deep sleep."

Elliot recoils. "What are you talking about? Why didn't you just tell me you wanted to meet your brother?" he asks then catches my eye and realizes the reason. "Ah," he says. "I see. You didn't want me to come with you."

Elliot pulls back and climbs out of bed faster than he had climbed in only a second ago. He shivers when his body hits the cool air of the room. Or maybe his anger has caused his body to tense. The latter isn't going to bode well for me in this spanking he's promised.

"Elliot, I…"

"On all fours or over my knee, Adams?"

"Wait, what? No…I…"

"On your knees or over mine," he grits out through gnashing teeth. "I won't ask again. You completely disobeyed me and broke one of the rules in your contract. You need to be punished, so I'll ask you one more time, over my…"

"Fine. Your knee, happy?"

"Not in the slightest. In fact, I'm so fucking *not* happy, that I don't think I can even look at you right now. I'm planning on spanking the shit out of your ass then taking you from behind, so I don't need to see your face while I'm fucking you."

I hiss in a hurt breath. This feels like more than a game, more than fun, kinky sex. This feels like what it really is, why I left in the first place. Ownership. A power play. His lack of understanding of my feelings over our budding relationship.

Elliot stands before me and strips his clothes off. My eyes rake over his toned body as they grow accustomed to the darkness. He sits on the edge of the bed and toes his Dom bag closer.

"How did you get into the house?"

Elliot laughs as he topples me over his knee, and I screech.

"After Bridget pulled her first stunt, which by the way, Ace sees as her second," Elliot rubs the round globe of my ass with his callused hand. "That island getaway pissed him off, too. Anyway, we looked into Joey to be sure he was legit and not some psycho perv. He happens to be best friends with Raina's best friend's new boyfriend. Guess where they live, Snowflake?"

"Next door."

"Right next door."

Slap.

Elliot laughs. "Easiest job the three of us ever did."

Slap. Slap. Smack.

"Three? Callan tagged along, of course."

"Mmm, hmmm."

Spank. Spank. Crack.

"Owww!"

"Shh, count or keep quiet."

Crack. Crack. Crack.

"Ten," I cry and squirm on his lap. "Shit, this room is freezing."

Elliot shifts his erection under me then reaches down into his bag. "Lay on your back quick then I want you on all fours with your knees wide open."

I obey his orders out of habit and because now that he's here, sure I'm still pissed off, but as his pheromones fill the room and make me as horny as a teenage boy, I forget a little bit of my anger and seek the pleasure only Elliot has ever been able to bring to my body.

He lowers his head to my right breast and sucks the nipple into his mouth. He pulls his head back, tugging the hard peak with him. He snaps my wet nipple from his mouth then grins at me. "This is going to hurt. Take a deep breath" he warns.

Before I have time to protest or question him, I scream out as he clamps my nipple with a pair of heavyweight clamps. I hear the squeak of the bed across the hall and raise my eyebrows.

"Sounds like Callan's hearing is still good. I should warn you, the constant stimulation to these perfect fucking nipples is a perfect choice for you. Lots of pull," he says as he tugs on the silver chain and I cry out again. "Shh, these walls are thin."

"Fuck," I arch my back into his body. Elliot pushes my body down by both hips then bites and tugs my other nipple. "No!" I protest, knowing the searing pain that is about to shoot through my other side.

Elliot attaches the other clamp then soothes me with a sweet kiss to my mouth. His covers mine and his tongue sweeps inside for a taste. "They'll start to feel good in a second. Breathe and process the pain," he says with his lips still covering mine. Then he bites my lower lip, flips me onto my stomach and slaps my ass with a demand for me to get onto my knees. "Spread wide for me. Going to fuck you until I'm not seeing red at the thought of you leaving me and why. Which we'll talk about while I'm fucking this tight pussy and getting off. Your answers will determine if you do too or not."

"Elliot, that's not fair."

"Never said I was a fair man, did I, Adams?"

My breasts hang down painfully in this position and brush the mattress. Every move causes them to further harden and I cry out in agony. Not pain any longer, but frustration because the clamps are now making my nipples super sensitive and so hard that they ache in a way that just might make me come if I can rub them on the sheets.

Elliot chuckles then slams into my body and snakes a hand under me to tug at the silver chain attached to both nipple clamps. That stops me in my tracks and draws his name from my lips.

"So motherfucking tight and hot, baby."

Elliot picks up his pace as we hear Ace grunting toward what sounds like an orgasm to end all in the next room. My sister cries out his name as Elliot leans his big body over my back and licks the shell of my ear. "Shh, Adams," he warns. "Or they'll hear every sound coming out of you. Do you want Callan to hear you come through the wall? Hmm, because I'm sure he's jerking off already to the sounds from them. You want him to finish off listening to you?"

I groan at the idea of exciting another man even though I know it's wrong. But is it? Callan isn't here watching or participating. Elliot is the man bringing me to orgasm, the man I...the man I love that doesn't seem to view me much differently than any other man has ever done, Callan included no matter what he might think.

Elliot grunts as he plunges deep, the crown of his dick rubbing that rough patch inside me and getting me ready to explode. He thrusts, each one harder, rougher than the last. With each thrust, he spanks my ass from below. It burns from the number of hits it's taken, and I know I must be bright red by now.

Elliot confirms my suspicions. "Red ass, so fucking hot. All mine. Tell me while I come."

He picks up his pace and I moan as his thumb finds and presses down on my clit. "Yours," I say in all honesty. No matter how I'm feeling about our relationship, I am his. All his. "Only yours."

Elliot roars at my admission then abruptly pulls out. Within seconds I feel the hot splash of his orgasm cover the skin on my back, my ass, my thighs. His hands join the warmth and rub his release into my flesh, easing the ache of my ass but doing nothing for the throbbing between my legs.

With one final slap to my ass, he says, "There's got to be something wrong with the furnace. Get under the covers. I'll be right back."

"I'm going to get all crusty and what about these clamps?"

Elliot laughs. "I'll clean you up in a hot bath once I know the house is warm. If something's wrong with the heat, there might not be any hot water."

"Can you take the clamps off so I can at least get dressed?"

"Sure, come here," Elliot reaches out for my body and cuddles me close to his chest for warmth. "Take a deep breathe and hold it. This is going to hurt" he warns while he releases the pressure of the clamp, causing blood to rush into my nipple and create a searing pain.

"Oww," I cry out. "That fucking hurt. Leave the other one on."

Elliot laughs then releases the other without even giving me a chance to recover from the removal of the first.

"Jesus Christ!" I swear and rub at my sore nipples to be sure they're still connected to my body because they sure as hell hurt like they'd been ripped clear off.

Elliot plants a gentle, distracting kiss to my mouth and I forget about the pain in my nipples as another ache begins to simmer between my legs.

"Get dressed," Elliot says as he readies himself to go in search of the source of our lack of heat.

After throwing on whatever clothes I find on the floor, I lay back under the blankets and watch Elliot tuck his cock, still slick from my body, into his jeans. "I'm going to make myself come while you're gone" I warn with an innocent smile.

Elliot chuckles. "Then I hope you're good with Callan watching. Black" he yells and within a blink of an eye, Callan Black is walking through the door of my bedroom, tucking his own erection into a pair of jeans with a dirty smirk on his face.

"What do you need, man?" he asks. "I was kind of in the middle of something."

"Make sure her hands stay above the covers while I check on the heat. And keep your hands where she can see them, too. Is it fucking cold in the whole house or just in here?"

"Whole house and I already checked. I was just waiting for you to finish up before I came in to tell you that everything is off. No heat, no power, no hot water. Generator is shot to shit and the snow drifts are blocking the door and the windows. We'll just need to sit tight for the night then see if we can get Justin's ass over here to shovel us a way out."

"Fuck!" Elliot says. "You'll freeze your balls off without body heat," he makes eye contact with me. "Stay with us, but don't try any shit."

Callan nods then locks eyes with me. "You good sharing a bed with me and your man, Court?"

"I'd rather see your balls be popsicles, but whateves."

"They don't need to be frozen treats for you to lick, sweetheart, here…"

"What did I just say about trying shit?" Elliot asks. "Knock it the fuck off. Climb in on that side," When Callan wiggles his eyebrows and thrusts his hips, Elliot adds, "With your back to her."

"Where's the fun in that?" Callan asks as he jumps on the bed making it dip under his weight. "Get Lyons and Bridge in here, then it'll be a real orgy."

"It's not an orgy, you ass!" I say then turn toward Elliot. "Send him back to freeze his tiny balls off alone in his room."

"Tiny? Baby, you didn't think they were tiny when you were gag…"

"Shut the fuck up, Black, or freezing your balls off will be the least of your issues with them."

31

I awake the next morning with Bridget smashed against my body and the guys nowhere in sight. "How'd you get in here?" I laugh. This is how we woke up almost every day of our childhood until "Uncle" Jim had moved in and I started locking the door between our rooms so Bridget wouldn't walk in on him forcing me to touch him.

"I don't know," she says confused. "Probably carried by Ace. He said something about no power or heat and the guys fixing it. Oh, shit! The guys are here."

"Yup. That didn't take long. Guess who Joey's best friend is dating?"

"The one that lives next door? Justin, right?"

"Yup."

"Haven't a clue," Bridget says as she snuggles closer to me and sticks her ice popsicle feet in between my calves. "Tell me."

I screech at the coldness then tell her the story Elliot shared with me about Raina's best friend, Amanda and Joey's best friend, Justin.

"Well, that was convenient for them, huh?"

"Yeah, um...can I ask you something about Ace?"

"Sure What do you want to know?"

I clear my throat to buy myself a minute while I figure out exactly what it is that I want to ask and how to word it. "The, um...the BDSM stuff. You're okay with that? He spanked you last night because you ran away again."

Bridget hugs me tighter and sniffs my hair. "You smell like a man."

"Yeah, well I slept with two last night, so..."

"What?" Bridget screeches. "You fucked Callan and Elliot? Together?"

I laugh. "Have you met Elliot Montgomery? No. Callan slept with us because it was so cold. He didn't come in here until after we...well, Elliot finished."

"Just Elliott? I thought you said he was great in bed?"

I scooch around on the mattress to try to alleviate the ache between my legs. "He was," I state. "I mean, he is, but I'm being punished," I say as annoyance rings in the air from my words. "Didn't Ace deny you an orgasm?"

Bridget laughs and tells me all about how things went down in her room last night. Apparently, much differently then in here by her contented sighing. Ace had listened to her pleading when he wanted to spank her for running away. He'd instead teased her then brought her to three orgasms, at the least. Bridget couldn't be sure, claiming she might have blacked out during a fourth. "The BDSM stuff is all about fun, kinky sex with him. I mean, yeah, he spanked me good that time I did leave without telling him," she shrugs. "But even then, it was fun, you know? Not serious. Why? Elliot is like all hardcore Dom?"

"Yup. No joke and it only makes me feel like I was justified in leaving and that I should ask him to go."

"Ask who to go where?" Callan Black asks. He's leaning on the door jam looking like a fucking sex god with his strong bicep muscle bulging in his t-shirt.

"Aren't you freezing like that?" I ask as I snuggle deeper into the blankets.

"We were trying to fix the furnace. Didn't end well. But I got hot, so…"

"Where's Ace?" Bridget asks. "Did he get hot too?"

Callan laughs. "It's disgusting the way you two are now. Can't we go back to the group sex days when everyone was happy?"

"I wasn't happy" I state.

"You don't look happy now either, sweetheart."

"That's because she's being punished and didn't get to come last night."

"Elliot!" I admonish.

"What?" he asks as he nudges me over on the bed then pulls me into his chest. He plants a kiss to my temple and says. "You smell like me. And sex. It's making me horny."

"I told her the same thing," Bridge says. "Well, not the horny part, but now that Ace is…aghhh" she screams as Ace picks her up and tosses her over his shoulder. He exits through the door between our rooms and slams and locks it before the rest of us can even react.

"You didn't make yourself come?" Elliot asks. "I wasn't sure if your sister being in here would stop you. Okay, time for Big Red to come out and play."

"Big Red?" I laugh. "You make fun of your hair, too?"

"Too?" Elliot smirks at me, knowing full well that I'm always calling him a red-headed nickname in my mind. "Nah, that's one of his," he nods at Callan. "Just giving him an early birthday present."

"For the record," Callan says. "I called it Little Red."

Elliot smiles then flips Callan off as he turns to leave us alone.

"What's happening with the heat?" I ask as Elliot nuzzles my neck. "I'm a crusty mess."

"Mmm, I like that you've been covered in me all this time."

I swat at him. "I stink and need a shower."

Elliot nibbles at my neck then lifts my shirt over my head and licks a nipple. "You taste fine though."

"Elliot!" I scold. "Seriously. What's going on with the house?"

"Amanda has a son, T.J. He's about three now and he has an ear infection. I didn't want to wake her and Justin in case they were up all night with the little guy. As soon as we hear Justin outside, we'll call over to him and get shoveled out. The furnace isn't something we're fixing so we'll need to call a guy or find someplace else to stay."

"Maybe you guys should go back to New York. Bridget and I can stay with Joey and Mallory."

"Joey's wife moved out weeks ago. They're getting divorced. It'll be finalized around Valentine's Day from what Amanda told me."

"You talk to Amanda a lot?"

Elliot pulls his shirt off over his head then lowers my pants. "You jealous again, Snowflake? Hmm? Because a few hours ago you were telling me that you left New York to get away from me. A second ago, you suggested that I leave you here. What is going on? Tell me what the problem is."

He kicks his pants off then pulls my body atop his. His hands go to my hips and help me adjust to fit perfectly against him and his cock effortlessly slides deep inside my wet heat.

I moan. "Are you going to finish me off this time or continue being an asshole?"

Elliot stretches up and bites my lip. "I love a woman with fire inside her."

"Is that another red-headed reference? I'm a natural brunette."

Elliot laughs as he thrusts his hips up. I groan and grind down onto him.

"You feel so good," he says as he finds a pace. "I'm sorry for whatever I did. Let's talk after I make you come all over my firestick," We both laugh and succumb to the pleasure coursing through our bodies as Elliot's hand snakes between us and the big pad of his thumb finds my clit. "I'll make it fast, baby. Relax and come for me."

That's all the encouragement I need to shatter around his cock. My pussy spasms so strongly, I'm afraid Big Red might have a concussion.

"You're fucking making me come," Elliot howls then with a load grunt, he finishes inside me. His hips never still, though. He rubs that first one out and continues the slow grind of our bodies. "Feels too good to stop. Hate it when it's over that fast."

I hum a noise and nuzzle into his neck. Elliot turns us so we're laying on our sides and places my leg on his hip. Still inside me, he thrusts deep and moans as his cock considers its options. After a few more thrusts, Big Red makes the right choice and I feel him harden.

"You want to go another round first or talk?"

"Both?"

Elliot chuckles. "Okay," he says with a strong push of his hips. "I'm so fucking deep like this. Feels good, baby?"

"Fuck, yeah," I say with a slight wince at the stretch. "I'm sorry I ran away without talking to you, but I was mad and confused. I still am."

"I'm not sure I know why."

"Yeah, which makes me all the more pissed off."

Elliot continues to slowly thrust inside me, really more just a slight grind of his hips, but he's rubbing the head of his dick over that spot that makes my eyes cross and my toes curl. One hand rests on my hip while the other finds it's way into my hair then to the nape of my neck allowing Elliot to pull me in close and seal his lips over mine.

He speaks with his mouth still covering mine. "I'm a difficult guy sometimes, baby. Can you give me a little slack when fucking this relationship stuff up, please? You came to me as a surprise. I wasn't looking for this right now, I'm not sure I know how to do this or if I'm ready for," Elliot clears his throat then starts over. "But I want us, I want *you* more than words."

I smile into his kiss and shake my head. "I guess" I mumble.

"I was away for a long time. The kind of shit I dealt with can fuck a guy up. It's going to take me a bit to get civilized again, okay?"

"That's not really what's bothering me."

"No? What then?" he asks then pushes in with a deep groan. "I've never had this. Slow. Making love. It's nice with you."

"Yeah?"

Elliot kisses my nose. "Yeah. Just because I'm making you stick to that contract you signed doesn't mean I don't have real feelings for you, okay, Snowflake? Trust me when I tell you, I do. I'm feeling things with you I had no idea existed."

"Oh…ah, oh, Elliot," I purr as he picks up his pace and begins to thrust into me. "Right there."

Elliot smiles. "I love making you come."

"Mmm."

And he does. Make me come. Twice before I finally admit to why I left New York. "I like when you get Dom on me. I love the spankings and the playing in the special room. The kinky sex is fucking hot and living together seems like it'll be fun. What I'm having a problem with is the ownership and the contract. And I know I signed it and if it were some random guy, God only knows what…"

He halts that line of conversation with a deep kiss and a pinch to one of my sore nipples. "Shh, do not mention being with another man to me.

Like I said, I've never been like this with anyone, but you mentioning that puts a picture in my head that makes me want to punch shit."

I giggle and Elliot groans as my pussy vibrates around his thick cock. "Do you really feel like I'm your property? Like it's okay for you to control everything I do, punish me every time you don't get your way?"

Elliot growls and slows his pace. "I like to be in control. I like order in my life and predictability. I've been a sexual Dominant for years, but it's only ever been about sex and practiced in the clubs. I've never had a relationship while being a Dom."

"When was the last time you had a girlfriend?"

Elliot smirks at me then grinds those hips again until my eyes roll back in my head.

"Don't avoid my question," I scold. "But keep doing that. Shit, that feels so good."

Elliot thrusts a few more times then slows again when I feel his cock growing harder with his need for another climax. "I've told you some already, right? I dated here and there in high school but nothing serious. I had a killer crush on an older girl who only saw me as Raina's pain in the ass "Idiot". God, that fucking nickname used to piss me off."

"You're not an idiot, Elliot."

"I know," he says and kisses my lips before he continues to tell me how he fell for a girl once. The same one he'd had a crush on since he was fourteen. "Her marriage was falling apart, and we had a secret thing for a few weeks. I guess I saw it as more than she did. It was stupid and wrong of me to fuck her while she was married, but I couldn't help myself."

"Did she stay with her husband?"

"No. She had this guy that she was hung up on since she was in college. Kind of like me with her," Elliot chuckles. "Ironic, I guess you could say. Anyway, they reconnected for a bit and she pushed me aside. I know she never meant to hurt me, and we ended things amicably, no one ever knew we were together, but the sting burned. I drowned my sorrows in the clubs," Elliot shrugs. "At the time, the BDSM stuff seemed like a perfect way to have sex and avoid any real commitment or feelings. Now," Elliot warns. "That's the wrong way to approach the lifestyle and with you, it's never been like that for me. I swear. Ohh," he sighs on a deep thrust. "I'm getting close."

"Mmm, me too. I can't believe how many times you're able to make me come in one session" I laugh.

"Is that a challenge?"

"If it is, I'm losing. Tell me what happened with this girl. She was married, had an affair with you then left you for another guy? Did she end up with the husband or the other guy?"

"Neither. And she's not a bad person. It's a complicated story. Honestly, she never should have married the guy she did. Her and the ex were meant to be together. Even I saw that."

"But you said she's not with him."

"Nah, it's a long story. I left for an assignment overseas to lick my wounds after she left town with him. When she got back, her and the husband divorced."

We both turn toward the window at the sound of a plow going by on the main street above our house. "Sounds like the Calvary is arriving," Elliot says. "I'm sure Justin will be up soon and shovel us out."

"It's not so bad in here."

"No, it's not."

"So, finish your story then we can focus on finishing you" I purr then nip at Elliot's ear.

He thrusts into me until I feel his muscles tensing and I know he's close. "When I got back from the assignment, she was with someone else that she met. A long time had passed, and they were happy, so I left it alone and never told anyone about us. We went back to being just friends. She tried to talk to me about it once or twice, but I stopped her. Baby, I need to come. I'm really fucking close."

"Then what happened?" I ask to force him into holding off on his pleasure so that when he does come, it'll be even better. A lesson he taught me and well.

"Then I met you. Adams, I don't care about the fucking contract. I thought you wanted me to be the way I was acting. Don't get me wrong, I want the upper hand and," he heaves in a deep sigh in frustration to hold off his need to fuck into me until he finds his release. "When you disobey me like this stunt you pulled, I full well plan to light your ass up good. I won't tolerate you even glancing in the direction of another guy and I expect you to stay with me in the apartment. No arguing over me buying you shit, paying for school, that kind of thing. But I promise to not be a jerk Dom again. I don't think of you as my property or something that I own. Well, anymore than you own me. And, baby, trust me, you own me."

We slowly make love as tears run down my face and Elliot kisses each of them away. At the sound of a snowblower kicking on, Elliot turns his head toward the window, and I do the same.

"Maybe I should yell out to Justin?"

"What? Before you finish? He'll still be out there when we're done."

Elliot's cock is inside me. It's solid but I can tell that his admission has taken the edge off his need to climax. I'm sure if I gave him the out, he'd go without coming. But then, we hear a loud, joyous female squeal and his dick twitches inside me. He hardens further, like when he's reached the point of no return and he momentarily pauses to enjoy the sensation for a quick second before he explodes.

"Did your dick just twitch?" I ask and glance in the direction of the window as my mind starts putting things into place.

Elliot pulls out and tries to drag my body under him instead of the spooning position we've been in since we began this session, but I resist and push at his chest. "Is that Amanda? Outside, is that Amanda with Justin? You heard her laugh and your dick twitched. Inside me! She's Raina's best friend, right? You met her when you moved to Florida when you were fourteen."

"Adams," Elliot warns. "It's not…"

"It was her, wasn't it? The girl you loved was Amanda" I accuse as I jump out of bed and wince at the freezing cold floor under my bare feet. I shiver from the coldness in the air, caused not only by the temperature in the room, but also from the tension now between Elliot and I, and wrap my arms protectively around myself.

Elliot leaps from the bed after me, his cock deflating in front of my eyes. "Snowfl…"

"Don't!" I warn with a hand going up between us.

"Let me explain," he begs. "Yes, it was Amanda but it's over and since I've met you…"

"No! I can't. I-I need to think. I need you to leave. Right now," I demand. "I need to be alone. Please."

"Adams, I can't. I can't leave you."

"Can't leave me? Did you even come here for me? Hmm, Elliot, or was this little trip to Maine to see her? Get out!" I demand. "I don't want to see you right now."

Elliot stands frozen for a second before he reaches for my clothes and hands them to me. "Get dressed or you'll freeze. I'll go downstairs and see if the guys and I can get us shoveled out, but I'm not leaving you. I'll give you some space, but then we need to talk this through."

I grab for my clothes and put them on while Elliot does the same then turns to leave. As he reaches for the door, he turns back to me and says, "I'm falling in love with you. Don't make more out of this thing with Amanda than it is. Come downstairs when you're ready to talk."

With that, I stand motionless and watch Elliot walk out of the room. Then I collapse to the floor and cry while I listen to Amanda happily laughing out my window.

I don't know how long I lay there or if my sister heard me crying, but I find myself wrapped in Bridget's arms in the coldness of my empty room. She smooths back my hair and takes me with her to the bed. She makes soothing sounds and doesn't ask what's upsetting me, instead, she offers her comfort without her judgment and that fact alone brings on more tears.

When I finally calm down enough to speak, I say, "Elliot and that girl next door had a thing. She's Raina's best friend and I think he still has it bad for her."

"What are you talking about?" Bridget asks. "He's crazy about you."

"His dick was getting soft while we were having sex. I mean, we had done it a few times already and we were just kind of slowly grinding just to not pull apart, but still. The minute he heard her laugh…Bam! Hard-on renewed!"

"Oh."

"Yeah, oh. I can't stay here. I need some space from him to think about this. It's why I left New York in the first place."

"We can leave as soon as the snow is cleared out."

"I think I kind of want to go alone. You should stay here with Ace and enjoy the snow. Go skiing, teach that city boy how us snow bunnies roll."

My sister sighs then says, "Okay, but promise you'll call me the second you get into the city."

"I will," I promise then let my own sigh escape. "But how am I going to keep Elliot from following me?"

32

I arrive back in the city alone with my anger still on the surface and my ego busted wide open. Bridget had wanted to come with me, but I'd made her stay in Maine with Ace, Callan, and Elliot. I needed the space away from all of them.

I enter the apartment in Stone Towers and fight off tears as I see Elliot's shirt laying over the arm of the sofa where he'd tossed it after ripping it off and charging after me. I'd let him catch me and we'd spent the next hour on the floor naked and in heaven. Now I wonder what he's doing in Maine. Maybe he really was there to reconnect with his schoolboy crush and he and Amanda are making love in front of a roaring fire. Maybe he isn't thinking about me like I am about him.

I search the apartment for my bag with my laptop and plug it in to charge while I take a shower and try to wash all thoughts of Elliot out of my head. I start classes in the morning and I still need to purchase my books and accessories. My first paycheck from CC arrived in my bank account in the nick of time. I had gotten the alert as I was driving through Connecticut.

After drying off and tossing on comfortable clothes, I open the fridge and frown at the food. Elliot always knew how to whip something delicious up for us to snack on. Me? I could maybe cut a few slices off the cheese block and throw them on crackers. Elliot should be the one going to school, not me. He has a talent for the culinary arts that he should pursue.

I open my account at NYU only to discover that Elliot has already purchased my textbooks and anything else I could possibly need as a new student beginning classes in the morning. I double check on the address of the bookstore and make sure to set my alarm so I can get there then to my early morning class on time.

I sigh and grab for my phone to send Elliot a quick text to thank him. When I'd left Maine, I'd promised to stay in touch, and he'd promised to give me space. I figure one text can't hurt.

Adams: *Thanks for buying my books. You didn't need to do that. I have money, you know.*

Elliot: *Regardless of what you think, I want to take care of you because I care about you. I didn't buy them to be a dick. I'm just trying to support you and make things as easy for you as possible. Going back to school isn't going to be easy.*

Adams: *I know. Thanks. Thanks for giving me some space. Talk soon.*

Why did he have to remind me that school was going to kick my ass? Now the butterflies set in, the typical first day nerves hitting me in the gut.

Elliot: *I miss you*

Adams: *Don't.*

I turn off my phone because I don't want to continue to argue with him over my leaving. I'm too worried over what tomorrow will bring to deal with our relationship right now.

The last time I attended school, I'd hardly ever shown up for class. The few I had gone to were only because there was a hot guy I wanted to bang, or the professor was yummy, and I wanted him to at least know my name when I showed up for his office hours in nothing but a trench coat. This time, I intend to keep my nose in the books and my vagina to myself.

I sigh and think that would be so much easier to do with Elliot here as I climb into bed and toss and turn until I finally fall asleep.

I awake the following day and head off to school with my stomach in my throat. I do the same over the course of the week and each night I delete all of Elliot's texts and voicemails without reading or listening to any.

Classes go great my first week. I met a few classmates and we hit it off. On Friday, we head out to celebrate our first week of classes at a pub. After happy hour ends, a few of them leave, saying they have dinner plans with their boyfriends or husbands. I stay on with the rest of the group, not wanting to go home to an empty apartment and the reminder of Elliot.

One pub leads to another and by the time the nightclubs are waking up, I'm at my second and alone, my classmates all gone now for a quiet night at home or out to eat with their partners. I order another drink at the bar and hit the dance floor where a group of guys join me and offer to get me another round. I accept, but after finishing that, they tell me about their plans to hit a new place just down the street and ask if I want to tag along.

I'm not in the club for more than ten minutes before I realize that I must either be drunker than I thought or maybe one of the dudes drugged me because standing with his arms folded directly in my line of vision, albeit shaky as it is, is none other than Callan Motherfucking Black. And he looks pissed off.

Callan stands with his arms folded over his chest and a scowl on his gorgeous face. He's just watching me. He watches as I sway on my feet while the guys, I headed to the club with, take turns dancing with me. They each grind into me and I slightly wince each time I feel one of their erections pressing into my ass or my stomach. I dance a little further away each time to put some space between us so I won't give them the wrong message.

Callan never moves. He just stands there with an evil glare for each of the guys and a disgusted look for me. Yeah, I disgust myself too, but I really am not doing anything wrong. It's not like I'm fucking any of them in the bathroom.

That thought has me shooting my eyes in Callan's direction as the memory takes root. I quickly scan the space and realize we're in the same club that Callan and I were in with Ace and Bridget not long before I took off for the island and met Elliot. The night that Callan and I had been here, we'd ended up fucking in the men's room in a stall while some creepy perv listened.

It had been hot at the time. Looking back, I'm embarrassed by my behavior.

I must have missed what the guys were saying while I was thinking about Callan and my romp in that bathroom because the next thing I know, one of them is pushing me along while two others have me flanked with my forearms in their strong holds.

"Hey, um, so.. ouch!" I screech. "Can you ease up?"

None of them answer my protests, but instead keep up their quick pace. By the time I realize that they're heading us in the direction of the exit through the side door, it's too late to call out for Callan's help because he's nowhere to be seen.

One of the guys pushes the door open as I start to protest. Another, the one behind me, covers my mouth with his hand as he hauls me through the door. I sputter as I'm catapulted onto the concrete, then movement from beside the door catches my eye.

I scramble to my ass and scoot myself as close to the brick building as I can as all hell breaks loose.

Callan Black takes out all three guys within the blink of an eye, leaving them each laying on the concrete I had just been tossed to.

I pull my bloodied scraped knees into my chest and start to shake as Callan is approaching me while talking into his cell and telling someone where we are. Then he bends down and picks me up into his arms and carries me out of the alleyway into a waiting black Escalade.

He plops me onto the seat then pushes me over as he climbs in next to me. I try to catch his eye to gage his disposition, but before I can make my eyes focus on him, he grabs my hand and turns it over to see the markings of each bar and nightclub I had been in.

"Bunch of cover charge stamps you got here, Court. All you need is one more color and you'd have yourself a full rainbow."

"I was in and out of every one of these bars. It's not like I spent the whole night drinking. I was out with some new friends I made at school after a full week of classes. We hopped around to a few places, no big deal."

Callan scoffs then rolls his eyes. "Hope those guys weren't your idea of friends from school."

"No," I say as I try to scoot away from him.

"This really how you want to act coming off a breakup? Be that girl again? I thought you wanted to change."

"Elliot and I didn't break up. Wait, does he think we broke up?"

Callan shrugs but I'm drunk enough to not understand his nonverbal communication. "What? What is that shrugging about?"

"You ran away from him, what do you want him to think? Do you even know about the accident?"

"Accident?" I ask. "Oh my God! Is he okay? What happened? Why didn't any of you call me if he got hurt?"

"Not him. Elliot's fine. His sister, brother-in-law, and niece. Some drunk asshole forced them off the road. It was an ice storm and the trees were covered in heavy snow and ice. Their car hit a tree, but they were all okay. Then the tree broke under the weight of the snow and ice and the impact from the car. It fell on the car and crushed the back where his niece was trapped in her car seat.

"Oh my God! Is she okay?"

Callan shrugs again and I punch him in the chest. He rubs at the spot then says, "She's fine. Pete and Elliot, not so much. They made them hospitalize her and Raina while they ran every possible test on them. They should be home by the end of the week. And I'd expect Elliot here a few hours later."

"How did I not know?"

"I'm good at my job. We kept it out of the media. I may have hacked into the hospital's computer system and wiped everything about Raina and Aubrey Roman clean."

We pull up outside of Stone Towers and I tumble fall out of the car before Callan makes his way around to open the door. "Thanks for the ride," I say. "See you around."

The heel of my shoe snags on a crack in the concrete and I come very close to faceplanting on the dirty New York City street. Lucky for me, Callan Black has quick reflexes and instead of my face hitting the ground, my legs are swung up into the air and I find myself cradled in his arms.

I giggle then hiccup which sends me into a great fit of laughter as Callan carries me through the door of the apartment building and up the one flight of stairs to 1-A. Poor Pedro doesn't know where to look or what to do, so he barely nods then lowers his head.

"You coming inside right now Cal is a bad idea."

Callan smirks at me. "You think that little of me, huh? You think I'd take advantage of the fact that you're drunk off your ass and your head is all fucked up over whatever in the hell you and Elliot got going on?"

"No, I," then I correct myself. "Well, yeah, I mean, kind of."

Callan chuckles as he punches in the security code on my door that way too many people seem to know for it to actually be a measure of security anymore. "Fair enough," he states. "But I'd never do that to Elliot. Or you, Court. I know I can be an asshole, but I'm not that bad. I like your man."

"I like him too" I admit then sway on my feet as Callan sets me down and nods toward my bedroom for me to go to bed.

"You staying here?"

"Yeah, I'll sleep in the kinky room," he says with a smirk. "Looks like you can use a friend and my place got sold underneath me, so it's a win-win."

"Okay," I say. "But we need to commemorate you moving in with one drink."

"I don't think that's a good idea, sweetheart. You're already plastered. I'm supposed to be a good guy now, remember?"

"You've always been a good guy; you were just a horny dick."

"Still horny, Court. That's why giving you any more to drink is a dumb idea."

I wave him off and turn some music on. "This is my jam" I say as I attempt to more to the beat and reach for the bottle of wine I had on the counter.

I'm bouncing around my living room like a pinball while singing, okay maybe not singing as much as fucking up every word of the song. I close my eyes as I dance to stop the room from spinning, but I feel Callan's stare hot on me. I smooth the top of my hair then bunch it into a ponytail and secure it with the band I always have on my wrist for times like this. I know my hair's probably a hot mess, but whateves. The fact that I can feel my boobs falling out of my dress is what I should be worried about because Callan can think he's changed all he wants, I'm the perfect example of how people cannot completely change their spots. If I'm being honest, all it would take right now is one move on his part, and I know we'd end up fucking into the morning. Not that I want to fuck him. I don't. I want Elliot. But with him not here, me drunk and missing him, Callan's right. He and I together are a recipe for disaster.

I reach for his left hand as I put his wine in his right. I tug so he'll dance with me. He smirks then shakes his head, but I shake my head too. "Dance with me, Black. Don't be a douche."

Callan laughs then lets me dance around him while he stands like a statue. "I got a job," he says out of the blue. "Mac needs me to look into this chick's company. That's why I came back. Elliot's going to be pissed when he knows I'm here. At your place."

"Yeah, well," I snort then cover my nose and laugh. "I'm not all that happy that he went running to Maine where the girl he's been crushing on since he was able to get a hard-on is."

"Wait, what?" Callan laughs again. "Who, Amanda?"

"Yes, Amanda. He had a crush on her then they had something, a fling, I don't really know all the details."

"I heard about what happened the morning you left. I gave him shit over it. But you have to know that he only went to Maine in the first place because he was chasing after your ass."

I roll my eyes. Guys are weird with each other. Girls would hug then cut the other down behind her back. It's evil, sure, but it's better than making fun of a poor guy about losing his erection in front of everyone.

"I've been avoiding his calls and texts."

"I know. He's a lunatic over you. When he finds out I'm here, it's going to drive him over the edge. I'm guessing you told him about us?"

"Not everything."

"Ah," Callan sighs. "So only that we fucked. You left out that I tried to make you mine."

I shake my head and cover my mouth as a strong yawn hits me. Then my legs are in the air again and Callan has me in his arms. He carries me to my room, and I have a moment of panic. I thought when it came down to this, I'd want to fuck him. It's been over a week since I've had sex and after crying to myself in bed every night, I've been too exhausted even for a good old fashion self-love session. The ache between my legs is strong and I know from experience that Callan Black is more than equipped to relieve the pain.

"Cal, I…hold up" I say, my voice growing more frantic as he slowly lowers me to my bed.

"Go to sleep, sweetheart. I'll be in the kink room hacking into Morgan's employee's lives if you need me."

Callan gently kisses my temple then turns toward the door to leave. "I had meant it, you know."

I raise my chin to him in question. "What?"

"That I wanted you to be mine. That I would have changed for you. Monti is one hell of a lucky guy. Give him a chance. You seemed happy, different with him. He's good for you and he's in love with you too."

Callan quietly shuts my bedroom door, leaving me to sleep all alone. I watch as the light from the apartment shines under my door. He's leaving the hall light on in case I need him in the middle of the night.

I moan as my head begins to throb. I reach for my phone even though I know drunk dialing is a very bad choice. I punch in Elliot's number and only need to wait for it to ring once before his voice fills my ears.

"Adams" his sweet deep baritone brings tears to my eyes.

"Elliot," I sigh. "It's like poison."

"Poison?" he asks. "What are you talking about?"

"You're full of questions tonight."

Elliot chuckles then asks, "Are you drunk?"

"I may have had a drink or two earlier tonight. I went out with some new friends that I made at school."

"It's going well, then?"

"Yeah, school's fine. I mean, it's only been a week, but..."

"I miss you, Ads. I want to come see you but I'm trying to give you space."

"I'm breaking my own rules and now Callan..."

Elliot interrupts me when he bellows, "Callan what?"

"Callan showed up here, he's..."

"What the fuck did he show up there for, Adams, hmm? What, to replace me in our bed?"

"I...no, Elliot...

"Don't treat me like a fool. He's been in love with you for months. You don't know what it feels like to fall in love with you, Adams or how easily that happens. I'm losing my mind without you and now you're telling me that another man who wants you is there while I'm five hundred miles away?"

"Calling you was a mistake. I can't do this. I'm hanging up, Elliot."

"Don't you dare hang..."

But I don't hear what he says next. I swipe to end the call before he finishes his sentence. I turn off my phone then I close my eyes and fall asleep.

33

I knew the day was coming when Elliot would be back on the concrete streets of New York and I'd have to figure out what to do. As much as I knew that day was coming, I hadn't prepared myself for the aftermath.

School has been my salvation and I can't believe my first semester is coming to an end. Elliot, even though we've barely spoken, set up and paid for summer courses, so I have those to look forward to. It's as if he knows I need something to keep my mind busy, or maybe he was trying to keep my body active in a non-sexual way. I know he's worried over Callan and me. I'd left that hanging in the air between us and I know that was wrong.

I understand his concern. He should be worried over Courtney and Callan, but I'm his Adams and he has nothing to fear from any man. If I could move past my own insecurities with men, Elliot and I wouldn't be apart. He's the only man I want, but after what happened that morning in Maine when I left, I can't seem to find comfort in considering a relationship with a man who is harboring feelings for another woman.

I knew it would happen sooner or later, knew he'd be back, and I'd have to face what we were doing.

Callan and I had fallen into a routine. He was working nonstop on his assignment with Morgan's company to find the culprit of their subterfuge and we barely had time to catch up between his schedule and my finals approaching. Joey, having moved to the city, was also taking up some of my time, and we'd choose to hang out with him and Morgan over remaining alone in our apartment and running the risk of falling into bed together.

Both Callan and I have moved past our sexual attraction, but we're both highly sexual creatures who know better than to tempt fate too many times. Living together, if we're not careful, can turn us back into fuck buddies, and that wouldn't help my situation with Elliot.

The first time we all hung out, I couldn't believe, that in a city of over eight million people, Joey's new girlfriend was the same woman that Callan was working for. The four of us fell into a companionable foursome and often had meals together or just hung out at one of our places.

The early Saturday morning get together at the coffee shop on our block wasn't planned. Morgan had remembered something she'd forgotten to mention to Callan before and had sent him a text asking to meet up. Callan had been heading to the coffee shop alone and suggested the location. Once Morgan mentioned that my brother was tagging along, I decided to do the same. Not wanting to hold them up, I went looking like I had just spent the night rolling around in bed with a man when in actuality, I'd been alone. Tossing and turning all night while thinking of

Elliot. And listening to my younger sister, Jordan, and Callan laughing and flirting in the main living space.

People can talk about that sexy hair look on a woman after having sex all they want. I don't need a romp in the hay to wake up with my hair all over the place. With my allergies kicking in, the last thing I wanted was to try to tame my heavy mane into a ponytail, so I left it down and looking a fright. My hair was too heavy, and my head couldn't take any more pressure. If people don't like it, they can look away. I wasn't trying to impress anyone, and I certainly didn't need any male attention to add to my life's current woes.

I'm standing in line when he catches my eye.

Elliot.

Here.

In New York City.

In our neighborhood.

In the coffee shop where I'm with my brother and his girlfriend and it'll look like I'm with Callan. On a date. After a night of sex. I knew I should have dragged Jordan's lazy ass with us. But she'd refused to wake up. I'm convinced she's in a sex-induced coma brought on by none other than my roommate, Mr. Callan Black. And I should know. I've experienced more than one of those comas. Lucky, that Jordan, while I'm over her ready to crawl out of my skin after four months without getting any, she's able to take a ride on the Black train anytime her pussy desires.

"Adams?" he questions as he comes up behind me and I don't need to turn at the sound of his voice to know it's him or that he's already spotted Callan and gotten the wrong idea. "Hey."

I slowly turn to face him as I heave in a deep breath when my eyes lock with his. "Elliot, I…" I murmur.

"Hey," he repeats. "Hi, Adams. How are you? You look great."

Great? He means I look like I've been fucking another man. But he won't say that. He's trying to not start an argument. But the fact that he's holding his jealousy back is pissing me off and about to begin one all the same.

"I'm doing fine, you? Are you here alone?"

I want an argument. I want him to tell me that he brought Amanda back to New York with him and I had been right to be worried. Wait, no! No, that's not what I want at all. I want Elliot to tell me he misses me, that I'm the only woman he sees in a room full of them. I want him to take me in his arms and kiss me, hike up my skirt, push my panties to the side and…is it hot in here?

I clear my throat.

Instead of doing any of those things, Elliot looks around and lifts his chin at Callan and Joey. "Yeah, more than I can say for you, though, huh?"

"It's not…"

"What the fuck are you thinking, Courtney?"

"What are you yelling at me for? And why are you calling me that? Don't call me that!"

"Because you're mine and…"

I roll my eyes and chuckle. "Really? You want to have that argument again?"

"You know what I mean" Elliot states.

Callan, like an asshole, waves at Elliot and then pats the seat next to him, asking me to come sit down. Acting as if we are here together. As a couple. See what an asshole he can be. Thank god my sister isn't here to see that for herself or he'd ruin his chances with her for sure.

"No. I really don't" I state.

"Have you told Damian you're breaking our contract? I should have known you two had unfinished shit going on. The unexplained glances, the way you smile when he says something ludicrous. I never gave it much thought. One thing never meant much, but when you add it all up, there's a flicker of something between the two of you that I fucking hate."

"I don't know what you're talk…"

"But I can forgive you, move past it, if there's hope that you'll come back to me. Adams, I l…"

Just as I think Elliot is about to confess his undying love for me, Callan, the asshole, sidles up next to us and wraps a possessive arm around my waist. I elbow him in the gut as casually as I can, but his amazing stomach muscles prevent him from feeling my jab.

"You here for good or just stopping by to see our girl real quick?"

Elliot growls and lunges for Callan who stands his ground and smirks.

"She's my girl, Black, not yours," Elliot says at Callan who is still holding his ground with a smirk that even I want to wipe off his smug face. "You have some fucking balls staying at the apartment without asking me. I thought you were better than that. I thought all those chicks in the service, the girlfriends and wives that you plowed through in more ways than one, were different because their boyfriends and husbands weren't your friends. I defended you to everyone. I guess I was wrong. I guess I didn't mean anything more to you than any of them."

Elliot flings Callan away from him then turns to address me. "Adams, this isn't over. I'll give you all the time in the world, but this," he points between us. "Isn't. Over."

Elliot's hand reaches out to brush a stray piece of hair from my face and I shiver at his touch.

"I'll-I-I-um," I stutter. "I'll talk to Damian in the morning and ask him to suspend our contract until we can figure this out."

Elliot nods. "I'll be at Pete and Raina's until you come to your senses."

"In Florida?" I ask with venom. "With the rest of their friends? Amanda?"

"No, Adams," Elliot says as he draws me to his body by my arms. "Not in Florida and not with Amanda. I'll be at their apartment here and the Amanda thing is nothing but a stupid misunderstanding that I'm not discussing here in public in front of him."

"Yeah, I don't think anyone here needs to hear about your inability to hold an erection, Monti" Callan teases as if they're still standing on friendly ground. He realizes his error when Elliot clocks him in the jaw.

Callan's head snaps back but he never fights back. Elliot laughs and turns his back on him. He rounds to face me one last time as my brother is approaching to stand by my side. "I'll text you later. I want to talk and explain. Alone."

I nod as the tears finally begin to fall. Elliot reaches out and wipes one away before he turns and walks out of the coffee shop.

34

Bridget and Ace have been my rocks since Elliot and I have been on a break. I guess that's what you'd call this, right? A break? I mean, we're not together, but we're not really broken up, right? I don't know, maybe we are. I don't look at us as broken up, but maybe he does. Maybe he thinks I'm with Callan and maybe he's been with other girls. That thought sends me into a tailspin that has my sister and Ace taking care of me like a small child unable to care for herself. I never doubted my sister's loyalty or her support, but I never expected it from Ace Lyons.

Ace has turned into another brother figure to me. I never asked for or wanted one growing up, and now here I am with a handful. Between Joey, Callan, and Ace, I'm never without one of them more than an arm's length away. I guess it's good. It's definitely kept other men from sniffing around. And they wouldn't have come sniffing. Guys have this sick radar for a jilted woman.

"Ace working out with Callan?" I ask my sister as it's one of the only times she and Ace aren't together.

"Yup, he said that we can go for ice cream if you want after they finish up."

"I'm not four, you realize I'm older than you, right?"

Bridget laughs. "I know, but who doesn't love an ice cream cone at this time of year? The weather is so nice. You should have come to the park with us yesterday."

I shrug. I hadn't been in the mood to take a walk with her and Ace because as much as they try their best to shield me from anything that they fear might upset me, they also don't realize that their own romantic gestures gut me. Watching Ace, a man that only a few months ago hadn't looked at the same woman twice, hold my sister's hand or carry her over a puddle like it's the middle ages or something…ick! It's enough to make me puke. And cry. Because that's what I want too. It's what I know I could have with Elliot.

"I'm going to take a quick shower," Bridget says. "Think about it, okay? We can go to that glass carousel you saw after."

"Okay," I say weakly then luckily I'm saved by the chirping of my phone and I wave my sister off when I see Elliot's sister on my screen.

Raina reaches out to me every few days. "Give him time," she says. "He's a good guy and the Amanda thing…" she trails off then clears her throat after gathering her thoughts. "Courtney, the Amanda thing started out as a young boy's fantasy. It was nothing more than that for years. They hooked up for a short amount of time and they'll both tell you that it wasn't all that great."

"Great," I say. "The sex was sucky so now what? I should believe they weren't meant to be together and trust that he won't leave me for her one day?"

I didn't mean for that to slip out. Especially not to Raina Montgomery-Roman.

Raina huffs in a deep sigh. "Courtney, listen, my brother really likes you. I've never seen him like this over any woman, not in high school, college, and not over Amanda, ever."

Raina continues to tell me the story of Elliot's upbringing and younger years while I wave to my sister and Callan as they walk out of the apartment with Callan's hand in the back pocket of Jordan's jeans. Jordan mouths, "We're meeting Joey and Morgan."

I wave them off and mouth back, "Have fun, I'm good."

They close the door as I hear Raina say, "Elliot was a really shy kid growing up. We moved around a lot when he was small, and my dad wasn't home a whole lot during those years."

"He never told me that."

"He doesn't like to think that it affects him, but it does. If he knew I was telling you about this, he'd flip his shit. But I don't care. I think you have a right to know."

Raina shares that her brother was the cutest red-headed kid she'd ever laid eyes on but that he had a hard time making friends because they moved around so often. He learned pretty quick not to bother putting himself out there at a new school with a new group of kids because he wouldn't be there long.

I remember how hard it had been for Bridget and I when we moved. I couldn't imagine doing that over and over like Elliot had been forced to do.

"My dad was undercover, so it sucked. We weren't military brats that had a base and other kids that got how it felt to be the new kid at school all the time. Back then, we had no idea what my dad did for a living. We just thought he had a job that made him not be able to be at home and one that kept us moving around."

"That sounds terrible," I state. "I'm sorry you guys grew up like that."

I can hear Raina's shrug through the phone. "It ended okay for me. Elliot's had a harder go of it. I hooked up with my group of friends, he never really had that. The closest he's come, is his military friends."

"Callan and Ace?"

"Well, right now, just Ace. He's pretty pissed off at Callan."

"Because of me?"

"What do you think? Anyway," Raina continues. "Elliot was kind of a loner in middle school and when we moved to Florida, he had no friends. I sort of left him high and dry once I met Amanda, Sof, and Tracey."

"Oh."

Raina tells me about that first summer that they lived in Florida and how she'd fell head over heels in love with Pete Roman. My mouth hangs open as she shares that her father set it all up with Pete's. They're friends and had worked together forever with Mac. She explains that Jonesie, the owner of the island where I met Elliot, is part of their tight-knit group as well.

After I recover from the shock of how much these people are tied together and the connection to my family, I listen as Raina laughs and says something about Amanda being nothing more than live porn for a fourteen-year-old Elliot.

"What?" I ask through a giggle. "What are you saying right now?"

"I'm saying that my brother had no friends and was going through puberty. He wasn't close with our dad and had no one to talk to about his body and emotions. He turned into this hot man overnight. I swear, one day he was a cute, freckled redhead, and the next he was a smoldering walking ball of testosterone."

She shares how Elliot used to watch her and her friends from his bedroom window and how she never gave it much thought. She'd still been thinking of him as a child and thought he was just too shy to come into the pool with them.

"Looking back, it kind of freaks me out that he was probably, you know…loving himself a lot back then. Probably while he was watching my friends swim."

"Mainly Amanda," I state. "She's really pretty."

"She is," Raina says. "And so are you."

I die a small death because Raina Fucking Roman just called me pretty. Don't snicker at me, you'd do the same.

Anyway, Raina goes on to tell me that Elliot grew into his body and grew close to their father when he joined the military and followed in his footsteps. It makes me wonder how Mr. Montgomery feels about him leaving the service to do…I haven't a clue what Elliot plans to do in the future.

"It's not about that though," Raina says, and it takes me a minute to remember that we were talking about Amanda and I being pretty. "He was never in love with Amanda and she was certainly never in love with him."

"How do you know?" I ask.

"Well, for starters, Amanda was in love with Todd. The fact that she insisted on letting him go to London, then the mess of not speaking to him for years, was ludicrous."

"I thought she was married when she and Elliot..." I can't bring myself to say the words to his sister.

"She was, on paper only. Her husband was a good guy until the end of their marriage. I don't blame him, but he walked away and never looked back. She's reached out to him to try to make amends and explain. He moved and changed his number."

I can't blame the guy either, so I keep silent and Raina continues.

"Amanda was in a horrible place after Todd died and she found out she was pregnant. She left her husband and had no clue what to do. Pete and Todd had been best friends forever and he was a mess, so I was trying to help him grieve while dealing with my own emotions. I'm sure Amanda felt slighted and left out. She turned to the only person she felt safe with."

"Elliot."

"Yeah," Raina admits. "They used to talk. She was always sweet to him."

I sigh into the phone and stand. I take it with me into my bedroom and put it on speaker so that I can get into my comfortable clothes while I listen to Raina explain that she thinks neither Amanda nor Elliot ever really liked the other one. She thinks they just fell into a quick romp in bed, that as she pointed out again, wasn't that great, to get past their loneliness.

"Oh," I sigh as I grab my laptop and cue up my school email. "Elliot was lonely?"

"I don't know for sure," Raina says. "I'm just guessing. He was probably worried over going into combat, too."

"Combat?" I ask with a shaky voice. "Elliot was in danger in the military?"

Raina laughs but there's no mirth in the sound. "Danger? That's an understatement. He was with our dad's group. They're like the special ops of special ops, they're so far undercover that no one ever knew where they were. I know from Pete that his father saw some really crazy shit and Elliot trained with Rick and his team, so I'm sure he saw stuff, too."

"He has nightmares," I state quietly. "He wouldn't talk about them with me though."

"He will. Give him time. Courtney, give my brother a chance" Raina begs.

We make a little small talk then hang up. I lie in bed and toss and turn all night while I think about the man who holds my heart.

35

Summer is hitting Manhattan with force this year and I can't tame my wild locks as the humidity wreaks havoc on my hair. My sister, Jordan, the lucky bitch, has poker straight hair that wouldn't dare curl or frizz while I look like one of those heads that you buy in Wal-Mart that grows grass where the hair should be.

Little Miss Perfect Locks kisses me on both cheeks before she turns to climb into the Uber waiting on the side of the street. "Tell Callan I'll be around later today if he's up for hanging out. He must've left really early today."

"I think he needed to be in court with Morgan."

"Oh," Jordan says. "Yeah, I do kind of remember him saying something about that now that you mention it. Have a good class."

I shrug and say that I'll try and promise to pass the message along to Callan if and when I see him.

My summer courses aren't holding my attention as much as the ones last semester had and I'm trying to convince myself that it's because of their subject matter and not that I truly don't have an attention span for knowledge. I manage to hand in my first assignment in my early class then grab a quick bite to eat before practically sleeping through my second and final class of the day.

When I meander toward the subway, I see Callan standing with a foot propped against a wall and his eyes scanning the area like the trained killer he is. Now that we're not having sex, we actually speak and learn things about the other. As I've grown closer with him, he's shed some light on not only his time in the military, but also Elliot's.

Elliot had worked hard to quickly move through his basic training and join the elite force that his father had headed up for years. Ace, Callan, and Elliot all trained in hand-to-hand combat and as snipers for Dave Montgomery's crew. They'd seen horrific things not long after arriving on solid ground in India. They'd been assigned to seek and recover young American girls believed to be part of a sex trafficking ring. Their mission hadn't taken long, but Callan expressed that the psychological impact was great.

They'd seen girls, as young as eight or nine being raped by men, and even a few killed in the process right in front of their eyes. As bad as it had been, Callan assured me that they'd accomplished well beyond their goals and had saved many girls from their demises. That didn't mean the toll was any less for Ace, Callan, or Elliot.

"What are you doing here? Did you testify today?"

"I did and Morgan's all set. You might want to call your brother later, though. I think he might have something to tell you."

"What?" I screech. "Did he ask her to marry him?"

"No. Something work related" Callan says and picks me up to twirl me around.

"You seem happier than normal," I state as I'm growing dizzy. "Put me down."

When Callan ignores my plea, I try to wriggle free and we both end up crashing onto the sidewalk in a fight of giggles.

At the sound of an angry male clearing his throat, I look up from the ground to see Elliot's not only pissed off, but also sad and tear-filled eyes. We lock on one another for a moment then he looks away from me, disgusted in the fact that I'm horse playing on the street with another man. Or so he thinks.

I mean, we were fooling around but not in a sexual manner. Callan is only as lighthearted as he is right now because of Jordan, his good-natured actions of spinning me around and laughing had nothing to do with his feelings for me, they were all thanks to the effect my sister has had on the hardened closed off man.

Elliot momentarily tilts his head and quizzically looks at me as if he sees that there's something that I'm trying to hide from him. He recovers quick enough and his chivalry wins out as he reaches for my hand to lift me from the grime of New York.

He leaves Callan smirking on the ground.

Elliot's hand is warm around mine, but his eyes are cold. He pulls away from me and I have to wonder, what's on his mind. Is he truly thinking that I'm this kind of girl? Does he honestly think Callan would betray him like this?

There's hurt behind his eyes, and I know that I've made a dumb mistake. I start to tremble, my body shaking like I'm back in the cold of Vermont as a little girl afraid of her "Uncle" Jim or a stupid adult in Maine who thinks the man she loves is going to leave her for his schoolboy crush.

My voice breaks when I say his name, "Elliot."

"Adams."

And just as I'm about to tell him this whole mess was my fault and not what he thought, Callan returns to the asshole he was before Jordan began transforming him into a decent human being. "I was just meeting Court after class, man. Want to come get food with us? I promise not to make her come under the table while you watch."

"Callan!" I scold. "Why the fuck would you do that?" Then I whip around to Elliot and try to repair the damage from Callan's careless joking. "Don't go, Elliot. Please stay. Don't listen to…"

"Yeah," Callan tries to help me out once he sees that I'm no longer interested in the charade of romantic relationship with him. "Man, I was joking. We're not..."

But it's too late because Elliot is walking away and I'm begging on my knees for him to listen to Callan.

Callan tries to yell out his name, but Elliot picks up his pace as he weaves between the busy New Yorkers.

"I can't watch him walk away from me" I cry into Callan's shoulder as he lifts me from the ground that I've spent too much time on today.

"It'll be okay," Callan tries to soothe me. "Let him go and blow off some steam. I'll track him down in a few hours and try to make everything right. He feels betrayed by the both of us. That's not going to be easy for him to shake off. His initial reaction was to walk away from you, Court, but he loves you, what he really wanted to do was stay, but he couldn't. He had to save face. Let him lick his wounds for the day, then I promise, I'll make him listen to me."

Later that night, I hear my sister bounding for the door and follow suit. Knowing that Callan was finally home from trying to find Elliot, I couldn't wait another minute to hear what had happened. I'm guessing it wasn't good, because if it were, wouldn't Elliot have called me as soon as Callan had explained?

Unless he's with him now.

I run out into the living space with my hopes high, but they're shattered when I find Callan standing there without Elliot waiting for me to jump into his arms and cover his face with kisses.

"Where is he? Did you find him?"

Callan nods. "Courtney, sit down. There's something I need to tell you and I know how you are. It's best if you can't hit the floor when you hear what I need to say."

"Oh, my God" I heave in a sob and collapse into the pillows of the sofa. Jordan curls me into her arms immediately then encourages Callan to break whatever news he has with me.

"Elliot left, um...the country."

"The country?" I question. "Where did he go? Oh, wait?" I smile. "Did he go back to the island where we met? Is he waiting for me to show up there? You know, like in Bailey Connors' romance novels?"

"Um," Jordan looks at Callan. "Honey," she says turning back to me and it hits me that she already knows where Elliot is. Callan must have texted to warn her. "Elliot isn't on the island."

"Then where is he?" I turn on Callan, raise to my feet and pound on his chest. "Where the fuck is he?"

"He went back in. When he thought we were together and it was over between you two for good, he reached out to our contact and asked for an assignment."

"An assignment?" I ask.

Callan nods. "He was coming to say good-bye to you today before leaving. I'm guessing that seeing us together only pissed him off worse."

"Where. Is. He?" I demand.

"I'm not sure yet" Callan says.

"When will you be sure."

Callan shrugs. "I'm not sure that I can…"

"Not sure that you can what?" I scream. "You can find out where he is, Callan. You *will* find out where he is and go get him."

"It's not that easy, Court. I can't just…"

"Yes, you can!" I yell then fall back down into a puddle of tears.

I hear Jordan talking on the phone to someone that I'm guessing is either Bridget or Joey while Callan lifts me into his strong arms and carries me into my bedroom and puts me under the covers like a child.

"Stay here," he orders. "I'll be back in a minute."

I hear a knock on the door and try to process how long it would have taken Joey or Bridget to make it here if Jordan had just called them. It doesn't seem to be long enough to make sense that it's either of them, but I lay down and wait for Callan to return because there's not much else I can do.

When I see a shadow enter, it's not a lone one. Jordan is side by side with Callan and she has an envelope in her hand. "Court, honey, you got a certified letter. Pedro said it was stuck under some other mail and he apologizes for bringing it up so late."

I hold out my hand and slice the letter open with a nail. I'm not sure what it can be or why I'm even opening it when Elliot is on his way into danger, but the serious tone of Jordan's voice and the somber stance of Callan has me doing it anyway.

It's a letter from Compatible Companions. I know what it's going to say before I read it, so my eyes only briefly scan down the paragraphs. I barely read a complete sentence.

Extenuating circumstances of Mr. Montgomery's career.

Can be reassigned with no penalty.

New match.

Sorry.

Then I glance down at the signature and see that the letter has been stamped by Damian Stone.

I fly out of my bed and rush into the bathroom, leaving the letter on my bed for Jordan and Callan to read while I brush my teeth and tame my hair.

I return to my room a girl on a mission.

"Where are you going?" Jordan asks.

"Upstairs" I say. "I need to speak to Damian."

"It's late, Court. Let's sleep on this tonight then talk about what to do in the morning?" Callan offers.

"Why are you still here? I ask. "Shouldn't you be out finding a way to learn where Elliot is?" I ask and I know my calm demeanor has him thinking I'm batshit crazy. He wouldn't be wrong.

I'd just heard about the level of danger Elliot sought out when in active duty from his sister and only minutes ago found out that he'd returned because of me. If anything happens to him, I'm to blame. I could never live with myself if I lost him forever. So, yes…Batshit crazy!

"Courtney," Callan tries to calm me with his stern voice, but I push past him and fling open my door. I'm in the elevator as he sticks his foot inside to stop the door from closing. "What are you going to tell Stone?"

"Let me worry about him, you just worry about finding where Elliot went."

Callan nods and removes his foot from the door. Our eyes catch as the door closes. We don't speak, but we both know that if Elliot doesn't return safely, we'll never forgive ourselves or the other.

36

Summer continued to be a difficult season for me. Elliot was still missing or avoiding everyone, no one was really sure, so when the leaves began to change colors and the autumn wind started to pull them from the trees, I was relieved to return to school. Because I had done a ton of course work over the summer, to keep my mind off Elliot and how badly I had fucked up, I was a semester ahead of where I should have been. I still had a long way to go, but it was made easier because of the man I pushed away. A man who had done nothing wrong.

But it was time to meet the first man who had.

Elliot had tried to encourage me to get closure with my biological father and my stepdad. At the time, I hadn't been receptive. If I recall correctly, I'd behaved like a petulant child with him. But after some self-reflection and digging deeper into my own psyche, I knew Elliot had been right to nudge me to speak to Kyle and ask Mac to track down Tom.

So, here I sit in my car in Maine, not far from where I ran to escape Elliot a few months back. If only he were here now for me to have a do-over with.

I push back those emotions and hold off the tears that fall for him each day and try to focus on the man who gave me life then chose his first family over us.

According to Joey, Kyle Collins isn't the awful dickhead I've created in my head. He agrees that what he did was shitty but insisted that I needed to hear him out and give him a chance to explain. It'd taken me all this time because, as my brother likes to point out, I'm as stubborn as our father.

The restaurant I agreed to meet Kyle at is on the property of one of Justin's marinas. He and Amanda asked me to stay with them. I thought about declining, but I didn't want to be rude. Amanda and I are still early days and our relationship is shaky at best. We've spoken almost daily about Elliot and forged a friendship, a bond of sorts, but if I turned down her hospitality, it might be viewed as more than it is. Amanda and Justin's wedding is approaching and she's finishing her first trimester of pregnancy, so I promised not to overstay my welcome. I also need to be back in New York in a day or two to prepare for the semester ahead of me. The time, face to face, with her will be good though. I kind of want to see her body language when she speaks about Elliot and watch the emotions that run behind her eyes. Because, yes, as much as I now know that what they had wasn't something that I should be concerned over, I was still jealous and knew protecting my heart was the smartest way to go.

I enter the eatery, an hour early so I'm sure to beat my father there. However, when I tell the girl at the door that I'm meeting someone there shortly, she seems to know exactly who I am and says, "Right this way. Mr. Collins is waiting for you."

"Wait…what?" I ask. "No…how?"

The hostess smiles and shrugs. "Said he was running early and to bring you back whenever you arrived. He described you perfectly."

Yeah, I'm sure he did. If I know my brother, he'd shared pictures and even shown our father my social media accounts that are now all but dead. I haven't been in the mood for selfies since Elliot left. I have all I can do to go on there every day to check his accounts or see if he messaged me through one of mine.

The girl stops and nods in the direction of a distinguished, older version of my brother, his spitting image. It's like one of those games on social media that you upload a current picture to see what you'll look like in thirty years. I'm literally looking at Joey in the future.

Kyle is handsome beyond good-looking and doesn't look a day out of his forties, even though he must be. I try to do the calculations in my head but end up feeling the beginnings of a headache, so I stop. I'm definitely more suited for words than numbers. As I rub a throbbing temple, he stands, and a smile covers his face.

"Courtney," he breathes. "My God, you're more stunning in person than I was prepared for."

"Joey shared my social media, huh?"

My father smiles and shrugs. "Don't be mad at your brother. He loves you and was only trying to help us. I've wanted to do this for a very long time. I should have…"

I raise a silencing hand. "Maybe we can have a drink first?"

"Yeah, sure. Here," he says pulling out a chair for me to sit. "Have a seat. What can I order you?"

"Nothing slushy," I say then heave in the sob that threatens to escape as I remember Elliot standing on the beach looking hotter than sin. "Um…sorry. Ah, how about a glass of white wine?"

"Sure," Kyle says and calls over our waitress with a finger. "My daughter would like a white wine, please. The best in the house."

I sit silent while Kyle gives me the once and twice over. Not in a creepy Uncle Jim kind of way, but in a dad critical eye sort of way. He's assessing the damage he's done and weighing how best to apologize.

I know what he sees. He sees a young woman who looks put together and ready to conquer the world. One who is self-assured and well-adjusted.

It's a cover.

Sure, gone are the slutty clothes and my wandering eyes, but the reason they were there in the first place, is still a strong pull. I no longer seek out men to fill a void because the only man who can help me isn't here. I know that it's not a dick I need to make me whole, it's Elliot. I know that now. Too bad I learned that lesson a little to late.

Kyle clears his throat. "You and your sister look so much like your mother."

I suck in air through my teeth and ask, "Who, Bridget? You've seen each other recently?"

"Yeah. She wasn't sure if you'd react well over it, so she held off telling you too much. She told me about your boyfriend. I'm sorry he's missing."

"He'll be back" I say with confidence I don't feel and irritation over my sister speaking about me to our father and hiding their time together from me.

Kyle nods then changes the subject. "I hear you're in school. NYU? That's impressive."

"That's because of Elliot. I never would have gotten in or even applied if he hadn't…"

"But he isn't here now and you're doing well, right? And doing it on your own."

"Well, sort of. He's paid for everyth…" It hits me before I can even finish my thought. Something I hadn't thought about. My coming semester and books had been paid for. Had that been something he'd set up in advance or had Elliot recently made a payment which would mean he was safe and well, possibly even in New York. I'll have to call the bursar's office when I get home and see what I can find out.

"What?" Kyle asks but I wave him off.

"Nothing. I look like my mom, huh?"

A smile crosses his face then something must enter his mind too because he sighs and says, "I'm sorry for the way I handled things. I hope you'll let me explain. I'm not expecting anything more than that from you, but Bridget said it did help her to know my reasons."

"I can't believe she didn't tell me."

"She's worried about you. Her and Ace, that Callan kid, too."

"Callan?" I ask.

Kyle nods. "Yeah, he did the drive up here with them. Tried to play it off that he was hanging out with his buddy the whole time. I might not be the smartest man, but I'm also not an idiot. He and Jordan are clearly fucking."

I choke on the wine that had been placed before me then smirk at my father. I guess I get my bluntness from him.

"I'm not really at liberty to discuss my sister's sex life with you."

Kyle chuckles. "I'm glad all of my girls are getting along. Jordan and Jenny can't stop talking about you and Bridget and you've had Joey wrapped around your little finger for months."

A smile spreads across my face. "They're all great. I was apprehensive at first, but I'm glad we found one another."

Kyle and I order then sit in silence for a few minutes while our food is prepared. It's not uncomfortable, but as the minutes continue to pass with neither of us speaking, the air begins to feel tight. Kyle breaks the tension with a clearing of his throat. "I loved your mother, Courtney. And you girls."

A lone tear falls and I wipe at it with the back of my hand.

"I was still in love with Shelly though, too. And Joey needed his father. It was a clusterfuck of my doing and I panicked. I made poor decisions that I'll stand by and take the blame for. But, please hear me out and then if you can find it in your heart, I'd love for you to be able to forgive me one day."

The waitress arrives with our lunch before I can respond and Kyle tucks into his while I push food around my plate. I haven't eaten a full meal since Elliot cooked me one. I eat enough to stay coherent, but food reminds me of him, and thoughts of Elliot rob me of an appetite.

"Courtney, honey, you need to eat. You're so skinny," my dad says. "I know you girls are always watching your weight, but you're wasting away."

I shrug. He has no right to lecture me on anything. But then my heart softens as I look into his eyes and see it is coming from a place of fatherly care and concern.

"Yeah, I know. The stress of school and Elliot…"

"I'm sure me popping up like this hasn't helped any."

I take a bite of my tasteless lunch and wonder if Elliot is somewhere making food for someone else. I sigh then place my fork back on the table and take a sip of my wine. "If you loved Shelly and wanted to be a father to Joey, why did you leave them?"

Kyle sighs deeply and pushes his plate into the center of the table. Placing his arms in front of it, he leans slightly forward and states, "Life is complicated and sometimes love isn't enough."

"Yeah, I'm learning that, too."

"I put work ahead of my family and money ahead of my happiness. I met Shelly when I was young, too young, and," Kyle clears his throat. "I, um…I was a dick to women back then. Your mother wasn't the first I stepped out on Shelly with."

"Oh."

"Yeah. I was never lacking for female attention," Kyle glances around the room and my eyes follow his. He may be getting on in years, but fuck if there weren't at least three women in the place eye fucking him right now. "I've learned it's not what's important and can handle it better now. Back then," he shrugs again. "I was weak and took advantage. It was shitty of me."

"Yeah, I've known a lot of guys like that. It is shitty. To the girlfriend or wife, but also to the girl that's nothing more than a quick one-night fuck...sorry."

"No," Kyle laughs. "I should be the one apologizing. And I am sorry, Courtney. When I met your mother, I was in a horrible place in my marriage. The stress of having Joey was taking its toll on Shelly and then she found me with another woman. As you can imagine, it only got worse from there. Then your mom walked into my life and brought the sun with her. I'd been living under a cloud of darkness and I couldn't resist her light."

"Wow!" I state in surprise. "I've never heard her described like that before. When we were growing up, she was always kind of sad and dark herself."

Kyle's lips turn down and sadness crosses his face. "That was my fault."

Kyle tells me how he and my mother had met and fallen in love, how he wooed her and how they'd been happy.

"What changed?" I ask.

"Me. I got sick. You wouldn't remember, but it affected me in a way I'm not proud of. It made me see how horrible of a person I had been. I was in an awful situation once I realized my mistakes. I wanted to be with Shelly and Joey, but I didn't want to leave Katrina and you girls. I tried to find a way to have us all be together, but..."

"Wait, you suggested what? A ménage? Like that sister bride kind of thing?"

Kyle laughs. "I don't know what I was suggesting, but, yeah, I guess that was it. It wasn't well received by your mother or Shelly."

"I bet."

"Anyway, I had surgery..."

"Wait, surgery? What was..."

"Open heart. I had a condition I didn't know about. Found it in the nick of time. Any longer and I'd be dead. During surgery, I had a vision, a dream, and I followed it back to Shelly and Joey a few months later. The day I left you girls was the hardest in my life. I didn't want to lose you. I tried to work out a way to see you..."

I cut him off again. "But my mother had a nervous breakdown and my Uncle Tate stepped in with his muscle, right?"

"He was only trying to protect you, all of you. I've never blamed him for that. He promised me he'd always be there for you."

"So, you just walked away?"

"I was out of options. My marriage to Shelly was legal, mine with Katrina was null and void, fake. Tate had money to spare and threatened to make my life very challenging in the court system if I ever tried to contact any of you. He took over your mother's care and Brook took you girls to Connecticut."

"I don't remember any of that."

"Good. I'm sorry you need to know any of it."

I chuckle, but it's not a happy sound. Then I push back from the table and mumble something about needing air. Before I know it, I'm in my father's arms on the concrete of the parking lot with tears running down my face.

Then it slips out. I didn't mean to tell him. I hadn't wanted to make him feel guilty or show me his expression of pity. I wasn't looking for attention or for Kyle to jump to my defense. I hadn't wanted any of those things, but I'd gotten them all when I'd said, "My stepfather had a best friend that touched me."

Once that was out, the flood gates opened, and I tell him everything while sitting in his lap like I used to do as a little girl. I tell my father about my mother changing after he left, how she was sad all the time. I explain how she'd been happy at first with Tom, so I hadn't wanted to make any waves. I cry as I describe my experiences with a man, one I was told was a safe adult and that I should listen to.

Before I know it, I'm telling him about every man I've ever been with. Well, not the details and I guess not every single one, I'm sure I missed a few along the way, but he got the idea. It isn't until I find myself sobbing over the only man that I've ever loved, that I realize what I've revealed.

Kyle gently kisses my temple and inhales my hair as he rocks my body in his arms and makes soothing sounds. He helps me to my feet and wipes the tears from my face and my matted hair out of my eyes. He places me in the passenger side of his car and drives me to my hotel.

"We should call your mother and talk to her."

"I've already told her. I told Elliot and Bridget too."

"And no one has thought to find, and fucking mutilate that fucking bastard?"

I shrug. I'm not sure. Things had all happened so fast back then. Shortly after, things with Elliot had fallen apart and that was all I was able to handle.

Then a thought crosses my father's features. "What did you say Elliot did before you met him?" he asks.

37

My visit with my father was good for me in many ways. First, it did help to hear how and why he'd left us. It didn't make his leaving right, or really make me forgive him anymore than I was currently capable of, but it did give me a little perspective and closure. It also brought him into my life at my darkest hour and when all was said and done, there are times a girl just needs her daddy.

It also helped me to appreciate Bobby more than I ever have. He's truly been a dad to me all these years, through so much of my shit. He never turned his back on me, and we've grown close again like any daughter and her father would after those horrific teen years pass.

Our family meeting had been emotional and uncomfortable at times, but it was also therapeutic and helped me to see things more clearly between my mom and Bobby. I hadn't been fair to him all these years and he deserved an apology. I'd asked for his forgiveness and we'd hugged, Bobby telling me that I didn't need to say anything, he's always loved me like his own and will continue to do so forever.

The most help Kyle has provided was in opening my eyes about Elliot. He planted a seed in my mind that's been cultivating and sprouting over the few weeks since we'd met for lunch in Maine.

Now back in New York, I walk into my living room to find Callan sprawling on the sofa with his phone in his hand. He's clearly texting Jordan by the smile on his face. Let's just hope they're not sexting or sending naked selfies. Finding Callan at full mast on the couch of my living room is really not my ideal way to wake up on a Saturday morning. Especially not this one.

And not after the blow up we'd had only a day ago. I'd finally let my pent-up anger at him, for that day on the street with Elliot, boil over. I'd yelled and cried, made horrible observations about his character, and called him every name in the book. He'd stood there and took it all in. Then he agreed with almost everything I said. Everything except the way he felt about me and Elliot. He honestly viewed Elliot as his brother and was as devastated over his absence as I was. He also defended his intentions as a man when it came to my sister.

I calmed down and apologized, we hugged, and I cried. Callan promised it was water under the bridge and putting it all out there on the table had made me feel a million times better.

But I have a plan and I can't let his dick get in the way. And yes, I'm well aware that at the size of it, it gets in the way often. But Callan and I are long past that. I think of him like I do Joey, like another annoying brother sitting at the ready to either piss me off or protect me without being asked.

"Hey Cal," I greet my roommate. "You sexting my little sis?"

Callan's smile grows wider. "Ah, yeah, earlier," he shifts his dick in his pants. "Sorry. Um, sit down. We need to talk about something."

"Great. I was about to say the same to you."

"You asking me to move out already? I thought I'd at least have a bed until Monti came back."

"I'm not sure he's coming back, Cal. I," I clear my throat. "We fucked up, big time, on this one."

"Yeah, I know. But that's what I wanted to talk to you about."

I raise an eyebrow. "Okay."

"We've been looking for him underground and in the hell holes where we'd been before he met you because when he first left, that's the intel I got. But I think he set that up to throw us off course."

"Okay, right," I say not understanding at all what he's getting at and only half listening because I was chomping at the bit to tell him my theory. "Yeah, and?"

Callan hands me his phone and states, "Look at this. Anyone you know?"

His phone falls out of my hands and thankfully lands on the plush area rug instead of shattering on the hardwood flooring. Who thought phones made from glass was a good idea? A man, I'm sure.

"Court?" Callan asks but his voice hits my ears sounding as if we're under water.

I look in the direction of the sound, but I can't process what he's saying while my mind is still running over the words I had read on the screen.

Jim DePoint had been arrested after turning himself into New Hampshire authorities following his hospitalization after what appeared to be a bar fight turned almost deadly. Sentencing was pending his trial, but the article stated the enormous number of women who had stepped up to testify had the authorities confident that he'd be convicted on several counts.

I hold my hand up to silence Callan.

My suspicions had been right about Elliot. He wasn't overseas in some hell hole; he was tracking down "Uncle" Jim and every girl he'd touched before and after me. He was talking them into testifying so I wouldn't need to. Then, in true trained killer style, Elliot had pounced and done to Jim what I couldn't. I'm sure he only kept him a breath away from death so that I'd have the closure and satisfaction of knowing he'd spend the rest of his life rotting in jail. But the story goes on to state that Jim was later found dead outside a nightclub.

"Oh, my God!" I cry as I plop back down on the sofa next to Callan. "I was going to tell you that Kyle mentioned something that got me to thinking. I was going to ask you if you thought it was a possibility that Elliot was playing vigilante on my behalf."

"I'd say there's a damn good chance."

"Holy shit," I exclaim as a smile spreads across my face. "He isn't dead. Elliot isn't dead."

TO BE CONTINUED...

Find out what happens in <u>My Forever Maybe</u> (Book 2)

<u>After You</u> (Book 3)

She's next to me. It's the middle of the night and we're in a New York City cab soaring through the streets on our way to somewhere. We're together so it doesn't matter the location in which we're heading. If I'm with her, I'd walk into the bowels of fucking hell.

I can smell her scent and feel the energy only Adams and I share.

But then I'm on my knees on the dirty concrete, begging her not to go, asking her to stay with me. "I can't stand to watch you walk away from me and go to him. Him!" I shout.

He was my friend. Sure, he was a known asshole to most, but not to me. To me, he'd always been loyal. Until he wasn't.

Now, *they're* walking together through the rain, droplets of water covering her teardrops as they fall down her beautiful face.

I want to snap every one of his fingers that skim her face to wipe them away.

It's my fault. All of it. I broke the rules, our contract. I did it for her. Everything I did was for her. But it wasn't what she needed or wanted no matter what she said or thought.

Could I make it right? Could I make her mine again?

She senses my presence like I do hers when I enter a room that she's in. She turns and looks at me, and I stand there like a fucking fool and do nothing but stare back. Because I know what it feels like to fall in love with her and I know the pain of being kept away. What I don't know is how to make things right, how to get back to us.

I feel her fingers reach for mine and curl ours together.

I must be losing my mind. I've lost my mind.

But here she is standing next to me. My eyes lock with hers and that's when I see it. She's about to wreck me forever. The look in her eyes say goodbye.

The intense feeling of betrayal hits as he appears on her other side and she leans into his body and kisses him.

I know I should walk away. Everything I know tells me that I should walk away. But I can't.

"Adams, you are my reason" I say right before my eyes fly open.

About the Author

Kitty Berry grew up an only child who never wished for a sibling in a small town in Connecticut. After graduating with a degree in Early Childhood Special Education, she began teaching in the field and started to raise a family. Her literary influences happened later in life when she stumbled upon The Pilot's Wife by Anita Shreve after seeing it featured on the Oprah Show. It was her late mother's (whose name she uses as a pen name) desire of becoming a writer that prompted Kitty to create a contemporary romantic series.

Being a creative person by nature who came into writing during a time in her life when the busy balance of career and family made her crave an escape into the world of romance, Kitty took that desire and turned it into a romantic series that offers the reader multidimensional characters.

In 2013, she published her first novel from The Stone Series, Sliding. Since then she has written 10 other novels in that series, among them Stoned, Second Chances, Surrender, Starting Over, and Silence. The final installment, Survivor was released in 2016. A holiday edition was released in late 2018.

Since then, Berry has released a trilogy titled, The Anatomy of Love and written a carry-over stand-alone novel, Vines of Ivy. In 2019, she will release the Compatible Companions trilogy.

Because angst-ridden, plot-driven, women's contemporary romances mesmerize Kitty, Berry writes only in that genre. While each book in The Stone Series can stand alone with its own story, Berry's intention was to create carry-over characters to satisfy the need of the reader to know more after each novel ends. As an avid reader herself, Kitty enjoys the feeling of being there with the characters inside the story and often finds herself wanting to know more about them, missing them when the story is over, and becoming excited all over again when she discovers those familiar characters in subsequent novels. It is her hope that The Stone Series will do the same for her readers.

Kitty is married to a man she met in graduate school and has three boys who are almost men.

Kitty recently founded RomantiConn and will host her first romance author signing event in Connecticut in 2019.

Visit Kitty's website @ www.kittyberryauthor.com

60086245R00148

Made in the USA
Middletown, DE
13 August 2019